MORGAN
LE FAY

SMALL THINGS AND GREAT

Jo-Anne Blanco was born in Brazil to an English mother and Spanish father. She graduated from the University of Edinburgh with an MA in languages and from the University of Glasgow with an MPhil in media and culture. As a teacher, she has spent much of her life travelling around the world. Her travels, together with her lifelong passions for reading, writing and storytelling, inspired her to embark upon her epic *Fata Morgana* series, about the life and adventures of Morgan le Fay. Mythology, fairy tales, and Arthurian legends are all major influences on her work, and her ongoing journeys to countries of great landscapes and folklore are never-ending sources of inspiration.

Also by Jo-Anne Blanco

THE FATA MORGANA SERIES
Morgan Le Fay: Children of This World
Morgan Le Fay: Giants in the Earth

MORGAN LE FAY

SMALL THINGS AND GREAT

BOOK I OF THE FATA MORGANA SERIES

JO-ANNE BLANCO

Published in the UK in 2021 by Argante Press

Copyright © Jo-Anne Blanco 2017

Second edition 2019
Third edition 2020
This fourth edition 2021

Cover art by Miriam Soriano

Paperback   ISBN 978-1-8384893-0-4
eBook   ISBN 978-1-8384893-1-1

Typeset by SpiffingCovers

For my mother Jane Blanco,
whose unfailing love, strength, support
and encouragement made this book possible.

"Just so, if one may compare small things with great, an innate love of getting drives these Attic bees each with his own function."

- Virgil, *Georgics* Book IV

CONTENTS

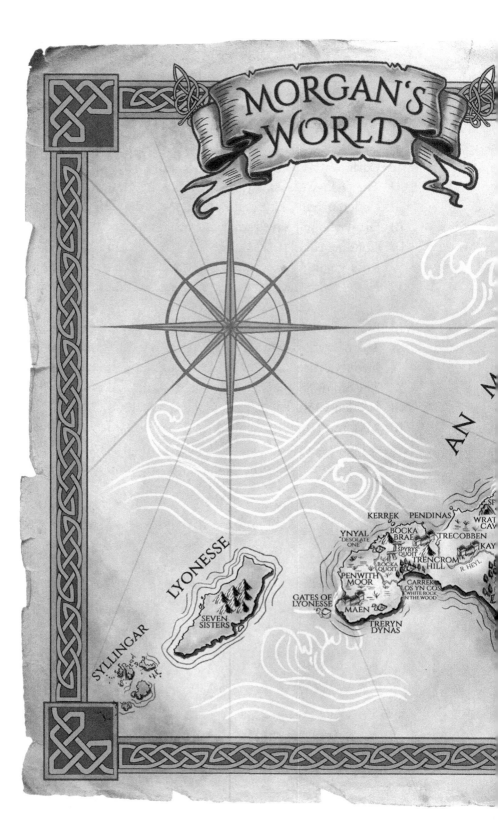

BOSKYNY
TINTAGEL
TREVANA
...TEK
R. KAMMEL
R. DINLONK
SELENA MOOR
R. TAMAR
R. TAVY
FOREST OF VERMILION
UNNAMED
VILLAGE
R. CLYVION
DIMILIOC
R. LINAR
R. GWYLES
WEST LOCH
EAST LOCH
R. SEYTHYN
TREDHINAS
TRENARREN
R. FALA

MOR BRETANNEK

BELERION

Prologue

Dark Waters

Morgan had never seen the sea like this.

The white-topped waves swirled and crashed beneath her, reaching up as if trying to grab her as she floated above the stormy ocean. She swayed to and fro in the wind, watching the long arms of the waves beneath her bare toes, feeling sick and terrified of the sea's anger below. The sea foam spray hit her face as the fierce wind propelled the waves upwards to form a mighty wall. She sensed the heavy black clouds above looming over her, ready to burst with fury.

On sunny days Morgan loved seeing reflections of the sky's different colours as they rippled across the sea, or gazing through the turquoise water to spot darting silver flashes of life under the surface. But now the waters gave back only darkness. The storm clouds were transforming the grey-green to an inky black and Morgan could see no light or life of any kind. The sky above her erupted, raining down bright swords and spears of light all around her, illuminating the darkness in brief snatches.

In the five years of her life, Morgan had never felt more helpless or frightened. She tried to shout but the roar of thunder that crashed around her drowned her cries. The wind gathered force and began blowing and battering Morgan in all different directions, carrying her through the air across the endless ocean. She tried to raise her arms to fight against the gale, but they seemed weighed down. Looking down, she saw that her small thin wrists were manacled together with irons, like her father's prisoners before they were cast into the dungeons. Morgan opened her mouth to scream and heard sounds of terror that did not come from inside her but from all around her, like echoes of her own panic.

She looked upwards and saw the dark sky was filled with people falling into the sea. At least she thought at first they were people;

but when she looked closer, Morgan saw that they all had large wings on their backs. She knew at once what they were, or at least what they were supposed to be – beautiful, noble beings of light who were calm and serene and pretty to look at.

But they did not look calm or serene or pretty now. They were frenzied with fear, ugly, frightening, howling in anguish and falling all around her. They appeared from on high beyond Morgan's vision, and as she watched in horror their wings caught fire and incinerated as they fell through the fiery circle that encompassed the dark sky. The heavens were raining down angels, hundreds of angels, as far as her eyes could see; falling and screaming, terrified and begging for mercy, streaking through the sky in red, white and gold flames like bolts of lightning and hailstones of fire.

As they landed in the water, frantically scrabbling and splashing in their attempts to stay afloat, they no longer looked to Morgan like angels but like demons, with faces contorted and agonised, their wings singed and burnt and reduced to nothing but stumps on their backs. Morgan knew she should fear them, that demons were supposed to be evil, but looking down at the tormented angels she realised with a shock that she was not afraid of them. Looking down from above, she felt heartsick watching the pitiful creatures flailing in the water, filling the air with their wretchedness and suffering. She felt their terror, their pain and also an overwhelming sense of despair she did not fully understand. Somehow she knew that there would be no comfort, no guidance, no safety for any of them ever again. Only never-ending confusion and darkness.

Struggling against the force of the wind, Morgan tried vainly to pull her hands free of the iron manacles that were rubbing her wrists raw. Desperately wanting to regain control of her arms and body, she reached out to the sea of screaming angels beneath her, but they were all lost in their own pain and oblivious to the helpless young child held aloft, being buffeted by the gale above them.

All but two. Two of the fallen angels stared up at her with ashen faces. They were holding on to each other, keeping each other afloat. Morgan could not see their faces clearly, for they were blurred by the sea spray and her own salt tears, but she could distinguish that one was a golden-haired man angel and the other a black-haired woman angel. In any other situation they would have been beautiful, far more radiant than any illustrations could hope to capture. But Morgan saw now that all light and hope and laughter in them had been cruelly extinguished, and that had destroyed their beauty. They looked old and frail and wizened, and they clung to each other as the last source of refuge from the darkness into which they had been cast.

As they turned away from Morgan and back to each other, the storm clouds parted for an instant. Morgan looked up and caught a glimpse of the Sun, frail and pale as the angels themselves. A dark circle was racing across it; an ominous shadow that moved in front of it with what seemed to Morgan like malice to block its path to the world and extinguish its light. Morgan watched in horror as the Sun turned black, with only a thin halo of light around it to suggest what it once had been. She had a sense of something far more terrible and powerful than the storm, which was still blasting across the ocean and throwing her every which way like one of her straw dolls.

She looked back down, trying to make out the two angels among the hundreds in the water. They were further away from her now. The woman angel was crying out in pain, making a horrible, unbearable sound Morgan had never heard before. Her raven hair was strewn across the angry waves like a dead animal, and Morgan was terrified that the angel herself was about to die. The man angel was desperately trying to help her, his golden hair dulled, his face twisted with distress and sympathy and another feeling Morgan could not identify, but which seemed to consume him from within. Morgan could not comprehend what she was seeing or sensing, but knew with a wrench of her heart that it was the unknown emotion of the male angel that made her feel more afraid than anything else.

Another furious thunderbolt shot down from the sky, almost striking Morgan. She braced herself for the inevitable subsequent crash; when it burst forth, it seemed to reverberate at the very core of her. She struggled to regain a form of control over her body. Her hands were still clasped together with irons; she pulled and strained against them trying to free herself until her wrists bled. A pleading, panicked voice from below called out to her, "Help us, little girl! Help us!"

Startled and fearful, she looked down once more to see a host of people staring up at her from the sea below, mouths agape, ready to cry out. Morgan realised at once that these people were different from those who had fallen from the sky. These were not angels. There were no charred wing stumps on their backs, only ragged clothes torn to shreds by the sea's rage. And Morgan could tell these people had never been beautiful or radiant; they were far too wrinkled and careworn and old looking.

Mixed in amongst the fallen angels, Morgan began to make out more and more humans alongside them, mortals of sagging and decaying flesh, awash and drowning in the waters just like the angels, but also, just like the angels, fighting against the waves that were impatient to pull them under. Morgan realised who the people were. Held and suspended above the sea by the storm winds in the sky, she strained her eyes for a glimpse of their ark of salvation, but she could see nothing. No boat, no ark, no land, no salvation. Nothing but hundreds, maybe even thousands of angels and humans united in terror, crying out as the dark waters swallowed them. She tried to find her two angels, the raven-haired woman and the golden-haired man, but she could no longer see them. They were lost forever in the darkness.

As Morgan watched the chaos of bodies mortal and divine, writhing and battling in the waves below her, she knew she could not remain just looking on, hovering in the sky above them like a bird on the wind. She saw children her own age and younger, grabbing at their parents, dragging them under and wailing, and her heart went out to them. Her first instinct was to help them. She didn't know how or why; she only knew that she had to help.

Still grappling with the metal bonds on her wrists, she kicked and squirmed against the wind, trying to fight her way down to join the people in the water. She wanted to be with them, to be one of them. Only as one of them could she help them. Striving against the invisible force that was holding her captive, Morgan beat the air with her bound arms, shrieking incoherently at it. Slowly, by sheer force of effort, she managed to lower herself to the water's surface.

Her bare feet hit the ice-cold water, then, with a sudden lurch forward, she plunged in. For a moment all went black and she stopped breathing. An enormous wave immediately swept her up, almost throwing her into the air once more, then pulled her down into the murky darkness. Morgan had lost control of her body again, but she fought ferociously to free herself.

Her head broke the surface and she gasped from the shock of the sudden gust of air and the blast of screams from those around her. The sound of terror never before imagined fell upon her and exploded in her ears like the discordant clang of a smith's hammer on an infernal anvil.

The storm clouds, now above Morgan's head, lit up again. Crooked swords of crackling light fell to earth once more. The crash of thunder that followed was so loud and wrathful that Morgan's terror emptied her mind of how cold and soaked and terrified of drowning she was.

In the same moment as the almighty roar, Morgan saw a silver shaft of light erupt from the clouds towards earth. This one was different from the other pale, twisted streaks. Visible only for a moment, it was shaped like a spear: straight, sleek, perfectly crafted and shining in the darkness. As Morgan watched, the silver spear fell from the sky, gleaming and purposeful. It pierced the water like a lance penetrating skin and then vanished.

At the point where it had struck, a dark liquid seeped out from under the water and spilled over onto the ocean's surface. It spread quickly across the waves, expanding and engulfing everything and anyone in its path. Desperately kicking to stay afloat, her hands helplessly shackled, Morgan watched as the dark liquid oozed its way towards her. As it came closer, she saw that the mysterious liquid was turning the waters red. She realised with horror that it was blood.

Frenzied with fear at the thought of it catching up with her, Morgan kicked under the water to push herself away from the oncoming terror. Her hands still manacled, fighting to keep her head above water, her legs endlessly kicking to prevent her from sinking, Morgan looked around for refuge; a piece of land, a rock, a floating bark – anything with which she could escape the ocean of blood rushing towards her.

A few yards away she caught sight of a small rock all by itself in the middle of the sea. Had it been there before? Morgan had often found that her thoughts would sometimes materialise in front of her; once, last spring, she had wished fervently for the daffodils to hurry up and bloom so she could pick them. Sebile had told her that it was too early, but then, suddenly, they had turned a corner on the path back to Tintagel and had been confronted with an array of bright yellow daffodils dancing in the wind. Morgan had been delighted and exclaimed that it was like magic. Sebile had said nothing, but looked at her strangely, half with pride and half with anxiety. Was this rock similar? Had it somehow appeared by magic? Morgan didn't care. She kicked her way towards it, using her bound arms to try and swim and keep her head above the waves. She reached the rock, placed her shackled hands upon it and hauled herself up. Her nightgown was sodden and her entire body shivered with the cold.

She lay on the rock exhausted, breathing heavily, looking up into the sky. She then looked at her wrists: they were still bleeding from the tightness of the irons. Suddenly angry and smarting with the pain, she tried to control her shaking and hauled herself up. Standing on the rock in her bare feet, her green nightgown soaked to her skin and strands of her drenched hair billowing in the wind, Morgan thought to herself that if she could make the daffodils grow and the rock appear just by thinking about them, then perhaps there were other things she could do. She had seen how her father's smiths worked with fire on metal; now she could try something similar.

Let the swords from the sky cut me loose, she thought, and held up her manacled hands in the air. The sky flashed and grumbled. Morgan tried again. I want the spears in the clouds to break these chains.

She took a deep breath, closed her eyes and concentrated, focusing her entire being on being free. She sensed an energy building in the dark clouds above her and instinctively raised her arms into the sky. She felt the lightning sizzle and the manacles crack in two. Her arms fell by her sides. Morgan opened her eyes and saw the chain broken and the irons on her wrist loosened. She tore them off and tossed them into the raging ocean.

Looking around, Morgan saw that she was entirely alone. Her rock, her refuge, was surrounded by a stormy crimson sea. The fallen angels and the condemned mortals had all disappeared, consumed by fire, water and blood. The screams had been silenced; the only sound she could hear now was the howl of the wind. Morgan gasped as the thick red waves lunged at her, inching up as she retreated to the very centre of her little island. She looked out again at the vast liquid redness, the emptiness, and in a panic wondered if there was anyone or anything left out there.

From the corner of her eye she spotted a movement in the water. Straining to see what it was, she tried to call out but somehow her voice would not work. The movement came closer and she could see that it was a person swimming.

It came into focus and she saw it was a little dark-haired boy of about her own age. He was swimming furiously towards her through the red sea, but his face and arms were somehow free from any kind of stain, as if he himself were swimming through ordinary water. Morgan watched him, fascinated and apprehensive.

As he drew closer, she saw that on his back clinging to him was a little girl. The little girl looked almost exactly like him, like a reflection of him, except that her dark hair was slightly longer and her wide open, filmy white eyes were sightless. Even though the girl was blind, she somehow seemed to see Morgan. The girl opened her mouth but no sound came out. She lifted up an arm and pointed at Morgan. The boy raised his head and saw her.

Morgan looked into fathomless dark eyes and her heart twisted. She stepped to the edge of her rock, fell to her knees and wordlessly held out her hand to help the boy. He trod water, staring at her, and did not move forward to take her outstretched hand. As Morgan and the boy stared at each other, motionless, the skies above them opened and began raining blood.

BELERION

I

THE DELUGE

Morgan woke with a start. She lay in bed, her heart racing, trying to make sense of the dream. She'd had bad dreams before, but nothing like this. Everything had felt so real – the cold, the wind, the burning angels, the drowning people, her terror.

Why had she dreamed such a horrible thing? She had certainly never seen anything like it in real life. As the eldest daughter of the Duke and Duchess of Belerion, and the apple of her father's eyes, the precocious five-year-old Morgan had always led a cosseted existence, safe behind the walls of Tintagel Castle. She was only allowed to venture out accompanied, either on a horseback ride with her father, Gorlois, or on walks with her tutor, Sebile. Her mother, Igraine, preferred to stay inside the castle walls or within the courtyard, and she liked it when her young daughter would stay in with her and show off her ever-improving reading and learning skills.

As Morgan lay in the darkness waiting for her heartbeat to return to normal, she became aware of a strange noise. It sounded like a ferocious beating and pummelling on the roof of the castle. She sat up. Listening closely, she realised it was water. Rain was beating down loudly and fiercely upon Tintagel. She could see it lashing against the window, blown savagely by a strong wind.

With a twinge of fear and still reeling from the intensity of her dream, Morgan got up and ran to the door. "Arcile!" she called, hoping to see her young maid at the door with a candle and her reassuring presence.

There was no one in the passage. A few of the torches were burning, but the light was dim. The noise of the rain on the roof seemed to be getting louder. Frowning, Morgan reached for a woollen wrap to cover her nightgown. She slipped into her shoes and ventured out into the deserted corridor.

"Morgan?" A small, scared voice made her turn and she saw her younger sister Blasine standing behind her in the passage. "Morgan, what is it?" Blasine asked her nervously. "Where is everyone?"

"I don't know," Morgan said. "There's a bad storm outside. Maybe they went to help the people in the village."

"Or maybe they all went to bed," another voice chimed in. Just behind Blasine stood her twin sister Anna. Anna and Blasine were a year younger than Morgan, but while Morgan loved Blasine, Anna annoyed her. Only when they were with their parents was Anna ever nice to Morgan. On those occasions Morgan tried to be nice back because she knew she should love her sister, but Anna made that very difficult.

"Not *all* of them went to bed," Morgan pointed out. "There's always a guard here at night. Something must have happened. I'm going to find out."

"Can we come?" asked Blasine timidly.

"No, you stay here," Morgan said. Out of the corner of her eye she saw Anna scowl.

Morgan ran down the passage to the stairwell. The noise of the wind and rain was becoming deafening. She went downstairs, running through the main corridor. The castle door was open and she felt powerful gusts of wind coursing through the building. At the door she stopped and looked out upon an astonishing sight.

The storm had caused flooding in parts of the courtyard and a number of her father's men, knee-deep in the water, were attempting to siphon it away. There were dead animals, chickens, rats, even a small puppy, floating in the debris. Morgan's stomach turned. There was panic everywhere; people were running in all directions as the storm whipped itself into a frenzy. A woman Morgan didn't recognise screamed and pointed upward. Morgan looked in the direction she indicated and saw some of her father's men standing sentinel on the castle battlements. Barely able to maintain their positions, they were bent double in the gale. As she looked, one of the men lost his balance and was swept off his feet into the sea. Morgan cried out in shock.

Lightning blazed and thunder crashed. In a panic, Morgan

looked for her father but she could not see him anywhere. Then she saw her father's page, a boy of about two years older than her, leaving the stables carrying a pile of ropes, running out of the courtyard as he cringed from the downpour. Morgan had only spoken to him a couple of times before. Maybe he could tell her where her father was.

"Taliesin!" she shouted, but he didn't hear her. Morgan ran out into the rain. It felt like sharp droplets of ice hitting her head and scratching her skin, but that didn't deter her. She negotiated her way round the edge of the courtyard to avoid the floodwater and caught up with the page as he reached the foregate. She grabbed his sleeve and he turned, startled.

"Morgan! I mean ... Lady Morgan!" the boy exclaimed. "What are you doing out here?"

"Where's my father, Taliesin?" she asked.

"Well, he's ..." Taliesin hesitated. "I'm not sure I should tell you, but ... he's down there." Taliesin pointed down toward the cliff path and the rocky cove below Tintagel.

Morgan was puzzled. "Why?"

The boy looked worried. "There's a wreck, Morgan ... Lady Morgan. A ship's been wrecked. They think it's the *Sea Queen*."

"What?" Morgan gasped.

The *Sea Queen* was the ship Tintagel had been expecting for two weeks now. Morgan had been so excited. Her mother had told her that Princess Blanchefleur of Ynys Môn, daughter of Igraine's sister Sardoine and her husband King Pellinore, was being sent to Tintagel to stay with them and to study with Sebile. "She will be your companion," Igraine had told Morgan. "She's your age and, like you, she's very, very clever, according to her mother." Igraine had stroked Morgan's hair and said softly, "It will do you good to have a friend."

Morgan had felt pleased, but said, "Why can't she study in Ynys Môn? Why does she have to go away from home and come here?"

Igraine had been silent for a moment and then said, "Well, your aunt Sardoine says she's very interested in learning about healing. You've started studying the healing arts with Sebile and you know there's no one with more knowledge than her." Morgan knew that was true. Sebile knew everything. And so Morgan had looked forward to Blanchefleur's arrival with anticipation and had made plans to show her where to find the best herbs to help concoct Sebile's remedies.

"It can't be! It can't be the *Sea Queen*!" Morgan said in horror.

She ran down to the cliff path with Taliesin running behind her shouting, "Morgan, wait!" At the top of the path, Morgan stared down into the cove and, with a sick feeling in her stomach, saw a sight that already looked frighteningly familiar.

In the sea below her was a heaving mass of people, screaming and shouting as the waves battered them onto the rocks. There were bodies broken, covered in blood; others, still alive, flailing and struggling, were fighting against the malevolent currents trying to pull them under into the black holes of the coastal caves, or fling them against the sharp jagged edges of the cove. The massive ship, torn almost in two by the rocks, was lying askew at the mouth of the cove, caught in the snare of the rocks around Tintagel's jutting island, being tossed and turned by the sea as pieces of its hull and mast were ripped away. The sails were long since gone.

Running around frantically like ants on the rocks, attempting to help the people in the water and salvage objects being thrown up by the waves, were some of Tintagel's soldiers, women from the castle and what looked like fishermen from the village. Bodies were being hauled away from the sea and laid out high up on the wide beach out of immediate harm's way. Morgan could not tell if any of them were dead or alive. She caught sight of Sebile's distinctive headdress and saw her going from person to person, kneeling down next to each one in turn with her bag of medicines. Morgan then saw her father, Gorlois, standing right on the edge of the rocks, shouting out orders, joining his men in throwing grappling hooks into the sea and helping drag people from the water.

"I have to go down there," said Taliesin at Morgan's shoulder. "He sent me to fetch these." The boy indicated the ropes over his shoulder. "You should go back to the castle, Lady Morgan." He ran past her and down towards the cove.

Morgan knew she could not go back inside. She followed Taliesin quickly down the steep cliff path to the rocky shore, stumbling as her soft shoes got snared on the stones. She held on fiercely to the cliff side while the wind tried to blow her over the side of the path. Her woollen wrap was already soaked through to her nightgown but she didn't care. People ran past her up and down the path, ignoring her in their attempts to help or to fetch help for those below. She descended as fast as she could.

As she arrived on the beach there was an almighty groan; the wounded ship out at sea split in two. People on the shore gasped as the wood from its hull snapped. Morgan ran out to the rocks at the side of the cove; she didn't want her father to see her. She watched Taliesin approach him and hand him the ropes. Morgan looked away and stared out to sea at the ship, helplessly watching its last dying throes as the sea swallowed it up. She felt desperately sad. It was like seeing an animal being eaten by an enormous monster.

The sky blazed once more with crackles of lightning. Thunder boomed out, like an ominous funeral bell tolling to signal death. The two halves of the ship rolled over and began to sink into the billowing waves. Standing on the shore in the aftermath of the ship's painful death, Morgan felt the immensity, power and force of the sea and the storm. Strangely, even though it made her feel sick because it reminded her of her terrible dream, she somehow at the same time felt an extraordinary sense of happiness that she couldn't understand. Deep inside her she felt a connection to the waters in the ocean and the sky, the currents and their pulses, the cloudbursts and their deluge, as if she were one with them. As if she were the waters themselves.

As she reeled from the sensation, just for an instant Morgan thought she saw the giant face of a man in the waters that parted the two sides of the ship; a face lined with ripples, surrounded by a head and beard of white foam and small dark whirlpools for eyes that seemed to look directly at her. She was stunned and afraid – what was that face? Had anyone else seen?

She looked around at the chaotic scene in the cove and then up at the sky. The black clouds swirling above her seemed to breathe fire; as Morgan watched, she began to see fiery eyes appearing one after the other, like evil stars, glaring down. Then, gradually, from within the murky depths, huge black figures materialised, mounted on horrifying horses the likes of which Morgan could never have imagined, roll-eyed and demonic, all teeth and eyes and saliva. Trailing them was a pack of red-eyed black dogs, foaming fire at the mouth.

Their leader was a powerful-looking huntsman with only one eye in his head. Where his other eye should have been there was nothing but a hollow socket. He had a long white beard blowing in the wind, a spiked steel helmet with feathered wings on each side, and a billowing cloak. He was wielding a spear that crackled with lightning. The spear's sharp pointy head gleamed in the darkness as the lightning bolts struck, while its slender shaft shone red and silver like steel dipped in blood.

The spear was the one Morgan had seen in her dream. The one that had fallen from the sky and pierced the ocean, making it turn into blood.

She heard the sinister laughter of the dark riders as they roared across the sky, observing the carnage and destruction of the wreck with glee. As they leered at the helpless victims below, Morgan could see what looked to her like small round pale lights hovering over the lifeless bodies. To her blurred eyes the lights almost seemed alive. They hovered helplessly while columns of what looked like smoke rose from the corpses and headed towards the fearsome huntsmen in the sky. Triumphant laughter rang out from the dark riders whenever one of the dead gave up its ghost. The lead huntsman's cackle rumbled like thunder and sent a chill straight to Morgan's soul. Petrified, she closed her eyes to banish the nightmare vision. "I'm still dreaming, please God," she prayed fervently. "I must be."

A high-pitched screaming nearby roused her. Morgan opened her eyes instinctively to see an injured woman lying on the rocks nearby, her head bleeding. Her right leg looked odd, askew at an unnatural angle. "Help me!" she screamed as she struggled to move on the slippery rocks. It looked to Morgan as if the woman was moving towards the water instead of away from it and was about to fall in. She ran forward, careless of the danger, and tugged the woman's arm.

"I'll help you! Come this way."

"My children!" the woman cried, staring wildly at Morgan. "Please! Help me find my children!"

"Morgan! What are you doing here?" Morgan would have recognised that voice anywhere. Sebile was running towards her, both fast and formidable for a woman of her advanced years. Morgan didn't know how old Sebile was. She gave the impression of being an old woman, but although her hair (for the most part hidden under her headdress) was white, her face was remarkably unlined. She had an aura of deep, abiding knowledge of which Morgan was in awe. Usually she carried herself with an air of serenity and dignity, but at this moment she was furious, her face strained with anxiety and exhaustion.

"What do you think you're doing?" Sebile demanded, grabbing Morgan by her shoulders and shaking her. "How dare you come out here in this storm? What were you thinking?"

"I wanted to help," Morgan protested, tears stinging her eyes.

"And what help could a child like you be? What good will it do anyone if you come to harm?"

"Also …" Morgan hesitated. Sebile looked shrewdly at her. "I had a dream," Morgan finished.

Sebile's eyes narrowed. "What kind of dream?"

"It was like this," Morgan said, indicating the terrible scene around them.

Something flickered behind Sebile's eyes. Then she turned her attention to the woman on the rocks. The force of the wind was still trying to blow them away into the sea, but it did not seem to worry her. Morgan felt her feet slither as she lost her balance and she knelt down, holding on with both hands. Lightning and thunder crashed around them again but Morgan dared not look up at the sky.

"It looks like her leg's been broken," Sebile said matter-of-factly. "It must have happened when she was flung upon these rocks."

"Can you make her better?" Morgan asked.

"It will take time … but yes." Sebile finished her brisk examination, then shouted out to some of the men on the beach. Morgan thought it was a miracle that anyone could hear her through the howl of the gale, but several people ran over to help. Sebile ordered them to take the woman up to the castle. As she was lifted up, the woman clasped Morgan's hand.

"Please," the woman begged Morgan, staring at her with wild eyes. "Find my children. They were together. A boy and a girl. Save my children." The woman's hand dropped Morgan's as she was carried away, but Morgan still felt its pressure.

"And you, Morgan," Sebile said as the woman was carried off. "You go back to the castle with them. Immediately."

Morgan suddenly felt angry. "She asked me to find her children," she retorted and without further ado jumped off the rocks and ran up the beach. Ignoring Sebile's infuriated shouts, she scurried along the stricken coast and shoreline, the wind buffeting her small body so hard that she couldn't walk straight. She searched for anything that might look like children from the ship.

There were fewer people in the water now and fewer cries being carried through the air. Morgan felt hollow in the pit of her stomach. Soon all she could hear was the wind. She reached the other end of the beach, further down from where most of the people had been driven by the currents. She looked back at all the figures and activity behind her. They suddenly seemed tiny and distant and very far away.

Then she did hear something faintly over the storm. An odd voice, unlike any she'd ever heard before. "Help us! Please help!" Morgan turned and saw a boy struggling to pull an injured little girl of about Morgan's age out of the crashing waves and onto the beach.

For a second Morgan thought she had found the wild-eyed woman's children, but then she knew at once that these could not be them. These children looked different from any Morgan had seen in her life. The boy was about eight years old, dark-skinned and dark-eyed, with short cropped black hair. The little girl was beautiful; her eyes were closed, her hair long, black and poker-straight, her skin smooth and perfect. Morgan was so startled that at first she didn't move. The boy managed to pull the girl up the beach just out of reach of the waves that were chasing them and behind a boulder to protect them from the worst of the storm. He looked at Morgan again and shouted, "Please!" He had a strange accent.

Morgan forced her legs to move, ran over and knelt down beside the unconscious girl. She laid her head upon the girl's chest as Sebile had taught her to do and heard a faint heartbeat.

"She's alive," Morgan told the boy. He nodded wearily, sank to his knees and rested against the rock on the wet sand next to her. "You saved her," Morgan said, looking at him in wonder.

The boy smiled sadly. "I don't think anyone will thank me."

"Why not?" Morgan asked.

The boy looked back at her and Morgan sensed that there was something unusual about him, something she could not quite put her finger on. "They'll be angry if they find out. I wasn't supposed to be on that ship," the boy said.

"You're a stowaway?" Morgan had heard of such people from her father. The merchant traders regarded them as a menace, no better than scavengers or rats. "Where have you come from?"

"A land far away," the boy said so quietly Morgan could barely hear him over the wind. He paused for a moment and then indicated the unconscious girl between them. "I'm a stowaway, but she's a princess."

Morgan gasped. "Are you sure?"

"It's the Princess Blanchefleur," said Sebile, looming over them. Morgan realised that Sebile had followed her up the beach and she withered under her tutor's angry glare. Sebile bent down to examine the girl while Morgan and the boy waited anxiously.

"Is she going to be alright?" Morgan asked.

Sebile frowned. "She's had a nasty knock on the head." The tutor indicated a bloody gash on the back of Blanchefleur's scalp. "We must get her up to the castle." She looked at the boy. "You, what's your name?"

"Safir, my lady," the boy replied.

"You're a Saracen," Sebile said. It wasn't a question.

"Yes, my lady," the boy said. Morgan was curious. What was a Saracen? The boy seemed about to say something else, but Sebile stopped him.

"I don't care how or why you're here, but I need your help now.

Do you think you can help me carry the princess down the beach, so we can take her to the castle with the rest of the survivors?"

"Yes, my lady," the boy repeated. Sebile gathered little Blanchefleur's head and shoulders in her arms, while the boy lifted the young princess' feet.

"And you, Morgan," Sebile commanded in a voice that would brook no transgression, "you are to follow us back and stay close. And do *not* disobey me again or there will be consequences."

Chastened and subdued, Morgan stood up shakily and followed Sebile and the boy Safir as they carried Blanchefleur back towards the teeming mass of people on the other side of the beach.

It seemed to Morgan that the anger of the storm was dying down a little; the wind seemed less strong and the noise of the thunder more distant. Chancing glances up at the sky, Morgan saw the terrifying hunter figures had gone. There were only the black storm clouds emanating fainter flickers of lightning as the tempest began to subside. The darkness was dissolving into an eerie light that began penetrating the clouds and shining down upon the beach. Increasingly aware of how cold, wet and tired she was, Morgan kept looking upwards to the sky, irresistibly drawn to the strange dawning light. The black clouds were slowly developing yellowish-tinged haloes as they appeared to shrink. Thunder still rumbled, but now it sounded as if it were coming from further away. Hurrying in Sebile's wake, Morgan's eye caught sight of something strange above them and she stopped short, startled.

On the edge of the cliff directly above the beach, she saw the tall silhouette of a man standing gazing out to sea, stark and imposing against the nascent light of the sky. Morgan's heart leapt. She didn't know if she was frightened or excited. What amazed her was her realisation that the standing man had the antlers of a stag growing out of his head. Against the light, he looked half-animal, half-man.

As Morgan's eyes adjusted to the new light, she could see the Horned Man wore a deerskin around his waist and a pointed beard on his chin. Images flashed through her exhausted young brain, trying to make sense of what she saw – everything from the illustrations of ancient satyrs in Sebile's story texts to the pictures of the Devil himself in the Christian books she had studied. Is this man the Devil? Morgan asked herself. Was he the one who started the storm that threw all the people into the sea and caused them all to die? Was he the one who led the angels she had seen in her dream, screaming as they streaked across the sky with their wings on fire before they fell into the raging darkness? Were those terrible sky hunters his servants, circling like crows over the dying, and collecting the souls of the helpless dead for him? Strangely, despite the wild thoughts swirling around her impressionable young mind, Morgan did not feel frightened. She wasn't sure if it was evil that she felt from the Horned Man. She knew that it was something unimaginably powerful. But was it evil?

As her thoughts coalesced, the Horned Man looked down from the cliff and directly at her. Morgan felt as if her heart had stopped. Everything around them seemed to grind down, as if time itself were slowing and stopping.

Morgan continued to stare up at the Horned Man. Somehow, even at a distance far below him, she was able to see into his black impenetrable eyes that seemed all-knowing. The Horned Man looked from Morgan out to sea, and then back to Morgan again. She sensed that he was silently trying to tell her something. He looked again at the sea and Morgan followed his gaze. The ocean that stretched out to the island and beyond was now empty. It seemed that everything and everyone had either been dragged ashore or swallowed down by the waves. Morgan looked up again at the Horned Man on the cliff edge, but he was no longer there. The skyline was unbroken. She looked back out to sea and her eye caught a movement in the water that she had missed before. As she stood beneath the cliff, she saw Sebile and Safir walking further away ahead of her, carrying Blanchefleur between them and getting smaller in the distance.

Feeling very alone, Morgan hesitated. If she disobeyed Sebile again, she knew she would be in trouble. She looked up again, but there was still no sign of the Horned Man. Whatever was moving towards her in the sea was coming closer. She had to know what it was. Instinctively, she ran towards the shore and felt her way across the rocks that cut through the beach and the water. There she stood upon a rock as the movement came into focus. Her heart began to race once more and time returned to its normal pace as she looked, astounded, upon a sight she had already seen in her mind.

A little dark-haired boy of about her own age was swimming determinedly towards the rocks. On his back, clinging to him, was a little girl who looked almost exactly like him except for her slightly longer dark hair. The little girl's eyes were pure white with no colour to their centre, wide open and watery. She was blind.

Morgan watched the two children with fascinated horror, unable to believe what she was seeing. Were they real, this boy and girl from her dream? How could she have dreamed about them without ever knowing them or seeing them before? The boy's wet hair was plastered to his head and his face was strained with the effort of swimming to shore while carrying the girl. Morgan remembered how he had refused to take her hand in her dream and how, after his refusal, the sky in her nightmare had rained down blood. She recoiled from the memory and for the first time in her life she hesitated whether to help or not. But then the girl raised her head and her sightless eyes seemed to look directly at Morgan. Still clinging to the boy, she pointed at her. The boy, still swimming, followed the girl's silent signal and saw Morgan. At once he almost imperceptibly changed direction, swimming straight towards her.

As they came closer, the pain and exhaustion on their faces was too much for Morgan to bear. With the strange sense of having entered her dream and done this before, she stepped to the edge of the rock, went down on her knees and held out her hand. This time, however, the boy did not stop. He swam all the way towards the rock until he reached her.

"Help me with my sister," was all he managed to gasp. Morgan leaned over, grabbed the little blind girl's arms and pulled. The boy pushed the girl from the water until between the two of them they got her out. The girl lay on the rock, her sightless eyes staring up into the sky. Morgan then held out her hand to the boy. He didn't hesitate, but took hold of her hand with one hand and the rock with the other. With Morgan pulling his arm the boy hauled himself up onto the rock and collapsed next to her.

"Are you alright?" Morgan asked them both.

The boy, out of breath, did not answer for a few seconds. "I think so," he eventually replied.

"What about you?" Morgan asked the girl, who was lying immobile but breathing on the rock.

"She can't answer you," the boy said, not looking at his sister. "She doesn't speak."

Morgan felt a surge of sadness for the little girl. "I'm sorry."

The boy looked at Morgan. Morgan felt a cold stab when she saw his dark eyes were exactly as she remembered in the dream. Before she could say anything, the boy said, "I know you."

"What?" Morgan gasped.

The boy didn't smile, just stated calmly, "I've seen you before."

"Where? How?" Morgan demanded. The boy said nothing, but merely looked at her.

"Morgan!" came Sebile's outraged voice.

Morgan started up and cried, "Sebile! I've found them! I've found the lady's children!"

"You saw our mother?" the boy asked, frowning. He tried to stand up, but his legs gave way. Morgan grabbed his arm to stop him from falling. The boy reacted with unexpected violence to her touch, almost as if she had wounded him. He pulled his arm away roughly and took a step back from her, almost cringing. Morgan was startled and hurt.

"She's alive. They've taken her to the castle," Morgan told him warily. The boy stood looking at Morgan, but this time, oddly, did not look into her eyes. "She asked me to find you," Morgan went on.

"How did you know it was us?" the boy asked.

"I knew as soon as I saw you," Morgan said. She couldn't explain how; she had just known. The boy then looked back at her again, appraisingly and interestedly. This time it was Morgan who looked away.

As Sebile came running up from the beach, Morgan negotiated her way back across the rocks. "It's them, Sebile!" she said breathlessly. "It's her children!"

The fury on Sebile's face subsided when she saw Morgan's

earnest, pleading expression. She looked at the boy standing shakily on the rock, and Morgan heard her sharp intake of breath. Sebile then saw the girl lying without moving, made her way across the rocks and picked her up. "Follow me," Sebile commanded Morgan and the boy, and they obeyed her. Together, Morgan and the boy walked the remaining length of the beach, now empty save for a few scattered remains of wreckage and clothing. The survivors and the dead alike were being carried up the cliff path towards Tintagel as the light grew brighter and the wind started to blow itself out.

At the foot of the cliff path, Morgan turned to look back once more at the sea. Like the wind, its anger and force were dissipating. The waves were still high, but not as ferocious as before and not as strong. Morgan thought with a shiver that it was as if the monster that was the sea had eaten until it was full and was now happy with the wreck and its passengers that it had taken that night.

"So you're Morgan," the boy said. He had stopped with her and was looking out at the sea as well.

"Yes. My father's the Duke of Belerion," Morgan told him.

"I know."

Morgan could not work out if the words were said with hostility or not. Before she could think of a suitable retort, the boy indicated his sister, who was being carried ahead of them by Sebile. "That's Ganieda. She's my twin."

"And who are you?" Morgan asked coldly.

The boy looked directly at her and this time she held his gaze. At this, the boy smiled for the first time.

"I'm Merlin."

II

UNDERCURRENTS

"How could you have done this?"

Morgan had never seen her mother this angry before. Igraine was always calm and patient, but today her fury was clear in the coldness with which she spoke to her daughter. Morgan quailed before her and could not reply.

"How could you have left the castle in such a storm? Anything could have happened to you," Igraine went on, her eyes not leaving Morgan's face. "You knew how dangerous it was. Sebile told you to return at once. How dare you be so disobedient?"

Morgan wanted to explain to her mother about her dream, about feeling the need to help that she didn't understand, but the words wouldn't come. Behind Igraine, Anna smirked, enjoying Morgan's discomfort and disgrace. Blasine, on the other hand, looked scared and tried to give Morgan a friendly smile when Anna wasn't looking.

"So you have nothing to say for yourself?" Igraine demanded as Morgan stayed silent. "No reason why you acted so foolishly, so selfishly, with no thought about what might happen, or how other people would feel?"

"I'm sorry, Mother," was all Morgan managed.

"That's not good enough. You will not be allowed out of the castle again until I allow you to go. And that will not be for a very long time."

"No!" Morgan exclaimed in dismay.

"Don't argue with me!" Igraine snapped. "If I hear one more word, you will not only stay inside the castle but in your room! That is the end of the matter."

Morgan's eyes stung as Igraine swept out of the room. Anna skipped after her, took one last triumphant look at Morgan and giggled as she left. Morgan's tears turned to anger when she heard

Anna's laughter and she wiped her eyes with her hand, determined not to let anyone see. She felt a hand take hers.

"I'm sorry, Morgan," Blasine said.

Morgan smiled and squeezed her younger sister's hand. "Come on."

The two little girls walked together out of the door and down the passageway to the castle's main hall. They entered to find that a large number of Gorlois' knights and Igraine's household were already present, as were a number of other noble-looking people Morgan didn't recognise.

As always, the room appeared huge and intimidating to the five-year-old's eyes, with its long stone walls divided by shafts of light entering from the largest windows in the castle, bathing the room and all those in it in a soft glow. Rich, floor-length tapestries hung on the walls between the windows. The long wooden tables and benches used for feasts had been taken apart and removed, and only the small wooden benches under the windows remained.

Gorlois sat on one of the two carved oak chairs on the raised stone dais at the far end of the hall, as he always did when receiving visiting nobles or granting an audience to his vassals. Morgan remembered from time to time seeing her father receive elegantly clothed noblemen and women calling themselves ambassadors. They came in from trade ships carrying goods from far-off lands and told her father that they wanted to be friends with the people of Tintagel. They offered goods and friendship in exchange for similar things from Belerion.

Igraine mounted the dais and sat next to him on the other chair. Little Anna, following with her blonde head held high, climbed up onto a smaller chair next to her mother. There were two other chairs the same size, one next to Gorlois and the other next to Anna. Blasine made a move forward towards the dais but Morgan pulled her sharply back. Blasine looked at her inquiringly and then nervously back at the dais. But Morgan didn't want to sit with Igraine or with Anna in front of the whole court of Tintagel after the scene she had just been through. Instead, she pulled Blasine behind a group of the well-dressed people she did not know and sat down quietly on a bench underneath one of the windows, hidden from view. With a show of reluctance, Blasine sat down next to her. All around them the adults talked and murmured, their chatter filling the hall with noise until one voice rose above the rest.

"Silence in the hall!"

Morgan strained to see through the crowd gathered in front of her and made out the tall figure of Sir Brastias, her father's seneschal. She knew Sir Brastias as Gorlois' most loyal friend and chief officer of the Tintagel guard. He was a thickly-built, imposing man who inspired a lot of respect and some fear, but Morgan thought of him as a kind and friendly greying uncle.

The noise in the hall died down almost at once. Morgan saw her parents seated together on the dais, looking every inch the reigning Duke and Duchess, and she felt a swell of pride despite her resentment at Igraine's harsh words. She watched Gorlois say something to Sir Brastias, who then turned to the assembled court and announced, "The Lord Gorlois calls forward Grand Master Cadwellon of the Druidical Order and Father Elfodd of the Christian Church."

The assembled people fell back on either side of the hall like a parting of the waters. In the centre, four men walked towards the dais. Two contrasting figures led the way. One was an old man whose age was clear from his long white hair and beard, which were almost the exact same colour as his robes and staff. However, the way in which he stood upright and straight-shouldered and walked with quick, purposeful steps seemed to Morgan to make him appear much younger than he was. Next to him walked a young man, hardly grown-up at all, with thick brown hair and a lean but handsome face. In contrast to the old man, the young man was dressed all in black, and moved in a slower way that made him seem very elegant and dignified.

Behind them walked two other men, a younger man behind the old man and an older man behind the young one. Seated by the window, Morgan was too far away to see them properly. She moved her head impatiently, looking in between one set of people and then another, trying to get the best view of the proceedings while remaining out of sight herself. The men stopped in front of the dais and Gorlois acknowledged them with a nod of his head.

"Welcome back to Tintagel, Grand Master Cadwellon. I'm sorry we have had to convene here in such tragic circumstances."

"My lord Gorlois." The old man inclined his head. "This storm was one of the worst we have witnessed for many years. And the loss of life in the shipwreck … truly terrible." He paused. "I need hardly tell you, my lord, that there are many among our Order who see this as an omen of a great tragedy that is to befall the people here."

Morgan heard the sharp intakes of breath around her and wondered what an omen was. It must be something bad because the people in the hall were looking worried and afraid. Except for her father. Gorlois was saying that he didn't believe in such things and asked the young man in black what he thought. Father Elfodd declared that no one could know the will of God. He looked at the old man next to him and said that some people believed they had ways of divining what would happen and of interpreting omens, but it was only blind speculation. The words didn't make sense to Morgan, but she carefully stored them in her memory so she could find out what they meant.

Through his tired-looking expression, Cadwellon gave a half-smile. "And yet, our young Father Elfodd would have us believe that his own Lord Jesus Christ foresaw both his own death and the manner of it. Was that just blind speculation on his part, too?"

The crowd in the hall tittered nervously. Morgan strained to see the young priest's face. He did not look angry or annoyed. He too half-smiled. Why was he smiling? Had Cadwellon said something funny?

"That was different, Grand Master. Christ was the Son of God. His divine nature enabled him to know and to see what we mortals can't."

"So, you admit at least that those of a divine nature can see into the future?" Cadwellon pressed him.

Morgan eagerly awaited Elfodd's answer, but Gorlois held up his hand. "Enough. Keep your religious disputes for another time. I've summoned you here to help us deal with the immediate situation concerning the survivors of the wreck. How many people were saved?"

"There were eleven survivors, including three children, my lord," Cadwellon said.

"One of them being the Princess Blanchefleur?"

"Yes, my lord."

"Thank the heavens," murmured Igraine.

Morgan was startled. That was wrong. There were *four* children survivors. Princess Blanchefleur, the twins Merlin and Ganieda, and the stowaway boy Safir. She wanted to shout out that they were wrong, but remembering how angry Igraine was with her, she kept quiet.

Gorlois was looking at Igraine and gently took her hand. "And what arrangements are being made for the poor souls who did not survive?" he asked.

Cadwellon and Elfodd exchanged glances. Morgan noticed that the look between the old Druid and the young priest was not unfriendly.

"Unfortunately, we don't know the faiths of the dead," Cadwellon said. "Father Elfodd and I wish to arrange their funeral rites according to their beliefs, but we have no way of knowing what those were."

"We thought perhaps we could honour them together, in similar fashion," Elfodd added.

Before Gorlois could respond, the older man standing behind Elfodd spoke up.

"I can tell you what their faith was, my lord."

Gorlois beckoned him forward. "Who are you?"

"My name is Blaes, my lord. I am one of the survivors," the man said. He was round-faced and middle-aged, dressed simply in a brown robe. "God saw fit to spare me from the waves."

"I take it you're a Christian?" Gorlois asked him.

"I am, my lord. Like the people of Gwynedd on the ship with me, may God have mercy on their souls."

The man shot a look at Cadwellon; Morgan was startled at the nastiness of it. "Gwynedd is a God-fearing country, my lord. King Einion banished the Devil worshippers from our land many years ago. The last remnants of that heathen scourge ran away to the far corner of Ynys Môn. If any of them return, they face the choice of conversion or death." He glanced at Elfodd beside him and anger entered his voice. "Unlike this boy priest you have here, our holy men of Christ never betray their calling to work alongside these evildoers."

"What's a Devil worshipper?" Blasine whispered in Morgan's ear.

"I think he means people like Grand Master Cadwellon and the Druids," Morgan murmured back.

"But what is it? Is Grand Master Cadwellon one?" Blasine persisted.

Morgan didn't know much about what Cadwellon and the Druids were. She had heard rumours and knew that they lived in the forests and mountains, away from the castle and the village. She had also heard some dark things about sacrifices, which made her afraid and which the storm eating the shipwreck in some strange way made her think about. But because she was too young, no one at Tintagel had told her anything and they probably wouldn't if she asked. She'd have to go to Sebile if she wanted to know more. But she didn't want Blasine to know that she didn't know either, so she silenced her with a "Shhhhhhh! I'll tell you later," and turned her attention back to the dais.

Gorlois was saying, "... so, in Belerion, Brother Blaes, the Christian followers and the Order of the Druids are all treated with respect. I myself am Christian and so is my wife, but many of our people follow Grand Master Cadwellon and his Order, and they live among us in peace. Father Elfodd understands that and I would advise you to do the same."

"I am aware of your ... views, my lord," Blaes said evenly. "That is why I accompanied the Lady Aldan all the way here to seek an audience with you."

"The Lady Aldan?" Igraine asked, as the people in the hall murmured excitedly at this news. "Do you mean King Einion's daughter? She was on the ship?" Morgan heard a strange tone in her mother's voice. "She survived?"

"Yes, my lady. She survived, thanks to the ministrations of your healer woman. She's here now, waiting outside. She wishes to speak with you and the Duke."

Igraine looked at Gorlois. Morgan thought she saw alarm in her mother's face. Gorlois nodded at Sir Brastias. "Of course. Show her in."

As one, the people in the hall turned towards the entrance door. Morgan turned her head with them. Sir Brastias made his way down the aisle and outside the hall, returning almost immediately. A woman seated on a chair carried on poles by four male servants followed him. The woman's right leg was tightly bandaged and stuck straight out in front of her, held rigid by attached wooden straps. So fascinated was Morgan by the treatment of the injury that she did not notice the woman's face until her chair passed close to where she was sitting. For the most part, the woman kept her eyes on the dais ahead of her, but occasionally she looked round at the gathering. When she looked in the direction where Morgan and Blasine were sitting half-hidden, Morgan could not contain a gasp. The eyes that had stared at her so wildly on the rocky shore the previous night were now calmer, though still full of pain.

Walking behind the woman were her children, the twins Merlin and Ganieda, the boy leading his blind sister with her arm through his. Paying no attention to the curious murmurings of the crowd, Merlin's dark eyes darted about the room as if he were looking for something or someone. Instinctively, Morgan shrank behind a tall nobleman standing in front of her. For some reason, she especially did not want Merlin to see her at that moment.

The party reached the dais. The servants set down the woman's chair directly in front of Gorlois and Igraine, who both rose to greet their guest. Anna, next to them, followed suit.

"Welcome to Tintagel, Lady Aldan," Gorlois addressed her. "We are very happy and relieved to see you alive in the wake of this tragedy."

"We did not know you were on the *Sea Queen*, Lady Aldan," said Igraine. "We would have made suitable arrangements for your arrival if we had known, but we had no word from your father that you would be journeying to Belerion."

"My lord Duke and lady Duchess." Aldan bowed her head. "Forgive me, but my father does not know that I am here. I had to leave Gwynedd in secret with the help of Brother Blaes."

"But why?" Gorlois inquired worriedly. "You are the King's

daughter!"

"That is why, my lord. I was no longer safe in Gwynedd. And nor were my children." Aldan indicated Merlin and Ganieda standing on her right-hand side.

"Surely King Einion would protect his grandchildren?" Igraine asked somewhat disbelievingly.

"He no longer acknowledges them, my lady," Aldan said quietly.

There was an outbreak of astonished muttering at this revelation. Morgan leaned forward to get a better look at the proceedings. She saw Merlin glance back towards the crowd and his eyes flashed. There was something chilling and dangerous in his stare.

Morgan then noticed the man standing behind Cadwellon, the younger, leaner, dark-haired Druid who had entered with him and who she had not seen properly before. The man seemed very interested in Merlin. He was watching him like a cat watching a mouse, never taking his eyes from the boy's face. Morgan could almost feel the man's tension and a strange excitement emanating from him. She was puzzled. Why was he so interested in Merlin?

Gorlois was asking Aldan questions. "Why would King Einion not accept his grandchildren? And why would you bring them here, my lady?"

"Perhaps the children are illegitimate, my lord," Cadwellon suggested. He looked at Blaes and then at Elfodd. "Pardon my bluntness, but we know how a Christian king might feel about grandchildren sired out of wedlock."

"Well, I can't deny that," Gorlois said with a sigh. He turned back to Aldan and said gently, "Is this the case, my lady?"

Aldan did not reply, but looked close to tears. Blaes stepped forward and said, "I believe I can tell you, my lord. But it is a very delicate matter that needs to be discussed in private."

With a flicker of his eyes towards Sir Brastias, Gorlois motioned a silent order. Sir Brastias immediately called out, "Clear the hall!"

The sound of mumbling and eager discussion filled the room as the crowd moved to find their way to the door. Blasine slipped off the seat next to Morgan and ran towards the door with the others, clearly bored by the proceedings and not curious to know anything more. Morgan, however, wanted to know everything. She needed to find out why Aldan, Merlin and Ganieda had come to Belerion. Ducking between the adults, she ran quickly in the opposite direction to one of the tapestries and hid behind it.

The room emptied quickly. Peering from behind the tapestry, Morgan saw that Anna had also been made to leave, almost certainly unwillingly, since Morgan knew that Anna always wanted to know everything, just like Morgan herself. Gorlois and Igraine remained with only Aldan, Blaes, Merlin and Ganieda as their audience, and Sir Brastias, Father Elfodd, Grand Master Cadwellon and the mysterious dark-haired Druid as witnesses.

"Well, Brother Blaes," Gorlois said. "Tell us why the Lady Aldan has come here."

Blaes hesitated and looked at Aldan. She nodded at him, turned in her chair and reached for her children, taking Ganieda's hand. The little girl's sightless white eyes were fixed straight ahead. Morgan wondered if Ganieda could even hear what was going on, or if she knew she was in the hall of a castle with people around her. Merlin was watching Blaes, his mouth pursed. Morgan could not read his expression.

"My lord," Blaes began. "Nearly six years ago, I was a hermit living in the mountains of Gwynedd. The Lady Aldan sought me out there to make her confession. She felt she could not confide in the priests of her father's court because what she had to confess was too horrifying for them to hear."

There was a pause. From behind the tapestry, Morgan strained to see the faces of the listeners at the dais. Cadwellon and Elfodd looked both interested and alarmed. Gorlois looked concerned, but Igraine, while also seeming worried, did not appear surprised. But Morgan's eyes were drawn to the dark-haired Druid. His predatory gaze was still riveted on Merlin.

"Go on," Gorlois said evenly.

Blaes took a deep breath. "The Lady Aldan confessed to me that she was with child. That she had been … taken against her will." He hesitated. "But this was no ordinary violation, my lord. The thing that impregnated her was no man. It was a demon, a monster, an incubus from the pit of Hell. It came to her in the night when she was alone and defenceless. At first I had no idea how to help her, my lord, so I bade her return to her father's court to wait for my counsel. Then I prayed to God to guide me."

He looked at Aldan. She did not return the look, but held tight to Ganieda's hand and watched Merlin. The boy did not take his eyes from Blaes' face.

"Is this true, Lady Aldan?" Gorlois asked.

Without meeting his eyes, Aldan replied, "It is true that the father of my children is no man, my lord."

"So what happened then, Brother Blaes?" Igraine's voice sounded unnaturally loud in the now still, almost empty hall.

"God gave me the answer, my lady. It was clear from Lady Aldan's description of the monster that defiled her that he was the Devil. I foresaw his plan to bring a powerful demonic child into the world and use this child born into a royal household to counter the spread of Christianity in our land. I went to King Einion's court to be at Lady Aldan's side during the child's birth. As soon as he was born, I baptised him in the name of Our Lord and drove the nature of his Devil father out of him."

"I'm sorry." The young priest Elfodd spoke up. "Forgive my interruption, my lord and lady, but I must speak. You cannot seriously believe what this man is saying? It's superstitious nonsense."

"How dare you!" Blaes' face was red with fury. "How dare you question me! What kind of priest do you call yourself?"

"One who doesn't think much of those who call themselves learned holy men and yet indulge in fairy tales such as this," Elfodd countered coolly. He turned to Gorlois and Igraine. "My lord, there are many of my fellow Christian priests who unfortunately cling to stories of devils and demons to try to explain what they cannot understand. But I assure you there is almost always a reasonable explanation for situations such as this. Perhaps the Lady Aldan was a participant in the heathen ritual of Beltane and that was where she became with child? I understand that the appearance of some of the men who dress up there would fit the description of the Devil."

"There are certainly similarities between some of our gods

and what Brother Blaes might consider demons," Cadwellon said wryly and, Morgan thought, almost as if he was making fun of Brother Blaes.

"Lady Aldan," Igraine said and the room went quiet again. Aldan looked up at her, and for a second Morgan saw something intangible flow between them, an undercurrent of what seemed like understanding. "Did you conceive at the Beltane fires?"

"No, Lady Igraine," Aldan replied. "I am a Christian woman."

"There you have it," said Blaes triumphantly. He indicated Merlin. "The boy is the child of the Devil. But I saved him when I baptised him as a new-born baby and thwarted the Devil's plan."

But what about Ganieda? Morgan thought, looking at the little blind girl standing next to her brother, staring at nothing. Her father was the same as Merlin's and she was born at the same time. *Did Blaes save her and baptise her too?*

No one at the dais seemed interested in that. Instead, Gorlois demanded, "Does King Einion know about any of this?"

Before Aldan could speak, Blaes responded, "We did not tell him, my lord. On my advice, the Lady Aldan let it be known that a visiting nobleman had taken advantage of her and left the kingdom soon after. King Einion was furious, of course, but at first he accepted our story and the children."

"So, what happened to change Einion's mind?" Gorlois queried.

Blaes and Aldan exchanged glances. It was Blaes who responded. "Regrettably, we could not convince everyone of the nobleman story, my lord. Rumours spread as to the children's parentage." He looked at Merlin and Ganieda, standing arm in arm. "Their ... afflictions were obvious from the beginning. The girl, of course, is blind, deaf and mute. She is cursed to live in darkness and silence. The boy ..." Blaes stopped.

"What about the boy, Brother Blaes?" It was the first time the dark-haired Druid had spoken. Morgan felt a shiver go down her back; she could not say why. There was something in his voice that made her immediately wary.

This time it was Aldan who spoke up. "My son has unusual gifts. He could speak when he was still a baby. He has visions of things that have not happened but that later come to pass. He has other gifts too, my lord and lady." A note of pleading entered her voice. "But they're not evil gifts, I promise you. They are wonderful gifts that can be used to help others. But the people in our country began to fear my son. They thought he was the Devil's child and that his gifts were those of the Devil." She stopped, unable to speak further.

Morgan saw Igraine whisper something urgently to Gorlois, while Blaes continued. "There were several attempts on the boy's life in Gwynedd, my lord, and even on the girl's too. Finally, a month ago, Lady Aldan was summoned before her father's judges and accused of consorting with the Devil. I argued in her defence, explaining that it had been against her will, and that the boy was baptised and was no danger to the realm. But they would not heed me. Thanks be to God, King Einion could not bring himself to execute his daughter or his grandchildren, so he ordered them into exile, never to return."

"So you came to Belerion," Gorlois said.

"I know of your tolerance and your goodness and your desire for peace among different faiths, my lord," said Aldan. She looked at Igraine. "And that of the Duchess, too, of course." Morgan saw her mother flinch momentarily and wondered if she was angry again. "I beg of you, let us stay," Aldan went on. "My son is still only a little boy. His education is in the hands of Brother Blaes, a good, Christian man. If you allow us to stay, I swear he will grow up to be an asset to the Duchy of Belerion."

"Naturally, Lady Aldan, you and your children may stay," Gorlois said kindly. "I would not for the world turn you away." He looked interestedly at Merlin, as if evaluating him. The little boy stared back at him impassively. "I'm sure the boy is gifted, though I'm afraid I tend to be as sceptical as Father Elfodd in these matters. Although I do have reason to believe there are many things in the world we don't yet understand."

Aldan looked up at Gorlois, her face shining with gratitude. "Thank you, my lord Duke. Thank you. For my children and for me."

"Welcome to Tintagel, Lady Aldan." Igraine stood up again and spoke to Sir Brastias. "Please call the servants back in. We'll take Lady Aldan and her children to my chambers and find them quarters in the castle."

Morgan watched as the group broke up. Cadwellon and Elfodd walked towards the door, talking together. Blaes observed the old Druid and the young priest as he followed them, his eyes narrowing. The dark-haired Druid made as if to follow Cadwellon, but lingered behind still watching Merlin. The boy paid him no attention at all, but guided his sister to turn and follow their mother being carried out on her chair with Igraine walking beside her. As he left, Merlin's eyes roamed around the room once more. His eyes caught the tapestry and Morgan quickly withdrew her head behind it at once, hoping he hadn't spotted her. She hid as the room emptied of everyone but her father and Sir Brastias.

"Do you think there will be consequences if King Einion finds out his daughter and her children are here?" she heard Sir Brastias ask.

"I doubt it. It seems from what we just heard that he's only too glad to be rid of them," Gorlois replied.

"And what of the suspicions surrounding the children, my lord? Do you not think the people of Belerion might come to fear them as well?"

"This is a land of very different beliefs," Gorlois said. "As long as they don't fight each other or kill each other, you know I'm prepared to let people follow whatever rituals they choose. This country has seen enough bloodshed, which is why we must help Vortigern succeed in this alliance with the Saxons. The last thing we need now is our own people fighting amongst themselves over which gods are the right ones and spreading fear of the others."

"Yes, my lord," murmured Brastias. Morgan heard footsteps walk briskly to the door. She peered out from behind the tapestry again and saw her father alone, stepping down from the dais and strapping on his sword belt.

"Father!" she called and ran towards him.

Gorlois was startled. "Morgan!" As Morgan reached him, he picked her up in his arms and hugged her affectionately. "I asked your mother where you were. Do you mean to tell me you were hiding there the whole time?"

"Mother was angry with me," Morgan said ruefully.

Gorlois looked intently at her. "Yes, she told me. She said you went out in the storm."

"I was on the beach, Father. I saw the wreck. I helped people. It was me who found Merlin and Ganieda. I saved them!"

Gorlois smiled. "I don't doubt you were very brave, Morgan. I wouldn't expect anything less." His voice became grave. "But you must understand why your mother was so worried. It was very dangerous and something very bad could have happened to you. I could not live with that." He kissed Morgan's cheek. "Promise me you won't do anything so dangerous again."

"Yes, Father," Morgan said.

"Off you go," Gorlois said, putting her down. "I'll see you at supper."

Happy that he wasn't angry with her, Morgan half-skipped, half-ran to the door. As she reached the entrance, she turned to wave goodbye. All of a sudden the room went dark. The shafts of light from the windows had gone, as if a veil had come down over her eyes. She saw her father dimly outlined in the darkness, alone at the dais, looking small and lonely in the vast hall. For a moment she thought she saw streaks of dark red on his tunic. They looked like blood.

"Father!" she cried and closed her eyes.

"What is it? Morgan!"

Morgan opened her eyes and the hall was as before. The daylight from the windows illuminated the room. Morgan saw Gorlois standing in the middle of the hall, looking tall and strong as ever. There were no red streaks on his tunic.

"I ... I thought I saw something," she stammered.

Gorlois smiled indulgently at her. "You're tired, that's all. You should have been asleep last night. Go and rest."

"Father!" Morgan cried again. She couldn't contain the fear in her voice.

"What is it, daughter?"

"Do you believe the story about Merlin? About his father being the Devil?"

Gorlois came towards Morgan, knelt down before her and took

her hands in his.

"No, Morgan, I don't believe it. And nor should you. Merlin's a little boy, nothing more. He's a child. Just like you."

III

DROWNED AND SAVED

"My goodness! You look a fright."

Sebile was mixing herbs on her long wooden table. A cloth-covered clay pot was hanging over the fire smelling strongly of seawater. Steam rose from the pot as the heated water evaporated, leaving behind white sea salt crystals. Morgan knew from her earliest lessons that salt was one of the most important things in the world, not just for food but for healing too. Putting salt onto wounds was painful but it would help them heal; drinking water with sea salt could cure stomach sicknesses and even some poisons. As usual, the aromas wafting from Sebile's concoctions mixed in the air, filling the room with an arresting scent found nowhere else.

Morgan had run straight from the hall to her tutor's rooms after talking to her father. She had so many questions to ask. But she was stung by Sebile's curt comment on her appearance, so she put her hands up to her unruly brown hair in an attempt to smooth it out and tried to adjust her crooked dress. She felt angry at her maid Arcile, who hadn't arrived at her room as she usually did every day to wake her up. *The next time I see her, I'll tell her off*, Morgan thought crossly.

"Arcile didn't come to attend to me today. I had to get ready myself and comb my own hair."

"Perhaps mastering those skills should be your next lesson, then," Sebile said with a half-smile as she picked up a small vial of medicine and left the table.

Morgan trotted after her through the arched doorway to the second chamber, then stopped abruptly. On a bed in the corner lay the little Princess Blanchefleur. Her head was bandaged with a piece of clean white linen. Even so, she still looked beautiful and most unusual. Her eyes were dark yet cat-like, her skin smooth, and her straight blue-black hair glistened in the light. Morgan felt more self-conscious than ever about her scruffiness and her own wild messy hair. But Blanchefleur didn't seem to notice; just observed her with an interested, friendly look.

"This is Morgan, the eldest daughter of the Duke and Duchess," Sebile told her.

"Hello, Morgan," the young princess said. She spoke in a sing-song voice, with a strange accent Morgan hadn't heard before. "Mother told me all about you."

"My mother told me about you too," Morgan replied. She was always shy around strangers, but remembered her manners. "It's nice to meet you, Lady Blanchefleur."

"Please, everyone calls me Fleur," the princess said. She smiled at Morgan and Morgan couldn't help but smile back. "My friends do, anyway."

"The two of you will be studying together." Sebile sat down on the bed to administer the medicine to Fleur. "You'll be pleased to hear, Morgan, that what we heard about Fleur is true – she shares your interest in all things healing. Ever since she woke up she's been asking me about the ingredients in the ointments and draughts I've been giving her. She asks almost as many questions as you do."

Morgan grinned. Fleur, swallowing the medicine, saw the grin, giggled and nearly choked. Morgan laughed too.

"All right, that's enough," Sebile said, taking the medicine back. "Now you need to rest."

"Will you come and see me again, Morgan?" Fleur asked eagerly.

"Yes!" Morgan said immediately. "I'll come every day till you're better."

Fleur smiled at her. Then her eyes widened as she looked past Morgan to the doorway. Morgan turned to follow her gaze and saw the boy Safir, who had saved Fleur, standing in the archway.

"I just came to see if she was alright," Safir said.

"Where have you been?" Sebile demanded, standing up. "You disappeared after we arrived at the castle. I was looking for you."

"I'm sorry, my lady. I didn't want anyone to see me."

"You've been hiding?" Morgan asked him.

"I was down in the cellars," Safir said. "No one else was there." He coughed and stumbled as Morgan took a step towards him.

"You're not well," Sebile said briskly. "You nearly drowned yesterday and then spending the rest of the night in the damp cellars … You've probably caught a chill. Morgan, help me get him onto that bed there and I'll have a look at him."

"No!" Safir exclaimed in a tone of such alarm that they were all startled. "Please, my lady! I am alright, I promise!"

"Nonsense," Sebile said, striding towards him and motioning to direct him to the bed opposite Fleur's. "Morgan, take his arm."

"No! Please!" the boy cried again, stepping away from them and staggering as he almost fell. Morgan noticed that his voice sounded different. Sebile stopped in her tracks at the sound and looked keenly at him.

"There's a lot more to you than meets the eye, isn't there, young Safir," she said softly.

Morgan didn't know what Sebile meant, but she sensed Safir's distress and spoke in what she hoped was a kind voice. "Sebile's going to help you. She can heal people. She's made Fleur better and she made Merlin's mother Lady Aldan better. She can help you too."

Safir looked at Morgan and, to her astonishment, a tear fell down his cheek. "You don't know me, Lady Morgan. You don't know what I am."

"I know you're a stowaway. You told me and I don't care. Please let Sebile help you."

Morgan moved slowly towards Safir and took him by the arm. The boy almost wilted at Morgan's touch and allowed her to steer him to the bed. Morgan looked up at Sebile, who was watching her with something akin to pride. Then, as Safir lay on the bed, Sebile went to his side and unbuttoned the boy's ragged tunic.

Morgan watched as Sebile examined Safir, checking his chest, listening to his heartbeat, feeling his bones and joints for injuries. She was always fascinated by the way Sebile knew the human body and how it worked, what made it move, how it could go wrong and what could be done to put it right. She saw how Sebile felt Safir's ribs, frowned, went for an ointment on one of her shelves to rub onto the boy's abdomen and then expertly bandaged his torso tightly with linen. Morgan glanced at Fleur, who was observing the proceedings with equal fascination. Fleur caught Morgan's eye and Morgan felt a swell of understanding pass between them.

"Now, let's get you out of these filthy clothes and into something clean," Sebile said. "Morgan, can you help?"

Morgan was surprised. She was supposed to help this boy remove his clothes? She looked at Sebile in some indignation, but before she could raise an objection, Sebile said, "If you want to learn how to be a healer, Morgan, you'll have to start by getting used to things like this."

Reluctantly, Morgan went forward and hesitantly began to take off the boy's breeches. Safir let out a sob as she did so. Morgan was bewildered and uncomfortable but continued until she had completed the task. Then she saw something that she did not expect and which startled her. Safir's naked body didn't look like the boys Morgan had seen swimming in the sea off Tintagel during the summer months. Instead, Safir's body looked like Morgan's. Fleur, watching from her bed opposite, let out a gasp.

"You're a girl!" Morgan exclaimed.

Another tear fell down Safir's cheek but she quickly brushed it away and did not reply.

"Yes, our young Saracen stowaway is a girl," Sebile said, not sounding at all surprised, and handed Morgan a linen shift. "Quickly, Morgan, put that on her."

Morgan hurriedly helped Safir pull the shift over her head. Sebile then covered Safir with a woollen blanket. The young girl looked at them both. "Are you going to tell them about me? Are you going to tell your father, Lady Morgan?"

"Why don't you tell us how you got here?" Sebile suggested kindly. "You must have come a long way and had a very difficult journey. Where are you from?"

"Babylon, my lady," Safir answered.

"Is Safir your real name?" Morgan asked.

Safir almost smiled at that. "No, Lady Morgan. My real name is Zafira."

"And how did you get here from Babylon?" Sebile demanded.

"It's on the other side of the world!"

"I came through Constantinople, my lady. I joined a train of merchant traders from Babylon, then in Constantinople I got on a ship to Venice."

"What's Venice?" Morgan asked.

"Venice is a city, my lady," Safir said. "A city built on water."

Morgan's eyes widened. "Built on water? But how ...?"

"Later, Morgan," Sebile said. And then, to Safir, "And you were disguised as a boy the whole time?"

"Yes, my lady. I borrowed my brother's clothes and cut my hair. Then I ran away from my home."

"I see," Sebile said.

"How can you speak our language?" Morgan wanted to know.

Safir looked at her and hesitated.

"I'm guessing that young Safir's father is a nobleman or a man of some importance," Sebile said. "I take it you were taught?"

"Yes, my lady," Safir acknowledged. "In Babylon we have the best scholars in the world. I learned different languages from my tutors."

"Alright, go on," Sebile encouraged.

"Well, on the ship to Venice I met a Frankish knight who gave me a position as a serving boy. I went with him to his castle and lands in Armor."

"Armor?" Morgan asked, turning to Sebile.

"Armorica," Sebile told her. "A land across the sea. In Gaul."

"Yes, my lady," Safir said. Her voice softened. "It was so different to anything I knew. So green and so cold. But I liked it. Even though people thought I looked strange, the knight and most of his household were kind to me."

"So why did you leave?" Sebile asked.

"The knight was killed, my lady," Safir said. Her voice bore no hint of emotion, yet Morgan could sense her pain inside. "I had to leave. I got on a trading ship as a servant to the captain. The work was very hard – there were only two of us. We had to run up and down the ship with messages to the crew, serve the captain, climb the rigging to fix the sails and keep a lookout sometimes. The sea was very stormy. One night the other boy who served with me was blown off the rigging by the wind. I never saw him again."

"By all the gods," Sebile murmured. There was both concern and admiration in her face as she regarded Safir. "So what happened after that?"

"We arrived in Gwynedd, my lady," Safir said. "The captain told me he didn't need me anymore, so I couldn't go back on the ship. We were in a port called Carn ... Carnar ..."

"Caernarfon," Fleur interjected helpfully. She had been listening in riveted silence to Safir's tale.

"Caernarfon, yes, thank you, my lady. It was so cold and grey and raining all the time. I heard from some sailors on the docks about the *Sea Queen* taking Princess Blanchefleur to Belerion in the south west, where they said the Sun shone. So I found the *Sea Queen* and got on board when no one was looking. I hid in the hold during the trip."

Morgan stared at Safir in awe. She couldn't imagine doing the things Safir had done or seeing the things she had seen. She wanted to ask her so many questions, about Babylon, Constantinople, Venice the city built on water, Armor – names and places she knew nothing about but the sounds of which thrilled her. But there was one question that remained unanswered, one that Safir hadn't talked about and that Sebile hadn't asked.

"Why?" Morgan said to her. "Why did you want to go away from your home?"

Safir looked at her. "Because of my father, my lady." For the first time Morgan heard a tremor of feeling in her voice.

Morgan thought of her own father, Gorlois. "What about him?"

"He ... didn't like me."

"Why?" Morgan said again.

Safir sighed. "I always wanted to be with my brothers. They used to practise sword fighting and learned to ride our horses. They were always outside in the Sun, training, riding, fighting. I wanted to train to be a knight, just like them." Safir's eyes hardened and her voice went cold. "But my father didn't want me to. He found me one day outside practising fighting with a sword like my brothers did. He beat me. He said that I was ... not natural. That I could never be a knight, that a girl could never do anything like that. He tried to lock me up like a prisoner until I was old enough to be married. So I ran away. I never want to see him again."

There was silence in the room. As she digested the revelation, Morgan tried to imagine what it would be like to have a father like Safir's. In the opposite bed, Fleur's eyes were wide with shock, but full of sympathy for Safir. Sebile said nothing, but laid her hand gently on Safir's head in what Morgan recognised as a sign of affection.

"Are you going to tell the Duke about me?" Safir asked, looking up at Sebile. Sebile caught Morgan's eye and smiled.

"No one here is going to tell anyone your secret," she said. "Isn't that right?"

"I won't tell," Morgan said at once.

"Nor will I." Fleur spoke up again. She looked at Safir admiringly. "You saved me."

Safir looked so relieved she was almost crying. "Thank you. Thank you. Can I stay here?"

"Of course. We'll worry about explanations later," Sebile said. "Now, you both need to rest."

As Fleur and Safir settled down, Morgan followed Sebile back to her table. "What are we going to say to people about Safir?" she asked.

"You're a clever girl, Morgan," Sebile replied. "I'm sure you'll think of something."

She smiled at Morgan, who felt proud at the praise. Her mind immediately raced ahead to possible explanations she could make up to explain Safir's presence at Tintagel.

"Now, run along," Sebile told her as she packed up several vials into a pouch. "There'll be no lessons with me today. I need to see to the other people who were wounded. We'll start again tomorrow."

"Yes, Sebile," Morgan said obediently, and left her tutor's chamber.

* * *

As she closed the heavy wooden door behind her, Morgan's imagination was already working wildly, spinning made-up tales of Safir's arrival.

First Morgan envisaged her as a runaway princess, before realising that Safir, who dressed up as a boy and loved sword fighting, would hate that. Even though she felt sorry for the horrible things Safir had endured, first from her father and then on her journey to Belerion, Morgan couldn't help feeling a little jealous of her. After all, Safir had seen things no one else in Tintagel had ever seen. Babylon, a mysterious, magical city on the other side of the world. Constantinople, the exotic capital city of the Roman Empire, an empire she had learned that other lands of Britain had once been a part of, but whose soldiers had left long before Morgan was born. And Venice, a name Morgan had never heard before. A city built on water! How could that be? Morgan loved water. Already her mind was envisaging castles and huts bobbing and floating on the sea surface, while ships and boats and swimmers darted to and fro between them in place of horses and carts.

So lost was she in her reverie that she didn't see there was someone waiting for her in the shadows of the passageway until he stepped out in front of her.

Morgan started. "Merlin!" she exclaimed.

"Hello," the boy said, gazing intently at her.

Morgan stared back at him. "What are you doing here?"

"I was looking for you. They told me you were in your tutor's chambers. So I waited for you."

Morgan felt a little unnerved by the boy's fixed stare. "Why?"

"I looked for you today in the hall," Merlin replied. His eyes roved over her face. "I didn't see you at first."

"I didn't want anyone to see me," Morgan said, a little defiantly.

"But I saw you, though. At the end."

So he had seen her hiding behind the tapestry. Morgan didn't know what to say to that. She simply acknowledged it with, "Yes, I was there."

"So you heard everything," Merlin said. When Morgan didn't reply, he continued, almost goading her. "Do you believe them, then? Blaes and my mother? That I'm the son of the Devil?"

"No," Morgan said, stung. She didn't like the way he was looking at her or speaking to her. "I think you're a little boy.

You're a child. Just like me."

"Just like you," the boy repeated.

The way he said it made Morgan curious. But she said nothing, only waited for him to speak.

When he did, he said something she did not expect. "You saw them, didn't you?"

"Saw what?" Morgan asked impatiently, getting somewhat annoyed with this strange boy and his equally odd conversation.

"The Furious Host," Merlin said. "The hunters in the sky."

Morgan was astounded. "*What?*"

"It's alright." Merlin frowned at her astonishment. "I saw them, too."

"I thought I dreamed them," Morgan gasped.

"No one else has ever seen them. That I know, anyway. You're the first."

"They're real?" Morgan said wonderingly. "But what are they? Where do they come from? Do you know?"

"My mother says they're the host of the dead. Hardly any people have ever seen them. They appear in the sky before a terrible thing is going to happen. Then they collect the souls of the living and take them to the land of the dead. When the ship hit the rocks, I heard them. I saw them flying above us when we fell into the water. They were waiting for us. I wasn't going to let them take us."

"You and Ganieda," Morgan said.

Merlin nodded. "So I swam with her to the shore. I heard them laughing all the way."

Morgan was horrified. Then a thought struck her. "Did you see the man in the sea, too?"

"What do you mean? What man?"

"I thought I saw ... well, it looked like a man, at least a man's face, except ... he was like a Giant. And made of water."

Merlin looked interested. "No. I didn't see that. What do you think it was?"

Morgan shrugged. She thought of telling Merlin about seeing the Horned Man on the cliff as well, but stopped herself. For some reason, she didn't quite trust this boy yet. Merlin seemed to notice that she was holding something back and his eyes narrowed.

Before he could say anything, Morgan heard a woman's voice calling her. Behind Merlin, she saw Halwynna, her mother's lady-in-waiting, approaching them. Halwynna was a young noblewoman who always appeared to Morgan to be rather cool and distant with everyone except Igraine. Now she seemed somewhat out of breath and anxious.

"Lady Morgan," she said as she came up to the two children. "Your lady mother requests that you join her in the courtyard immediately."

"The courtyard?" Morgan asked incredulously. But, looking at Halwynna's face, Morgan realised with a sinking heart that it was serious. Was she in more trouble? She dreaded another telling off about her going out into the storm the day before. Still, she wasn't going to let Merlin know about that.

"I have to go," Morgan said to him imperiously. She stalked past Merlin without looking back, but was still very much aware of his eyes on her as she left. She didn't look around until she and Halwynna were out of sight and on their way down the staircase.

"Why does my mother want to see me?"

"She'll tell you, my lady." Something in Halwynna's tone made Morgan look at her sharply, but Halwynna kept her eyes ahead, with one hand on Morgan's shoulder.

As they stepped out into the courtyard, Morgan hesitated, remembering the scene of chaos the previous night. The ground was still damp and muddy, with holes and hollows in the ground filled with pools of dirty water. The stones were darkened by the excess water, reflecting the day's pale light with a damp sheen. There was an unpleasant smell in the air – dank and rotten and heavy, a lingering reminder. Morgan saw heaps of debris piled up in the corners of the yard and being loaded onto wooden carts by servants in an attempt to get the castle back to normal. In amongst the refuse, Morgan saw the carcasses of small, drowned animals being thrown carelessly onto the piles to be carted away.

Averting her eyes, she caught sight of her mother standing in the centre of the courtyard looking sombre. For a moment Morgan marvelled at the sight of Igraine's beauty amidst so much ugliness. Her mother's braided golden hair gleamed and her richly coloured gown stood out against the darkened greys and browns of the storm's aftermath. It wasn't until she looked down that Morgan saw the two rows of dirty linen sacks lying on the ground behind Igraine.

"Here she is, my lady," Halwynna said, gently pushing Morgan forward.

"Thank you, Halwynna." Igraine held out her hand. "Morgan, come here, my darling."

Thankful that Igraine wasn't angry anymore, Morgan ran to her. Igraine bent down and drew her daughter to her.

"I have some bad news," Igraine said softly. "Something terrible has happened."

"What is it?" Morgan asked in alarm.

"Your maid, Arcile." Igraine stopped, as if searching for the right words.

"Arcile? She didn't come to attend to me today." Morgan remembered with anger how ashamed she had been after trying to dress herself. But when she looked at her mother's face, she was suddenly scared. "Where is she? What's happened?"

"During the storm last night, there were very bad floods here in the castle and down in the village," Igraine told her kindly. "The waters rose because of all the rain and wind, and a lot of people were taken away. The water was too strong." She gave a barely perceptible glance towards the linen sacks, but Morgan noticed at once.

"Arcile?" Morgan could barely get her voice out.

"Arcile was in the village last night. When the storm came, she was on her way back to the castle." Igraine paused, her eyes full of concern as she looked at her daughter. "She was taken by the flood. They found her this morning. She's dead, Morgan."

Morgan thought she hadn't heard properly. "What do you mean, Mother?"

Igraine sighed. "Now, I want you to be brave." She stood up and led Morgan by the hand over to one of the linen sacks. She nodded at Halwynna, who was standing next to it. Without a word, Halwynna leaned over and opened the top of the sack.

Staring down, Morgan saw the motionless face of her maid. A

girl of about ten years old, not much older than Morgan herself, Arcile was a pretty, chirpy soul with a toothy grin and a face full of freckles, who could make Morgan laugh with her funny sayings. Seeing her now, lying with closed eyes in the dirty sack on the muddy ground, white and cold and immobile, Morgan hardly recognised her.

Images from the previous night flashed before her eyes: bodies laid out upon the beach, Fleur lying soaked and unconscious behind the rock. Merlin swimming while carrying Ganieda with her sightless staring eyes. The dark demonic huntsmen pursuing them from the sky. Instinctively, Morgan fell to her knees, pulled open the sack, looked into Arcile's unmoving face, and put her ear up to the ice-cold chest to listen for a heartbeat. It was hard and silent. She looked up at Igraine, unable to speak.

"I'm so sorry, my darling," Igraine said, holding out her arms. Morgan couldn't feel anything. She stood up stiffly but didn't go to her mother. Instead she asked, "Will she come back?"

Igraine looked sad. "No, Morgan, I'm afraid not. She's gone."

"Gone where?" Morgan asked. Her voice didn't sound like her own.

"To Heaven, of course. Arcile was a good girl. God will welcome her as one of his own."

"Which God?"

Igraine's expression changed from sadness to shock. "What are you talking about?"

"Which God will welcome her?" Morgan asked. She realised that she didn't really know anything about Arcile. She had never talked to her properly. What was her favourite colour? What were her parents like? Would she like being in Heaven? And would she be welcomed by Cadwellon's God? Or Father Elfodd's?

"Now, Morgan ..." Igraine began, but Morgan didn't want to listen anymore. She turned and walked away. Behind her, she heard Halwynna say in a low voice, "Perhaps she's still too young for this, my lady."

"No, the sooner Morgan understands, the better," she heard Igraine say quietly and sadly. "She's going to have to get used to people dying around her. I wish I could protect her from it, but I can't. She's going to outlive all of us. Death will always surround her. She'll forever be alone in the end."

Frightened and confused, Morgan broke into a run. Running as fast as she could, she left the courtyard and headed for the cliffs, not caring if her mother was angry or came after her for disobeying her order to stay inside the castle. She felt as if she couldn't breathe and was running towards the air. The open sky was filled with grey clouds, the daylight was dim and the wind was blowing gustily as an afterthought from the night before. Morgan stood at the cliff's edge, staring down at the still turbulent greyish-green sea. She watched as the waves crashed, white and foaming, against the rocks.

Arcile was gone. Taken by the waters of the storm. She remembered she had felt angry with Arcile that morning and a painful wrench of sorrow and remorse hit her. *Death will always surround me*, she thought. *Is that why Arcile is dead? Because of me?* The wind stung her face and her eyes brimmed with tears. If Arcile was dead because of her … Watching the waves buffeting the rocky shore beneath her, Morgan remembered her dream. The vision of the angels and people drowning below her as she floated above them filled her head. While she had been dreaming, the *Sea Queen* had been wrecked, people had drowned, Fleur and Safir and Ganieda and Merlin had all nearly died, the floods had risen, Arcile had died. "Death will always surround her," her mother had said. What did she mean?

A horrible thought struck Morgan. Was the storm her fault too? Had she somehow made her dream real? She felt sick to her stomach.

But if I can make bad things happen, maybe I can make good things happen too, a small voice said inside her head. The daffodils. Morgan remembered wishing for daffodils before they appeared in front of her that past spring. The iron manacles binding her hands in her dream. Controlling the lightning, cutting the manacles loose. *I freed myself*, Morgan thought. *I thought it and I freed myself. Maybe I can free Arcile if I think about it. Bring her back.* Morgan closed her eyes, feeling the wind and sea-spray on her face mixing with her tears. *Come back, Arcile*, she half-thought, half-prayed, concentrating hard.

After a minute or two, she sensed a fluttering near her face, like a bird or a butterfly. Opening her eyes, she saw nothing but the cliffs, the rocks and the crashing sea in front of her. Then, in the corner of her eye, there was a flash of sparkling white. It was a small, hovering, round white light like the ones she had seen during the storm flickering over the dead bodies of the people on the beach. The strange white light glowed like a candle, but no warmth came from it. As it glided about Morgan's head, she spun round to follow it, not taking her eyes off it as it ruffled stray strands of her hair with what felt like the fast and tiny wings of a hummingbird. But when Morgan reached for it, the light darted just out of her reach.

"What are you?" she demanded aloud. Her question was lost upon the wind, but Morgan thought she could hear faint peals of laughter.

"Lady Morgan!" a voice shouted.

Morgan jumped, startled. Running towards her along the cliff path was Taliesin, her father's page boy, his fair curls blowing in the breeze. Morgan turned quickly back to the small white light, but it had vanished.

Taliesin came up to her. "Lady Morgan," he said again. "Are you alright?"

"Yes," Morgan said uncertainly. "I just thought I saw ..."

"What?"

"Nothing." Morgan didn't know how to explain the white light and decided not to mention it.

Taliesin looked at her closely. "You've been crying," he said.

Morgan didn't deny it. She wiped her tears with the back of her hand. "My maid died in the storm last night. She was in the village."

"I'm so sorry, my lady," Taliesin said. "My father was in the village last night, too. He tried to get to the beach to help with the people in the wreck, but he couldn't because of the flood."

"Is he alright?" Morgan asked in a panic, feeling the tears about to fall again.

"Yes, he's well, thank you," the boy said and smiled at her. His kindness made Morgan feel a little better. "My father's a fisherman. He's survived many storms."

"So why didn't you become a fisherman, too? How come you're a page?" Morgan asked, wiping her hand across her eyes again.

"He wanted something better for me," Taliesin said. "I got a position in the castle because of his friend who works there ..." He paused. "Can I ask: what are you doing out here, Morgan ... sorry, Lady Morgan? After last night, shouldn't you be in the castle resting?"

"I don't need to rest," Morgan said. She looked at him and softened. "And you can call me Morgan, if you like. I just wanted to get out of the castle."

"Well, I'm going to the village to see my father," Taliesin said. He looked at Morgan thoughtfully. "If you ever need to go somewhere away from the castle, you could come to the village with me. I go there a lot to see my father and his friends. You'd have to ask your father or mother for permission. But I know my father would be honoured to receive you ... Morgan."

Morgan felt a warm feeling beginning to banish the loneliness, fear and sickness inside her. "I'd like that," she said. "Thank you."

"Thank you for what?" said a sharp voice behind them.

There on the cliff path stood Merlin. He was regarding them with a cool and unfriendly eye.

Taliesin bowed to him at once. "My lord."

"Why are you talking to her?" Merlin demanded. "Aren't you the Duke's page boy? I just heard you call her 'Morgan'. Do you always talk to the Duke's daughter that way?"

Taliesin said nothing, but he looked upset. Morgan felt sorry for him and was immediately angry with Merlin. "Taliesin can talk to me however he wants!" she retorted. "He's my friend."

Merlin's eyes went cold and his mouth twisted. Taliesin saw the look and said hastily, "I should go, Lady Morgan. I'll be back before nightfall."

"Yes, go, page boy," Merlin said before Morgan could reply. "No one will miss you."

Taliesin flinched, but did not say a word. He bowed to Morgan and set off quickly down the path to the village. Morgan turned to

Merlin.

"What are you doing here, anyway?" she asked him indignantly. "Are you following me?"

"Is that boy really your friend?" Merlin asked, ignoring her questions and her manner.

"Yes, he is! So what?"

"Why? Why is he your friend?"

What a strange question, Morgan thought. She had barely spoken to Taliesin before the previous night, but it didn't matter. "Because he's kind to me. And I like him."

Merlin said nothing. He was looking at her in that odd way he had, gazing at her but avoiding looking directly into her eyes. It made Morgan uncomfortable.

"We should go back to the castle," she said, attempting to walk around him. Merlin stepped in front of her, blocking her path.

"I told you I'd seen you before," he said. "Before we met yesterday, I mean ..."

"Yes," Morgan interrupted him. "I saw you before yesterday, too..."

"... in a dream," both children said together.

Morgan stared at Merlin. "You saw me in a dream, too?"

Merlin nodded. "It was the night of the wreck. Before it happened. I saw you in my dream, standing there on the shore." He indicated the beach below them. Morgan looked down, her eyes drawn to the distant spot where she had stood that night and seen Merlin for the first time. She looked back at him. He was still observing her in that intense, curious way. "In my dream you were watching me swimming with Ganieda towards you," he continued.

Morgan was stunned to hear this. Could it be they had had the same dream? "Yes!" she said, eager to share. "But then the sea turned red, like blood. You were swimming in it, towards me. I held out my hand and ..." She stopped abruptly as she remembered.

"And what?" Merlin asked.

Morgan looked at him accusingly. "You wouldn't take my hand. You just stared at me and wouldn't let me help you."

"That's not what happened in my dream," the boy said.

"What happened in your dream, then?"

"In my dream, I swam towards you and you just stared at me. You didn't hold out your hand. You didn't try to help us. You didn't do anything. You just stood there and watched us drown."

Morgan felt sick to her stomach again. "That's not true."

"It's what happened in my dream," Merlin stated matter-of-factly.

His seeming lack of emotion disturbed Morgan. She felt angry with him again and baffled by him at the same time. "But that isn't what happened. I helped you. I saved you. You know I did."

When Merlin didn't reply, she cast a look of triumph at him. "*My* dream is what happened, Merlin. You see? You were wrong. I was right."

And with that, Morgan turned on her heel and stalked back towards Tintagel. She didn't look back, but somehow she knew that he was watching her all the way. In her mind's eye she saw him smile when she wasn't looking.

IV

Confluence

The sea of the storm night seemed far away, like a distant dream. As she and Fleur walked the rocky coastal path together, Morgan marvelled at the ocean's changeable moods. Today the sea glimmered a deep turquoise, moving slowly, gently and steadily, all the while sparkling in the late afternoon Sun. Warm vapours from the blue-green waters below swept up and over the cliffs, carrying with them salt-scented breezes and white sea-birds that cawed plaintively as they hovered overhead, gliding on the gusts of early autumn air.

The land along the coastline was varied, with green-speckled rocky headland lying alongside patches of long-stemmed grass, and bracken dotted here and there with the bright pink of foxgloves. For the past two weeks Morgan had been permitted to take Fleur out walking along the coast within sight of Tintagel Castle – as part of her recovery, Sebile had said. Morgan felt happy inside, knowing that Sebile had helped her get around Igraine's plan to keep her inside the castle by using Fleur as the perfect excuse. It was the first time she had been allowed to go walking outside Tintagel without a guard or an escort, and it made her feel very grown-up and important.

"It's so beautiful," Fleur said wonderingly. She was no longer wearing the linen bandage around her head and her long straight black hair glistened in the sunlight. Sebile had said that Fleur's wound had healed fast and that she was ready to begin lessons.

Morgan had visited Fleur every day in Sebile's rooms since the day they had discovered Safir's secret and the two little girls found that they enjoyed each other's company. Like Morgan, Fleur was hungry for knowledge and wanted to know all about Sebile's healing methods and remedies. They had spent many an hour talking eagerly about herbs like woundwort and comfrey

56

that Sebile used in the ointment for the compresses on Fleur's head wound. Morgan had been allowed to change them from time to time. She had also helped Sebile boil animal fat and mix in marigold petals to apply to Safir's bruised ribs. Sebile had taught Morgan to simmer, strain and cool the mixture while Fleur had watched, fascinated.

Looking around at the sunny shoreline of stark rocky cliffs and deep azure sea, Morgan agreed that it was beautiful. "What's Ynys Môn like?" she asked, wondering if Fleur missed her home.

Fleur thought for a minute. "It's different," she said finally. "It's a bit like here, but ... darker maybe. And colder."

"You mean the sky's darker?" Morgan said, glancing up at the pale blue expanse above their heads. She remembered the black swirling clouds of the storm and the one-eyed hunter and his wicked followers emerging from them. She shivered involuntarily despite the day's warmth.

"The sky and the sea are darker," Fleur told her. "The sea doesn't look like this. I've never seen it this colour before. And the land's darker, too, I think." She looked at the pretty green grasses and pink flowers around them. "It just feels different."

Morgan was intrigued. "I'd really like to see it. I've never been anywhere outside Tintagel before."

Fleur smiled at her. "Maybe you'll come back with me to see my parents someday." Her smile faded at the mention of her family. Morgan felt sorry and bit back another question she was going to ask about Fleur's home. But Fleur seemed to want to talk to her about it.

"You see ... Ynys Môn is my home, but it's not my real home," Fleur said after a pause.

"What do you mean?"

"I'm not my parents' daughter. I mean, I am, they adopted me, but I wasn't born in Ynys Môn."

Morgan thought about her aunt Queen Sardoine and Sardoine's husband King Pellinore, neither of whom she had ever met. "How do you know that? Where were you born then?"

"I don't know. Mother told me was that I was found." Fleur looked out at the sea. "My parents were at the monastery on Holy

Island when it happened. Mother said that a strange ship came in with the tide. It didn't look like any ship they'd ever seen before and it was carrying spices Father said were from the East. But the really strange thing was that there was no one on it. The ship was abandoned. Mother said it was like a ghost ship. They found me in a cot – the only person left. I was just a baby."

Morgan was fascinated. "And you don't know where the ship came from?"

"There was no one to ask. Father said it must have come from eastern lands because of the cargo. So I must have come from there, too. Mother wanted children and she said she loved me the moment she saw me. She asked Father to let her keep me, so they adopted me."

"Is that why you look so different?" Morgan wanted to know.

Fleur looked wistfully back at her. "I suppose so."

Morgan sensed Fleur's sadness. "Do you think about your real parents?"

"Sometimes," Fleur replied. "Mother and Father are very good to me. I know they love me. But sometimes …"

Morgan understood. She felt bad for Fleur, not knowing who her parents were or indeed who she really was. She thought of Fleur as a tiny little helpless baby, sailing alone in a ship into an unknown harbour. Her mind went back to the sea and to what she had seen in the storm.

She wondered again why she and Merlin had been the only two to see the hunters in the sky. It made her nervous being the only one besides him to have seen them, and the only one to know about the Horned Man on the cliff and the old man's face in the sea. Listening now to her friend tell the strange story of how she came to Ynys Môn made her realise that Fleur had secrets too, even if they were secrets she didn't know about yet.

Not for the first time, Morgan considered confessing to Fleur what she had seen that day. She hadn't told her parents because she was afraid they would think she was making it up. Igraine always said she had a wild imagination and Gorlois would think she had just dreamed it. She hadn't told her little sisters, either; she wasn't going to give Anna a reason to laugh at her and Blasine would probably be scared. She had thought many times of telling Sebile, but the same thing held her back from telling her tutor as it did Fleur. Morgan feared she wouldn't be able to explain or describe what she had seen properly. Or, worse, that they wouldn't believe her. Or they would think she was mad.

"Maybe when you grow up, you can find out where that ship came from," she said to Fleur instead.

Fleur smiled at her. "Maybe."

They walked back to Tintagel in the late afternoon Sun. As they walked, a slight breeze picked up along the coastal path, sweeping through the grasses and delivering an unexpected chill. Morgan glanced up at the sky and stopped walking.

"Look!" she said to Fleur, pointing upward.

There above them, standing out against the bright blue of the sky, was the Moon. It was like the slenderest of fingernails, perfectly curved and gleaming white.

"The Moon!" Fleur gasped. "But how come we can see it? It's daytime!"

"I don't know," Morgan said, puzzled but excited. She looked at the slowly descending Sun and the sliver of the Moon higher in the sky, and she felt oddly exhilarated. "I've never seen the Sun and the Moon together before."

"Do you think it means something?"

"I don't know."

They watched the yellow orb and the white crescent in the sky for a few minutes until the daylight glow began to turn slightly reddish. Then they made their way back to the castle, talking animatedly.

Fleur had already moved out of Sebile's rooms and into Morgan's chamber. They would be spending time in Igraine and Gorlois' quarters that night, and Morgan hoped she would be able to read aloud to everyone, as she often did, with her father's help. As they discussed what book she should read from (Fleur wanted the Bible, Morgan was hoping to read from one of Sebile's history books), they entered the courtyard. Morgan couldn't walk in there without remembering Arcile and her cold body lying in its dirty sack on the hard stony ground. As Fleur continued to chatter happily, Morgan fell silent. A strange dark shadow seemed to fall between them, and Morgan felt a wave of sickness and dizziness wash over her just as she had done that terrible day.

Just then she saw that in the corner of the courtyard Merlin was sitting on a wooden box near the shelter for the message pigeons. He had a book in his hands. Morgan had barely spoken to him and hadn't wanted to since they had talked about their shared dream and its differences. Alongside her never-failing annoyance at his presence and peculiar behaviour, a feeling of distinct discomfort now arose in Morgan at the sight of him. She tried to avoid him as much as possible, though she noticed that it was becoming more and more difficult. Out of the corner of her eye, she could see him watching them, but as soon as she looked directly at him he looked down at his book with concentration as if he hadn't seen them.

Morgan was irritated. "Why does he do that?"

Fleur turned and saw Merlin reading. "What?"

Exasperated, Morgan tried to explain. "He's always near me. Wherever I go, he's there. He's always staring when he thinks I'm not looking. But then when I look at him, he doesn't look back. He hardly ever speaks to me. But when he does, he's just really unfriendly and mean."

"Maybe he doesn't know how to talk to people," Fleur suggested.

Morgan frowned. "I don't think so. He's just annoying. I don't like him."

They went inside and made their way to Sebile's chambers. Sebile was on her rounds, but Safir was there looking out of the window towards the sea. She too had recovered and she had been like a bird in a cage shut inside for the past week. She still looked like a boy with her short, cropped hair and wearing her freshly laundered boy's attire. They had managed to keep her a secret up till now, but Safir had repeatedly expressed her wish to leave Sebile's rooms and find a position in the castle. She greeted Morgan and Fleur with relief.

"I am so happy to see you! Lady Morgan, have you thought of how I can stay here at Tintagel?"

"You can call me Morgan," Morgan said. She was finding that

she didn't enjoy people calling her by her title, especially people she considered friends. "Yes, I've thought of something you can do."

"It's brilliant!" Fleur said eagerly.

Safir's face lit up. "What is it?" Then her smile faded. "Will I have to be a lady's maid? Or work in the kitchens?"

Morgan grinned at her. "No. It's something only a boy can do." She waited a moment for Safir's silent but delighted reaction and continued. "I'm going to ask my father to make you his squire. He doesn't have a squire anymore because the one before was made a knight."

"It's perfect," Fleur said. "Then you can stay a boy *and* learn to be a knight."

Safir's eyes shone. Then her face fell again. "Will your father let me, though? I mean, I'm a Saracen – I'm not from here. Why would he choose me instead of one of his nobleman's sons?"

"Don't worry," Morgan said, exchanging a glance of complicity with Fleur. "We have to go to my parents' chambers this evening and my father will be there. I'll talk to him then."

Safir moved towards her and looked into Morgan's eyes. "Thank you, Morgan," she said quietly. "I'll never forget this."

Morgan smiled and took both Safir's hands. A warm feeling crept through her as she stood there with her two friends. *This is what it feels like to help people*, she thought proudly.

* * *

A fire was blazing in the hearth in Gorlois and Igraine's chambers when Morgan and Fleur got there. Igraine was seated in her chair sewing, while Anna and Blasine sat at her feet. Morgan hated sewing. She knew her mother and other noblewomen had spent the last two weeks making clothes for villagers in Tintagel who had lost all their belongings in the floods. Morgan admired this, but not enough to want to take up needlework herself. Blasine was fingering the material and observing Igraine, while Anna held a small child's dress that she was attempting to sew together with Igraine's encouragement. Morgan knew Anna hated sewing as well

– she only did it because she knew their mother would be pleased with her.

Igraine looked up as Morgan and Fleur came in and smiled. "Hello, girls. Did you have a good day?"

"Yes, thank you, Mother," Morgan replied.

"Come and sit down. Your father will be along shortly." As Igraine spoke, Anna let out a cry. She had pricked her finger with the needle and there was a trickle of blood. Igraine tutted and staunched it with a white handkerchief.

"You must be more careful, darling. You always try to finish things too fast. Slow down and concentrate on what you're doing."

Morgan smirked. Anna saw and scowled at her.

As Morgan and Fleur sat down by the fire, Gorlois entered looking somewhat weary. "Good evening, Igraine, girls."

Igraine stood up. "Gorlois." She embraced him warmly and took his cloak as he sat down in the chair opposite hers. "Is everything alright?"

"We've managed to rebuild the west wall beyond the kitchen," Gorlois told her. "Some of the houses in the town are being reconstructed. I ordered the men to the quarry so we could build the houses with stone instead of wood this time, the way the Romans used to. The stone houses should survive any future storms we may face."

"That's a blessed relief," Igraine said. Gorlois looked down at Morgan sitting in front of the fire. "Hello, sweetheart. All well?"

Morgan got up and hugged him. "We're well, Father," she said. "Fleur and I went for a walk along the cliffs again."

"That's good," Gorlois said, patting her head somewhat absently. He nodded respectfully at Fleur. "Lady Blanchefleur." Then he turned back to Igraine. "What of the Lady Aldan and her children? How are they adjusting to their life here? Are they happy with their quarters? You put them in the domestic rooms above the stables, is that right?"

"Yes," Igraine said shortly. Morgan noticed once again her mother's cool reaction to Aldan. She wondered why Igraine didn't like Merlin's mother.

"And?" Gorlois asked.

"I've visited her," Igraine told him. "Lady Aldan seems to be recovering from the injury to her leg, though Sebile says it may never fully heal. The boy is attending his lessons with Brother Blaes and the girl ... well, I think she is mostly confined to their rooms."

"Have you invited them here to your chambers, Lady Igraine?" asked Fleur.

Gorlois and Igraine both looked at Fleur in surprise. Fleur blushed.

"I just thought ... I'm here with you. I thought you could invite them, too."

"I think they prefer to be left alone," Igraine told Fleur in a kindly tone. But Morgan sensed the tension behind her voice. Fleur must have felt it too, for she said no more. Morgan was glad. She really didn't want to have to see Merlin in the evenings as well.

"So, Morgan, are we going to read together tonight?" Gorlois asked her.

"Yes, Father," Morgan said. "But first, can I ask something?" She sat back on her heels to face him, glanced sideways at Fleur who nodded encouragingly at her, and began. "I'm helping Sebile with someone from the wreck. He's a boy, a bit older than me. He wants to stay in Tintagel."

"There was a fourth child survivor?" Gorlois said, looking at Igraine. "Why didn't I know about this?"

"Nobody did," Morgan said quickly, before Igraine could respond. "He's staying in Sebile's rooms until he's better. He was squire to a knight, but his master ... died in the sea that night."

"Do you know who the knight was?" Gorlois asked.

Morgan was alarmed. She hadn't thought of that. But Fleur came to her rescue.

"The boy came onto our ship at Caernarfon," Fleur said without missing a beat. *At least that's true*, thought Morgan. Then Fleur added a couple of white lies to help out. "The knight was from Gwynedd. I saw the boy with his master on the ship."

"I see," Gorlois commented, looking back at his daughter intently. "So what do you want to ask, Morgan?"

"He wants to stay in Tintagel," Morgan said. "I thought ... because you haven't got a squire anymore, he could be your squire."

"Morgan, we don't know anything about this boy," Igraine said severely. "To be a squire is a position of honour. Especially to your father, the Duke. Many families would like their sons to have that post."

"But he would be the best!" Morgan protested. "He's very clever and he loves sword fighting." She saw her parents smile at each other.

"He's very brave," Fleur said. "He saved my life."

Gorlois looked impressed. "Did he indeed?"

Morgan could sense his growing interest. "Yes, Father," she said eagerly. "He got Fleur out of the sea. He rescued her. That's how I met him." She stopped, remembering her mother's anger about her going out in the storm. But Igraine was looking at her fondly and, Morgan thought, with a touch of pride.

"Very well," Gorlois said. "Bring the boy to me tomorrow. I'll take a look at him."

Morgan was delighted. "Thank you, Father!" she cried, jumping up and hugging him again. Gorlois laughed as he embraced her back, exclaiming, "Now, now! I haven't promised anything yet."

That's true, thought Morgan. Her initial happiness gave way to nervousness at the thought of presenting Safir to her father. What if Gorlois didn't accept Safir? What if he saw straight away that she was a girl and punished both Safir and Morgan for daring to try to pretend that she wasn't?

"Now, Morgan." Igraine's voice broke into her thoughts. "A little decorum, please. Why don't you read to us now?"

"Yes, Mother," Morgan said. Fleur grinned at her encouragingly and Morgan smiled back. She picked up one of the two books she had brought and sat down on her father's lap. She had made a bargain with Fleur: Morgan would first read a chapter from Fleur's favourite book, the Book of Genesis in the Bible. ("Mother reads it to me all the time," Fleur had explained.) Then she would read from one of Sebile's very old books that she knew came from a far distant land. Morgan opened the Bible so that she and Gorlois could both see the pages and started to read, with Gorlois' prompting and encouragement as he helped her with the words she didn't recognise.

"*In the ... beginning,*" Morgan began, her eyes scrutinising the large black Latin letters and tracing the lines with her finger, "*when God created the heavens and the earth, the earth was a formless void, and darkness covered the face of the deep, while a wind from God swept over the waters. Then God said, 'Let there be light'; and there was light. And God saw that the light was good. And God separated the light from the darkness. God called the light Day, and the darkness he called Night. And there was evening and there was morning, the first day ...*"

As Morgan read, her mind's eye wandered to the images she was reading about. She saw a vast empty darkness suddenly illuminated by a great light that chased the shadows to the far corners of the world. She saw the great dome that God called the sky stretched out to separate the waters above and the waters below. She watched as the waters gathered together, crashing and churning, to form the seas, and the land bursting forth from them. She observed seeds opening and rising to form trees filled with fruit, and buds blazing to life with flowers of every size and colour. She saw how the waters below brought creatures small and huge to life, and how birds flew across the dome of the sky through the clouds above.

"*... God made the two great lights – the bigger light to rule the day and the smaller light to rule the night – and the stars. God set them in the dome of the sky to give light upon the earth, to rule over the day and over the night, and to separate the light from the darkness. And God saw that it was good. And there was evening and there was morning, the fourth day ...*"

When Morgan had finished reading the seventh day, she stopped. "That was excellent, Morgan!" Gorlois said proudly. He looked at his wife. "She's learning very fast."

"Yes, she is," Igraine agreed. Morgan was surprised that she sounded almost sad and looked questioningly at her. Igraine caught her eye, instantly put on a smile and said, "That was very good, my darling."

Morgan saw Anna looking sulkily at her behind their mother's back and it made her determined to do even better with the second book. It was an old, dusty tome that Sebile said came from a library in a far-off country where it hardly ever rained and there were no trees. Morgan couldn't imagine such a place.

She picked up the book. It fell open at a page marked with a thin strip of parchment. Was it Sebile's? Morgan looked at the page and then at her father. Gorlois nodded at her, so Morgan clasped the parchment strip in her hand and began, hesitatingly, to read. She found this book much more difficult. It was written in an unusual script not like the one used by the monks, and in a different style, with many shorter lines together making up a kind of rhythm. With Gorlois again helping her decipher the strange words, Morgan began:

> *"Hail, daughters of Zeus! Give me sweet song*
> *To celebrate the holy race of gods*
> *Who live forever, sons of starry Heaven*
> *And Earth, and gloomy Night, and salty Sea.*
> *Tell how the gods and earth arose at first,*
> *And rivers and the boundless swollen sea*
> *And shining stars, and the broad heaven above,*
> *And how the gods divided up their wealth*
> *And how they shared their honours, how they first*
> *Captured Olympus with its many folds.*
> *Tell me these things, Olympian Muses, tell*
> *From the beginning, which first came to be?"*[1]

Morgan's imagination returned to the beginning of the world – the sea, the sky, the land, the animals, the stars, the Sun and the Moon, all laid out and placed together in harmony and splendour. But this time it was different. This time she saw figures moving amongst it all, like people, but bigger, grander, more beautiful. The figures were hazy, almost shadow-like, but she could see them as they strode up the mountains and danced through the woods, lurked in dark caves and watched the earth from the sky.

---

[1] Hesiod and Theognis, *Theogony, Works and Days and Elegies*, trans. Dorothea Wender (1973), ed. Betty Radice (London: Penguin Classics, 1973), 104 – 115.

"Chaos was first of all, but next appeared
Broad-bosomed Earth, sure standing-place for all
The gods who live on snowy Olympus's peak
And misty Tartarus, in a recess
Of broad-pathed earth, and Love, most beautiful
Of all the deathless gods. He makes men weak,
He overpowers the clever mind and tames
The spirit in the breasts of men and gods.
From Chaos came black Night and Erebos.
And Night in turn gave birth to Day and Space
Whom she conceived in love to Erebos …"[2]

"Enough!" Igraine interrupted, reacting so suddenly that her sewing fell to the floor. Morgan looked up, startled out of her reverie by her mother's agitation and the sharpness of her tone.

"The children are far too young for this," Igraine said angrily to Gorlois. "What is this book? Where did she get it?"

"Sebile gave it to me," Morgan said, puzzled.

"*Theogony*," Gorlois read. "Hesiod. One of the scholars of the old world, it seems."

"I shall have to talk to Sebile." Igraine picked up her sewing again. "I don't want Morgan reading this kind of thing."

Morgan noticed a look pass between her parents. They seemed worried about something. What was so bad about the book?

"It's time you girls were in bed," Igraine said to them. Anna immediately protested, but Fleur and Blasine rose obediently to go. As Anna pleaded with their mother to be allowed to stay, Morgan closed Sebile's book, stood up and looked at her father inquiringly. Gorlois smiled reassuringly at her.

"Why is the book bad, Father?" Morgan asked.

"It's not bad, Morgan," Gorlois told her. "It's just a book for grown-ups. Not for you."

"But why? It's the same story," Morgan said.

"What do you mean?"

"The beginning of the world. It's telling the same story as the Bible, isn't it?"

[2] Ibid., 116 – 126

Morgan looked over at her mother and saw that Igraine looked almost alarmed. Gorlois' face was solemn. He hugged her and said quietly, "I think one day you'll understand, sweetheart."

"I'll take the book, Morgan," Igraine said, holding out her hand. However, observing Morgan's stricken face, Gorlois intervened.

"I think Morgan should take it back to Sebile tomorrow," he said. "You'll do that, won't you, Morgan?"

"Oh, yes, Father, I will," Morgan replied fervently.

As the four little girls left the chamber, Morgan heard Gorlois say to Igraine in a low voice, "Don't worry. It's very difficult for her. I doubt she'll be able to read any more of it without help."

Once they were outside in the passage, Anna turned on Morgan. "It's your fault!" she hissed. "Your stupid book!"

"Be quiet!" Morgan said angrily.

Anna's dark eyes flashed and for a moment it looked as if she was going to hit Morgan. Morgan braced herself to hit back, but Fleur stepped in.

"Please don't quarrel, you two," she said gently.

"Yes, don't," Blasine echoed nervously.

Morgan and Anna stared at each other for a few moments, then Morgan turned on her heel and stalked off to her room, still holding Sebile's book. Fleur followed her, carrying the Bible.

"She's always so hateful," Morgan said, thinking about Anna.

"She doesn't like it when your parents are happy with you," Fleur observed.

"She's always being the good girl in front of Mother, but I know she's not good. She's horrible."

Morgan changed into her nightgown. In the weeks since the storm, she had learned to dress, undress, wash and comb her hair without a maid, but every time she did she thought of Arcile. Morgan tried very hard to remember her as she was when she was alive: laughing, joking, colourful, warm. But the terrible image of the cold, stiff, empty, closed-eyed Arcile kept rearing up in her mind and blocking out her memory of the living one. She hadn't tried to call Arcile back since she had seen the small white light on the cliff path – in truth, she was afraid of what might happen if she did.

Fleur was already in the large bed, turning the pages of the Bible and gazing at the illuminated pictures. The gold from the pages glittered in the faint glow of the candles. Morgan clambered up onto the other side of the bed, brushing up against the hangings and pushing them back. She had left Sebile's old book on top of the coverlet. Sitting up, she lifted it again. It was heavy. *"Theogony,"* she read, remembering the way Gorlois said it.

Fleur looked up. "I didn't like that book."

"Why not?" Morgan asked.

"It's not right. You said it was the same story, but it's not."

Morgan knew she had understood the *Theogony* story as describing the beginning of the world like the Book of Genesis. "It's not exactly the same," she admitted. She opened the book at the page she and her father had read together. "But it talks about the Earth and the sea and Night and Day, just like the Bible. Only this book has gods in it, like people."

"That's why it's wrong," Fleur said earnestly. "There's only one God."

Morgan couldn't argue that, so she said nothing. She looked again at the page written in the unfamiliar script and traced her finger along the lines to try and read aloud hesitantly to herself some more, straining her eyes to make out the words in the dim candlelight.

"... And Earth bore starry Heaven, first, to be
An equal to herself, to cover her
All over, and to be a resting place,
Always secure, for all the blessed gods.
Then she brought forth long hills, the lovely homes
Of goddesses, the Nymphs who live among
The mountain clefts. Then, without pleasant love,
She bore the barren sea with its swollen waves,
Pontus. And then she lay with Heaven, and bore
Deep-whirling Oceanus and Koios; then ..."[3]

Morgan took a deep breath at the daunting list of names that

[3] Ibid., 127 – 136

followed. Her tongue stumbled over the difficult clusters of letters:

"Kreius, Iapetos, Hyperion,
Theia, Rhea, Themis, Mnemosyne,
Lovely Tethys, and Phoebe, golden-crowned."[4]

Who were all these names, she asked herself? These gods? Where were they? What did they do?

"Last, after these, most terrible of sons,
The crooked-scheming Kronos came to birth
Who was his vigorous father's enemy."[5]

Morgan didn't understand all the words she was reading, nor did she know if she was saying them correctly. But somehow, the meaning, she knew. "The crooked-scheming Kronos," she thought. "Most terrible of sons." Was he like the Devil? Morgan knew the Devil was God's enemy. And Kronos? Who was his father? And why was he his enemy?

She turned to Fleur to talk to her about it, but the princess had fallen asleep, the Bible still open beside her. Morgan noted the difference between the two open books. The Bible's pages were beautiful, elegant and rich, and even though most of the candles had gone out, Morgan could see the gold paint that illustrated the pages still shining in the dark. The *Theogony* had no such beauty or images or illumination: its bare pages were stiff and worn and cracked at the edges, its letters simple and stark. *And yet*, Morgan thought stubbornly, *they* are *telling the same story.* She just couldn't say how.

The wind rustled outside the window, bringing with it a chill breeze. For an instant, Morgan's mind went back to the coastal path amongst the grasses and foxgloves, to the moment where she had seen the slender white Moon shining so strangely in the blue sky of day. She slipped out of bed as the last of the candles burnt out and the room plunged into darkness. Morgan made her way

---

[4] Ibid., 137 – 139

[5] Ibid., 140 – 142

unseeing to the window and peered out.

There was no sign of the crescent Moon. The sky was black as ink, save for a few faint white stars that could just be glimpsed through swirling dark clouds. Morgan heard the sound of the sea swelling far beneath her at the foot of the cliff; a moving, living thing that smelled of salt and seaweed. There was a hush in the air outside the window, as if someone or something were holding its breath. As she stared out into the night, Morgan felt a growing apprehension that something was coming.

Something flickered in the distance. A white object was approaching the castle, heading towards Morgan's window. Morgan wondered, *Is it a bird?* It seemed to be flying, floating towards her on the breeze. She thought of the small white light that had come to her when she had called Arcile – had it returned? But this was much bigger.

As it flew nearer, Morgan could see that the white looked like a robe. Then she saw a head. Arms. Legs. It was a man. A man floating towards her. She could see his head and then his face. He was looking directly at her and she saw his teeth as his lips parted in a grin.

Morgan was paralysed with terror. She opened her mouth to scream but nothing came out. She couldn't cry out; she couldn't move even to turn to Fleur asleep in the bed behind her. She stood, helpless, as the man came towards her, white-robed, grinning, all the way up to the window. He looked intently at her.

"Hello, Morgan," he said.

His voice sounded like the chiming of bells. Morgan felt her heart pounding hard and she couldn't respond. All she could do was stare at him. He looked young but seemed old; his hair was black and curly and his eyes were a strange type of yellow-brown. He observed Morgan staring at him as he hovered outside her window and grinned again, showing chalk-white teeth.

"Don't be afraid, little girl," he said to her. "You must be brave."

Morgan found her voice. "Who ... wha ... What are you?"

"I'm a herald."

"What's that?"

He laughed and the bell-sound grew louder. "A messenger, little

Morgan. I'm a messenger. My name is Dyonas. And I've come to bring you a message."

Morgan felt her racing heart start to slow down. "A message from who?"

Dyonas looked at her keenly. "Someone very important. Someone who wants to know you."

"Me? Why?"

"You'll find out." His voice grew sombre. "Tonight is the darkest night of the year. The Moon awakens during the day and sleeps at night. Tomorrow night you must wait on the battlements of the castle, after everyone has gone to sleep. Your visitor will meet you there." Morgan didn't take her eyes off Dyonas' face. His expression changed and he looked stern. "And you cannot speak of this to anyone. Do you understand?"

"Yes," Morgan said at once, though in reality she understood very little of what was happening. Amidst her confusion and fear, he fascinated her. "Are you a ghost?"

Dyonas laughed again. "No. Not at all."

"So what are you?"

"You'll find out."

Morgan was feeling bolder. "Who am I going to meet tomorrow night?"

"I was told you'd ask a lot of questions," Dyonas said. "As I said, you'll find out."

A thought struck Morgan.

"Why does the Moon awaken during the day? Is that why I saw it in the daytime? Why can't I see it now?"

Dyonas floated closer to the window and Morgan resisted the urge to shrink back. *I must be brave*, she thought. As if he were reading her thoughts, Dyonas smiled.

"Tonight, Morgan, the Moon is on the same side of the world as the Sun. Tomorrow is the first night of the waxing Moon and that is when she will arise."

Morgan felt the breeze on her face again as it ruffled the herald's white robe. "She?"

Dyonas nodded at her. "Until tomorrow."

Morgan watched in wonder as he floated away from her. Up

and above the roof of the castle, the young man flew, his white robe growing fainter and fainter in the blackness of the night until he disappeared altogether. Morgan was left trembling at the window, blinking her eyes in the darkness and wondering if what she had just seen and heard was real.

V

KINDRED SPIRITS

"So this is the boy."

Gorlois appraised the young Saracen child standing nervously before him. Safir was wearing her boy's clothes. Her hair had been cut very short again by Sebile to maintain her disguise.

Morgan stood beside Safir in her father's council chamber next to the main hall. Following the encounter with Dyonas, she hadn't slept at all and was so tired that she was beginning to wonder whether it had all been a dream. But now she had to pay attention to her father, and make sure he didn't find out or suspect that Safir was a girl.

"You didn't tell me the boy was a Saracen, Morgan," Gorlois said to her. Morgan detected a severity in his voice and felt nervous herself.

"No, Father," she said. "But he was a squire like I told you … and he speaks our language." She looked appealingly at Safir.

"Yes, my lord," Safir said in her slightly accented tones. "I was a squire to a very noble knight called Sir Gorlagon."

"And how did you meet this Sir Gorlagon?" Gorlois asked.

"On a ship from Constantinople to Venice, my lord. I came from Babylon."

As Safir told Gorlois her story as truthfully as she could, without revealing her secret and carefully omitting all mention of Armorica, Morgan watched her father and his seneschal, Sir Brastias. Brastias was frowning as he listened to Safir's account. Morgan thought with a sinking heart that he didn't like Safir. Could it be that he knew Safir was really a girl? She looked back at her father anxiously, wondering how he would act if he was told that the child who wanted to be his squire was a girl, like her.

"So," Gorlois said when Safir had finished. "The first thing you ask is to stay in Tintagel, even though you came here under false pretences as a stowaway. And now that you're here, you ask to be made my squire, no less."

Safir and Morgan exchanged looks. "Yes, my lord," Safir said again. "If it please you."

"Well, I can't fault your ambition, boy," Gorlois said. "But to be my squire is a very important position." He looked at Morgan. "It seems you have befriended my daughter, but that's not enough for me to give you the position."

Safir looked crestfallen. Morgan opened her mouth to protest, but Brastias spoke.

"Pardon me, my lord, but I think you would do well to consider the boy."

Gorlois turned to him in some surprise. "You think so?"

"That was quite a journey he had for such a young lad," Brastias said. He looked at Safir and frowned again. "He's obviously strong if he managed to travel so far and survive all that. And the boy's got courage, no doubt about that."

Morgan was stunned. She had been wrong! Next to her, Safir was trying to stifle a hopeful smile.

"Yes, I suppose so," Gorlois said uncertainly. He looked closely at Safir again.

Morgan couldn't contain herself. "Please, Father," she begged.

Gorlois chuckled. "Very well, then. We'll give it a try." He nodded at Safir. "You know how to saddle up my horse ... Safir?"

"Yes, my lord," Safir said eagerly.

"Go out to the stables, groom my horse, polish the saddle and my riding boots, and have everything ready within the hour."

"I'll take him to the stables, my lord," Brastias said.

"Thank you, my lord." Safir bent her knee before Gorlois. "I swear to you, you will not be sorry."

"Go on with you," Gorlois said. Safir stood up and went out of the room with Brastias, exchanging a delighted look with Morgan as she left.

"Thank you, Father," Morgan said gratefully.

Gorlois nodded. "Remember, Morgan, he's only on trial. If he's no good, I'll have to think of what to do with him."

"He'll be a good squire," Morgan told him confidently.

Gorlois gave her an odd look with a half-smile. "Oh, Morgan. How is it that someone so young can sometimes seem so old?" His smile faded. "I hope you always keep your faith in people, Morgan." Before Morgan could puzzle over his meaning, he said briskly, "Time for you to go. You have lessons today, I believe."

"Yes, Father. With Fleur," Morgan replied.

As Morgan walked down the passage to Sebile's rooms, she thought again about Dyonas and what he had said to her. He had told her not to tell anyone, but Morgan wished she could have told Gorlois. She always felt safe with her father. Knowing about Dyonas and having to keep him a secret made her feel frightened and alone. She was scared about the "visitor" she had to meet on the battlements that night – "She." Would "She" be like Dyonas? Or something different?

Fleur was already seated when Morgan entered. Sebile was carrying several books from her collection to the table and Morgan went to help her.

"You look tired, Morgan," Sebile said as Morgan took a couple of the books from her.

"I didn't sleep," Morgan said.

"She was reading," Fleur told Sebile.

Morgan put the books down on the table. She looked up to see Sebile watching her with a smile. "What?" she asked, somewhat defensively.

"Now, don't be rude, child," Sebile said, setting down the rest of the books. "If you're tired, we'll study this morning and then you can rest this afternoon."

Looking at the books on the table, Morgan saw that Sebile's lesson was going to be about herbs and healing potions. Interested as she was in this, Morgan had a more important question to which she wanted to know the answer.

"Sebile, can I ask you about that book you gave me?"

"I've given you lots of books, Morgan," Sebile replied.

"The *Theogony* book. The one about the beginning of the world."

Sebile sat down on the other side of the table. "Ah, yes. Did you see the passage I marked for you?"

So the scrap of parchment had been Sebile's. "I read it with Father last night," Morgan informed her.

"We read the Book of Genesis first," Fleur said.

"It was the same story, wasn't it?" Morgan asked. "Fleur doesn't think so, but I do."

"The Book of Genesis is true," Fleur objected. "The other one isn't."

"So, you both see it in different ways," Sebile said. "That's something very important to think about. The story of the creation of the world is just one example – each of those books has a different way of looking at the same thing and understanding it." She looked at Fleur. "The Genesis story may be true for you. But the *Theogony* story may be true for others."

"But which one *is* true?" Morgan asked, frustrated with Sebile's answer.

"Perhaps both. Perhaps neither. Perhaps the creation of the world was bigger and more difficult than either of these stories," Sebile said, turning back to Morgan. "The point is to understand that there are many different ways of looking at things. The way you look at something, the way you understand something, and understanding how others may look at the same thing and understand it differently is very important."

Morgan's tiredness made Sebile suddenly look strange to her – was there a light in her face? Sebile's pale, watery-blue eyes seemed larger and brighter as they looked into Morgan's. "You need to remember that there are different ways of understanding things before you make decisions in your life."

Morgan tried to make sense of this in her mind. Fleur, however, seemed upset.

"But that's ...! That's blasph ... blasph ..."

"Blasphemy," Sebile finished for her. "No doubt the priests would say so."

"Which priests?" Morgan asked, thinking of Father Elfodd and Brother Blaes, and then of Grand Master Cadwellon and his dark-haired Druid companion.

Sebile smiled at her. "Which, indeed."

The old woman opened one of the books to begin tutoring

her pupils. As the lesson progressed, Fleur paid close attention, occasionally writing down lists of herbs for remedies on her roll of parchment with Sebile's help. Morgan attempted to do the same, but her head was hazy and her eyelids felt heavy. She felt as if she couldn't breathe and took several gulps of air, remembering again the sensation of the breeze along the cliff path on that sunny afternoon.

All of a sudden she desperately wanted to be outside again, in the open salt-smelling air, not in Sebile's rooms surrounded by musty books and heady potions. In her mind she kept remembering the nocturnal meeting with Dyonas, which seemed ever more like a dream. As she examined an illustration of the yarrow flower, she thought about going to the battlements in the darkness of night and felt scared again. She had an urge to tell Sebile what she had seen and ask her what to do – but then, she again heard Dyonas' warning, "You cannot speak of this to anyone." As Sebile explained how yarrow or achillea could be used on wounds and cuts, Morgan had the sudden wild impulse to ignore Dyonas and tell her tutor everything. She didn't want to go on being the only person to know about the strange flying man. And she didn't want to have to face "She" alone. Taking a deep breath, she opened her mouth to speak.

Don't tell her, a voice said in her head.

Morgan was startled. She knew the voice wasn't her own.

Don't tell her, the voice said again. *She can't help you.*

What? Morgan demanded, almost in panic. *What do you mean? Who are you?* The image of Dyonas, floating towards her window all in white, his teeth bared, loomed over her again in her mind.

I can see him, the voice continued. *You're scared of him.*

How do you know? Morgan asked. *How can you see him?*

He's in your mind. I can see him there.

The back of Morgan's neck prickled. She stood up and whirled round so fast that she knocked over her chair.

"Morgan!" Sebile looked at her in concern. "What are you doing?"

Morgan didn't answer. She stared into the corner of the room where the milky-eyed twin sister of Merlin was sitting quietly behind her, her sightless gaze fixed straight ahead. It seemed to Morgan that Ganieda's blind eyes were looking at her, even though she knew the little girl couldn't see.

"Ah, yes. Ganieda," Sebile said. "Her mother asked me if she could sit with us during your lessons, while her brother studies with that monk from Gwynedd. I thought the two of you wouldn't mind."

"But she can't hear us or see us, can she?" Fleur asked.

"No, she is blind and deaf, and thus mute as well," Sebile said. "Born that way, it seems. But she may recognise companionship, even if she can't see us or hear us or talk."

Morgan didn't take her eyes off Ganieda. *Is that you?* she thought, cautiously.

In shock, Morgan saw the corners of Ganieda's mouth rise slightly, almost in a smile.

Yes, said the voice in her head. *It's me.*

So you can *hear*, Morgan thought.

I can hear your mind. Not your voice.

Morgan took a deep breath. *And you can see my mind?*

What's in your mind. Yes.

And you know me?

You're Morgan.

How do you know that?

My brother told me about you. He showed me.

Merlin, Morgan thought with the annoyance and unease she always felt when she thought of him. Then, with a start, she realised that Ganieda could feel what she felt too.

He's the only person who can hear me, Ganieda's voice said. *The only person who can see things for me. But now you can too.*

"Morgan?" Fleur was looking at her, puzzled and wary. "What is it?"

Morgan made an effort to stay calm. "Nothing." She picked up her chair and slowly sat down again, very aware of Ganieda's white eyes seeming to bore into her. "I was just surprised to see her." She caught Sebile's eye and noticed a glint of something she couldn't comprehend.

The lesson resumed, but Morgan wasn't paying attention. She

stared at the picture of the white yarrow flower, trying to grasp what had just happened. Then a thought occurred to her.

Can you still hear me? she asked Ganieda.

Yes, she heard Ganieda's voice reply.

And you can see what I see? In my mind?

Yes, Ganieda said again.

What am I looking at now? Morgan asked, fixing her eyes on the yarrow picture and thinking about it.

There was a pause. Then Ganieda said, *It's a white flower.*

It's a picture of a white flower, Morgan told her. *It's called yarrow. It's a herb you use for healing cuts.*

Again there was a silence. Morgan could sense that Ganieda was confused.

Why are you telling me this? Ganieda finally asked.

Don't you know? Morgan said to her. *If you can see what I see, you can learn what I learn. You can study too.*

Another silence. *I can study?* Ganieda asked. Morgan could feel the girl's wonderment. And something else. It was a moment before Morgan recognised what it was. Happiness. Immense happiness.

"Sebile?" Morgan said, interrupting her tutor's flow of words.

"What is it, Morgan?" Sebile asked. It seemed to Morgan that the tutor was trying to stifle a smile.

"Can Ganieda sit with us? Here, at the table? It's not fair that she's sitting all by herself."

"Well, of course," Sebile said. "Is that alright, Fleur?"

"Yes," Fleur said, though looking a little nervously at Ganieda.

Morgan stood up and went over to the silent blind girl. Ganieda rose before Morgan reached her and stretched out her hand. Morgan took it and gently led her over to the table. She pulled up a chair and eased Ganieda into it.

"How did she know?" Fleur asked in amazement. "How did she know to stand up if she can't hear us?"

"Where I come from, they used to say that if a person is blind or deaf, they develop other senses," Sebile said. "Perhaps she felt Morgan come over to her. Maybe she sensed that you were inviting her to share your table with her."

Morgan said nothing. How could she explain? As she sat

back down, she saw Fleur looking curiously but not unkindly at Ganieda. Sebile, however, was not looking at Ganieda, but at Morgan. Morgan realised from her tutor's expression that at that moment Sebile was feeling very proud of her. Morgan thought it must be because she had done something kind. She had an odd sense of having passed a kind of test. But when she saw Ganieda's face, she felt a swell of pride herself. The little girl with the sightless eyes was smiling directly at her.

Morgan smiled back. For the first time since her encounter with Dyonas, she didn't feel afraid. She had obeyed the night messenger and not told anyone about him, but now someone else knew and had seen him too. She wasn't alone.

* * *

Morgan hadn't seen much of Taliesin since the day she had found out about Arcile's death. He had been performing his normal duties as page, which meant that she didn't meet him often. But she had not forgotten how kind he had been to her, nor his invitation to go to the village with him and meet his father the fisherman. When the morning lesson finished, and Sebile told them there would be no lessons that afternoon so that she and Fleur could both rest, Morgan's mind went to Taliesin. She wondered if he was going to the village that afternoon and whether he would take her with him. Her need to get out of the castle had grown stronger.

"Shall I take Ganieda back to her mother?" Morgan asked.

"Certainly," Sebile said.

Did you like the lesson? Morgan thought to Ganieda. She was sure she could see Ganieda's blank eyes shine with an unusual light.

Oh, yes! Thank you, thank you, the little girl replied in her mind. *I never had a lesson before.*

What about your brother? Doesn't he have lessons?

Ganieda's eyes faded. *Yes. But he doesn't show them to me.*

Knowing that Ganieda was listening inside her head, Morgan tried not to think what she felt about Merlin at that moment. But she could see Ganieda had felt it too. The girl's face fell.

"I'll come, too," Fleur said. She and Morgan went either side of Ganieda and guided her slowly towards the door. Morgan concentrated on the view in front of her so that Ganieda could see what she was seeing through her mind.

"I'll see you both later," Sebile said. She was busily packing up her bag with vials of medicines, preparing to visit patients both inside and outside the castle. "Perhaps after the next lesson, the two of you could accompany me. That way you'll see the practical side of healing as well."

Morgan and Fleur walked with Ganieda down the passage and through the main hall towards the courtyard.

"I'd like to see her healing people," Fleur commented.

"It's really good," Morgan said as they went outside and crossed the yard towards the stables. "I want to make people better like her."

She caught sight of Taliesin at the far side of the courtyard, drawing water from the well.

"Taliesin!" she shouted at once. Turning to Fleur, she asked, "Can you take Ganieda back? I want to speak to Taliesin."

"Um... alright. Yes, I will," Fleur said, looking surprised. Morgan looked at Ganieda. *I have to go*, she told her. *Fleur will take you back. I'll see you tomorrow in the lesson.*

She gave Ganieda a quick smile and let go of her arm. There was a change of expression in the girl's face. Was she upset? But she couldn't be, Morgan reasoned – she'd just had her first lesson which she'd enjoyed. Morgan dismissed it and turned away from Ganieda and Fleur. She ran over to Taliesin.

"Hello, Morgan," the boy said. He was clearly happy to see her, though he looked around cautiously to see if anyone was watching them talk.

Morgan wasn't concerned about that. "Are you going to the village this afternoon?" she asked him abruptly.

Taliesin looked taken aback. "I was going tomorrow. My father wants to see me about something. Why?"

"I don't have a lesson this afternoon," Morgan told him. "I want to get out of the castle. I could come with you to the village to see your father today, if you like."

"I have to ask permission if I want to go," Taliesin said. "But your father's gone out with Sir Brastias and his men and that new squire – the Saracen boy."

"Safir," Morgan said. She felt impatient with him. "Can you ask someone else? Or I can ask for you."

"Well … maybe Halwynna. She knows my father."

"So, ask her. I'll wait for you."

"You want to go now?" Taliesin asked incredulously. "Don't you have to ask your mother?"

To her surprise, Morgan found that she didn't care about Igraine's permission the way she once might have. "She thinks I'm in lessons." She saw Taliesin's anxious face and tried to reassure him. "Don't worry. We'll come back before it's night."

"I'll go and find her then," Taliesin said. He still looked a little uncertain but he left carrying his bucket of water and disappeared into the castle.

Morgan waited for him by the well, watching the people and activities in the courtyard. Several individual horses were tethered to iron rings in the wall and a number of newly arrived horse-drawn carts filled with sacks were being unloaded. A few black crows fluttered hopefully around the carts and hopped alongside as the sacks were carried into the stables, pecking on the ground at spilled seeds that only the birds themselves could see.

As Morgan watched, she observed an especially large sack being lifted off one of the carts. Her mind, unbidden, went back to the image of Arcile lying lifeless in a similar sack on the cobbled ground. The familiar feeling of sickness and sadness welled up in her. Just then she saw Fleur emerging from the stables above which Lady Aldan's family was quartered. Behind her was Merlin. Morgan took a deep breath to dispel both the memory of Arcile and the feelings it brought. She didn't want Merlin to know about it.

The two children came up to where Morgan was standing. "Merlin was there when I took Ganieda back," Fleur said to Morgan, almost apologetically.

"Hello," Merlin said.

"Don't you have lessons now?" Morgan asked, without returning his greeting.

"No, Brother Blaes has gone to see the priest," Merlin replied. "He's angry with him."

"What are we going to do?" Fleur asked Morgan. "Shall we go for another walk?"

"Taliesin's gone to ask permission to go to the village to see his father," Morgan said. She glanced at Merlin to see how he would react, but he just gave her an unreadable look. "We can go with him."

"Oh, yes! I'd like that," Fleur exclaimed eagerly.

"So would I," Merlin said.

After a few more minutes, Taliesin reappeared with Halwynna by his side. They were both carrying several bundles. "Lady Morgan," Taliesin called, careful to use her title in front of Igraine's lady-in-waiting. Morgan, Fleur and Merlin went over to them.

"Lady Morgan, you can accompany me to the village to deliver these provisions," Halwynna said. "Taliesin came to see me and I've informed your mother that you will be with me. She is in council with some of your father's tenants."

"Thank you," Morgan said. Halwynna handed her and Fleur small bundles to carry, then looked at Merlin. "You're coming, too, Master Merlin?"

"Yes," Merlin said without further explanation. Halwynna nodded at Taliesin, who held out a larger bundle for Merlin to carry. Merlin stared at him for an instant. Then he silently took it and slung it over his shoulder.

"Well then, let's go, children." Halwynna led the way out of the yard and down the winding path to the village.

Morgan had only been to the village once before in her life and never on foot. She knew it was called Trevana and was the closest town to Tintagel Castle. Many of the castle servants came from there. Like Arcile. *No*, thought Morgan, pushing the memory back. She concentrated on the path before them.

"Will your father be fishing now?" she asked Taliesin.

"He starts early in the morning, so he'll be back now," the boy told her. He stole a glance at Halwynna ahead of them. "He knows Lady Halwynna's coming because she sent a message yesterday. So I expect he'll be there."

"What's his name?" Morgan wanted to know.

"Elffin," Taliesin told her.

"How do he and Halwynna know each other?" Fleur asked.

"My father sometimes delivers fish to the castle, my lady," Taliesin said. "He and Lady Halwynna met about a year ago. She was in the kitchens when he was making a delivery."

"So that's how you got a position in the castle," Merlin said. "Through her."

Morgan gave him a sharp look, but Taliesin responded quickly. "Yes, my lord. But I started out as a kitchen boy. Now I work as page to the Duke himself. *This* position I got on my own."

Morgan caught Fleur's eye and they both grinned. Merlin looked sour, but didn't say another word until they had reached the village. From a distance, Morgan could see the small round houses clustered close together with smoke rising from some of the roof-holes. Surrounding the village were green meadows with sheep and cows grazing, and fields of dull-gold wheat stalks that looked somewhat battered. A number of people were gathering the wheat that remained into sheaves.

The four children and Halwynna made their way down the road. As they got closer, they saw several men and women mixing clay and stacking stones as they pulled out rotting planks of wood in the walls of the buildings and filled in the jagged holes. In the centre of the village they could see a few animal pens grouped together surrounded by fences of wooden stakes.

"They're rebuilding the houses," Halwynna said. "A lot of the wood from the houses' walls was torn down by the storm."

"Now they'll be made of stone," Morgan said, looking around at the small houses grouped along the road, and remembering Gorlois' words from the previous evening.

"Yes," Halwynna said. "They're bringing the stone locally from the quarry."

"Stone houses, like the Romans," Merlin mused.

"My father says some people use slate now instead of thatch for their roofs," said Taliesin.

"That's right," Halwynna said. "Most of the thatch was blown away by the wind as well."

"What's that smell?" Fleur asked, wrinkling up her nose.

Halwynna smiled. "Trevana is an unusual village, my lady. People here keep livestock, like cows and pigs and chickens, but some of them, like Taliesin's father, are also fishermen. They keep their boats in the bay and bring their catch back to the village to be cleaned and sold. That's why the air here can be a little …"

"Stinky?" Merlin said. Morgan couldn't help chuckling. Fleur giggled too, but Taliesin looked a little downcast. Halwynna nodded.

"Yes. But remember, Master Merlin – the people here work very hard. This is one of the villages in Belerion that provides much of the land's wealth and food."

A clanging noise told Morgan that they were passing the smithy. She peered inside as they went past. The bright red and orange sparks from the blacksmith's fires were a sharp contrast to the browns, greens and greys of the town around them.

"Father!" Taliesin suddenly shouted. He broke into a run towards a man who laughed and gathered the little boy up in a bear hug.

Morgan was surprised to discover that Taliesin's father was not at all as she had imagined him. She had seen him in her mind's eye as a greying, older, slightly wrinkled figure. But Elffin was a young man, though very different from his son. Tall, black-haired and dark-eyed, with skin browned by the Sun, he couldn't have been more different from the fair-haired, hazel-eyed Taliesin, whose skin was the palest Morgan had ever seen.

"Lady Halwynna." Elffin greeted the lady-in-waiting with a happy smile, bowing deferentially to her and kissing her hand. Halwynna seemed suddenly superior and greeted him coolly.

"We have brought provisions," she said, handing him her bundle and indicating the smaller ones carried by the children. "I trust you will distribute them accordingly."

"Yes, my lady," Elffin said and beckoned to several women standing nearby. Morgan noticed for the first time that their arrival in the village had caused some excitement. The people working on the houses and in the smithy had stopped and were staring at them with interest.

"Thank you, my lady. We are most grateful to the Duke and Duchess," one of the women said as they came forward to take the provisions from the children.

"The Duchess regrets that she could not come herself, but she has business to attend to at the castle," Halwynna said. She turned back to Elffin. "I trust he is here?"

"Yes, my lady. He arrived last night," Elffin said. "I received your message. But we were expecting you to come alone today. My son wasn't due until tomorrow."

"Things changed," Halwynna told him.

"Father," Taliesin said, tugging at his arm. "This is Lady Morgan, the Duke and Duchess' daughter."

Morgan stepped forward and held out her hand as she had seen Halwynna do. "Hello, Elffin," she said primly.

"Lady Morgan. It is an honour." Elffin took her hand and bowed again.

"And this is Princess Blanchefleur of Ynys Môn," Halwynna said. Fleur gave Elffin a friendly smile as he bowed to her. "And Merlin, son of the Lady Aldan of Gwynedd," Halwynna said after a pause, as if she were not sure how to introduce the boy. Merlin looked at Elffin seemingly without interest, but Morgan could tell he was curious.

"Come, please," Elffin said, placing his arm around his young son's shoulders. "I've prepared some food. There should be enough for all of you." He looked back at Halwynna, then at the children. "And I have a very important guest who I know would like to meet you all." He looked down at his son. "Especially you, Taliesin."

"Why me?" Taliesin asked, surprised.

Elffin seemed about to say something else, but Halwynna interrupted. "No. Let him tell the boy."

"Why would somebody important go to a fisherman's house?" Morgan whispered to Fleur.

"Maybe he's one of your father's men," Fleur whispered back.

"Or maybe he's a town leader," Merlin said from behind them, listening.

They followed Elffin, Taliesin and Halwynna to one of the round houses at the end of the village. There were nets lying on the ground outside and a distinct smell of fish about the place. The house itself was small like the others, and the walls were a patched mixture of layered stone and mud – Elffin's house must have been hit by the storm and rebuilt, thought Morgan. It had a thatch roof which looked new and a narrow stone chimney. Morgan had never been inside a village house before, so she approached the entrance with some excitement. Elffin stepped back to allow Halwynna to enter first; both grown-ups had to bend down to get through the door. Morgan saw Taliesin trying to catch her eye. He smiled and indicated that she should go in ahead of him.

At first the single room seemed so dark and smoky that Morgan could barely see in front of her. As her eyes grew accustomed to the gloom, she saw a stone hearth on the right-hand side, with smoke from a lit fire rising up through the chimney and partly filling the room. Opposite the door stood a simple straw mattress bed with no posters or hangings. Next to the entrance was a row of soft-looking sacks that looked as if they had been slept on. On the other side of the room was a large round wooden water container next to which lay a pile of freshly caught fish. A solitary cow chewed on a scattering of hay in the far corner as it solemnly observed the proceedings.

From the smoke, the stench of the fish and the smell of the cow in the corner, Morgan could hardly breathe. She had an overwhelming urge to run back outside again, but realised that would be very rude. Putting her hand up to her nose, she turned towards the hearth and saw a wooden table on one side next to the window.

Then she almost jumped out of her skin.

Sitting there very still, watching her every move, was an old man. Through the haze of the hearth-smoke, she dimly recognised who he was.

VI

FAERIE FAITH

"Grand Master Cadwellon," Halwynna said, bending her knee before him.

"Bless you, child," said the old man, placing his hand on her head in greeting. He looked at the children standing before him. "And who are these?"

Halwynna beckoned them forward. "This is the Princess Blanchefleur. My lady, this is Grand Master Cadwellon, the head of our Druidical Order."

"A Druid?" Fleur asked, alarmed.

Cadwellon smiled at her. "It's alright. I'm not dangerous, my lady."

"And this is Merlin," Halwynna said, looking in the boy's direction.

"I remember him," Cadwellon nodded. He looked keenly into Merlin's eyes. "How are you and your mother and sister faring at Tintagel, Merlin?"

"We're well, sir," Merlin replied, returning Cadwellon's gaze.

"Hmm." Cadwellon looked from him to Morgan. "And this is…?"

"Morgan," Halwynna said. Something in her voice made Morgan stare at her, startled.

A light shone in Cadwellon's eyes. "Of course!" he exclaimed. "Has it really been five years already?" He observed Morgan as he had Merlin – deep, penetrating blue eyes looking into hers. "This is really her? The child herself?"

"Yes, it's me," Morgan said, before Halwynna could respond. "The Duke of Belerion is my father."

"Remarkable." The old man smiled. "It's wonderful to see you here among us, my dear."

Morgan couldn't contain her curiosity any longer. "Grand

Master Cadwellon, why are you here? Shouldn't you come to the castle to see my father?"

"Lady Morgan!" Halwynna sounded nervous. "You mustn't question the Grand Master in that way. He has his reasons for doing things."

"It's alright, Halwynna," Cadwellon said. Then, to Morgan: "I am here to see your father, Lady Morgan. I have an audience with him tomorrow and I have to deliver a very important message for him. But I am here in the village for another very important reason. Halwynna was kind enough to help me with this task."

"How do you know the Grand Master, Halwynna?" Morgan asked before the obvious explanation struck her. Her eyes widened. "Are you a Druid?"

"Yes, my lady," Halwynna told her. "I was an acolyte when I was a young girl." Seeing Morgan's uncomprehending expression, she explained. "An acolyte is a pupil of the Druidical Order. The way you are a pupil of Lady Sebile."

"I'm of the Druidic faith, too, Lady Morgan," said Elffin. "And so is my son."

Taliesin gave a shy smile. For the first time Cadwellon looked at him. "He's here already? Well, well."

"This is him, Grand Master," Elffin said. He placed his hands on the boy's shoulders and pushed him gently forward.

"Wha ... what do you want with me, sir?" Taliesin asked the old man.

"Have you not talked to him about this?" Cadwellon asked Elffin.

"No, sir. I thought it would be best if you told him."

"What, Father?" Taliesin asked anxiously.

Cadwellon fixed his piercing gaze on him. "I would like you to join our Order, young man. To become one of us."

"Me? A Druid?" Taliesin gasped. He looked round at the others and his eyes met Morgan's. "But, sir! How?"

"You would start as my apprentice, Taliesin. You would learn everything I have to teach you."

"But ... I'm only a page boy," Taliesin said.

"No, my boy, you are much more than that. And you can be

much more than that, if you choose to be."

"Come," Elffin said to Halwynna and the children. "Please sit down and have some food. Taliesin, help me."

As they chose places on wooden stools around the table, Morgan made sure that she sat next to Cadwellon. She was fascinated by him and had all kinds of questions she wanted to ask. As soon as she sat down, Merlin pulled up a stool next to her and sat down on her other side. Fleur sat opposite them and Halwynna sat next to her. Morgan noticed that Elffin paid a lot of attention to Halwynna, taking her cloak, pulling out a stool for her, glancing her way frequently. Was something wrong, Morgan wondered? Why was he staring at Halwynna all the time?

Just as she was thinking this, she caught Merlin watching her. But once again, as soon as she realised he was looking at her, he averted his gaze. Before Morgan had time to get annoyed and discomforted again, Elffin brought over to the table a pot he had lifted from where it had been hanging above the fire. Inside the pot something was boiling that had a very a strong smell. "It's fish stew," Elffin told them, as Taliesin handed round bowls. The boy still looked stunned at the news the Grand Master had brought.

Observing the father and son as they sat down to table, Morgan couldn't resist asking a question that was on her mind. "Elffin," she said. "Can I ask why Taliesin doesn't look like you?"

Elffin stopped ladling out portions of stew for a moment. "Ah, Lady Morgan," he said. "Taliesin is a special boy."

"Maybe he looks like his mother," Fleur suggested.

"I wouldn't know, Lady Blanchefleur. I never knew Taliesin's mother."

All the bowls were filled with steaming hot stew. Cadwellon picked up his wooden spoon and began to eat. The others followed suit. Morgan dipped her spoon into the pungent-smelling bowl and tentatively tasted the stew. To her surprise, it was very good. For a few minutes, nobody said anything but ate in silence.

Taliesin was the first to speak. "Father didn't know my mother because he found me."

"He found you?" Morgan asked, surprised.

"That's right, my lady," Elffin acknowledged. "I found him

on the beach when he was a baby. He was in a leather bag that had washed up on the shore. When I opened it, I couldn't believe my eyes. I'd never seen a child so fair, so beautiful, so happy. He laughed all the time." He ruffled Taliesin's hair affectionately. "I brought him to the village, but no one seemed to know who he was. When no one claimed him, I took him into my home and adopted him as my son."

Morgan couldn't contain herself. "But that's like Fleur!" she exclaimed, turning to her friend.

Fleur's eyes were shining. "Yes, my parents found me, too. I was on a ship when I was a baby, the only person on board. My parents adopted me as well."

"It doesn't surprise me to hear it, my lady," Cadwellon said to her. "From the way you look, I'd have said you were a changeling child."

"What's that?" Morgan asked before Fleur could react.

Cadwellon smiled at her. "Have you ever heard of the faeries, Lady Morgan?"

Morgan hadn't. She shook her head.

"The faeries are what the Christians would call spirits," the old man said. "There are many different kinds and they live in all sorts of different places – in the woods, in the mountains, under the hills, in caves, in streams and in rivers, sometimes even in the air above us. It is all around us, the faerie world; on earth and yet not of this earth. The faeries vary in size and in the clothes they wear, and in looks too. Some look just like people; others look quite different from us. Many of them are like us in other ways, too. They have kings and queens, courts and castles, realms and communities, like us, though often with different rules. Sometimes they kidnap a human child and replace it with one of their own. That child is called a changeling."

Morgan's mind reeled. She thought back to Dyonas, the floating man in his white robe. He must be a faerie. The memory of him brought back the spectre of "She" who she was supposed to meet that night. "She" must also be something Cadwellon said was "not of this earth", like the horrible hunters in the sky or the Horned Man. She glanced at Fleur across the table and was shocked to see that her friend's expression had changed completely. Fleur looked as if she was going to be sick.

"You think I'm a changeling?" Fleur said in a shaky voice.

Cadwellon looked at her and spoke gently. "Who knows my lady? Changeling children sometimes look different from the rest of us, as you do a little bit, but often they can look the same. They are different in other ways as well. They have powers – magic, we call it. They can, for example, move things with their minds or see the future in dreams or speak with the tongue of an adult when they are only a baby." He smiled kindly at Fleur. "As far as you know, do you have any of those things?"

"No," Fleur said thankfully. She was almost crying. Morgan shot her a look of sympathy. But her own mind was still spinning. She had seen the storm and Merlin in her dreams. And she had made daffodils appear when she wanted them. And the white light had appeared when she had called Arcile. All of a sudden she could no longer taste her food.

"I have those things," Merlin said before Morgan could find her voice. It was the first time he had spoken since they had sat down at the table. "My mother says that I could talk when I was a baby."

"So could I," Taliesin spoke up. He turned to his father, his eyes wide. "You said that I talked like a grown-up when I was a baby."

"Yes, son," Elffin said. "But after I found you and you stayed with me, you stopped. After a while you weren't able to do that anymore."

"It often happens when changelings live with humans," Cadwellon said. "They adapt."

"So am I a changeling?" Taliesin asked the Druid Master.

"We shall have to find that out," the old man said. "If you come with me and agree to be my apprentice, we'll see what you're really capable of."

What about me? Morgan thought.

"What about me?" Merlin said, echoing her own unasked question. He was looking at Cadwellon keenly. "Could I be a changeling? I could talk when I was a baby." He stopped, as if not wanting to say too much. "I can ... do other things as well. Can I come with you and be an apprentice too?"

Cadwellon turned to him. "But I thought you had been claimed by the Christians, young man," he said. "Is not the monk from Gwynedd teaching you?" Before Merlin could reply, the Grand Master continued: "Each Druid can only have one apprentice, Master Merlin. Our teachings are many and varied, and our knowledge is wide. It takes many years both to teach and to learn everything there is to know. That is why there can only be one apprentice for each Druid. And I have chosen Taliesin."

Taliesin's face glowed. Morgan saw that Merlin's face and lips had gone white. She suddenly felt a surge of feeling, of anger. But she knew, instinctively, that the anger she felt at that moment didn't come from her.

"Grand Master, can girls be apprentices?" she asked cautiously. She wasn't sure if she wanted to put the changeling question to him herself.

"They can be apprentices to Druid priestesses, Lady Morgan," Cadwellon told her. "As Halwynna was. As the Lady Igraine was."

"My mother?" Morgan gasped.

"Ah." Cadwellon exchanged glances with Halwynna. "The child doesn't know?"

"No, Grand Master," Halwynna said. She looked at Morgan. "The Duchess was an acolyte as I was. She was apprenticed to the High Priestess Birôg of the Mountain, when we were girls."

"But that's not true!" Fleur blurted out. Everyone at the table turned to her. "Lady Igraine is a Christian," Fleur said indignantly. "She's my mother's sister. And Mother is a Christian."

"Lady Igraine is a Christian now," Halwynna said. "Like her mother was. But her father was not. And she was taught by the Druidical Order when she was a child."

Morgan struggled with this idea. "But ... but ... how can you be a Christian *and* a Druid?"

Cadwellon laughed. "Ah, that's the question, child! No one has yet found the answer, to my knowledge. The two cannot be reconciled. In this world, you believe one thing or you believe the other."

"What do you believe?" Morgan asked him.

Cadwellon fixed his bright blue eyes on her once again. They looked much too young for his face.

"That takes many years to explain, Morgan," he said softly. Morgan noticed that he hadn't called her by her title, but the solemn way he said her name made her wary. "And it takes many more years to understand. In essence, we believe in the power of nature, of the world all around us. Trees, groves, lakes, rivers, hills, the sea, the sky, animals, plants – for us there is not only one God but many gods, who protect us and shape all natural things and fill the earth. After all, with all the riches in this world, how can our gods not reflect this richness and abundance but through their own infinite varieties and incarnations?"

Morgan remembered the words from the conversation she had witnessed in the Great Hall between the Druid Master and the young Christian priest Father Elfodd. "What's an omen, Grand Master? What's interpreting an omen? What does divining what will happen mean?"

Cadwellon gave her a delighted smile. "So you know something about us then, child! Divination is one of our most sacred and profound teachings. It means being able to predict what will happen in the future. Omens are signs; things that happen in nature which are messages from the gods, like the stars in the night sky and the movements they make. Interpreting them means reading the messages contained in them, just as you would read a book."

He stopped, looked at Fleur who appeared upset, and then back at Morgan, who was listening intently to his every word. "I should also say, Morgan, that we do not believe life ends only once. Like the Christians, we too believe that people's souls are immortal, that they will last forever. Unlike them, we don't believe that the soul leaves earth after death."

"What are people's souls?" Morgan asked.

"A soul is like a person's spirit, his thoughts, his mind, his feelings, his being." The old man rolled up his sleeve and pinched his arm between his thumb and forefinger. "Whatever is not of a human person's body, young Morgan, whatever is not this skin, is not these bones and blood, is his soul. Some time after death, we believe that the soul enters another body, to live again."

"So you don't believe that people's souls go to God in Heaven?" Fleur said incredulously.

"Don't you have a God in Heaven?" Morgan asked.

Cadwellon gave Morgan a strange look, pursing his lips. Morgan thought with a stab of fear that he was angry at her question.

"Among our many gods, we worship the Great God and the Great Goddess of Light and Life," the old man said at last. "They are held in supreme honour and veneration." He looked strangely at Morgan again. "They go by many names. He is sometimes called Belenos, the Lord of Light, and she is sometimes Limnatis, the Lady of the Lake, of the Shining Water. Together, water and light bring forth life."

While Morgan absorbed this, Fleur said nothing but seemed close to tears again. "Perhaps we had better not talk about this further," Cadwellon said gently.

"But ..." Morgan objected.

"No, Lady Morgan," Halwynna interjected firmly, also glancing concernedly at Fleur next to her. "Let the Grand Master finish his meal in peace."

When they had all finished, Elffin collected up the bowls and Taliesin took them over to the water container to be washed. Halwynna stood up and addressed Cadwellon.

"I should be taking the children back to the castle," she said. "Thank you for everything, Grand Master."

"Of course, Halwynna," the Druid Master said. He looked at the children. "I expect I shall see you all tomorrow."

"Yes, Grand Master," Morgan said eagerly. Fleur said nothing. Merlin didn't even look at the old man, but got up abruptly to leave.

"Thank you, Elffin, for the meal," Fleur said to the fisherman. Morgan quickly added her thanks and Elffin bowed to them both.

Taliesin joined them at the door. Cadwellon put his hand on the boy's shoulder. "Remember, I shall be leaving Tintagel in a few weeks," the Druid Master told him. "You'll need to decide if you are to leave with me."

"Yes, sir," Taliesin said. He looked fondly at his father and the two embraced. Elffin placed Halwynna's cloak gently over her shoulders and looked directly into her eyes as she left. Halwynna didn't say anything in parting, but Morgan noticed that the lady-in-waiting's cheeks were decidedly pink as the party made their way through the village and up the path to Tintagel.

As Halwynna led them back, Morgan fell behind the others. She walked slowly, trying to digest both the fish stew and all the things that Cadwellon had told them. Was that why she could do and see all these strange things that other people couldn't? Was she a changeling? Did she really belong to the faeries?

Her mind rejected the idea. It was impossible, she reasoned to herself, trying to stop the breathless pounding of her heart. She was a human girl, "a child," her father had said, the daughter of Gorlois and Igraine. The Duke and Duchess of Belerion were the most important people in their part of the land. They would never have a changeling child for their daughter. It wasn't real. It *couldn't* be real. And Merlin was only a child, too. "Just like you," her father had said to her that day in the Great Hall.

The Sun was descending in the late afternoon sky and the rolling hills around them were bathed in a golden-yellow glow. Fleur and Taliesin were walking together ahead of her. Morgan could see the young princess talking earnestly to the page boy but she couldn't hear what they were saying.

Merlin had fallen in step with Morgan and was walking alongside her at the same pace. "You liked the old man, didn't you?" he said.

"Yes, I thought he was really nice," Morgan replied, wishing Merlin would leave her alone.

"Do you believe all those things he said?"

"I don't know. Do you?"

"I don't know, either," Merlin said. "Brother Blaes says people like that old man are Devil worshippers. But he says I'm the son of the Devil." As Morgan looked at him, alarmed, he changed the subject suddenly, as he often did. "Maybe those hunters we saw in the sky, the Furious Host, are some of the gods the old Druid was talking about."

Morgan shuddered. She didn't want to think about that. "I hope not. They were horrible. They frightened me. Anyway, I thought gods were supposed to be beautiful."

"I don't think gods are always beautiful," Merlin said. He was looking sideways at her. "I studied a story in the Bible with Brother Blaes. The Christian God destroyed two whole cities because he was angry with them. Brother Blaes said the people in them were sinners, so they deserved to be killed. The God killed them with fire raining from the sky, all the people, every single one." Merlin paused. "The Christian God was really angry and horrible in that story. Like a monster."

Morgan was taken aback. An image flashed into her mind of fire from the sky. Raining fire. Raining blood. "Did you say that to Brother Blaes?" she asked, trying to rid her mind of the image.

"Yes." The corner of Merlin's mouth twisted. "He got angry. He shouted at me and told me I didn't understand. He's such a fool."

Thinking of Blaes' round red face and his nasty looks to Cadwellon and Elfodd during the audience in the Great Hall, Morgan couldn't help silently agreeing. Her eyes met Merlin's and she felt oddly comforted. Both children smiled.

As they came within sight of the turquoise-green ribbon of the sea along the horizon and the smell of the salty breeze began to waft over the hillside, they saw the thin sliver of the white Moon rise up before them, like a tear in the fabric of the fading daylight sky. Noisy groups of black crows and white sea-birds mingled together as they circled over the rocky cliffs.

Merlin was watching Taliesin ahead of them. "You know you said the page boy didn't look like his father?"

"Yes, and he told us why. Elffin isn't his real father."

Merlin gave her an artful look. "I think the same about you."

"What do you mean?" Morgan asked, both puzzled and irritated.

"You don't look like any of your family. Your father's got red hair and brown eyes and your mother's got fair hair and dark blue eyes. Even your sisters have fair hair and brown eyes – they look like your mother and father. You don't."

Merlin turned and gazed straight into Morgan's face. "Your hair's brown, your eyes are … light blue, light green. Like different colours of the sea. You look different from them."

Morgan had never even thought about it before. She pictured her father with his red hair and beard, her fair-haired mother and sisters, and then she thought of changeling children. Her stomach turned over at Merlin's words.

Before she could form an answer, Taliesin came back towards them. Fleur, some way ahead, was staring at him in a way that was very unlike her. She seemed unfriendly all of a sudden. Taliesin's face looked the way Morgan felt: worried, nervous and not sure about something.

"What do you want?" Merlin asked abruptly. Once again, Morgan heard a harsh tone in his voice.

"Merlin ..." she began, but Taliesin interrupted. "I'm sorry, but I was going to ask Morgan if I could walk with her." He seemed different somehow – he hadn't addressed Morgan or Merlin by their titles. "I'd like to walk with you, Morgan, if that's alright."

"Of course," Morgan said. She saw Fleur turn away and continue walking up the path.

Morgan and the two boys walked along in silence. With Merlin and Taliesin on either side of her, Morgan couldn't think of anything to say. Though she tried to stay calm and dismiss the idea as stupid, she was horrified at the thought Merlin had planted in her head: that she wasn't like the rest of her family, not even in looks. And what about the fact that only she could talk to Ganieda in her mind like Merlin, but no one else apart from them could? She wanted to talk to Merlin about being able to share her thoughts with his twin sister, but didn't feel that she could speak about something so strange and mad-sounding with Taliesin there as well.

She really wanted to know if Taliesin thought he was a changeling after everything he had found out, and if he was going to become Cadwellon's apprentice, but she knew that would make Merlin angry again. So she said nothing to either of them, but focused her attention first on the path in front of them and then on the sky above their heads, attempting to lull the thoughts rising and falling in her mind.

When grey-stoned Tintagel came into view, she gave a little

gasp at the sight of the crescent Moon curving gracefully in the sky above the castle, standing sentinel in the oncoming twilight like a protector – a god? or God? – in Heaven.

Just then she heard soft laughter, like the tinkling of small bells. She looked first at Taliesin, then at Merlin, but neither of them were smiling or making a sound. Merlin returned her gaze and in one gleam of his eye, she knew he heard it also.

A spark of white, a quick flutter; something butterfly-like hummed and danced in the early evening air. The flickering round white light was back, bobbing up and down some way away from them on the side of the path. The bell-like laughter seemed to grow louder. It was coming from the small light.

Morgan stepped hurriedly towards it, but no sooner had her foot left the path than the light vanished and the laughter died. Turning back, she realised Merlin had followed her off the path into the grass and was standing by her side. Taliesin remained on the path and kept his eyes firmly on the castle ahead, but from the look on his face Morgan knew he had seen and heard it too.

VII

She

⌐etting ready for bed, Morgan started to feel scared again. She didn't dare disobey Dyonas' order to wait for "She" on the battlements, but she was frightened at the thought of meeting whoever or whatever "She" was by herself, in the darkness.

She wished she could at least tell Fleur. The young princess, who was already in bed, had hardly said a word since the visit to Trevana. She was sitting up against the pillows holding the big Bible, her little hands balled tightly into fists as she clutched the pages. Normally, Morgan would have asked her what was wrong, but she was too worried about everything she had learned that day and what she had to face that night to think about what was upsetting Fleur. As she pulled her nightgown over her head, she thought again of Arcile and the laughing white light hovering off the path. She wondered if it was laughing at her. The idea made her feel uneasy.

Igraine entered the room, followed by Sebile. As always, the Duchess' presence seemed to illuminate the room as much as the candles did. Her braided golden hair shone in the dim light and her deep violet gown was almost the same colour as her eyes. Looking down at the ends of her own brown hair, Morgan thought again about what Merlin had said to her on the path.

"Mother?" she asked. "Why don't I look like you?"

Igraine looked surprised. Then another, unreadable expression crossed her face. "I couldn't say, darling," she said eventually.

"Children don't always look like their parents, Morgan," Sebile said.

"I didn't look like my mother," Igraine said. "She was dark-haired, like you. I got my fair hair from my father."

But I don't look like Father either, Morgan thought. There was no time to ask further questions. Igraine guided her young daughter to bed and tucked the sheets gently around her. Sebile went around the room putting out candles. The shadows followed her.

"Halwynna tells me you enjoyed your visit to the village," Igraine said.

"Yes, Mother," Morgan said sombrely.

"I didn't." Fleur spoke up. "There was an old Druid man there. He was saying things, Aunt Igraine. Horrible things. He said you were a Druid and a heathen and that you learned heathen things."

"Ah." Igraine reached over and took the princess' hand. "That was a long time ago, Fleur. That's over now."

Fleur seemed a little comforted. She closed the Bible and lay down. Sebile picked up the book and her eyes met Morgan's. The tutor nodded at her briefly but Morgan didn't understand. Did Sebile want her to do something?

"Goodnight, darling." Igraine kissed her. "I'll see you tomorrow."

"I've left a few of the candles burning, Morgan," Sebile said. "They should last till morning."

The Duchess and the tutor left the chamber. "Goodnight, Morgan," Fleur said sleepily and turned over, away from her. Morgan didn't answer. Her whole being was concentrated on the meeting ahead of her.

She waited for what seemed a very long time. Fleur was soon asleep next to her, breathing slowly and deeply, but Morgan wanted to be sure that everyone in the castle was sleeping before she made her way to the battlements. After a long while, she slipped out of the bed and crept up to the door. Placing her ear upon it, she could hear nothing but silence. She lifted the latch, which was very high and heavy for her to handle, and swung the door open. It squeaked a little and Morgan flinched, shutting her eyes tight. When nothing happened, she peered out down the passageway. There was a solitary guard seated on a stool in the corridor outside. As Morgan tiptoed towards him, she saw that he had dozed off and was snoring lightly. Slowly and quietly, she stepped past him and hurried down the passage.

Aside from the night of the storm, she had never been alone outside her room in the castle at night before. It was a different place, larger and wider, full of nooks and hidey holes where shadows waited to pounce. The passages and stairwells were dimly lit with torches along the walls, and even the tiniest noise sounded loud and seemed like footfalls tapping towards her.

Morgan sensed the echoes of the people who had been walking around the castle during the day. There was the lady-in-waiting, with the lingering scent of her flower-like perfume in the air. There was the man-at-arms, the smell of steel and sweat trailing behind him. There was the maid, carrying with her the fresh-air-and-water smell of newly washed linen. The people were gone, yet something of them remained in the air they left behind. But as Morgan made her way through the castle, she was highly aware of something other than the leftover smells of the people who lived and moved and walked there from day to day. Her skin prickled as she looked into the shadows, into the dark corners which the torchlight could not reach. She stared into them and knew with a leap of her heart that there were things there staring back at her. Things she couldn't see, but she could feel their gaze.

With an effort, the little girl clambered the steep stairs to the castle battlements. Cool, crisp night air hit her face as she emerged onto the platform and the familiar salt smell of the ocean filled her nostrils. Morgan was too small to see over the parapet, so she stood on tiptoe to look at the sea through one of the crenels. The shimmering blue-black mass held the reflections of a few bright stars that shone clear in the sky like beacons. Directly below, the sparkling white waves rose and fell gently upon the rocks, their splashing sound enriching the silence. Above her, the Moon was starting to pierce through the darkness, like a thin white fingernail. Morgan stepped back from the parapet, transfixed. Her fears were momentarily quelled. The sea, the waves, the stars and the sliver of the Moon all seemed in her mind to go together perfectly; just like the threads of the tapestries in the Great Hall went together to form a picture of beauty.

The sound of the waves began to change. Amidst the rise and fall, Morgan could hear the sound of horses' hooves galloping. But instead of being on the ground, it seemed to be coming from across the sea. From the sky. Morgan's memory went back to the hunters on the night of the storm, the dark evil figures with their one-eyed leader and spit-mouthed horses and red-eyed dogs. Her heart missed a beat.

Out across the sea and sky above, other white lights started to appear alongside the stars. Moving through the air towards the castle, they came closer, gradually revealing themselves as the shapes of horses and riders. But they were not the storm riders. These were different.

The horses looked like ordinary horses except that they galloped through the air. The beauty of the animals was stunning, their coats and manes glistening grey and white and silver. And the company that rode them were the most beautiful creatures Morgan had ever seen.

Unlike the hunters of the Furious Host who had all looked the same, these riders were many different kinds of beings in size and appearance. There were children riding bareback, barely older than Morgan herself, with flying curls and ruddy cheeks; young maidens with flowing hair that ranged in colour from coal-black to foam-white, with shades of sunset-red to sea-green in between; young men whose handsome looks and warrior bodies were marred only by bloody scars across their luminous flesh. Some of these figures Morgan at first mistook for human-type riders like the others, but on closer observation she saw that their upper bodies joined with the lower bodies of the horses to form single beings. Scattered among them were other strange creatures as well; in the vanguard Morgan saw two beings that had men's bodies, but one had the head of a dog and the other the head of a stag.

The shock stopped her breathing. Her small knees gave way and she collapsed trembling against the wall, unable to speak or cry out.

The company skimmed over the battlements, surrounding Morgan in the air above her. She could see them shining against the dark sky, and heard their inhuman laughter and excited chatter as they arrayed themselves over her. A familiar figure with black curls and grinning white teeth soared above the rest. The herald Dyonas bore a silver trumpet and as he put his lips to it an unearthly sound blasted forth. For a terrified instant Morgan thought he would awaken the entire castle. But no one came.

The floating company parted. Arising from the throng came a silver chariot pulled by winged horses, one white and one black. Driving the chariot was a young woman. Her beauty surpassed that of any in the company and anything Morgan could ever have imagined. Her hair and eyes were black as the night sky, her skin the colour and texture of moonlight. She was wearing a soft, flowing white gown that seemed to Morgan as if it was made of mist, and she was carrying what looked like the white fingernail Moon itself. She had gleaming silver horns and a quiver full of arrows slung over her shoulder. Alongside her chariot, not leaving her side, stalked a large green-eyed black dog and a white brown-eyed stag.

The beautiful woman's depthless dark eyes looked directly into Morgan's as her chariot landed soundlessly on the battlements and drew close to the cowering child. She held out her hand in invitation and smiled, lighting up the night.

"Morgan," she said.

But Morgan couldn't answer. The vision before her faded and the world went dark.

* * *

When Morgan opened her eyes, she felt the cold wind on her face. The salt smell of the air had changed. It was thinner and harder to breathe. She sensed that she was moving very fast and that something was holding her tight. Her blurred vision came into focus. Ahead of her she saw the black and white winged horses pulling her along and she dimly realised she was inside the silver chariot. They were flying through the night. The beautiful woman was holding Morgan in one arm while with the other she gracefully steered the horses. Morgan stared at her, mouth agape. She was too weak to struggle. But as the woman looked down at her and smiled her radiant smile, Morgan realised she didn't want to resist. Her hair whipped back from her face in the icy air and her teeth chattered. But overwhelming curiosity and excitement had momentarily banished her fear.

They were flying across the ocean. The dark blue sea far below glittered with rhythms and patterns that seemed to be pulled irresistibly by the white-clad woman's silver chariot as she glided over them. Behind them streamed the procession of beings – men, women, children, animals and animal-people, trailing shards of light and exhilarated laughter. The stars round about weren't the far-off pointed dots of light Morgan had seen so many times before, but had turned into circular shining spheres spinning round them. The former fingernail Moon became a huge, blindingly bright crescent, cutting through the black veil of the sky as surely as their silver chariot streaked through the night air like a shooting star.

Morgan glanced at the woman as they crossed the Moon's white arch. The silver horns on her head caught the light for an instant and Morgan saw that they weren't horns after all, but a silver crown shaped like the arched Moon. Looking down again, she saw they were passing over a coastline with rocky cliffs and sandy bays. They flew over night-darkened forests and fields, sprinkling what looked like silver dust as some of the riders and horses skimmed along the surface of the land itself. Then, all together, they rose up again, like a wave in the sky. Straight ahead of them was a jagged mountain range covered with glittering snow-capped peaks. The woman loosened her hold on Morgan and with both slender white hands expertly directed the winged horses towards the slopes of the highest mountain.

Below them was a group of trees assembled in a wide circle surrounded by a thicket of dark forest. The young woman guided the chariot down into the centre of the grove. Morgan barely felt the landing, so lightly did the chariot touch down. The lady let her go and she stumbled out of the chariot onto the solid earth, her legs so shaky they could barely hold her up.

As the procession of beings landed effortlessly around them, still chattering and laughing in their strange sonorous voices, the light that shone from them began to illuminate the grove. To Morgan's eyes it seemed like the grand hall of a palace, with the tall columns and twisted trunks of the trees like pillars and walls, the interlacing finger-like branches and silken leaves like carvings and tapestries, and leafy overhanging bows high above her head like a roof through which the winking eyes of the stars and the slender Moon could just be spotted. The fresh and heady green fragrance of the forest wafted through the clearing, and a familiar rushing sound and coolness in the air told her there was water nearby.

The crowd of beings fell silent and bowed deferentially to the beautiful young woman as she descended from her chariot. As the creatures parted to allow her through, Morgan saw on the slope behind her a sparkling waterfall cascading into a glassy lake.

The young woman approached the child and stood above her, her dark hair and eyes glistening with silver, and her misty white dress shimmering in the mountain breeze. Holding out a slim white hand, she smiled again. "Don't be afraid, Morgan," she said.

Morgan dared not speak.

The herald Dyonas came up and stood at the young woman's left. The creature with the man's body and stag's head appeared on the woman's right. Morgan was terrified again at the sight of him up close. She tried to shrink away.

"I think it's Smertullos who's frightening her," Dyonas said to the young woman, indicating the stag's head man.

"Me?" the creature named Smertullos asked, sounding surprised. "Why me? I'd have thought any child would like me. I look better than you, Dyonas, at any rate."

The young woman looked at Morgan. "You have nothing to fear from him, child," she said gently in her musical tones. But Morgan thought she sounded amused. The thought actually made her forget her fear and begin to feel angered. Anger always made her bold.

"I'm not ..." Morgan found she could hardly talk. She swallowed and began again. "I'm not afraid," she said, her voice sounding oddly loud and out of place in this forest that was unlike any she'd ever known or believed could exist. She pointed at Smertullos. "I've seen him before."

The young woman looked interestedly at her. "Really?" She turned to Smertullos. "*Has* Morgan ever seen you?"

"Not likely, my Queen," Smertullos said. His brown stag eyes looked at Morgan and she felt faint again at the sight and sound of an animal's head talking like a person. "I never set eyes on the child before tonight."

The young woman and her entire entourage looked back at Morgan in silence. She was finding it difficult to breathe but found her voice again. "I saw him the night of the storm," she said hoarsely. "When the ship was wrecked. On the cliff. A man with horns."

The company seemed to breathe a collective sigh. "Oh no, little Morgan," Smertullos said. "That wasn't me. I can see how you'd confuse us from a distance. But the man you saw is just like a man all over, including his head. Only his horns are those of a stag."

"So Cernunnos was there that night," Morgan heard Dyonas murmur to the young woman.

"It was inevitable," the young woman said. "He was bound to have an interest in that ship." Her black-as-night eyes found Morgan again. "This is the first time we meet, Morgan," she said, kind but at the same time firm. She gestured around her. "These are my people. Dyonas you know and the others you will come to know in time – as if you were one of us. No one here will hurt you, I swear it."

She smiled her moonbeam smile again and Morgan caught her breath. She reached up almost instinctively to grasp the young woman's hand and was surprised to find that it was warm and smooth, like a human hand. At once a cheer went up from the assembly as the young woman led Morgan by the hand over to the biggest and oldest-looking tree in the grove; a massive, twisted dome with grey bark and lobed leaves. To Morgan's astonishment, two silver chairs appeared out of thin air in the clearing at the foot of the tree – a glorious ornamented one for the young woman and a smaller one for Morgan herself.

When they sat down a strange melodious music broke out, and sounds of laughter and chatter once more filled the air. Musicians sat at the side of the grove in a half-circle like the fingernail Moon. Underneath a row of leaf-tapered trees with forked branches forming a canopy over their heads, they eased out a felicitous harmony of drums and pipes and harps and violas that filled all ears with a rapturous joy. Twinkling yellow lights and round orange lanterns descended from the trees and the company began to dance.

Morgan sat stock still on her chair and watched the revellers, mesmerised. Everyone was dancing – the cherubic children, the young maidens with hair all colours of the rainbow, the handsome young men with their battle scars. Elegant older ladies and gentlemen, all dressed similarly to the courtiers at Tintagel in bright colours and rich fabrics, glittering with jewels and masks that hid their faces, but you could still see their unnaturally shining skin and button-bright eyes.

Behind them, as they danced, the midnight blue lake glimmered with the reflected gold of the lights. There were other creatures, too: the half-men-half-horse beings and others, like Smertullos, with animal heads: there was the one with the dog's head she had seen earlier, another with a cat's, another with a bull's, another with a hedgehog's, and even, to Morgan's momentary horror and then fascination, a creature with what looked like a man-size grasshopper head, with huge insect eyes and large grasshopper wings on its back. Her mouth open in wonder, Morgan looked over at the young woman next to her. The young woman had not taken her eyes from Morgan and was still smiling at her.

"Can I ask, my lady … what's your name?" Morgan said at last.

"I have many names," the young woman replied. "The Romans called me Diana. Many of the people living in your country now still call me that."

"Are you a faerie?" Morgan asked, remembering Cadwellon.

Diana laughed. It was a beautiful sound. "Some call us that. But again, we are called many things."

"Why did you bring me here?" Morgan suddenly remembered something else and felt as if cold water had been thrown on her. "Am I going to stay here? Are you going to put a changeling in my place?"

For the first time, Diana looked surprised. "A changeling? In *your* place? Heavens, child, no! What makes you think that?"

"The Druid Grand Master told me about changelings," Morgan said in a small voice.

"Ah, the Druids," Diana said. "They would know." She shook

her head. "You are not to stay with us here, Morgan. At least, not yet."

"Then … why?" Morgan asked.

Diana leaned towards her and took the child's chin gently in her hand. "Have you ever been able to do strange things, Morgan? Different from other people? Things that you can't talk about?"

"Yes!" Morgan said at once. "Yes, my lady. Things I can't talk about. I can do things that aren't like other people. Things happen to me and I don't know why." She looked into Diana's lovely face and felt she had to ask her the question she could not ask the Druid Master. "Is it because *I'm* a changeling?"

"You? A changeling?" Diana said. She sounded almost angry for a moment. "You were not exchanged for anyone, Morgan. You can do all of these things because you are special. Unique. One day you will understand. There is no one else like you, my child, and there will never be anyone else like you. You were kissed by all the Fates when you were born, and you were granted many gifts. You have not come into most of them yet, but you will. And I can help you, if you will help me."

What did she mean? What gifts? Morgan wasn't aware of any presents she had been given, except for those her parents had given her sometimes. Kissed by all the Fates? Who or what are the Fates, Morgan wondered? Why did they kiss her when she was born? It didn't make sense. And how did Diana know about her?

"I've been watching you all your life," Diana said, answering Morgan's unspoken question. "I know everything there is to know about you."

"How old are you?"

Diana laughed. "I'm older than the earth, child." She indicated the dancing company before them. "Do you see who they are, Morgan? They are many and varied – spirits of the earth, of the sky, of the forest. I am the Huntress and they follow me in the Hunt. Then there are the human spirits of all kinds who have joined us. Young people who have died before their time, when they are still of too young an age or through violent means, or Christian children who have died unbaptised and as such cannot leave this world. I take them in and they all follow me."

Morgan's mind had focused on only one thing. *"Died?"*

Diana said nothing but inclined her head in acknowledgement.

"So you're … you're … like the Furious Host?" Morgan said with horror, remembering the evil huntsmen galloping through the storm.

"So you know about them, too," Diana remarked. "Well. We're not like them, Morgan. There is more than one Wild Hunt and many of us ride the skies at night." She smiled reassuringly at the little girl. "But we are different. My Hunt saves souls. As you see. The Furious Host is led by a very different hunter and if a soul is captured by them, it is condemned. Once a person is taken by the Furious Host, they are forever damned."

Morgan thought about this for a moment. "But that's not fair," she said at last.

"No, it's not fair," Diana said. Morgan looked up at her to see the young woman's dark eyes had turned cold. "There are many things in this world and beyond that are intolerably cruel and unjust. But, remember, you must never stop fighting to make those unjust things right. You have the power to do that, Morgan. Or, at least, you will have the power one day."

"I try to help people," Morgan said, eager to please. She thought of Safir and Ganieda and Fleur. And Merlin and the night of the storm.

"You're like me then," Diana said. She was smiling again and she stroked Morgan's hair. "I helped people when they first walked on the earth. I taught them to hunt, to find food and make clothing when they were cast out into the wilderness. First I taught them with my spear, crafted from the rays of the Moon – my beautiful spear of silver which always found its target, but which was stolen from me long ago. Then I taught them with my bow and arrows. I taught them to aim with skill and grace for everything they ever wanted. To be strong and independent and beholden to no one."

Her smile faded. "But remember too, Morgan, you must be careful and keep a watchful eye. People are not always loyal. You can help them and teach them and fight for them, and still they will turn on you … as they did me."

Diana fell silent and turned her attention to the revellers.

Morgan didn't know what to say. She watched the dancers too, and listened to the unearthly music weaving its spell in the air around her. She felt an overwhelming urge to stand up and dance, swaying as she sat in her chair while the notes washed over her. As the festive lights became blurred, she noticed several familiar dots of light like white moths bobbing and fluttering amongst the lanterns and branches.

"The lights!" she exclaimed. She pointed at them. "I've seen one of them before!"

"The Wisps," Diana said. "They are the souls of those who have recently joined us."

"They're ghosts?" Morgan asked, astonished.

"That is not a word we use, but, yes, you can call them that, if you wish. They sometimes show themselves to the living in the form you see because they like to visit those they have left behind." Diana beckoned and one of the white lights fluttered towards them. "This is the one you have seen before."

The white light grew larger, expanding and stretching as if it were pushing from the inside. Arms and legs appeared, followed by a head with reddish-brown hair, a freckled face and a wide grin with lots of teeth. Morgan's jaw dropped when she saw the young girl standing in front of her, clad in a pretty green dress. She felt as if her heart had stopped.

"Arcile!"

Her former maid laughed, sounding exactly as she had the last time Morgan had seen her alive. "Hello, Morgan," she said. "Are you surprised to see me?"

Morgan didn't answer. She stood up from the chair and ran to Arcile. Then she stopped in front of her, unsure. "Are you real?" she asked.

Arcile looked at her affectionately. "I'm here, Morgan. You can see me. Just as you remember me. That makes me real."

Morgan was so happy she threw her arms around her. Arcile hugged her back. The young maid felt warm and soft and alive – so different from the cold and stiff body that terrible day in the courtyard.

"My Queen." Arcile curtseyed before Diana. "May Morgan

come and dance with us?"

Morgan looked eagerly at Diana. "By all means," the Queen smiled.

Arcile grabbed Morgan's hand and pulled her along into the mass of revellers. Before she knew it, Morgan was caught up in the whirling sea of dancers, most of them towering above her. Arcile took both her hands, and the two girls skipped and danced and twirled amongst the strange merrymakers. On one side of the clearing, Dyonas was standing with a group of youths and maidens, drinking a thickly flowing yellow liquid from a golden chalice. He raised his cup to Morgan when she went past.

As she and Arcile skirted near the edge of the company, Morgan saw a long, elaborately prepared table laden with a banquet of roasted game and frosted sweetmeats. The appearance and smell of the food was almost unbearably tempting, and made her want to reach for it and fill her mouth with as many of the delicacies as possible. But Arcile had a strong grip on her hands and Morgan was forced to dance quickly by without stopping.

"Hello there, young Morgan!" shouted a voice, and Morgan looked up to see Smertullos dancing alongside her with his companion, the dog-headed man. Before she knew it, Smertullos had picked her up and was swinging her around in the air. She felt as if she was flying. Giddy with excitement, Morgan laughed aloud, carried away by the music. Smertullos put her back down on the ground and bowed.

"This is my friend, Dando," he said, gesturing to the dog-headed man. "Dando, meet the Lady Morgan."

"My lady," the dog's head acknowledged. Hearing a human-like voice emerge from the snout of a dog no longer seemed strange to Morgan somehow. Her head felt light and her heart was pounding. She held out her hand to Dando, who took it and seemed to smile with his dog's mouth and teeth.

Arcile took Morgan's other hand again. "She's with me, Dando. Don't frighten her. She's very young and she's never been here before."

"Wouldn't dream of it," Dando said, and with a bow and a flourish the dog's-head man danced off into the crowd. Smertullos winked at Morgan before dancing away too.

"Are they your friends?" Morgan asked. She had to shout to be heard above the music, which seemed to be getting louder.

"Everyone here is my friend," Arcile told her.

"Even Diana?" Morgan said, seeing the beautiful young woman on her silver throne watching them as they danced.

Arcile smiled and her eyes brightened. "Diana is our Queen. You know, she's one of the Eternals. She's been worshipped as the Goddess of the Moon for as long as the earth has been alive. She's the Goddess of the hunt, of the lake, of the forest, and of horses and wild animals too. You can see all the animals here with us in this grove. Do you see there the dog? The stag? The wolf? The owl? She's the Goddess of all these things."

"Yes, she told me," Morgan said, looking dutifully at the animals but distracted by the smells coming from the table full of food as they danced towards it once more. "She told me she taught people how to hunt for food." Then a thought struck her as she stared at the tantalising spread. "But if the people here are dead, why do you need food?"

Arcile laughed. "We don't *need* it, Morgan darling. We just enjoy it."

Morgan looked at her laughing maid, who seemed so alive ... and yet she wasn't. "But if you're dead, why are you here, Arcile? Why aren't you in Heaven?"

Arcile's laughter quietened. "Oh, Morgan." She hesitated for a moment, then pulled Morgan to the side of the dancing company. The two girls stood for a few moments catching their breath and watching the dancers. Edging nearer to the table, Morgan couldn't resist secretly plucking a small sweetmeat from one of the dishes. Not wanting to eat it in front of Arcile, and feeling naughty because she hadn't been invited to have any of the food, Morgan hid it in the sleeve of her gown for later.

"I'm a Christian, Morgan," Arcile said at last. "You didn't know that, did you? My parents were Christian and they taught me to read the Bible before they died. I learned about Jesus and his disciples, and I learned to love him and everything that he said. But my parents didn't baptise me in the Church. I don't know why.

When I died I was unchristened. That's why my soul can't leave this earth."

Morgan's heart hurt at the sadness in her maid's voice. "But aren't you happy here, Arcile?" she asked, placing her hand on Arcile's arm.

Arcile smiled again but the smile didn't reach her eyes. "Oh, yes. As happy as I can be in this world, as I am now. Our Queen Diana makes this possible. She saved me, as she saves so many others. She makes our life after death here as happy and beautiful as she can. But I think it makes her angry, that she can't do more for us or find a way for us to enter Heaven."

This puzzled Morgan. "Do you know what's in Heaven?"

Arcile shook her head. "Not really. I can't explain it to you, Morgan. It's more a feeling, a longing that we have. Everyone here feels it. Even Diana, I think. We long for Heaven, but we aren't allowed to go there."

Morgan hesitated. She wasn't sure how to ask, but her curiosity got the better of her. "Arcile ... do you remember dying? What did it feel like?"

Arcile pondered for a while. "Do you know, I really don't remember," she said at last. "I remember the water all around me, covering me, dragging me away with it. I remember feeling really, really frightened and trying to push my way out. But I only sank deeper. Then ... it was like going to sleep. The next thing I knew Diana was in front of me. I didn't feel frightened anymore when I saw her."

"So it didn't hurt?" Morgan asked in a small voice.

"No. Not for me."

"But it does for some," said a voice next to them. A tall, older-looking man with a pointed beard was standing next to them. "Not all deaths are like your friend's," he said to Morgan.

"What do you mean?" Morgan asked, surprised.

"For some of us it did hurt," the man said. He was looking at Morgan so keenly that he made her nervous. "Do you want to know how I died?"

Morgan didn't like the man. "No, I don't," she said and turned away. But the man grabbed her arm roughly and turned her back to look at him. He bent down and put his face close to hers.

"I was tortured to death, little lady," he hissed, showing his teeth. "And I'll show you how."

Up close to her face, the man's skin began to turn red. Horrible welts and boils erupted from his face and neck and hands. His skin started to peel off, layer by layer. His eyes began to bulge and sizzle in his head. And yet, through all this, the man's teeth were still displayed in a horrible grin.

"I was burned in boiling water," he chortled. "This is what it felt like."

Morgan screamed in terror. The music ceased abruptly and the company stopped dancing, muttering in confusion. Arcile tried to pull Morgan away.

"Stop!"

The command echoed through the grove and across the mountain. Through her fear, Morgan saw Diana rise from her throne, float up in the air and swoop down like an angry bird towards where they were standing, the diaphanous sleeves of her gown outspread as menacing wings.

"What do you think you are doing, Bormovo?" the Queen demanded in that terrible voice.

"Forgive me, my Queen," the man called Bormovo pleaded, going down on one knee as Diana stood glowering before him. His appearance had returned to normal. "The little girl asked what it felt like to die. I sought to inform her about how I died, that is all."

Diana's anger seemed to subside as she observed the creature before her. "She is a young child," the Queen said in a stern but less terrifying voice. "She is neither ready nor able to know about such things. Be conscious of that, Bormovo."

"Yes, my Queen," Bormovo said, his head lowered.

Diana took Morgan's hand and led her back to the chairs. Arcile followed them. With one flick of the Queen's hand, the music started up again. It seemed quieter this time and the revellers, although they continued dancing, appeared more subdued. When Morgan sat down on her silver chair, she realised she was trembling. She felt embarrassed at having screamed so loudly and tears stung her eyes.

"Who was that horrible man?" she asked Diana, her voice shaking. "Why did he do that?"

Diana's beautiful face looked sympathetic. "Bormovo is a very old soul, Morgan. He has been with us for a long time. Sometimes, as the ages pass, a soul gets restless, often bitter." She looked toward her dancing courtiers and Morgan followed her gaze. "A tormented soul that stays in one place for too long can feel a lot of pain," Diana said. "Sometimes the anguish becomes too much for them to bear and their behaviour becomes ... ungentle. Spiteful. Even harmful. You must learn to be on your guard."

Morgan wondered. If the man was in pain from the way he had died, why didn't Diana make him better, the same way Sebile made people better? But before she could ask this, Diana held out her slender hand. The sweetmeat Morgan had taken from the table shot out of her sleeve and into the Queen's grasp. Morgan felt scared and her face grew hot.

"Morgan!" Arcile exclaimed reproachfully.

"I'm sorry!" Morgan said in a panic. She looked at Diana, whose dark eyes were piercing right through her. "I didn't mean it! The food looked so nice."

"There is a reason you were not offered any of it," the Queen told her. "If you had eaten this cake, you would never have been able to leave us."

Morgan stared at her, round-eyed with shock.

"Anyone who eats our food has to stay with us forever," Arcile said. "You wouldn't be able to go home to Tintagel and your family and friends ever again."

"And that is always the way," Diana said. "Remember, Morgan: any time you visit a court like this one – of any beings that are not of the human world – do not eat or drink anything they offer you. That is how they will keep you prisoner and make you one of them. This is very important. Never forget. Never trust a fae."

"I won't," Morgan said. "I promise I'll do what you say, Queen Diana."

Diana's cold look turned to warmth as she observed Morgan. "That's good, child," she said. "Because you will see many other courts like this one – and some of them very soon, too. Why do you think I brought you here tonight?"

"I don't know, my lady."

"I brought you here tonight for a purpose, Morgan. I showed you our world that exists alongside the mortal one sooner than I intended for a very important reason. I need you to do something for me."

Morgan was stunned. "But what can I do?"

The music had stopped again and the assembly had gone quiet. The entire grove was still as they listened to Diana's words.

"You can go where I cannot," the Queen said. "I need you to enter the realms of the Small Ones."

"Who are they?"

"They are creatures humans also regard as faeries, but they are very different from us. They are beings of our world who exist within and without the world of mortals, as we do, but they are much closer to humankind. I cannot enter the realms of these creatures because my world, as you can see, is wide open space, filled with skies and stars and woods and waters. But the world of these creatures is a hidden one, deep within the confines of the earth, inside holes and hillocks. They live in mounds and caves, under hills and stones. They are as small as insects and resemble them in many ways, yet their existence is bound to that of living mortals much more than ours."

Morgan tried to imagine this. "But how will I go to them? How will I find them?"

"Are you willing to help me, then?" Diana asked. "I cannot force you, my child. You must choose."

"Yes!" Morgan said immediately. She couldn't fathom what the Small Ones or their realms might be, but she knew she would do anything for Diana. "What shall I do?"

The Queen placed her hand on Morgan's cheek. "There is someone there you must find and bring him to me. He was stolen by these creatures before I could reach him, but he was meant for me to save." She gestured towards Morgan's maid, who was standing silently in front of them. "Arcile will guide you and be with you all the time in her guise as a Wisp. On the night of the full Moon, thirteen days from now, she will come to you and tell you what to do. Listen to her. She will guide you to where you need to go."

"Who do I have to find?" Morgan asked.

"You will know him when you see him," Diana said. "Arcile will tell you more when the time comes. But there is one thing you must promise me, Morgan."

"What, my lady?"

"I am entrusting you with this task. It is yours and only yours. You must do this alone. Promise me."

"I promise," Morgan said again. Her head felt lighter than ever and her whole body was tingling. She heard animated murmuring coming from the company once again.

"And now," Diana declared, smiling once more, "it is time to take you back to Tintagel, my child."

Morgan's heart sank. She didn't want to go home yet. Any fears or doubts she had felt to begin with had disappeared. The time spent in Diana's grove felt as if it had both lasted forever and gone by in an instant. Part of her wanted to stay and ride through the sky in Diana's chariot and dance in the grove every night. She almost wished she had eaten the cake after all.

"Do I have to go already?" she asked. "Will I ever come back here again?"

Diana laughed. Her courtiers joined in, and the echoes of their uncanny laughter passed through the trees and rang out across the mountainside.

"Oh yes, Morgan. You will come back."

VIII

INTERCESSION

Today is the day?

Morgan heard Ganieda's voice in her head as she crossed off the number XIII on her secret parchment. She knew Ganieda could see it through her eyes.

Yes, it's today, Morgan told her. *Arcile will come tonight.*

She had been keeping a watchful eye on the Moon from her window night after night, watching the fingernail grow to half a circle to almost a full beaming sphere in the sky. She had carefully written out the numbers I to XIII on her parchment and dutifully marked each number as the days went by.

What do you think the Small Ones are, Morgan? How will you find them?

After the encounter with Diana and her Wild Hunt in the mountain grove, Morgan had spoken of it to no one. No one except the little blind girl, who was the only person to whom she could show everything that had happened to her without describing it. Ganieda had seen the images and memories in Morgan's mind and had held her breath in amazement, occasionally opening her mouth silently in shock. Since then, they had talked in their thoughts every day before lessons.

Once, at Ganieda's suggestion, Morgan had even ventured to ask Sebile what the faeries known as the Small Ones were. Sebile had said she was not a native of Belerion, but that she knew of a local belief in small invisible beings who lived in hills and under barrows. She had told the children that, wherever people lived, there was a belief in races that were not human or divine but very like human beings, that those spirits existed in a different way to people, and that sometimes people could encounter those spirits who had crossed over into the human world.

"Like angels?" Fleur had asked. Sebile had hesitated for a

moment and answered, "Like angels, yes."

Morgan had asked her for pictures, but Sebile had said there were none, because people hardly ever saw them. The tutor had looked hard at Morgan then and told her that if people ever did see them, they rarely lived or returned to tell the tale.

Arcile will show me how to find them, Morgan told Ganieda. She had complete faith in Arcile. Arcile would know what to do.

But you can't go by yourself, Ganieda protested. *Sebile said people don't live after they've seen them.*

The thought made Morgan nervous. But she knew she had to do what Diana wanted. She wanted to see Diana again. She wanted the beautiful black-haired Moon Queen to be proud of her.

Arcile will protect me, Morgan thought. *She won't let anything happen to me.*

Maybe I could go with you, Ganieda said. *I could help you.*

Morgan was taken aback. No. *Diana said I have to go alone.*

But Diana wouldn't mind if I went.

You can't come, Morgan said, irritated now. *You can't see or hear or speak or walk without someone there to help you. You can't help me and I won't be able to help you. I have to find the person Diana wants and bring him back. I can't be helping you at the same time.*

Ganieda didn't reply, but Morgan sensed something simmering beneath the silence in her head. She tried to look into Ganieda's mind but something was stopping her. *Don't worry*, she told the girl. *I'll show you everything when I get back.*

Still silence. Morgan was puzzling over her sudden inability to communicate with the blind girl through her mind when Fleur arrived, carrying her books and a quill. The little princess looked surprised when she saw Morgan with Ganieda.

"Morgan! I was waiting for you! I didn't know you were here already."

"Sorry. I just thought I'd go and get Ganieda from Lady Aldan's rooms before the lesson."

Fleur looked reproachful. "Why do you spend so much time with her?" She looked at the white-eyed girl sitting seemingly expressionless before them. "She can't hear you or talk to you,

you know."

"I know." Morgan felt as if she was lying, but it was true that Ganieda *couldn't* hear her or talk to her like everyone else could. "I feel sorry for her, that's all. She doesn't have any friends. Not like us." She watched Ganieda's eyebrows lower in a frown.

Fleur seemed satisfied and seated herself at the table. Morgan wondered again if she should tell Fleur the truth. She hated not telling her friend. But something made her keep the meeting with Diana and the flying chariot and the dancing in the mountain grove and the task Diana had set her a secret from the princess. Morgan remembered how upset Fleur had been two weeks before with Grand Master Cadwellon and his explanation of the Druid beliefs. She didn't know how to begin to talk to Fleur about everything she had seen and heard and done.

Cadwellon had arrived at Tintagel the day after they had seen him at Elffin's house. He had had a private audience with Gorlois and his closest advisers and the whole castle was buzzing with it. Morgan had heard snippets of conversations with the words "High King" and "council" and she sensed preparations were being made for something.

Fleur never wanted to speak about Cadwellon; in fact, since his arrival, she had been spending a lot of time with Father Elfodd, who was giving her lessons in the afternoons on Christian catechism up at the chapel. Fleur had asked Morgan if she would like to meet the priest and join in her lesson, and Morgan had agreed. Sebile was teaching them about the Christian religion as well, but Morgan had a lot of questions, much like the ones she had asked Cadwellon, that she wanted Elfodd to answer.

The lessons with Sebile seemed to drag on endlessly that morning. Morgan usually enjoyed immersing herself in the pages and pictures Sebile provided for them, soaking up the seemingly endless new information and images. In Sebile's rooms Morgan's mind often forgot about the outside world. But today was different. Arcile coming that night and the unknown task Diana had set were all Morgan could think about. History and geography sailed by, with Morgan paying next to no attention, but fixing her eyes upon Sebile whilst her thoughts wandered. Once or twice, her tutor looked sharply at her, but did not comment. While Sebile was talking about the Romans in Britain, Morgan came back down to earth when her tutor told them they had brought new types of religion, even though the people of Belerion had still kept many of their own beliefs and traditions. Like the Small Ones, Morgan thought.

After history and geography came reading and writing practice, for which they turned to the New Testament. They had been reading parables told by Jesus Christ, who Morgan knew the Christians said was the son of their God. Today they read and copied out a story from the Book of Luke. The Bible said Jesus told the story to show his followers how they must always pray and never give up. In the parable, there was a bad judge who did not like God or people, and a lady kept coming to him to ask him to grant her justice. At first he kept refusing, but in the end he got tired of her coming to see him so he granted her justice. At the end of the story, Jesus said, *"Listen to what the unjust judge says. And will not God grant justice to his chosen ones who cry to him day and night? Will he delay long in helping them? I tell you, he will quickly grant justice to them."*

Morgan thought of how unfair it was that Arcile, riding the skies with the Wild Hunt and dancing in the mountain grove, was not able to go to Heaven. She wanted to go, but she couldn't because she hadn't been baptised. It wasn't Arcile's fault that her parents didn't baptise her, Morgan reasoned. Why shouldn't she be allowed to go to Heaven? *"I tell you, he will quickly grant justice to them."* Would God grant justice to Arcile? Morgan stored the parable in her memory to ask Father Elfodd about the story and unbaptised souls that afternoon.

Then came healing and herbs. It was one of her favourite subjects, but still Morgan couldn't concentrate. She glanced at Ganieda seated at the table next to them, staring at nothingness. She could feel Ganieda following the lessons through her mind and eyes, but the girl had not communicated a single thought since Morgan had told her she couldn't come with her to the Small Ones.

Ganieda's silence pricked at Morgan's conscience and made her annoyed. What was she so sulky about? It was obvious that she wouldn't be able to go with her, even if Diana allowed it. It wasn't as if Morgan had kept anything from her. She had talked to her about it every day for the last thirteen days. She had shown her all the amazing things she had seen through the memories in her mind – things that no one else had seen and that she had told no one else about. And, besides, if it wasn't for Morgan, the blind deaf-mute girl wouldn't know anything or be able to do anything, especially not follow their lessons. How could she be so horrid all of a sudden?

After some meat broth was brought to them from the kitchens (Morgan could scarcely eat a bite), they accompanied the tutor on her physician's rounds through Tintagel Castle. Since the storm there had been few serious injuries or illnesses to deal with, save for a couple of lingering cases of ague (to be treated with groundsel in a linen bag close to the skin, Morgan remembered, despite herself) and of course Lady Aldan's broken leg. Lady Aldan was the first visit on their rounds, partly because they had to take Ganieda back to her mother. Morgan and Fleur walked on either side of her. Still Ganieda did not communicate with Morgan. Morgan was so vexed with her at this point that she no longer wanted to talk to her either and concentrated on blocking her own thoughts from the blind girl.

Lady Aldan's two rooms across the courtyard above the stables were much smaller than the high and wide rooms of the main castle. The walls were of grey stone mixed with wood with a low ceiling and a thatched and timbered roof. A four-poster bed had been squeezed in for Lady Aldan as befitted her status. She had spent much of her time at Tintagel lying in that bed as her leg healed, although Sebile insisted on her being turned over and made to stand up and walk around on crutches from time to time; because, as she explained to Morgan and Fleur, the patient would get terrible bed sores and her blood would stop flowing if she remained in one position for too long. Merlin and Ganieda slept on a rudimentary bed in a corner of the same room as their mother. A chair had been set up for Ganieda by a small window that brought in little light.

As Sebile knocked and they entered, Morgan detected the now-familiar odours of hay and horses wafting up from the stables mixed with the fouler smell of dung. Once inside the room, she dropped Ganieda's arm immediately and allowed Fleur to take the girl over to her chair by herself. She didn't see why she should help Ganieda when she was being so horrible.

"Lady Sebile," Lady Aldan greeted her from the bed. "I am glad to see you."

"And how are you today, my lady?" Sebile asked her, handing her bag of vials to Morgan before approaching her patient.

As the older woman and the younger exchanged pleasantries and discussed the state of the latter's health, Morgan watched as Sebile examined the patient. Lady Aldan's right leg was still held straight and immobile by the attached wooden straps that Morgan now knew were called splints. Lying in the bed, her leg was held in what Sebile called "traction", by a lead weight suspended from a pulley and fastened to the patient's foot. While Morgan stood at her side and Fleur watched from the foot of the bed, Sebile set about changing the linen bandages on the leg. She had explained to Morgan and Fleur that it was very important not to wrap the bandages around a broken leg or arm too tightly, because it could cause the limb to heal in a bad position and result in the limb being forever malformed.

Morgan's preoccupation with what was to come that night made her mind drift again, so she didn't really listen to the conversation. However, her attention was soon caught by Aldan's mention of the name of her son.

"... he seems always to be asking the wrong questions," Aldan was saying. "Brother Blaes is quite despairing of him. He says Merlin is very clever, but that he applies himself in the wrong way."

"Perhaps your son is simply asking questions the good monk cannot answer," Sebile suggested.

"Brother Blaes says he is always asking about the Druids and their heathen religion. He tries to teach my son the truth of Jesus Christ, and he says that Merlin listens and then asks questions like what Jesus the merciful would think of the Old Testament God who punishes people with cruelty and wrath. Or what would Jesus think about the Druids and their many gods instead of just one."

"They seem like valid questions," Sebile said. "Rather like the kind Morgan here would ask." Morgan thought she could see a hint of a smile around her tutor's eyes.

Aldan looked at Morgan. "But she is different from my son, is she not? She is the daughter of the Duke and Duchess, the heir of Belerion. She has nothing to fear, unlike my fatherless son. How will he find a place in the world if he doesn't learn from Brother Blaes' example?"

Morgan felt oddly proud to hear Aldan acknowledge her as the heir of Belerion. These days any reminder of the fact that the world knew and thought of her as Gorlois and Igraine's daughter gave her comfort. But Sebile didn't respond and changed the subject.

After they had finished the rounds with Sebile, Morgan and Fleur thanked their tutor, who sent them on their way with praise for the work they had done that day. Upon leaving Sebile, the two little girls made their way to Father Elfodd's chapel, where Morgan was to meet the young priest for the first time.

"I think it's horrible that Lady Aldan should have to live in those rooms," Fleur said.

Morgan was startled out of her thoughts. "Why?"

"Because they're awful. They're small and they're cramped and they smell bad."

Morgan couldn't deny that. "Well ... that's true," she said awkwardly. "But we don't have a lot of guest rooms at Tintagel. And most guests don't stay here for a long time. Sometimes they have to sleep in the main hall or the guards' rooms or the other buildings outside. At least Lady Aldan has somewhere she can stay all the time."

They walked outside the foregate and along the cliff path. Out above the ocean, birds were circling, cawing, nesting in the grey cliffs. The great blue and white-foamed sea churned against the rocky coves tucked away far below. Occasionally Morgan would catch a glimpse of a stony bay or small stretch of sand at the bottom of a sheer drop through a break in the cliffs. Winding down to these inlets were perilously steep and narrow paths, some carved naturally into the cliff-face, others mere animal tracks. Morgan knew that local people hardly ever used those paths – if they had to go into the bays, which was rare, they would go by boat. She and Fleur were of course forbidden to go anywhere near the paths leading down to the bays.

The Christian chapel was the newest building of Tintagel, built by Gorlois himself as a young man. It stood alone on the cliffs between the castle and Trevana village, a simple rectangular building made of the same grey stone as the castle, with a stone cross outside that always looked to Morgan more like a wheel, with the four separate sections of the cross forming part of a circle and carved with a pretty knotwork pattern.

As they climbed towards the chapel, the long green grasses around the building swayed in the breeze. The land round about was patterned with grey headstones and a solitary purple foxglove danced and bowed as if in greeting. A spectacular view of the endless sea beyond the shore met them as they walked up the winding path to the chapel door. Morgan's father and mother attended daily morning Mass, but she had only accompanied them previously on special occasions: Christmas, Easter and Holy Days.

The priest before Father Elfodd had been a nasty man who had always seemed to Morgan very mean and shouty, talking in a very loud voice about things called hellfire and damnation. She had never paid much attention to him or the surroundings. But now, as she tried to banish the fluttery nervous feelings in her stomach and took the time to drink in the peaceful beauty, soothing calm and unfussy look of the place, she understood why the new young priest seemed to prefer to stay out here rather than live in the castle. She remembered him arguing quietly but also being friendly with Cadwellon in the Great Hall all those weeks ago, and she was keen finally to meet him.

Fleur reached up, grabbed the handle of the heavy door and pushed it open. Its groan echoed through the interior of the chapel. Inside the building it was cool and fragrant. The smooth grey walls seemed to create a silence and tranquillity unbroken by the rays of light that spilled in through the windows. At the far end was the wooden altar with an unadorned cross on top and wooden benches arranged in rows in front of it. Several lit candles had been placed at the foot of the altar below the raised stone platform. The hand-painted carved statues standing up against the walls seemed to follow Morgan with their eyes as she and Fleur walked down the aisle towards the altar.

"Good afternoon, Lady Fleur," a voice greeted them. Father Elfodd emerged from a side door just before the altar. He looked just as Morgan remembered him: young, thin and handsome, dressed plainly in dignified black.

"Hello, Father," Fleur said. "This is Morgan."

The young priest smiled and bowed. "My lady."

Morgan inclined her head politely, as she had been taught to do. "Hello, Father. Thank you for letting me come here today."

"Not at all." Elfodd mounted the steps to the altar and laid a heavy-looking Bible down upon it. "I understand you want to join us in the lesson this afternoon?"

For the first time Morgan noticed that Elfodd's sing-song accent sounded quite similar to Fleur's. "Yes, Father," she said and then turned to Fleur. "He sounds like you," she said to her friend.

"Father Elfodd is from Ynys Môn, too," Fleur told her.

"That's right," Elfodd said, joining them by the first row of benches. "I arrived here when Father Goeznovius came to Ynys Môn to become abbot of our monastery. He sent me here in his place."

"Do you like it here?" Morgan asked.

Elfodd looked surprised. "Why, yes. Of course." He looked curiously but not unkindly at the little girl. "Why do you ask?"

"You don't come to the castle much," Morgan said.

"Oh." Elfodd nodded. "True. I go much more among the ordinary people, Lady Morgan, as Jesus Christ did. I spend most of my time among the people who work the land and the poor who have very little and are hungry. They need me a lot more than the people who live in the castle do." He smiled again. "Although I am here for whoever wants me or needs me. I am just a humble servant of God, but God always speaks to those who come to him and are prepared to listen to him. So long as you are ready to speak and listen."

Morgan was fascinated. "I am ready!" she said eagerly. "Can I speak to God?"

The priest laughed. "Well, perhaps not immediately! But you

Intercession

can speak to him through me, if you wish."

"I have a lot of questions, Father," Morgan said apologetically. She didn't want to annoy the priest just after she had met him.

"That's all right," Elfodd said amiably. "That's what I'm here for." He sat down on the bench and indicated that she and Fleur should sit down too. The girls sat on either side of him.

"So, ask away," Elfodd said.

Morgan had so many questions that she decided to begin with the easy one. "We read a parable today," she began. "About the lady and the judge." She told Elfodd what they had read and how at the end Jesus had said, "*I tell you, he will quickly grant justice to them.*" Morgan wanted Elfodd to know that she understood that Jesus was saying that God was just and that they must always pray to him and not give up. When she had finished, Elfodd, who had been listening attentively, nodded.

"That's very good, Lady Morgan. So what's your question?"

Morgan hesitated. "It's about children who have died who haven't been baptised," she said finally. "They can't go to Heaven."

Elfodd looked startled. "Where did you hear this?"

"Someone told me," Morgan said truthfully. "It's just that ... it's not fair that they shouldn't go to Heaven because they weren't baptised. It's not their fault. How can God be just if he won't let them into Heaven?"

Elfodd sat silent for a moment. "You're right, of course," he said eventually. Morgan was relieved to hear there was no anger in his voice, only kindness and interest. "If what you say were true, it would be unfair. But there is nothing in our Christian teachings to say that unbaptised children cannot go to Heaven."

Morgan was stunned. "Really?"

"Oh, yes. Many of our cleverest and most learned men and women have opinions about it, of course. But our Holy Church has no position on this." The priest looked intently at her. "And Jesus never said anything about children not getting into Heaven, I assure you. Just the opposite."

Morgan liked the way he talked to her, seriously and earnestly, as if she were a grown-up. "What did he say?"

Elfodd smiled again. "If you had read on from your parable,

129

you would have seen it. After Our Lord had told the people the story, they started bringing their children to him so that he might bless them. Jesus' disciples, his followers, ordered them to stop. But Jesus said, '*Let the little children come to me, and do not stop them; for it is to such as these that the kingdom of God belongs. Truly I tell you, whoever does not receive the kingdom of God as a little child will never enter it.*' What he means by that is that the kingdom of God – Heaven – and the love of God belong to children like you. All children belong to God and are all sanctified by God to Jesus. And you're right – they are not responsible for what their parents do or do not do."

Morgan was happy to hear this. Then, thinking of Arcile's situation, she felt even more confused. If Arcile was wrong about not being able to go to Heaven...

"But, Father Elfodd, why should a soul stay here on earth if there's no reason?" she asked him. "If they aren't being stopped from going to Heaven, why should they stay here?"

The priest observed her with interest. "Why are you asking this?"

"Yes, why?" Fleur inquired, sounding curious.

"Have you seen something?" Elfodd asked.

Morgan felt suddenly nervous under Elfodd's sharp-eyed gaze. "No," she said at once, lowering her eyes. "It's just ... my maid, Arcile, died in the storm. She was ten. She was Christian, but she wasn't baptised."

"I see," Elfodd said slowly. "And you're afraid she's not in Heaven."

Morgan looked up and into the priest's eyes. "I know she's not."

"You never told me!" Fleur exclaimed, surprised. "I didn't know your maid had died. Why didn't you tell me?"

"I expect it was very painful for Lady Morgan," Elfodd commented, still watching her.

"I'm really sorry, Morgan," Fleur said. "I wish you'd told me."

"I'm sorry, too," Morgan replied. She felt bad about keeping things from Fleur. Perhaps she should trust her more.

"Why do you say you know she's not in Heaven?" Elfodd asked.

Morgan thought quickly. "Sometimes I think she's still here," she told him. "I can feel her near me." She lowered her eyes again. "Some people say spirits of dead people come back to visit us. That they're here with us. Is it true?"

"The Church doesn't believe in ghosts," Fleur said. "Isn't that right, Father?"

"In a manner of speaking," Elfodd replied. "Certainly not ghosts as you would describe them." He continued to observe Morgan with consideration. "The spirits that some people believe they see may well be real and not imagined, but they are much more likely to be demons disguising themselves as ghosts to trick people. As it says in Corinthians, '*And no wonder, for Satan himself masquerades as an angel of light.*'"

Angels, Morgan thought. "Can spirits be angels, too?"

"Most certainly," Elfodd said. "You see, Lady Morgan, as Christians, we do believe that spirits exist." He made a sweeping gesture with his arm to the walls around them. "There is the visible physical world that we see here before us, but also around us, unseen, is the spiritual world." He smiled at Morgan. "'*So we fix our eyes not on what is seen but what is unseen. For what is seen is temporary, but what is unseen is eternal.*' This spiritual world is inhabited by our God, our Father, his Son and the Holy Spirit, our Blessed Mother Mary, all his saints, and the angels and demons. It is part of us, but it is greater than us. And the souls of those who have died are part of this spiritual world, but they are not allowed to come back to visit people without the permission of God."

Morgan was elated. "So you believe it's true?"

"Yes, we believe that," Elfodd conceded. "But remember, Lady Morgan: once a person's soul dies, it is judged immediately. After death, a soul is judged and can be either saved or damned. There are no souls that are lost in the sense that they are trapped between death and eternity, and are unable to cross over to the other side. A damned soul is in Hell. A saved soul is either in Heaven or Purgatory."

Heaven and Hell Morgan knew about. "What's Purgatory?"

"Purgatory is a place between Heaven and Hell, where people's souls go to be purged – to rid themselves of any sins they committed in life. It's where they go to wait and pray and repent – and wait for those still living to pray for them – before they enter Heaven."

Elfodd paused as he looked at the little girl listening fiercely to his every word. "But it's not a place for children, Lady Morgan. Children don't have sins and cannot repent. They are innocent." He hesitated again. "I can tell you that Purgatory might in some way involve the life a person lived here on earth. It is not un-Christian to believe that a soul's purgation might involve revisiting people or places that were meaningful to us in our earthly lives. It may even be that sometimes God allows people to see such souls in order to inspire prayers for them or in some way teach a lesson to the people who see them." He watched as Morgan pondered this information. "Does this help you, my lady?"

"Yes!" Morgan said fervently. Her mind was on Arcile. Arcile must be still on earth because God wanted her, Morgan, to pray for her and maybe to teach her a lesson, too. Perhaps the lesson Arcile was supposed to teach her was to help her with what Diana wanted her to do. After that, Morgan thought, she would pray really hard for her and then Arcile could go to Heaven where she longed to be.

"If you are worried about your maid, we can pray for her," the priest said gently, as if reading her thoughts. "We call it intercession. We pray to God for the person who is departed. We intercede for them and pray for their sins to be forgiven and help them get into Heaven."

"Thank you," Morgan said. "I'd like to do that."

"Very well," Elfodd said. Fleur at once knelt down before the wooden altar and cross. Elfodd did the same and Morgan followed. They each made the sign of the cross. Elfodd began a beautiful prayer asking God and Jesus and Mother Mary to take the young maid into Heaven, and all the saints to pray for her. Morgan felt lighter, happier and more at ease than she had in a while. For the first time she was as confident that she could help Arcile as she was that Arcile could help her.

* * *

Morgan enjoyed Father Elfodd's lesson, which consisted of Fleur and then Morgan reading aloud passages from the Bible the priest had placed on the altar. It made her feel calmer somehow, more at peace. She began to believe that whatever she and Arcile had to do that night, she would have the strength to do it. Elfodd stood beside them as they read and helped the one reading with the words she did not recognise, while the other sat on the front bench listening as if she were at a Mass.

After the readings, they all sat on the benches together while Elfodd asked the children questions about what they had read and what they thought about it. He then explained the parts of the passage they didn't understand. Morgan especially liked how the young priest seemed interested in what they had to say. He wanted them to talk to him and to hear what questions they had to ask. In some ways he reminded her of Sebile, who also always encouraged her to ask questions, but her old tutor was much stricter and more formal when she talked to them or taught them. Elfodd spoke to them as if they were friends.

At the end of the lesson, Morgan said, "Can I come with Fleur every afternoon?"

Father Elfodd looked at her kindly. "Of course, Lady Morgan."

"Perhaps you should ask the Duke," a voice said from the direction of the main door. "I'm sure he won't want his priest wasting time teaching girls."

They all turned to see Brother Blaes walking up the aisle towards them. Morgan noticed that he had his usual red face and sour expression.

"I have the Duke's permission to instruct Lady Blanchefleur, at her father King Pellinore's express wishes," Elfodd said. He seemed unworried by Blaes' appearance or his remarks. "I have no doubt the Duke will be pleased to know his daughter has the same opportunity to learn."

Morgan couldn't contain herself. "But you teach Merlin, Brother Blaes," she said somewhat indignantly. "Why shouldn't Father Elfodd teach us?"

"Don't be impertinent, girl," the monk said irritably. "The boy Merlin will make his way in the Church – so long as I can get certain misguided ideas out of his head. You and the Princess

Blanchefleur, on the other hand, have no need of learning."

"You should be getting back to the castle now, Lady Morgan," Elfodd said evenly. Morgan and Fleur exchanged looks. They thanked the priest and made their way towards the door. As they left, Morgan heard Blaes say to Elfodd, "I presume you know those Druid friends of yours are convening their heathen council at Vortigern's request."

"I wouldn't call them my friends, though I have no quarrel with them," she heard Elfodd murmur in reply. "Yes, I've heard something of it."

Fleur pushed open the heavy door and Morgan followed her out. Once back outside in the fresh air, Morgan plucked at Fleur's sleeve and pulled her to the door jamb. She put her finger to her lips and pressed her ear against it. Fleur, understanding, did the same. The two little girls strained with all their might to hear what was said next.

Blaes sounded furious. "And you're going to do nothing? You will not speak to the Duke?"

"What good will it do?" Elfodd reasoned. "Vortigern is a follower of the Druidic faith. The Duke has no influence over that."

"He should not have allied himself with such a man! This usurper allows these barbarian Saxons to rampage freely through this land, bringing wretched demons they call gods into the lives of good Christian people. They are monstrous blasphemers. The Duke should dissociate himself from this traitor king immediately."

"Take heed, Brother," they heard Elfodd say in a low voice of concern. Morgan and Fleur looked at each other, alarmed. Did he know they were there? "You realise the Duchess is half-Saxon?" Elfodd went on. "Both the Duke and the High King are tied to the Saxon chieftain by marriage. And, besides, what was the Duke supposed to do? Ally himself with Constantine's sons and be sent into exile alongside them? Or be killed? At least Vortigern achieved a measure of peace by inviting the Saxons in."

"You know nothing of the world, boy," Blaes sneered. Morgan was shocked at the ugly tone the monk used to address the priest. "I've told you before you're not fit for this position. If you continue in this way, you are worthless to God's cause and the Church. I am leaving for Cambria today to consult with Germanus, and I will be taking the matter up with him."

Fleur tugged at Morgan's arm and pulled her up the path away from the chapel.

"They're talking about the High King!" she said to Morgan in alarm.

"I know," Morgan said. She remembered her father mentioning Vortigern on occasion, but neither he nor her mother talked about him much in front of her. "I think something's happening."

"Do you suppose he's coming here?" Fleur asked, wide-eyed.

"I don't know. Let's find Safir. She'll know."

Walking back along the cliff's edge, Morgan found she had Fleur's sympathetic words about Arcile's death on her mind. She felt guilty for not telling her friend about Arcile and for keeping all the other things from her. Musing on Fleur's bad feelings about the Druids, Morgan wondered if telling her the truth about Diana and Arcile might make the princess feel happier with what Cadwellon had told them. If she knew that the things the Druids believed were true, just like the things the Christians believed were true, she wouldn't be so upset, Morgan reasoned. After all, Elfodd telling her the truth about what the Christians believed made Morgan feel much better about Arcile.

By the time they got back to the castle, Morgan had resolved to tell Fleur everything about Diana and the faeries and the task she had been set once she had completed it. More than anything, she wanted a real friend to talk to properly. Not like Ganieda. Especially now that Ganieda was being so moody and mean. She was too much like her brother.

As they entered the main courtyard, they saw Safir going into the stables. Since becoming Gorlois' squire, the young Saracen girl had been working hard at the duties required of her. The stabling and care of Gorlois' horse was one of the main ones. She also had to keep the Duke's clothing fresh and clean, run errands to his soldiers, carry messages to his servants, look after his sword, lance and bow and arrows, clean his chain mail, and help him put it on when required.

Morgan couldn't understand how or why anyone would enjoy

such duties, but Safir was thriving on it. Her eyes were bright, her child's body slender and strengthened, and she walked with a sprightly confidence and her head held high. She was envied by the squires of Gorlois' knights, all of them nobleman's sons, taller and older than her. Morgan had heard some unpleasant whispers behind Safir's back about what she looked like – specifically the colour of her skin. It bewildered her and made her indignant. But when she had told Safir, the squire had merely shrugged her shoulders and said she had heard many similar things said about her in Venice and Armorica.

Gorlois was apparently very pleased with Safir and had praised her in view of his men on several occasions. Because of her position, Safir was present at all the Duke's meetings and was at his side at all times. Her friendship and loyalty to Morgan made her more than willing to share information and news. Morgan always worried that someone might still find out that Safir was a girl, but, with Sebile's help, so far no one suspected. Sebile cropped Safir's hair once every week, regularly provided her with new items of boy's clothing and allowed her to bathe in private in her chambers once a week so she could avoid discovery.

Inside the stables a couple of servant boys were sweeping up bits of hay and had thrown buckets of fresh water on the floor to clean up the dung. At least ten different horses, most of them rounceys, were standing in their stalls, blinking at the girls as they passed by. Some of the stalls were empty; several of Gorlois' men were most likely off hunting or patrolling the land round about the castle.

Safir was in one of the far stalls with Gorlois' brown courser horse Swiftback, a more elegant animal than the rest, light and sleek with an arched neck. She was standing on a wooden stool and murmuring to the horse as she groomed him with a distinctive steel curry-comb that had loose rings on it. She had previously told Morgan that she had brought the comb from her home in Babylon, and that the rings clinking together made a sound that calmed the horse as it was being groomed.

"There you are," Morgan greeted her as she and Fleur entered the stall. "Have you been out with my father today?"

"We haven't gone out yet," Safir said. "Your father had work to do in the castle." She stroked the horse. "Although it's odd. Swiftback is supposed to be rested, but he seems tired."

"What do you mean?"

"Look," Safir said, sounding mystified. She stepped down from the stool and pointed to the horse's coat. It was streaked with mud and sweat. "I groomed him yesterday evening and he was clean when I left. But look at him now. I came out here this morning and it seemed like Swiftback had been running all last night. He's still exhausted. I was lucky your father didn't go out to ride this morning. I didn't know what to tell him. I only was able to get away now to come and groom the horse again. The saddle and bridle over there are still clean from yesterday. This horse has not been ridden."

Morgan noticed that as well as being sweaty and dirty, the horse's eyes were wide and rolling. "He's frightened of something," she said.

"I know," Safir agreed. "And look here." She indicated the horse's mane. Morgan and Fleur moved closer to see. Swiftback's mane was messy and tangled. Strands of it were tied together in strange complicated knots with loops. "I combed out his mane yesterday," Safir said. "How did those come to be?"

"Maybe one of the Duke's men rode him without the saddle this morning," Fleur suggested.

"Who?" Safir asked.

Morgan didn't believe that. "None of them would dare!" she said. She reached up and patted the horse's neck. He whinnied in response.

"So, what can I tell your father?" Safir wondered.

"Don't tell him anything," Morgan said. She detected a force emanating from around the horse that she couldn't explain. It was an eerie sensation. She knew Swiftback had been in the presence of something that was familiar to her. Remembrance of night shadows in the castle watching her with unseen eyes reared up for a second in her mind. It was something she couldn't talk to Safir or Fleur about just yet.

"We've just come from Father Elfodd up at the chapel," Fleur told Safir.

"And Brother Blaes was there, too, talking about High King Vortigern," Morgan said. "He said something about Vortigern and the Druids and a council. What's happening?"

"The Grand Master Cadwellon told your father that the Council of Twelve Druid advisers has been called by the High King again," Safir said. "The Grand Master says he is the leader of the council. He said that the High King is trying to get together all the rulers of the tribes of Britain because he is worried about their loyalty to him. There is something about the Christians being angry with Vortigern and the Saxon leader, Hengist."

"Hengist," Morgan repeated. She had vaguely heard the name before, but knew nothing about him.

"But it's true the Saxons are heathens," Fleur said. "They're dangerous. That's what my father says."

"And it's not only the Saxons," Safir said. "Cadwellon says the High King is expecting there will be an attack from an army in Armorica."

"An army? From Armorica?" Morgan asked, alarmed.

"Yes. An army led by a man called … Ambrosius? That's it. Ambrosius. And his brother. A man called Uther."

A veil came down over Morgan's vision. It was suddenly so dark she could hardly see in front of her. Safir, Fleur, Swiftback, the other horses and the stables all blended together in one large blur before disappearing. Heartsick, she put her hands over her eyes and felt herself sway on the spot as if she were going to faint.

"Morgan!" Safir's voice tore through the veil and the light came rushing back. Morgan uncovered her eyes to find herself sitting on the stool next to the horse. Safir was looking concernedly into her eyes, while Fleur knelt on the ground next to her, holding her hand.

"I'm alright," Morgan said.

"Maybe I shouldn't tell you these things anymore," Safir remarked.

"No!" Morgan forced herself to stand up. "Please, Safir. I want to know. Who are they? The men from Armorica?"

"Ambrosius and Uther? All I know is that Sir Brastias called them the sons of Constantine. Whoever he is."

"Constantine's sons," Fleur said, recognising the name. "Father Elfodd talked about them. Remember, Morgan?"

Morgan nodded. She must ask Sebile who Constantine was.

"If there is going to be a war, maybe your father will let me start training to fight," Safir said to Morgan. "He says for now I'm too young. Only in two or three years, he says. But maybe now I can start early."

"I would hate to fight with a sword," Morgan said with distaste.

Safir laughed. "Come on! You're not scared of sword fighting, Morgan?"

"No!" Morgan said at once. She didn't like swords or fighting, but she wouldn't admit to being scared of anything.

"Is that why you fainted when I told you about the army coming?" Safir teased.

"No!" Morgan said again and pushed Safir playfully. "I didn't faint!"

"Oh, yes, you did. You are scared," Safir taunted her, grinning.

"No, I'm not!" Morgan retorted. "Shut up! You're just as bad as a boy!"

She lunged at Safir, but the squire was too quick for her. Safir dodged her grasp and ran out of the stables laughing, with Morgan on her heels. Once outside she stopped so abruptly that Morgan ran into her.

"Got you!" Morgan said breathlessly.

Safir stepped away from her and put her finger to her lips. She looked across the courtyard and Morgan followed her gaze. As Fleur came out of the stable door behind them, they saw Merlin on the far side of the yard. He was with the lean, dark-haired Druid, who was talking earnestly to the boy. The Druid had the same cat-watching-a-mouse look as he had had the first time Morgan had seen him staring at Merlin in the Great Hall. Merlin was looking up at him and listening with what appeared to be a disdainful frown on his face, but Morgan could tell he was interested in what the man had to say.

"I didn't know he was here!" she exclaimed.

"You know that man?" Fleur asked.

"He's a Druid. He was with Cadwellon before."

"They call him Myrddin," Safir told them. "They say he is Grand Master Cadwellon's right hand. He is always very quiet. Hardly ever says anything in council. He only does what the Grand Master tells him."

Morgan looked at the squire, quick to pick up on the tone in her voice. "Don't you like him?"

"I don't know," Safir said pensively. "There is something about that man. I don't ..." She trailed off.

"I wonder why he's talking to Merlin," Fleur said. "Does he know him?"

Morgan wondered as well. They watched as Merlin gave Myrddin a short reply and the dark-haired Druid bowed to the boy in response. Merlin turned to walk away and he caught sight of Morgan. His face went red, as if he was suddenly hot. Morgan felt her cheeks flush too and averted her eyes.

When she looked again, Merlin had turned his back on her and was walking into the castle. But she saw that the Druid Myrddin was now watching her. He was staring at her, in the same way that he had stared at Merlin, seeing her for the first time. The blood drained from Morgan's cheeks and she suddenly shivered as she felt an icy chill hit her. She realised that this man who she did not know and who did not know her was now very much aware of her. And in that instant she knew that he did not like her at all.

IX

The Moon Moor

Breathless, Morgan waited beside the window in her chambers. She had quietly put on her dress, shoes and cloak and carefully snuffed out all the candles once she was certain Fleur had fallen asleep. The darkness of the room made the full Moon outside look brighter than ever, its reflection over the ocean below broken up into glittering shards over the black water. Morgan could see dark patterns like water stains across its smooth surface. Staring at the dark patchy surface of the huge white orb that seemed closer to her than ever, she idly wondered what the marks on it were that made the Moon look not as perfect as it should be.

There was no sound coming from anywhere inside the castle. It must be very late. She felt afraid. No one except Ganieda knew what she was about to do and the mute girl couldn't tell anybody. Sebile didn't know. Fleur didn't know. Igraine and Gorlois didn't know. Morgan had no idea where she would be going or how long she would be away. Would they miss her? Would her father send out his soldiers to look for her? When would she come back? She wavered in her resolve – should she do this? Everyone would worry. They would be angry. It might be frightening. It might be dangerous.

But then her mind went back to Diana and the night ride through the sky. The dancing in the mountain grove. The faeries. "Some call us that," Diana had said. The sweetmeats you couldn't eat. The magic. The spiritual world. "It is part of us, but it is greater than us," Father Elfodd had said. What Diana wanted must be important. Morgan took a deep breath and tried to calm her thoughts. She had to do this. She didn't know how Arcile would be coming to her, but she knew this was the night of the thirteenth day since she had seen Diana. Arcile would come.

A small round white light fluttering wafts of air against her face told her that the moment had arrived. The Wisp was hovering outside the window like a tiny vision of the Moon itself. "Arcile!" Morgan whispered.

"Reach out, Morgan." Arcile's voice came from inside the little light. "Reach out your hand."

Morgan stretched out her arm as far as she could outside the window until the tips of her fingers touched the white light. With a shock, she felt her feet leave the ground as she was lifted up and carried out into the night. Momentarily dizzy, she looked down in fear at the cliff plummeting below her. There was nothing to break the drop between her and the jagged rocky shore. The Wisp twined round her hand and she felt Arcile holding on tightly as they glided effortlessly around the castle, up over the tower and across the battlements down towards the courtyard.

As they descended, a cold sea breeze ruffled Morgan's hair and cloak. She stared in awe at the bird's-eye view of her home's weather-beaten high walls. She had often imagined what it would be like to fly, but she hadn't known that it would somehow make the world look smaller and make her feel bigger.

Abruptly landing on the cobblestones of the yard, Morgan stumbled a little. The world went back to its normal size. But walking suddenly seemed to her clumsy and awkward. The Wisp was bobbing anxiously next to her.

"Aren't you going to turn into you?" Morgan whispered.

"I can't here," Arcile's bell-like voice said, much softer, quieter and stranger than her normal voice. "I'll be with you all the way, but only like this."

Morgan looked around nervously to see if there was anyone about, but the yard seemed empty.

"The guards are asleep," Arcile said. "You must go to the stables and get your father's horse."

"Swiftback?" Morgan said, astonished. "But why?"

"He was taken last night by the Small Ones. They like to take horses and ride them all through the night. He knows the way to them. With my help, he'll take you there."

Morgan crept into the stables and made her way to Swiftback's stall. He was standing as if he was expecting her, all sleekly groomed and clean thanks to Safir's efforts earlier that day. Morgan was too small to be able to saddle and bridle him, even if she had known how. She would have to ride bareback. Climbing up onto the large horse was daunting, but Morgan was determined. She fetched the wooden stool Safir had used for grooming, placed it next to Swiftback and climbed onto it, preparing to haul herself up onto the horse's back. Then, just as she reached up to grab Swiftback's mane, a voice said: "So you're going there on your father's horse."

Morgan gasped and almost fell off the stool.

"Merlin! You scared me! What are you doing here?"

"I've been waiting for you," the boy said. He was standing at the edge of the stall entrance, watching her.

"What do you mean? How did you know?"

"Ganieda told me."

Ganieda. Morgan's thoughts flashed back to the little girl's sullen silence after Morgan had told her she couldn't go with her to the Small Ones. So, what, now she had told her brother what Morgan was going to do because she was cross?

"She wasn't supposed to tell anyone," Morgan said angrily. "It was supposed to be a secret."

"I can hear her thoughts, like you," Merlin said. "And I can see what's in her mind, like she can see in yours. She showed me everything."

"Everything?"

"Everything. Diana, Dyonas, the Hunt creatures, the trees, the dancing, the feast. Arcile. What Diana wants you to do." Merlin came forward into the stall. "You could have told me."

"Why should I?" Morgan demanded. Her heart began to beat quickly and she wished she could make Merlin go away somehow. And not tell anyone what he had seen.

"I've told you things," Merlin said. He sounded annoyed, but underneath Morgan sensed something else. "I've told you things I haven't told anyone. I told you about the Furious Host. I told you about my dream – the same dream you had. And I saw the white light on the path that day when you did." He looked around the stables. "Is she here?"

"Arcile? Yes, she is," Morgan said. She couldn't see the Wisp at the moment though; Arcile must be hiding from Merlin. "I have to go."

She turned back to the horse, but Merlin stepped forward quickly. "You can't go by yourself, Morgan."

"I have to," Morgan told him. "Diana said I must."

"But you don't know where you're going. You don't know where the Small Ones are. You don't know *what* they are. You don't know what will happen." To Morgan's surprise, Merlin not only sounded annoyed, but anxious and tense. "You need someone to go with you."

"I don't." Morgan was firm, though Merlin's words made her uncertain. She hesitated for an instant, then stood on tiptoe on the stool, grasped Swiftback's mane and heaved herself onto his back. "The Small Ones took Swiftback last night. He'll take me to where they are."

Merlin stepped up onto the stool next to her. "Let me come with you, Morgan. I can help you."

"No," Morgan said. She gave Swiftback a sharp kick with her heel as her father had taught her and the horse moved forward, walking out of the stall, through the stables and out into the yard. His hooves made a loud clacketing sound on the stones, echoing in the night's silence. Morgan, afraid someone would hear, looked around again for Arcile. The Wisp was nowhere to be seen. But ahead of her was Merlin. He must have run through the stables and around Swiftback, for he was standing in front of the horse, blocking their path.

"Morgan – you've *got* to let me come with you! Something could happen to you!"

"I can't!" Morgan hissed. She was more afraid than ever that one of the guards – or worse, Gorlois – would be roused. "You get out of my way!"

She gave Swiftback two more nudges with her heel and the horse shot forward. Merlin jumped aside as the horse cantered towards the foregate. But then Morgan suddenly pulled hard on Swiftback's mane and the horse slowed to a walk. She'd forgotten about the guards outside the castle! What if they stopped her? She considered galloping straight past them, but then they'd send riders after her and catch her. Gorlois himself would come after her.

Morgan held her breath as they approached the foregate. There seemed to be four guards on duty. In the light from two burning torches on sconces, she could just see their silhouettes, shadows slumped against the wall. All snoring lightly. Arcile was right; they were asleep. Swiftback passed them slowly at a walk until they were outside the castle. Then the horse speeded up its pace to a canter, carrying Morgan up onto the hills beyond Tintagel.

Away from the surroundings of home, the horse's canter surged to a gallop and the world around them rushed by. Time ebbed and flowed ... the hills and valleys blended together; the air and the earth were as one. Morgan's fears and doubts washed away as her heart beat in rhythm with the horse's hooves. She held on tightly to Swiftback's mane, feeling an exhilaration she had known only once before. It was as if she was back in Diana's chariot, flying through the sky on the wind, and she laughed excitedly into the darkness.

The open night land before them glowed forest green and stone grey in the moonlight. Occasional shadowy trees loomed up and fell back against the sky; here and there a silvery pool shimmered, capturing the moonshine in its ripples as they rode past. The sound of Swiftback's hooves was all Morgan could hear as she and the horse pounded along, more muffled now against the grass. The horse seemed to know when the castle was far enough behind them, for gradually he slowed first to a canter, then to a walk.

"Arcile!"

"I'm here."

The Wisp was fluttering beside her. Morgan, steadying herself on the horse, breathed a sigh of relief.

"Where were you?"

"I thought that boy might see me."

"He's already seen you," Morgan said, thinking of the day on the path.

"It's a good thing you didn't let him come with us."

Morgan said nothing. The elation of the night ride started to evaporate, and her fears and uncertainties slowly began flowing back. Although she had felt triumphant that she hadn't let Merlin come with her, now that she was out here by herself in the night, she was having mixed feelings about leaving him behind. In his odd way, he had seemed to be trying to be her friend when she was starting to feel more and more alone. He knew about the strange things she could see and do, and he didn't think she was mad or not believe her – after all, he could see and do the strange things, too. Why was he also special, as Diana had called it? Why could they do these things that other people couldn't? How could they talk in their minds to Ganieda? Dream the future? See the Furious Host and Diana's Wild Hunt and Wisps like Arcile? Thoughts raced around Morgan's mind as Swiftback walked onwards.

For the first time she began to notice strange noises coming from all around her – noises she at first thought she had never heard before that startled her. Then she realised they were sounds she had heard many times when out on her walks beyond the castle, sounds she hadn't noticed in daylight with the Sun shining so brightly and brashly. But at night, with the Moon shining so much more softly and quietly, they were impossible to miss. Everything was louder, clearer, easier to hear. The sound of an otter diving into water. The snap of a twig or a branch. The croak of a frog. The screech of a bat. The cough of a nearby cow. The hoot of an owl. The whitter of a woodpecker rudely awoken, protesting in alarm from a nearby tree.

Unnerved, Morgan looked up at the Moon, wondering where Diana was. Could she see her? Was she watching her? Would she come to help her if she got into trouble? Arcile was there, but the fact that she was only a Wisp and couldn't or wouldn't turn into herself made Morgan doubt how much help she could really be. The Wisp bobbed beside her, just a tiny pale reflection of the round sphere in the sky. They stayed silent for some time as the horse walked along, needing no direction.

Then, out of the dark empty land around them, Morgan heard what she thought was an echo. It sounded like the noise of Swiftback's hooves on the ground, distant and muted, but as she listened the noise gradually grew louder and faster. A thrill of fright hit her. It was another horse! Someone was coming. Someone was chasing her.

"Arcile!" Morgan said urgently. "Someone's following us!"

"It can't be!" Arcile's voice said, sounding alarmed.

Morgan tried to urge Swiftback on to a gallop once more. This time, however, the horse did not respond. He seemed to want only to go at a very slow walk, as if he was being careful where he trod. In desperation, Morgan looked behind her. She saw the black silhouette of a horse approaching through the moonlit night, but she couldn't see a rider. Since Swiftback was not prepared to outrun the other horse, Morgan pulled on his mane to draw him to a stop. Whoever or whatever it was, Morgan would have to face them and think of a way either to make them go away or get away from them herself. Maybe in that way Arcile as a Wisp could help her.

As the other horse came closer, Morgan saw that a small person of about her own size was riding it. She thought for a wild instant how funny she must look – such a small person on the back of a large animal. Then, with another thrill, she knew who the other rider was. It had to be.

The other horse slowed to a canter and then a walk as it drew up towards them. The small rider, also riding bareback, pulled on the mane to make the horse stop just as Morgan had.

"Is that you, Morgan?" Merlin's voice said after a few moments.

"You know it's me," Morgan said. "How did you find us?"

As the other horse stopped alongside Swiftback, Morgan saw Merlin clearly. "This is Sir Brastias' horse, Windbane," Merlin said. "I knew he'd be able to follow your father's horse wherever it went." He stopped and stared above Morgan's head at the Wisp hovering there. "Is that Arcile?"

"Go away!" Arcile's voice hissed at him. "You can't be here!"

"Listen, Morgan," Merlin said, looking back at her and straight into her eyes for the first time. "I know Diana said you have to do this alone. But the Small Ones, the faeries, you're going to find … you don't know what they're like. I knew things about faeries back in Gwynedd; we have them there, too. They're not always nice. They can be nasty. They can be dangerous. If I go with you, you'll have someone to help you if things get bad."

Morgan was touched, despite herself. It gave her a warm feeling inside to think that Merlin had done all of this to help her and make sure she was alright. And being out alone in the night with nothing but the Wisp for company had changed her mind about a few things. If Merlin was right and the Small Ones turned out to be nasty or dangerous, it would be good to have a friend – a real, live friend who knew about her and could do the same things she could. Maybe she had been wrong about him.

"Alright then," she said. "You can come."

She expected him to smile at her, or at least show himself to be happy. But Merlin just continued looking intently at her and simply nodded. He did not react further.

"No!" Arcile whirred in front of Morgan's face. "You promised Diana you would do this alone!"

"I will do it alone," Morgan said. "I'll do what Diana wants me to. I'll find who she wants me to find. But I never said I would *go* alone. Merlin's coming with me."

"But ..." Arcile protested, but Morgan didn't want to hear any more. She held up her hand and for the first time since Arcile's passing spoke as the Duke's daughter to her former maid.

"No! Merlin's coming with me. I want him to. That's all."

The Wisp stopped fluttering for a moment, then went silent. Arcile floated up and ahead of them as Morgan urged Swiftback on with her heel. Merlin followed suit with Windbane and the children rode on together, side by side.

"Do you and Ganieda always talk to each other in your mind?" Morgan asked him, after riding along in silence for a few minutes.

"Yes," Merlin replied.

Their voices sounded loud in the stillness of the night. Morgan waited for Merlin to say something else. He did not. So she tried again.

"Do you know how you can do it?"

Merlin was silent for a moment. Then he said, somewhat shortly, "No, I don't really. I thought it was because she's my twin. I'm her brother. I've always been able to hear her."

"And she can hear you."

"When I want her to."

Morgan struggled with this. "But why can *I* hear her? She's not *my* twin, or my sister."

Merlin eyed her askance. "Maybe because you're like me. We had the same dream ... apart from the end. We both see things other people can't."

"The spiritual world," Morgan said, remembering Father Elfodd.

"The faerie world."

Morgan glanced at him sharply. "You said you knew about faeries in Gwynedd. Have you seen faeries before?"

"Once. In Gwynedd."

Again, he said no more. Morgan prompted him. "What happened? Tell me."

"I saw a lady with long gold hair standing on a boat in a lake. She spoke to me and asked me to go with her to her home. She said I had a great destiny and she would teach me everything I needed to know."

"Were you afraid?"

"Yes," the boy said. He wasn't looking at Morgan but kept his eyes firmly on the lonely path ahead of them. "She made me feel bad somehow. There was something ... nasty about her. Scary."

"Why?" Morgan asked, fascinated. "Was she very ugly?"

"No. She was very pretty. It was something else about her that scared me. I ran away. I didn't see her again."

"But why?" Morgan wanted to know. "Why did she come to you? Why did Diana come to me? Diana said that I'm special ... but why?"

"I'm supposed to be the son of the Devil," Merlin said. "Maybe that's why."

Morgan was having difficulty staying on her horse's back. Without a saddle to sit on, she was finding it slippery and uncomfortable, feeling herself sliding from one side to the other. She feared she would fall off and hurt herself, sitting so high above the ground. She held on tighter to Swiftback's mane in an effort to keep her balance as she absorbed the shock of what Merlin had just said. She was stunned at the casual way he had spoken, as if he didn't care.

"I don't believe that!" she said indignantly. "Anyway, *I'm* the daughter of the Duke and Duchess, and they're normal people. So why do the faeries come to me? Why can I see these things?"

"That old Druid man said your mother studied with the Druids when she was young. Maybe she can see these things, too. Like you."

A gauze of misty cloud floated across the Moon. The darkness around them thickened. The air felt colder. Endless black open countryside stretched away from them on all sides. Morgan's heart began to beat faster and she was grateful for Merlin's presence, even though she didn't much like what he was saying. She thought about Igraine. Was her beautiful, devoted, Christian mother secretly magical? It would explain why she, Morgan, was. But something in Merlin's tone irked her.

"Why do you talk about Grand Master Cadwellon like that? Are you still cross because he wanted Taliesin for his apprentice and not you?"

She heard Merlin's horse stumble in the darkness and the boy's sudden exclamation.

"No!" Morgan felt oddly pleased to hear Merlin sound angry. "I don't need him anyway," the boy said. "I'm going to be a Druid without his help."

"How?"

"Another Druid asked me to be his apprentice."

Morgan remembered seeing Merlin in the courtyard the previous afternoon. "Myrddin?"

"How do you know him?"

"I've seen him," Morgan said. She almost added, "And I don't like him", but stopped herself.

"He's going to make me his apprentice. I'm going to study with him and learn everything the Druids learn."

"What about Brother Blaes?"

Merlin pursed his lips. "I have to keep learning with him. My mother says so. But I'll study with Master Myrddin, too." He looked almost fiercely at Morgan. "No one knows, not even my sister. Only you. And you can't tell anyone. I keep your secrets; you have to keep mine."

"All right, I will," Morgan said coolly. She couldn't understand why Merlin wanted to study with Myrddin. The dark-haired Druid gave her a bad feeling. But she thought it best not to tell Merlin what she really thought of his new Druid Master.

The gauze of cloud lifted and the Moon shone unhindered upon the landscape once more. Morgan's arms began to ache from holding on to Swiftback's mane so tightly and the horsehair was making her hands itch.

All of a sudden the horses came to a standstill.

"What is it?" Morgan said, looking ahead.

Ahead the ground rose sharply above them. The soil had been torn away by wind and rain, littering the hillside with granite rock-piles. Looming in front of them in the Moon-dappled darkness, it looked like the stern and forbidding wall of a fortress – completely unlike the gently rolling hills, richly grassed valleys, and flower-flecked green fields, woods and hedgerows of the countryside around Tintagel that Morgan was used to. This hill was cold and jagged and unadorned.

"We're here," Arcile's voice snapped. The Wisp was hovering next to Morgan's head again. She sounded grumpy as if still annoyed at Morgan's insistence on Merlin coming with them. "Out here you will find the Small Ones. Or they will find you."

"Where are we?" Morgan asked.

"People call this place Selena Moor," Arcile said. "The Moon Moor. There are few paths that enter its heart. You can only go in on foot."

Morgan was startled. "But we can't! Swiftback has to take us there."

"Swiftback will lead you," she heard Arcile reply. "But you can't ride him. The moorland is too soft and light to hold you both – it will swallow you if you try. You have to get off the horse here and follow him along the path."

With reluctance, Morgan swung her legs over Swiftback and slid the considerable distance from the horse's back to the ground. With a soft thud, Merlin dismounted next to her. The children watched, fascinated, as the shining white Wisp floated in front of Swiftback's head. Morgan heard Arcile whisper into the horse's ear a strange rhyme, most of which she could not hear, and what she did hear she could not understand. The Wisp's glowing light expanded and swirled around the horse's head, engulfing it. When Arcile floated back to her, Morgan asked, "What did you say to him?"

"I've enchanted him," Arcile said. "He'll lead us along the path he was ridden last night when he was taken. The Small Ones hide themselves well, even from us, but they love to come out and dance when the Moon is full. Swiftback's memory will take us to where they are."

"What about Windbane?" Merlin asked.

Arcile didn't answer him. It seemed she had decided to ignore Merlin. Morgan felt frustrated with her.

"I suppose we'd better leave him here," she said to Merlin. "He can wait for us."

"For how long? How long will we be?"

Morgan took a deep breath. "I don't know."

She reached up to give Windbane a pat on the nose, turned and began to walk up the slope carefully and deliberately so as not to lose her footing in the darkness. She shifted her eyes back and forth from the ground to the shape and sound of Swiftback, who was plodding fixedly up towards the moor ahead as if in a stupor. Windbane whinnied behind them, his cry sounding stark in the wilderness. Morgan felt bad. She looked back in sympathy at the other horse standing at the bottom of the hill. He was staring mournfully after them, a lonely figure growing smaller as she climbed higher. Merlin was edging up the steep hillside beside her. He did not look back.

* * *

When they reached the top of the hill, the air turned cooler and the world changed. The night lands of the Moon Moor stretched out before them, wild and weather-beaten and seemingly never-ending. Amidst tufts of bushes, rocky outcrops and the occasional solitary tree, vast swathes of grass clogged with glimmering pools of water covered the earth in a patchwork display as far as the dim light allowed them to see. There were no fields that Morgan could see; no houses, no hedgerows, no farms. It was as if nobody lived there at all. The place was bleak and empty. The sky, larger and wider than Morgan had ever seen it, hung heavily over them. The moor itself waited in brooding silence; unfriendly, hostile, even threatening. Morgan got the distinct sense that wherever they were going they would not be welcome.

"This is where the Small Ones are?" she asked Arcile in a hushed tone.

"This is where they live," Arcile replied. "They do like to go into the mortal world sometimes – usually to cause people trouble. But this is where they prefer to be. This is their domain."

Swiftback was already walking across the dark moor in front of them, his hooves making a softer squelching sound instead of the usual clopping.

"Take care," Morgan heard Arcile whisper to her. "Make sure you follow Swiftback and don't stray from the path he takes you on. The moor's covered with bogs and you have to know your way through. If you leave the path, the mud will take you and pull you under. You'll never get out."

Morgan was convinced that Merlin hadn't heard what Arcile had said and, moreover, that the Wisp hadn't meant him to. "We have to follow Swiftback," she told him in a louder tone that echoed in the empty air. "If we don't stay on the path, we'll sink in the mud."

"Right," Merlin said. Morgan sensed Arcile fluttering around her again and was sure that if the Wisp's face were visible, she would be scowling in annoyance.

The children set off in single file, Morgan in front keeping her eyes on Swiftback's retreating shape, with Merlin so close behind her she could hear his fast breathing. She was aware he was as nervous and afraid as she was, though she knew him well enough by now to know that he would never admit it. Ahead of them lay the moor, a vast swampy marshland with shadows everywhere and a silence broken only by the odd distant shriek and cry that made Morgan's heart jump. But she went on bravely and determinedly, stepping gingerly along the path Swiftback trod for them that criss-crossed the rivulets and pools of murky mire all around. The huge expanse of dark blue sky above was splashed with an ocean-spray of stars dominated by the enormous round white Moon, its water-stained surface starker than ever. Its silvery light lit up the moor's gleaming marsh-ponds, sporadic rocky banks overgrown with tussock grass and gorse, and sharp silhouettes of hunchbacked, wind-battered trees, their tangled branches splayed sideways and frozen against the night sky as if in mid-gust.

As they walked deeper and deeper into the moor, the unearthly silence grew stronger, save for the occasional *glug-glug* of quivering mud. Morgan tried to keep up her courage, but the stillness and emptiness of the wide open land seemed to press heavily upon her. The quiet and the dark began to get her down, and she yearned for a light or promised warmth of a house or any sign of people living in this lonely place. Unknown, unseen things continued their bloodcurdling screeches from time to time. They were starting to seem bolder and louder, and sounded as if they were coming nearer. Once Morgan thought she saw a shadow with shining eyes gliding across a moonlit pool a little way off and her heart hammered so fast she felt it would burst.

The thrill of the adventure had waned. She was cold and tired and scared, and her legs were aching. What was she doing out here on this dark and creepy moor, late at night, far away from home? Watching Arcile's small white shape bobbing in front of her, she wondered why the Wisp would not turn back into her human self. Somehow she would feel so much better and safer if she could just see the older girl; if she knew she was truly with her as a person, or, rather, the shape of a person, and not as a Wisp. Just being a round white light made Arcile strange to her, unfamiliar, something other than human. Like the Small Ones. Up until then, Morgan had been so focused on getting to the Small Ones that she had put off thinking about who or what she would actually face when she encountered them. But now, following the plodding horse, treading lightly on the tufty path and feeling the eerie darkness closing in around her, her mind went forward to the Small Ones themselves.

"Have you ever seen the Small Ones?" she asked the fluttering white light ahead of her.

The Wisp floated back to her side.

"No," came Arcile's voice. "I heard them when I was little, though. They came out at night and scratched on our door and knocked on the walls. I remember hearing them laughing. I was frightened. Father used to get angry and curse them. He said prayers to keep them away. People in the village are still afraid of them. I heard stories of people being chased and bitten by small horrid things they can't see. Sometimes they move things around in the house – you can't see the Small Ones but you can see the things moving and flying around the room. But Mother always left a dish of milk out for them so they wouldn't harm us or curse our house. She said they used to steal human children and leave their own children in their place."

It was strange to hear their voices breaking the quiet of the lonely moorland around them. The shadows seemed to be getting longer and the silence ever more intense.

"Changelings," Morgan said, remembering.

"Yes. There used to be a little boy in the village who looked really strange. He didn't look … human. His face was all hairy and wrinkled like an old man but he was only a little boy. He was about your age."

"Really?" Morgan was intrigued. "Was he a Small One? What happened to him?"

"He died," Arcile said, a note of sadness in her voice. "His parents hated him. They would hit him and kick him and didn't give him food. His skin was awfully burned because they'd thrown him on the fire when he was a baby."

"On the fire?" Morgan asked in horror. "Why?"

"People believe it's a way to make a changeling turn back into a faerie. They say if you throw it on the fire, it will fly up the chimney. But he didn't. Everyone in the village was afraid of him and would run away from him. I was scared of him, too, but I felt sorry for him. Sometimes I brought him food from the castle and left it for him to find. One day his parents locked him outside in the winter snow and wouldn't let him back in the house. They thought he was a changeling, so they thought the Small Ones would come and take him back. But they didn't. They found him the next day, dead under a tree."

Morgan was aghast at the thought. "That's horrible! Poor boy."

The uneven path they were walking on was beginning to seem spiteful and mean. It was muddy and peppered with stones that weren't easy to see in the semi-darkness. The nasty stones kept twisting Morgan's feet and ankles unmercifully, trying to trip her and make her stumble or slip. The outline of a solitary, wind-broken tree loomed up in front of her against the bleak moorland horizon, its snapped branches raised like swords as if to strike.

She shivered. Then a thought struck her.

"But … how come he died? If he was a changeling, he would be a – a spirit, wouldn't he? Like you."

There was a silence. Morgan wondered if Arcile was offended. The moor itself seemed to be listening intently, hanging on to their every word.

"Maybe he wasn't a changeling," Arcile said finally. "Maybe he was just a strange-looking human boy – born that way. But then maybe he was one of the Small Ones and he was able to leave this world to go on to another." She paused again. "I don't really understand everything about this new world I'm in, Morgan. Diana has explained some things to me and I can see some things much more clearly, but I don't understand everything yet. And that's why telling you about your task is going to be difficult."

At the mention of her task ahead, Morgan stopped suddenly, causing Merlin to bump into her. She fell forward, slipped on a stone and took a quick step to keep her balance. Her foot touched ground that felt different – softer and squelchy, as if it would give way at any moment. She realised with horror that she had stepped off the path into the mire. With a squeal, she hastily grabbed hold of Merlin and pulled her foot back. Breathing rapidly, she steadied herself and looked around for Arcile's small light.

"Diana said you would tell me what to do. Are you going to tell me now? What it is she wants?"

"I told you that the Small Ones steal human children," Arcile said. "I didn't tell you that some of them also *are* children. Dead children."

Morgan was horrified. She heard Merlin's sharp intake of

breath behind her.

"What do you mean, dead children?" She hesitated awkwardly, still concerned about offending Arcile. "Like you, you mean?"

"No," Arcile's voice came back abruptly. "Not like me. They're children who never lived. Some babies, Morgan, are born dead. They come into this world dead. Some are meant to never enter the world; they leave for Heaven and never come back. Others are meant to have their souls be born again, so they can have another chance at life."

Morgan turned to Merlin. "Cadwellon told us about that," she said to him. "He said the Druids believe the soul goes into another body."

"Yes." Merlin nodded.

"So that's what happens to the souls of children who are born dead?" Morgan asked Arcile.

"That's right," Arcile said. "It's one of the gifts Diana can give – the gift of life. She's the ancient Goddess of the Moon and she's the Goddess who helps women when they have children. When they give birth. She's helped babies be born since the beginning of time. And she can give the soul of a child who dies before it can ever live another chance at life. She saves it and makes it possible for it to be born again."

Morgan was stunned into silence. Her mind couldn't grasp how this could happen or why it even had to happen. It was Merlin who spoke for her.

"But if Diana can do this, why does she need Morgan? What's Morgan supposed to do?"

Arcile didn't reply. The silence of the open moor lingered once more in the air.

"Tell us!" Morgan insisted. Her voice sounded unnaturally loud, echoing in the vast stillness of the night. She was getting tired of the Wisp's unfriendly attitude to Merlin.

"Like I told you, some of the Small Ones are the souls of dead children," Arcile snapped back, clearly resentful at Morgan's tone. Then her voice softened. "They steal them away before they have a chance to go anywhere else and so they become one of them. Only this time they've taken someone very important. A little baby boy whom Diana had to save. He was born dead – stillborn, it's called – but the Small Ones came and took away his soul before Diana could reach him. She needs this boy's soul. He has to be reborn. He's with the Small Ones now and it's your task to go into their realm to find him and bring him to Diana."

"*What?*" Morgan gasped after she had found her voice. She struggled to find words. "But ... but ... how shall I do that? How will I know him? How will I get him out? What if the Small Ones don't let me?"

The enormity of what she was supposed to do suddenly terrified her. Was *this* the spiritual world Elfodd had told her of? Alone now with only Merlin and the Wisp, standing on the cheerless dark expanse of moor that seemed to spread out forever, it appeared ugly and terrifying to her. Not at all like Diana's beautiful forest grove with the music and dancing and sweetmeats. And not at all like the lovely angels and saints she had been imagining after her talk with Elfodd. But then, she remembered, he had talked about demons, too. "Demons disguising themselves as ghosts to trick people," was what he had said. She remembered Bormovo at Diana's court. A normal-looking spirit who in life had been tortured to death in boiling water. She recalled how scared she had been when he had showed her how he died, revealing his hideous burnt flesh and boils. His true appearance.

She shivered again. Was that what the Small Ones were like, only worse? Were they demons tricking people? A terrible thought flashed through her mind: what if that was what Arcile was? And even Diana too? She let souls like Bormovo stay at her court, after all. If Elfodd was right, could she trust them? What if they were tricking *her*?

"You're worried, Morgan," Arcile's voice said, as if reading her thoughts. "You think you can't trust me."

"I don't know anymore," Morgan said shakily. She was scared but now also felt angry. "Can I?"

The Wisp remained quiet for a moment, flickering silently in the darkness. Then Arcile's voice replied, clear and steady. "What's important is that you trust yourself, Morgan. I know it's hard to trust me and understand everything. You're still so young ... as

I was once. But trust yourself. Trust what you can do when the time comes – and you *can* do it. Diana needs someone to go into the court of the Small Ones, where she can't go. Nor can I in my human form. But you can and you will. And there's something else you must do when we find them. I'll help you with it."

Morgan felt numb. Her head and heart were heavy, and she didn't know what to say. But she knew there was only one thing to do. They were all the way out on the moor, in the night, a long way from home. They couldn't go back now. They had to go on.

X

Into the Mire

Trudging along the path, Morgan's thoughts were such a whirlpool that she had to make a great effort to concentrate hard on continuing along the narrow track. It was getting harder to avoid the treacherous rocks and slippery mud patches despite the Moon's silvery-white light. The first inkling she had that something was wrong was when Merlin pushed past her.

"What are you doing?"

"Wait." Merlin had stopped and was looking ahead. Something in his voice alarmed her.

"What is it?"

"The horse. He's gone."

The path immediately before them was empty and petered off into the bogs. Swiftback had disappeared. There was no sign of him anywhere on the marshes before them; no reassuring sound of his hooves in the distance.

"But that can't be!" Morgan protested in desperation. "Where's he gone? How are we going to find our way now?"

"The Small Ones can't be far," Arcile said. For the first time Morgan thought she heard fear in the Wisp's voice. "We shouldn't have stopped. We'll have to go on on our own. Be very careful."

Morgan and Merlin looked at each other. "I'll go first," Morgan said.

"No." Merlin shook his head, his eyes not quite meeting hers. "We'll go together."

Morgan didn't reply, but wrapped her cloak more tightly around her and set off once again across the moor. Merlin kept pace beside her as they felt their way along the rough clumps of grass, avoiding the fetid growth of rushes and patches of sinking mud. Merlin exclaimed as he took a wrong step and his foot sank into muddy soil; instinctively, Morgan grabbed his hand to pull him back up.

As usual, Merlin flinched at her touch, but once back on the path he did not let go of her hand. The children did not speak, but the feeling of Merlin's warm hand in hers comforted Morgan a little.

Arcile's tiny white light still fluttered alongside them, but the shadows around them were growing longer. Veiled black clouds slowly crept across the bright face of the Moon and its light dimmed again. Morgan started to make out the shapes of rocky hillocks overgrown with furze and withy trees, looking like small islands pushed up by the surrounding marsh bog. Snow-white seed-heads of cotton grass shone in the fading moonlight, acting like little beacons warning of the dangerous patches of quaking mire. As Morgan and Merlin climbed hand in hand over the rocks, twisted roots rose up from the ground to trap their feet and trip them up. Cruel brambles clawed at them with hooked thorny nails. Morgan felt fingers brushing against her face that were as cold as frost. Adjusting her eyes to the growing darkness, she could see crooked-fingered misty hands looking like trails of smoke gathering round them.

Then, as she was about to cry out, a stone turned under her foot and she fell, letting go of Merlin's hand and putting out her other hand to save herself. As soon as she touched the ground, a bramble sprang up and wound itself around her fingers, holding her tightly and tearing at her skin. The pain made her yell.

"Merlin! Arcile!" she shouted, struggling to free herself. Arcile hummed agitatedly around her trapped hand. Morgan could feel the tiny Wisp tugging at the thorns trying to pry the bramble loose. But Merlin stood as if mesmerised, staring across the moor.

"Look," he said. "It's Swiftback."

Morgan looked up and saw the silhouette of a horse standing on the marsh amongst the cotton grass. But she knew something was not right. The horse stood rigid, stock still. He made no sound. And how, Morgan wondered wildly, was the horse able to stand right in the middle of the bog without sinking?

"Merlin ..." Morgan began, but before she could say any more she heard a noise that made her heart miss a beat. A single-voiced, high-pitched laugh rang out in the dark. Another followed. Then another. And another. Soon the air was filled with a cacophony of manic shrieking laughter. But whoever was laughing seemed invisible.

"It's them," Arcile whispered. Now Morgan knew she hadn't imagined the change in Arcile's voice. The Wisp was afraid.

Through the stunted branches of a broken-down tree nearby, Morgan saw two tiny lights glinting. They weren't white like Arcile, but of different colours, one bright red, the other bright blue. They flickered briefly for a moment, then vanished. The mad laughter vanished with them.

"Did you see that?" Merlin called. He was still gazing across the marsh.

"Merlin, it's them!" Morgan cried. "It's the Small Ones!"

Merlin didn't seem to hear her. "I'm going to get Swiftback," he said and walked towards the horse.

"No!" Morgan tried to stand up but the bramble tore viciously at her hand again and held her fast. "Arcile, get me out of this!"

The Wisp pinched at the thorns, trying to pluck them out as Morgan attempted to pull her hand away. But the more she tried, the more the bramble grew. Rising from the ground, it snaked its way round and round up her arm, winding itself all the way to her shoulder until she was held in a vice-like grip. With shock she realised that another bramble had risen from the ground and was winding itself around her ankle and up her leg. The thorns digging into her hand had drawn blood. It stung.

Out on the moor, the small red and blue lights reappeared, further away this time, floating enticingly near the unmoving figure of the horse. The horse's coat gleamed with the reflection of the unearthly red and blue lights above, shining out in the dark. Merlin began to make his way toward them and Morgan heard the chorus of mocking laughter once more.

"They're leading him into the mire," Arcile said.

"No! Merlin! *Merlin!*" Try as she might, Morgan couldn't get free from the brambles. She could only watch helplessly as Merlin stumbled towards the red and blue lights, lured further and further away into the marshes. As Merlin walked towards it, the shape of the horse faded away into the night. Morgan knew Swiftback had never been there. It was a trick. But Merlin continued to follow the brilliantly-coloured red and blue lights as if he was being pulled by them. Ignoring Morgan's screams and yells, he walked fixedly on, his gait growing slower and his feet heavier, drenched in the thick boggy soil.

Soon he stood completely still, dazed and worn out, no longer able to lift his legs to take any further steps. Morgan could see creeping black shadows approaching the boy and surrounding him. Long-tapered misty-grey fingers were reaching out for him. With a shock she thought Merlin had begun shrinking. Then she realised with terror that he was being pulled down into the mud. The lights hovered above him, bathing the boy's helpless figure in their eerie blue and red glow as he began sinking into the blackness of the marsh. Laughter emanated from them all the while and from the shadows round about.

As the laughing mockery rang louder and louder in her ears, Morgan grew so angry and sorry that she determined to push her fear to one side and save Merlin. She was not going to let these horrible things get her friend. Or her.

"We have to do something!" she hissed at Arcile.

"I can't help the boy," the Wisp protested.

"What? You have to!"

"I can't! I'm bound only to help you. I promised!"

"Well then, help me!" Morgan said urgently. "Help me help Merlin!"

Arcile was quiet a moment, as if thinking what to do. Then she said, "The shadows hate light."

"What?"

"The shadows hate light. The Moon. They run away from her and try to block her. Her bright light hurts them." The Wisp's own small white light hovered above Morgan's head as she sat trapped on the ground. Directly above Arcile's light, like a reflection, Morgan saw the faint outline of the Moon, now smothered in black cloud.

"Trust what you can do, Morgan. Remember the daffodils? Remember your dream? Remember how you freed yourself? Free yourself now. Bring back the light."

Morgan didn't have time to think. She saw that Merlin was

down almost to his waist in the muddy mire, fast disappearing from her sight. Recalling in an instant the lightning from her dream, she threw back her head to glimpse the blackened Moon, closed her eyes with the afterimage burned onto her brain, and focused her whole being on bringing back the light. "Make the clouds go away. Let the Moon shine again. Make the shadows run away," she murmured to herself over and over.

She felt cold fingers touch her face and cloak again. Other creeping, twining, nipping plants sprang up to bind her, joining the brambles holding her arm and leg in their biting grip, but she kept her focus on the Moon in her mind and paid them no heed. She concentrated on the memory of the huge crescent she had ridden past in Diana's chariot, on how over the nights that followed the thin fingernail expanded into a half-circle, and finally on how it shone out bright as a shining full circle, streaming all its light into the darkness. She thought of Diana, and her beauty and her brightness. From behind her closed eyes the blackness grew whiter, like a lantern being lit and gradually glowing into full flame.

Opening her eyes, she saw the veils of black cloud had parted and the Moon was shining down from the heavens, lighting up the moor once again. She heard howling and gibbering as the shadows slunk away into their dark crevices. The brambles holding her prisoner sputtered and moaned and unwound, releasing their grasp and hastily withdrawing back into the earth. Morgan shook them off violently and scrambled to her feet, stamping on any brambles she could still see and cradling her blood-stained hand as she looked frantically for Merlin. At that moment the boy let out a yell. He seemed to have suddenly woken up and was looking about him in panic, sunk deep in the mud. He flailed and struggled, plunging blindly through the bog trying to find the path.

"Help! Morgan! How did I get here? Morgan, where are you? Help me!"

From her vantage point on the rocky island, Morgan saw the true path shining ahead of him. "Merlin!" she shouted. The boy turned, straining to see her.

"This way!" Morgan called, running down towards the path to meet him.

"Go slowly," Morgan heard Arcile mutter, too quietly for Merlin to hear. "If you go too quickly, you'll sink."

"Go slowly, Merlin!" Morgan repeated, shouting the words. "Don't go too fast or you'll sink!"

She knelt at the edge of the path and watched him, just as she had on the rocky shore the night of the storm. This time Merlin was not weighed down with his sister on his back, but with the sucking mud of the mire pulling him down. He heeded Morgan's advice and struck out slowly for the path, pushing his way through the thick sludge and keeping his eyes on her. Morgan gazed steadily back, concentrating the entirety of her own mind on getting him back to safety. Both children were so focused on Merlin's return that all fear and weariness was forgotten. A couple of times, the boy seemed to lose his footing and sank further, until the mire reached his chest. However, Morgan sensed that through the combined force of her mind and a vivid energy of his own, Merlin managed to raise himself back up far enough to be able to keep moving forward. He eventually managed to reach the path and, taking Morgan's hand once more, between them they hauled him back up onto firm ground.

"Clever."

The voice behind them had a twangy, unpleasant sound. The red light and the blue light had appeared on the path with them and were flickering malignantly before their eyes.

"Clever girl, to get rid of the shadows like that," the same voice said. It came from the red light and sounded like a boy, but with an inhuman timbre Morgan had never heard before.

"Who are you?" Morgan demanded.

The raucous laughter rang out again – not just from the red and blue lights, but from all around them. Morgan became angry again.

"Be quiet!" she shouted.

The laughter ceased abruptly. "Bossy, isn't it?" said another nasty-sounding voice, this time a girl's one coming from the blue light. "What does it think it is? A princess?"

"*She* asked you a question," Arcile's voice snapped. The white Wisp was floating next to Morgan.

There was a sudden change in the air.

"Oooh, what's this then?" the red light chortled. Darting forward, the red and blue lights glided either side of Arcile and began spinning round her, faster and faster. Arcile squealed.

"No! Stop!"

"Leave her alone!" Morgan tried to swat them away, but the red and blue lights continued whirring round the white Wisp, forcing her to spin like a tiny top, their laughter shrieking in Morgan's ears. She was about to focus angrily on making them stop with her mind, but before she could do anything, the shrieks of laughter turned suddenly to pain.

"Arrrrggggghhhhh! Stop it! Stop it!"

It came from the blue light. It was burning whiter and whiter, giving off waves of heat, and seemed to turn in on itself. The cries turned to screams of agony.

"Don't!" the voice from the red light screeched in sudden fear. "What are you doing?"

"Nothing," Morgan said in bewilderment. Then her eye caught Merlin. Caked with mud to his elbows, his face streaked with dirt, the little boy exuded the same energy Morgan had sensed while he was making his way through the mire to the path. But now he was free it was much stronger. His face shone in a strange way, mirroring the white heat of the pulsing blue light. But his expression was dark with fury and his eyes were ice-cold as he stared at the blue light with the same kind of focus Morgan employed to make things happen with her mind.

The voice from the blue light screamed even louder as it burned hotter and sparks began to fly. It sounded less uncanny and more like a human.

"You're destroying her!" the red light cried. He sounded desperate.

"Merlin, stop it," Morgan urged in a low tone.

The boy didn't seem to hear her. His eyes glinted with a determined ferocity that Morgan found alarming.

"Merlin!" she exclaimed, grabbing his arm. Merlin whipped round to face her. The spell was broken.

"They tried to kill me," he said. His voice shook with anger.

"No! No, we didn't!" the red light protested. The blue light had resumed its original size and colour, and was bobbing next to the red, audibly sobbing. "We weren't trying to kill you! It was just a bit of fun! Nothing wrong with that, is there, Princess Light-Eyes?" The red light seemed to appeal to Morgan, before emitting a sharp "Owwww!" sound. Arcile's white light appeared to bump into the red; she seemed to have smacked the red light in some way.

"You're evil tricksters!" Arcile said angrily. "These children could have died!"

"Are you the Small Ones?" Morgan asked.

"I suppose so," the red light said, sounding aggrieved and resentful. "You Big People call us the Small People, I believe. *We* don't call ourselves that, though. There are many of us and we're all different, so there! Why are you here, anyway? What do you want?"

Morgan was thrown for a moment. Then she had an idea. "I'm looking for the Small People who took my father's horse," she said. "He led us out here, so it must have been you."

"Oh. Yes," the red light said dismissively. "We did that. So what? We enjoy it."

"So, what are your people called?" Morgan asked, somewhat exasperated.

"We are the Piskies, Princess Light-Eyes," the red light said. "What is it you want with us? Your *Highness*?"

Morgan knew it was making fun of her and felt angry again. "Careful," Arcile whispered in her ear.

Morgan took a deep breath. "I have a message," she said in an even tone. "I need to speak to all of you."

The red light floated up to her and hovered in front of her face. "Aha! You want to appear before our court?"

"Yes," Morgan said boldly.

"Very well, then. We'll take you there."

Morgan squinted at the small red light, trying to see what was inside it. "What's your name?"

She thought she sensed a mocking grin from the tiny being. "I'm Jack, Princess Light-Eyes. Delighted to meet you."

"And who's that?" She pointed to the little blue light, which had gone silent.

"That's Joan," Jack said. The blue light floated to his side.

"Hello, Princess Light-Eyes," Joan sniffed.

"Well, now," Jack said. "Let's go then."

He gave a crazy-sounding giggle, the sound of which Morgan didn't like at all. The red and blue lights fluttered away over the rocks. Before setting off after them, Morgan turned to Merlin. "Are you alright?" she asked.

"You can't trust these creatures," Merlin said. He wasn't looking directly at her, but ahead of them, his eyes following the lights. "Not after what they did."

"Of course I don't trust them! But we came here to find them. We have to go with them."

"I know."

* * *

Morgan and Merlin went after Jack and Joan, following the winking coloured lights across the rock-tipped moor. The land rose higher as more trees and plants and shrubs began appearing along the path. Soon it was overgrown with rough herbage. As they walked, Morgan spotted some familiar silvery-white flower heads in the moonlight. She leaned over and picked one to rub against the scratches from the brambles. She was about to pick another when Merlin bent down and picked it first, handing it to her.

"Yarrow," he said. "For your hand."

"You knew," Morgan said, smiling in surprise.

To her amazement, Merlin smiled back. "You showed it to Ganieda. I learned it from her."

Morgan rubbed the yarrow onto her skin to stem the bleeding. Something else was worrying her, though, and she looked round for Arcile. The Wisp was floating beside them as they made their way up the steep incline.

"You said there was something else I had to do when we found them," Morgan said to the Wisp. "You said you'd help me with it."

"Yes," the Wisp agreed.

"Well? What is it?"

The Wisp hesitated.

"You won't be able to go into the Piskie court as you are," she said eventually. "You have to make yourself small enough to talk to them properly. Get down to their size so you can actually see them."

Morgan stopped in her tracks. Merlin also stopped walking. His expression was quizzical as he stared at the Wisp.

"That's mad!" Morgan exclaimed angrily. "How are we supposed to do that?"

"Why is it mad?" Arcile asked. She sounded irritated. "Haven't you realised *anything* yet, Morgan? You just made the clouds go away and the Moon shine again! Don't you understand that you have the power to *make* things happen if you really want to?"

"But this is different!" Morgan objected. "The clouds move with the wind. It's normal."

"You're not normal," the Wisp said sharply. Morgan winced. She didn't want to think about that. But Arcile continued. "If you'd stop pretending to be 'normal', you'd know how to get small instead of only knowing how to get big."

"But it's natural to get big." Merlin addressed Arcile directly. "All children do. It's not natural to get small. So of course Morgan and I don't know how to."

"It's natural to the Moon, Morgan," the Wisp said, directing her words to her former young mistress and ignoring Merlin again. "You've seen it. The Moon grows bigger and smaller. Sometimes she can disappear altogether."

"Well, that's stupid because I'm not the Moon!" Morgan said crossly. "And I can't grow small."

"In that case, you won't be able to go into the Piskie realm. You won't be able to do what Diana wants. So you've come all the way out here for nothing."

Morgan was torn. She really wanted to do what Diana had asked, but at the same time she again felt the fear deep inside herself that she couldn't explain. She hadn't thought that she would have to change so much, and see and do so many things that weren't normal in order to complete Diana's task. The more she did and the closer she came, the more it made her feel fearful. Just like when Arcile had lifted her out of the window at Tintagel earlier that night and she had looked downwards, with nothing but emptiness between her and the dangerous rocks far below. Nothing to stop her fall. Nothing to catch her.

Merlin was watching her in the pale moonlight. His expression as he looked at her was, as always, one of interest and curiosity and ... something else. Something Morgan couldn't put into words. She wasn't sure she wanted to. It made her almost as uneasy as the idea that she had this power to make things happen with her mind.

"You'll help me do it?" she asked Arcile.

"Of course!" the Wisp said eagerly.

"But I don't want to *stay* small," Morgan told her.

"Don't worry. It'll be easy for you to get big again."

"What about you, Merlin?" Morgan asked him.

"If you're going to do it, so am I," the boy said. "If you can do it, I can."

His words weren't said in a friendly way. They were almost a challenge, with a hint of a tone Morgan recognised – a tone she had often heard her little sister Anna use when she spoke to her. She didn't have time to wonder about it further; the little red and blue lights were flying further and further away, taking their strange soft flares with them.

"Quick!" she said breathlessly and started to run towards them before they disappeared from sight. They followed Jack and Joan up to the top of the moonlit tor where a copse of mangle-branched trees opened onto a glade. In the middle of the grass was a smooth round earthen circle. A dim flicker of light filled the circle with an uncanny glow. Small sinuous figures appeared to be moving on it. Morgan heard the sounds of bells and pipes, and a similar malicious laughter to that which earlier had echoed out across the moor.

The children stared in fascination. Morgan's excitement was such that her fear paled against her curiosity and desire to see the Piskies up close. She had an overwhelming feeling that she must join them.

"Arcile!" she whispered, turning to the Wisp beside her. "Help me now!"

"Think of the Moon, Morgan," she heard the Wisp's urgent reply. "Think of how she grows from big to small, from the circle to the fingernail. Then close your eyes and say after me ..."

Morgan closed her eyes tight and concentrated on the image of the waning Moon in her mind, repeating the words Arcile chanted.

"By the glow of the Moon's full light
Give me the will to change this night
Wise true ancients, hear my call
Shift my shape and make me small."

The Moon's rays bathed her in a light she could feel with her eyes closed. Gradually her legs began to fold up underneath her. Her arms started to shrivel. Her stomach closed in on itself. Her head felt like it was being crushed from the inside. Her eyes rolled into the back of her head. It was as if something from the very core of her was pulling her down with a rope and letting all the air escape out of her. She tried to cry out in shock and pain, but her voice wouldn't work.

When everything had stopped and she dared to open her eyes again, the blades of grass she had been standing on were like slender fledgling trees that had grown a head taller than her. She looked around in amazement. Instead of the moonlit rocky glade with bare trees and patches of grass, the land surrounding her had transformed into something else. She was standing in what appeared to be a dark but lush woodland. Nonetheless, there was something decidedly odd about it. Long grasses had become like trees; sticks and twigs had grown to become as big as logs and branches. She saw three-leaf clovers the size of bushes and spotty mushrooms the size of rocks.

"I did it," Morgan murmured in wonder. She gasped and then laughed with the thrill. "Arcile! I did it!"

"I know," said Arcile's voice. Morgan turned and saw her former maid standing a little way away from her. She still glowed faintly white, but she was there in her human form, smiling, as a little girl, all red-brown curls and teeth and freckles.

"I can see you!" Morgan exclaimed.

"Yes," Arcile nodded. "You're the same size as me now."

Morgan laughed again in excitement. Arcile grinned at her affectionately. Then her smile turned to one of triumph. "At least we got rid of that boy at last."

"What?" Morgan stopped laughing at once. "Did we? Merlin? Where is he?"

"Here," said Merlin's voice. There was a rustling sound and Merlin appeared, pushing aside the tall blades of grass. He was still covered with dry mud, but his dark eyes shone brightly. He was the same size as they were.

"What!" Arcile was furious. "How did you ...?"

"I said the spell when you did," Merlin said to Morgan, ignoring Arcile the way she had previously ignored him.

"And it worked," Morgan said, pleased. "Did you think of the Moon, too?"

"No," Merlin said after a moment's pause. "I thought of other things. Small things."

"Like what?"

"Like that." Merlin pointed to something large that was moving through the large blades of grass. Morgan stepped forward to take a closer look. Then she jumped back in horror and screamed. The hideous thing moving alongside them was long and slimy, like a grass snake she had seen once, but this was much bigger. It was a reddish colour and had no eyes or legs but grooves all down its body. It looked monstrous.

Merlin laughed. It was the first time Morgan had ever heard him laugh, but she knew it wasn't meant kindly. "Don't you know what that is? It's an earthworm!"

"It's horrible!" Morgan fired back in disgust. "Is that what you thought about to grow small? Earthworms?"

"And other things," Merlin said, his smile fading. "Ants. Spiders. Like I said, small things."

"Horrible!" Morgan said angrily again. The earthworm was now making a revolting gurgling sound and started to burrow slowly into the earth. Morgan stared at the ugly thing with distaste, then looked away. "We need to go. We have to get to the Piskies."

"We're here!" cackled a voice behind them.

Turning round fast, they beheld two extraordinary creatures, the same size as themselves. One was similar to a very thin and pale little boy, except he had sharply pointed ears, nose, eyes and bare feet that each ended in a single pointed toe. He was wearing nothing. The other looked like an older girl, also unclothed, with grey-hued skin, wild hair that was the texture and colour of green moss, sharp-pointed ears similar to the boy's and huge black eyes with no whites. They stood not three yards away, regarding the children intensely.

Morgan didn't like the looks of them at all. They looked wicked and unfriendly and very ugly. However, she was determined to be brave and gazed upon the creatures with a serious expression.

"Are you Piskies?" she inquired.

"Yes, we are," the thin boy Piskie answered. His voice sounded vaguely familiar. "Don't you know us, Princess Light-Eyes?"

With a grin the boy held up a red lantern, glowing red just like the light on the moor. Next to him, the girl brought forth a shining blue torch that reflected on her skin, turning her flesh blue.

"Jack and Joan!"

"That's us," the girl Piskie said. She had a permanent frown on her face that made her look very disagreeable. "You'll get there faster if you let us take you."

Before they knew it, the blue Piskie had darted forward and grabbed Morgan by the shoulder. There was a whirr and a hum, and Morgan found herself lifted up into the air just above the tips of the grass. Jack, the red Piskie, had picked Merlin up by the shoulder and with the red lantern in his other hand was flying across the grass carrying the boy. The two Piskies didn't rise up gently to fly like birds or butterflies, since they had no wings. Instead, they took bounding leaps like hares or squirrels, and propelled themselves forward while staying in the air.

The look of shock on Merlin's face soon turned to fascination. Held aloft, Morgan twisted around looking for Arcile. "Here, Morgan," Arcile called. The former Wisp was flying alongside them, no longer just a white light but as a little faerie girl this time, also without wings but much more graceful. Joan the Piskie scowled at her, but Arcile was undaunted and stared haughtily back.

The five of them flew towards the patch of land upon which dozens of Piskies were dancing and singing in a ring. As they flew closer, skimming the tops of the grasses, they were out in the moonlight once more. Now so much smaller and closer to the ground, Morgan was mesmerised by the constant movement. The whole of the still, silent earth was teeming with life. What she thought was a bristle-backed hedgehog lying under some leaves unfolded itself to reveal talon-nailed human arms and legs and Piskie pointed ears. A creature looking up at them from a mushroom had a Piskie head, grinning teeth, insect wings, and squatted on brown-spotted frog's legs.

As they approached the Piskie ring, a dark green-and-brown-skinned Piskie crouched at the edge of the earthen circle wearing a flat acorn hat and a tuft of moor grass sprouting out of his back. Morgan heard the ring of Piskies singing in a weird but unusually pretty melody that captivated her and made her want to join them.

We are the Piskies up on the tor
Spirits of the night and rulers of the moor
By the light of the Moon we dance and play
In the shadows of the Night we'll lead you astray

As we dance round about, little urchins all
The frost will bite and the dew will fall
Our false fires lead you far from your path
You'll join our revels or you'll feel our wrath

We work all day and we ride all night
We'll steal your children if you don't do right
We'll take them below into the hollow hill
Turn them into Piskies and bend them to our will

Morgan closed her eyes, feeling the shimmer of the moonlight and the music melded together in a soothing harmony. Everything seemed very far away. Even Arcile's anxious "Morgan? Morgan!" reached her as if from a great distance. She hung suspended serenely in the air, her memory fading, her eyelids heavy.

Then suddenly she came back to earth with a thud. Joan had dropped her unceremoniously into the middle of the Piskie ring. The girl Piskie's shriek of laughter and the rude surprise of the fall brought her sharply out of her reverie. Merlin landed next to her, having been dropped just as roughly by Jack. As Morgan glared up at the boy Piskie, he grinned at her and called out, "Behold, everyone! We have guests!"

Morgan and Merlin looked at each other. Merlin got to his feet first. He held out his hand to Morgan, something he had never done before. Morgan took it and stood up. The children looked around. They found themselves surrounded by a crowd of such strange beings that they stared, speechless with shock, into the sea of faces that confronted them.

The myriad of creatures around them was truly extraordinary. Wizened, hunched, twisted, blemished, bestial; some squint-eyed, some sharp-toothed, some with animal features, some with plants growing out of their bodies instead of limbs – they all looked ill-willed and vicious and terrifyingly ugly. Morgan had never seen or imagined anything like them in the worst of her dreams.

The expressions on the Piskies' faces at the two children falling unannounced into their midst changed quickly from surprise to curiosity to malevolence. Leering, menacing, chuckling, the crowd of Piskies edged nearer and nearer to the children, encircling them until they were trapped. Morgan and Merlin instinctively moved closer to each other and clasped hands.

XI

The Small People

As she stared at the sea of grinning and grimacing faces of the Piskies around her, all Morgan could think of were the demons Elfodd had told her about. These creatures must be what he meant. There was nothing pretty or nice or holy about these scrawny, withered, monstrous-looking things. Her fear was mixed with fury at both Diana and Arcile. Why hadn't they told her what the Small People were really like? And *why* had Arcile made her and Merlin grow small so they were now the same size as them? At least if they had been their normal size they might not be in so much danger.

"That's not true," she heard Arcile murmur next to her.

"What?"

"They're dangerous, no matter how big or small you are. If you were normal size, they'd see you as more dangerous and be even meaner."

"Great," Merlin said.

A naked green figure with a flat pinched face, grass-like hair and wearing a hat that looked like a dead flower came leaping over the crowd to land in front of them. He squinted at them with beady black eyes and in a harsh voice demanded:

"Who are you? What are you doing here?"

Morgan hastily gathered her courage and thoughts to focus on the idea she had been forming. "We're from the Big People. We have a message for all of you."

"They're lying." A tiny figure spoke shrilly. It was the size of a toddler child in Piskie terms, even smaller than the others, but with the wrinkled face of an old man and corn-yellow hair growing from its head and chin. "They're Muryans. They've come to spy on us."

"I don't think so." Jack landed next to him. "They *were* big. Then they made themselves small."

"There you are then!" the yellow-haired Piskie shrieked. "They're Muryans! Shape-shifting to look like Big People, then changing back!"

"No!" Morgan exclaimed amongst the excited chatter of the crowd. "We *are* Big People! Jack's right. We just made ourselves small."

"How?" the green figure demanded.

Morgan hesitated and looked at Merlin and Arcile. "Um ... with the power of the Moon, I think."

"With magic," Merlin declared defiantly.

"Rubbish! Big People can't do magic," the green figure scoffed. But the little yellow-haired Piskie was looking at them curiously.

"Where are you from then?"

"Tintagel Castle," Morgan said. "It's in the land of Belerion."

"Well, I've never heard of Belerion, so it might be true," the green figure conceded, addressing itself to Jack.

"You're *in* Belerion!" Morgan said indignantly. "This is part of it, anyway. My father is the Duke. He rules this land. That means he rules you too."

There was a roar of laughter at this. All the Piskies who stood or crouched around them laughed. Only the little yellow-haired Piskie did not join in. He watched the children with narrow eyes.

"So you *are* a bit like a princess, after all, Princess Light-Eyes," Joan said mockingly.

"I'd like to hear what Twadell says when she tells him her father rules us," Jack chuckled.

"Ha, ha! Tee, hee! Yes!" the creatures answered in various piping tones.

"Who's Twadell?" Morgan asked.

"He'll tell you that," the green figure replied. "You've broken the laws of our realm by coming here uninvited. Whatever you are, Twadell will decide how you're to be punished. Take them!"

This last was addressed to the creatures round about. Morgan felt a flurry of bony hands and claw-like nails grab her arms and pull her along. Alongside her, Merlin and Arcile were dragged in the same way by the crowd of spindle-shanked creatures towards an opening in the ground a little way away from the Piskie ring.

The hollow was framed by two stones on either side joined by a longer stone on top, forming a doorway. The stones were as large as boulders to the Piskies, but could easily have been dismissed as just a pile of pebbles by any normal-sized mortal passing by.

"Morgan!" A strange light was shining in Merlin's face as he caught her eye while being jostled along. It was a light she had seen before, not so long ago. With a flash of memory, Morgan went back to the image of him tormenting the blue-light Piskie Joan through the force of his mind, and she knew instantly what he was suggesting they try to do together. She shook her head at him. As horrible as the Piskies appeared, she didn't want to try to escape yet. An overwhelming curiosity had taken hold of her, as well as a determination to carry out Diana's task. She wanted to see this Twadell, who was supposed to be so powerful. Pulled along next to her, Arcile nodded at her in encouragement.

The Piskies took them through the doorway, which opened onto a cavernous passage leading down into the earth. The passage was eerily illuminated, but Morgan could see no torches or candles anywhere. The walls were built of packed brown earth and spiked grey stones woven tightly together with winding roots and tendrils coiled over their heads. At first she and the others were squashed together tightly as they were pushed and shoved along by the dozens of Piskies. Gradually the corridor grew wider as they went deeper into the hill, until finally they reached a vast chamber. It was so huge it seemed almost to be the size of the hill outside. It was as light as day inside the chamber, but Morgan could still not see where the light was coming from. There were no windows or openings of any kind leading to the outside, and even if there had been, it was still night-time.

The chamber ceiling overhead was covered with stalactites hanging down. Morgan had seen such things in the caves around the Tintagel coast, but because she was now so small these stalactites looked like enormous sharp-pointed swords suspended ominously above their heads. Underground rivers of running water ran through the vaulted cavern; around them were grouped what seemed to be numerous dwellings like burrows or hollows carved into the rock. They were all different: some were chalice-shaped, some bell-shaped, some circular, some oval, all with small holes and crevices that served as doors and windows. To Morgan's astonishment, they all looked lovely, bedecked very prettily with flowers and blossoms and berries in an array of colours. She even spotted small household things like vessels made out of acorn heads and chairs built with twigs.

In the middle of the chamber a group of rocky stalagmites rose up from the ground together like a many-turreted castle. Morgan, Merlin and Arcile were taken towards it and led through a corridor into a main hall similar to the one at Tintagel, except that it was ornamented with spirals of leaves and flowers rather than tapestries.

"Wait here," commanded the green Piskie. The crowd around them pushed them onto a stone bench, where they sat and waited for Twadell to appear.

"Are you alright, Morgan?" Merlin asked her in a low voice, as the Piskies settled down around them, chattering and laughing in eager anticipation.

Morgan was taken aback at his concern. "Yes," she said under her breath. "I want to meet Twadell. If what Cadwellon said is true, and the faeries have courts and realms just like we do, he must be their King."

"What are you going to say to him?" inquired Merlin.

"Morgan has a plan – don't you, Morgan?" Arcile said proudly.

But Morgan was still angry with Arcile.

"You and Diana should have *told* me what the Small People were really like," she said indignantly. "You never said they were like this!"

"Like what?"

"Well … like this! That they were so …"

"What?" Arcile demanded, also indignant now. "Ugly? Scary? Mean? And what if we had told you? Wouldn't you have come? Would you have refused to do what Diana asked?"

Before Morgan had time to reply, the green Piskie reappeared, followed by another Piskie unlike any of the others they had seen so far. He too was lean and spindly, but he looked older than the rest, with big green pointed ears, a dull-grey wrinkled face and a white wispy beard. He was clad with green leaves around his waist and wore the tall bell of a dead foxglove flower on his head. The slits of his squinty eyes were a bright blue and the expression on his face was suspicious and cunning. He made his way to a throne carved out of rock and seated himself upon it, beckoning the children forward with a crooked finger. Morgan, Merlin and Arcile rose to greet him and stood before him in the centre of the Piskie court.

"So these are the intruders, eh," he said in a husky voice.

"Are you Twadell?" Morgan asked.

"I am *King* Twadell," the old Piskie corrected her. "I rule this realm. My word is law here."

Morgan stepped forward and bowed, just as she had seen the ambassadors from far-off lands do when presented to her father in the main hall at Tintagel.

"Greetings, King Twadell," she said formally. "I am from Tintagel Castle in Belerion and I am here to …"

"Wait!" commanded the green Piskie, who was standing next to Twadell. "The girl says they're from the Big People, but we're not so sure. Jack! Joan!"

Jack and Joan emerged from the throng and stood before Twadell.

"Jack here says he saw them big, but then they made themselves small," the green Piskie continued. "It sounds to us like Muryan magic."

"Muryans, eh?" Twadell mused. He looked at Morgan, Merlin and Arcile with interest. "Pretty children. They're certainly pretty enough to be Muryans."

"We're not Muryans!" Morgan protested. "We don't even know what they are!"

"Oh, you don't, eh?" said Twadell. He chuckled.

"Careful with that one, Sire," Jack interjected, jerking his head towards Morgan. "That's Princess Light-Eyes. That's a clever one. She chased the shadows away. Got the Moon to come out again."

"Did she now?" Twadell leaned forward.

"And *that* one," said Joan, pointing angrily at Merlin. "*That* one tried to kill me!"

"Tried to kill you, eh?" Twadell's squinty blue eyes bored into Merlin. "Yes. Yes. I see. This one's a heart of stone."

Merlin pursed his lips, but otherwise did not react. "They tried to kill me first," he said evenly. "They tricked me into the marshes. I nearly died."

Manic laughter broke out around him. "Into the marshes! Ha, ha! Nearly died! Tee, hee! Piskie-led! Ho, ho!"

Twadell held up his skinny hand and the laughter died down.

"So they have magic, eh?" he said to the green Piskie.

"It would seem so, Sire."

"So they must be Muryans. Have you ever known Big People with our kind of magic, eh?"

"What does it matter?" The small yellow-haired Piskie pushed his way to the front to face the King. His face was mottled with anger. "What does it matter what they are? Big People? Muryans? Who cares? They entered the Piskie ring at the full Moon. You know that can only mean one thing."

The Piskies around them began to hiss and chant. "Death. *Death*. DEATH."

"Death." Twadell's slit eyes had turned cold and nasty. The crowd of frightful faces stopped grinning and became grisly as they leered at the children, moving closer to them as if to trap them once more.

Morgan's heart pounded. "Stop!" she cried. She stared in shock at the small yellow-haired Piskie, whose creepy little eyes were sparkling at the thought of them being killed. Then she took a deep breath and stepped closer to Twadell's throne.

"You didn't let me finish," she said, trying to keep her voice from trembling. "I told you I'm from Tintagel Castle in Belerion. I'm an ambassador from the Big People to you, the Sma – the Piskies. I'm here to – to offer you the chance to be friends with us."

"To be *what*? *Friends* with you?" Twadell sounded disbelieving.

"Yes." Morgan quickly remembered what Arcile had told her about the Small Ones. "You frighten people and throw things around their houses and steal their … things. But why? Why should you make us hate you? You could be friends with us instead."

There was complete silence for a moment. Morgan wondered

wildly if Twadell had heard her properly.

"And why would we want to do that, eh?" the King said eventually. His expression had changed to one of astonishment and curiosity.

"Because we can help you," Morgan said, her mind going back to the ambassadors, trying to remember how they had offered things to Gorlois and how he had given them something in exchange. "Friends help each other. We're Big People, so there are things we can do that you can't. You're Sma – Piskies; you can do things we can't. We can give you something and you can give us something."

"Also, we have magic," Merlin said. He had quickly grasped what she was trying to do and joined in. "Jack and Joan saw what we can do. Anything you need, we can help you."

"Any problems you have," Morgan continued, glancing gratefully at Merlin, "we can help you with."

Twadell sat back and contemplated them. The green Piskie whispered into his ear. The other Piskies also looked startled, but remained silent, waiting. Morgan saw Jack watching her; when he caught her eye, he nodded knowingly. She glanced at Arcile standing next to her. Her former maid had stayed quiet the entire time, leaving everything to Morgan and Merlin. She looked pale but firm. Morgan wondered what she was thinking.

"So," Twadell said finally. "You say you can help us with any problems we have, eh? Well, Princess Light-Eyes, we have a very big problem. The Muryans."

"Who are they?" Morgan asked.

"The Muryans are our enemies. They are what you'd call Small People, like us, eh, but they're very different. They attack us and raid us and plunder our realm and crush our people. They have vowed to destroy us but I intend to destroy them first. I will crush every last one of them until there are no more of them on this earth."

Twadell's eyes gleamed cruelly and his face looked fierce and wicked as the entire Piskie court shouted out their support. Morgan and Merlin looked at each other anxiously.

"I am very sorry," Morgan said with as much sympathy as she could when the yelling had ceased. "Why do they want to destroy you?"

"Their Queen is evil. She steals children and keeps them to be her slaves. We've tried to stop her, but she sends her soldiers and they take our children away from us." Twadell then looked beyond Morgan and Merlin instead of directly at them. "She and her Muryans also steal away human children. Children of the Big People. Children like you, eh. Sometimes the children are alive. Sometimes when they die unprotected she steals their souls so they cannot escape her."

Morgan was astounded. Had they come upon the wrong faerie realm? She hadn't bargained on there being more than one type of Small People. Were the Muryans the ones who had stolen the soul of the child Diana wanted, and not the Piskies after all? She looked meaningfully at Arcile, who mouthed, "Don't trust him" at her.

"So … you don't steal human children?" Morgan asked.

There was a hostile muttering among the Piskies.

"Our children are stolen from *us*," Twadell said angrily and his eyes flashed again. "Our two most precious children were taken from us by the Muryans just recently. A boy and a girl. Much like the two of you, eh, only younger. And that's how you can help us."

"How?"

"We can't go into the Muryans' realm. We can change our shape to look like beasts or plants, but we can't make ourselves look like Muryans. They've protected themselves against it with magic. But you look like them, eh. You'll easily pass for Muryans. You can go into their realm in secret and get back our children for us."

"Wait a minute," Merlin interrupted. "How will we get there?"

Twadell snapped his fingers. Jack and Joan both bounded forward to stand either side of Morgan and Merlin.

"Jack and Joan will take you and Princess Light-Eyes to the borders of the Muryans' realm, Prince Stone-Heart," Twadell asserted. "If you're discovered there, you pretend to be Muryans yourselves, eh. Fool them long enough to get our children back. You'll know them when you see them. They're twins, golden-haired, and they look like human babies. They're called Mabon and Maglore."

Morgan was immediately suspicious. If the children looked

like human babies, how could they be Piskie children? But she didn't say anything, just glanced again at Arcile and was startled. Arcile had a smile on her face and her eyes were shining. Suddenly Morgan knew. The golden-haired boy child must be the soul Diana wanted her to find.

"Alright," she said. "We'll do it."

"No!" The little yellow-haired Piskie suddenly leapt in front of Twadell. "Sire! These creatures have broken our laws! Invaded our kingdom! Defiled the sanctity of the circle! They *must* die!"

Twadell dismissed him with a wave of his hand. "If they return Mabon and Maglore to us, the debt will be paid. Oh, and one more thing, eh?" he said, addressing himself again to Morgan. "Just to make sure you keep your word, Princess Light-Eyes – we'll take *that* as our prisoner."

There was a terrified scream. Before they knew what was happening, Arcile had been seized from behind by a group of Piskies. They twisted her arms behind her back so tightly she cried out in pain. The green Piskie sidled up in front of her.

"No! Wait!" Morgan protested.

"Did you think we didn't know she wasn't like you and Prince Stone-Heart here, eh?" Twadell said. "She's not a Muryan and she's not one of the Big People, as you claim to be. What is she?"

"She's a W – " Morgan began, but Arcile frantically shook her head at her. "Woman," she finished hastily. "I mean, a girl. She's a girl. Just like me."

"Rubbish!" the green Piskie scoffed.

"Liar!" the yellow-haired Piskie shrieked at her.

The other Piskies started screeching too, but were silenced again by Twadell. "Whatever she is, she stays here until you return with our children," the King said. "If you don't ..." His eyes went cold once more and he nodded to the green Piskie. The creature moved close to Arcile, lifted a stick-like finger and ran a thorny nail across Arcile's throat, leaving a thin red line of blood. The Wisp whimpered. Tears fell down her cheeks. Morgan was shocked and horrified. How could Arcile, a spirit, be harmed?

"Oh, we have ways of killing anything, whatever she might be," Twadell asserted, as if reading Morgan's thoughts. "And in the meantime, there are plenty of ways to hurt her if you don't help us, eh."

"No!" Morgan cried as Arcile sobbed. Merlin put his hand on Morgan's arm and she looked at him, tears stinging her eyes.

"Let's go," he said quietly.

Morgan glared furiously at Twadell. "Don't hurt her! We'll come back with your children! Just don't hurt her!"

Twadell grinned and rose up from his throne to give Morgan a mock bow. "Until you return, she'll be our guest, eh. We'll be waiting, Princess Light-Eyes." Then, with an unpleasant laugh, he ordered, "Take her away!"

"Morgan!" Arcile screamed as the gang of crowing Piskies dragged her out of the room. Morgan stood in the middle of the hall in terror and despair. What could she do? Surely Diana could not have seen that anything like this would happen.

Twadell left his throne and departed from the hall without a backward glance. The remaining Piskies got up chattering excitedly and began leaving the hall too. Only Jack and Joan and the little yellow-haired Piskie stayed behind, the latter scowling at them. There was nothing else to do. Morgan fought back the tears, refusing to cry, and turned to Merlin.

"You're right. We have to go."

Merlin nodded. "Take us to the Muryans," he said brusquely to Jack.

Without a word, Jack conjured his red lantern back into his hand and led the way out of the hall. Similarly, Joan's blue torch magically appeared and, with a glower at the children, she followed. Morgan and Merlin made their way out of the hall together. When Morgan looked back, she saw the yellow-haired Piskie still staring after them with unmistakable hatred and malice.

* * *

Hurrying back along the passageway following the blue torch and red lantern, Morgan found herself trembling. Just ahead of her, Merlin hastened after the two Piskies without saying a word. Morgan desperately wanted to speak to him about everything that was happening and most of all Arcile, but she didn't want Jack and Joan to hear. For an instant she wished it were Ganieda who was with her instead; at least she could talk to her through her mind without anyone else listening.

Then she had a brainwave. If both she and Merlin could talk to Ganieda in their thoughts, why couldn't they talk to each other in the same way? *Merlin, Merlin, Merlin,* she tried repeating in her mind over and over again, concentrating with all her might on the boy and willing him to hear her. But there was no response. All she heard were the echoes of her own thoughts inside her head.

They emerged outside into the night through the doorway of stones. The blazes of the Piskies' red and blue flames were stark against the moonlight's soft shimmery white. Standing once again on the flat earthen Piskie ring, to her diminutive eyes bigger than the courtyard at Tintagel, Morgan could just see the forest of tall grassland beyond, swaying in the night breeze.

"So, where do we go?" Merlin asked.

"It'll be faster if we take you," Jack replied. "Getting to the Muryans is a difficult business. And we can't let them see us."

Joan said nothing, but stepped forward to Morgan and took hold of her shoulder. Once again, Morgan was borne aloft as the Piskie leapt with her into the air, brandishing the blue torch, and flew with her over the hill down towards the moor. The world looked so gigantic from the tiny size she was now that Morgan wondered how they had ever managed to walk up the huge hill to the Piskie kingdom. The scrubby slope they had climbed soon gave way to the immense outstretch of moor below, scattered with its lakes of bog water, marsh mud and slabs of rock.

The Moon was still beaming round and bright in the sky. Morgan looked across at Merlin, who was being carried through the air by Jack with his red lantern, and she thought of how she had made herself small through the power of the Moon. Maybe that magic could help her this time too. *Merlin,* she thought again, half-closing her eyes and willing herself to soak up the moonlight. She concentrated on going into Merlin's mind as she had Ganieda's. *Can you hear me? Merlin!*

The Piskies swooped down towards a grassy green hill rising

sharply from the marshes round about. It was very different from the rest of the moor and the stunted trees and herbage of the Piskie realm. As they approached, Morgan and Merlin saw that this hill was lush and fertile, covered with rich foliage. They landed in the midst of a woodland of massive trees that towered into the sky above the shrunk-sized children; of ferns that were to them as big as oaks; berry bushes the size of hornbeams; and flowers drooping like willows, whose scented petals were furled to the night air.

Morgan steadied herself on the ground and looked about her. She couldn't see any path through the densely thicketed forest of grass and leafy plants. But Jack held up his lantern in front of her, shining its light directly on her face.

"Follow us, Princess Light-Eyes," he said. "We've been here before."

Joan had already started to make her way through the grass, pushing aside the tall blades, her torch bobbing ahead of them. Jack went after her and Morgan followed, with Merlin bringing up the rear. They had to pick their way carefully through the grass blades that reached higher than their heads. Down so low on the ground, the moonlight barely penetrated and it was dim and gloomy. Morgan couldn't see what was ahead of them or from side to side. There was nothing to see but enormous grass stalks, an occasional three-leaf clover as large as a shrub, or the lower stems of plants as tall as birch trees. Even though the nimble-footed Piskies seemed to prance ahead of them with confidence, Morgan began to be afraid that they would get lost.

Suddenly there was an exclamation, then a shriek from Joan.

"What is it?" Morgan cried, rushing forward. Merlin followed her and they struggled forward through the grass. Then there was a yell from Jack.

"No! No! Go back!"

It was too late. Before they knew it, the children had run straight into something Morgan at first thought were ropes. But these were unlike any ropes she had ever seen. They were soft and sticky, and shone with droplets of water that glittered like jewels. The ropes were threaded in an intricate pattern and had been woven around the blades of grass. Try as she might, Morgan couldn't free herself. The more she fought, the tighter the silken ropes bound her, attaching themselves to her arms and legs. She saw that Merlin and the two Piskies had been ensnared too.

Merlin's expression was scared and angry again as he tried to free himself in a panic, attempting to pull the ropes apart with his hands.

"What are we going to do?" he hissed at Morgan.

Morgan looked over at the Piskies, also bound by the ropes and trying frantically to escape. "Maybe we could use magic again," she said urgently.

"How?"

"I don't know."

Before Morgan could rack her brains to think of a solution, she heard a rustling in the grass. Straining to turn and see what it was, she heard a strident voice.

"What have we here, then?"

Into her line of vision came crawling the most terrifying creature Morgan had ever seen. It was the size of a dog and had a long, huge head, with eight horrible black eyes set close together in a circle and two sharp fangs. From its bulky and hairy brown body, eight long yellowish legs protruded outwards. Trapped in the silken ropes, Morgan's mouth went dry. She felt her heart had stopped beating and she couldn't utter a sound or move from fright. The disgusting hideousness of the creature made her feel so ill she thought she would be sick. *NO! PLEASE!* she screamed in her head, reaching out with her mind and praying to anything – God, Diana, the angels, the faeries, anything – that could hear her or save her from this monster. Anything that could get her out of this.

Morgan! She heard the voice in her mind, echoing her own terror. An invisible door had suddenly swung open and she could hear Merlin's voice. Like her, he hadn't spoken a word, but she knew that somehow together they had unlocked the invisible door and could hear each other in their minds. The knowledge calmed her, helping her swallow her nausea and gather her thoughts again. She realised now what the creature was, but of course she had never seen them this big or this close.

Spider, she thought to Merlin.

He did not answer, but she could feel his agreement and his own attempts to stifle his fear.

"They look like Piskies," another voice said. A different spider, equally hideous and revolting, was crawling around the captured Jack and Joan.

"Aha! Enemy intruders!" said the first spider. "The Queen shall know of this!"

"You'd better let us go!" Jack shrieked in his high-pitched voice. "Our King will kill you all if you harm us!"

"Your King has no power here," the first spider said lazily. "You Piskies aren't long for this world if the Queen has her way. And you're our prisoners now."

Morgan found her voice and steadied it. "Do you know the Muryan Queen?" she asked the first spider.

The spider's black eyes turned back and appraised her at length. "I serve the Queen of the Muryans," it said at last. "All of us do; my sons and daughters, and my brothers and sisters."

Morgan thought fast. "We're here to find her. We're Muryans, too."

"If that's true, then what are you doing with Piskies?"

"We captured them," Merlin asserted before Morgan could answer. His voice shook and he took a deep breath to steady it. "We were bringing them to her when we got caught here in your webs."

Morgan heard more rustling and over a dozen spiders emerged from the surrounding grass. She tried again to will away the sick feeling that welled up in her at the sight of them.

The first spider looked suspicious. "I don't believe you. Muryans, you say? Well, I say you're Piskies and we should take you to the Queen!"

"No," said another spider. "Why bother her? We could keep them here and feed on them. The Queen would reward us for getting rid of them. She wouldn't have to deal with them then."

Jack and Joan both screamed in terror. The two Piskies squirmed frantically and vainly to free themselves as the spiders laughed.

Morgan! She heard Merlin's voice in her head again. *We have to make them believe that we're Muryans. They're going to kill us!*

No, they won't. Morgan decided to try something else – something she had seen Igraine do sometimes. "How dare you say that!" she exclaimed in an angry voice. "We've come to see the Queen of the Muryans! We *are* Muryans! We're ambassadors from a Muryan land far away from here and we've come to be friends with her. The Queen will kill you if you hurt us!"

The spiders all stopped. They seemed surprised.

"How do we know you're not Piskies?" the first spider asked after a pause.

"Yes!" the other spiders cried. "How do we know? Prove it!"

"Because Piskies can't make themselves look like Muryans," Morgan said, remembering Twadell's words. "Muryans have protected themselves against it with magic."

"And if Piskies could make themselves look like Muryans, then those two would have as well," Merlin added, indicating Jack and Joan.

The first spider lifted up one of its front legs and scratched its head. "Hmm," it said to the others. "Let's see if they're really Muryans, shall we."

Four of the spiders crawled towards the children, opening the pincers in their heads as if to grab them and bite down on them. They came closer and closer, their curved jaws clacking in greedy anticipation. The gleam in their ugly black eyes was the last thing Morgan saw before she closed her own.

She felt them right up close. The hair on their disgusting bodies. The touch of their legs on her skin. The sick rose up in her throat again. Her terror froze her.

Dimly she heard a snapping sound.

The silken ropes fell away from her arms and legs. When she dared to open her eyes again, she and Merlin were standing free.

An overwhelming sense of relief washed over her, a relief she could feel in her mind that she and Merlin shared. The children's eyes met and an undercurrent of understanding flowed between them. The fear wasn't gone, but it was easier to bear now they could feel it together.

"What about them?" one of the spiders said, pointing a claw-like leg towards Jack and Joan. "Can't we at least keep them to eat?"

"No!" Morgan exclaimed. "They're our prisoners, not yours. They have to come with us."

"Release them," the first spider said to the other. "But keep hold of them."

As the spiders went snapping their fangs towards the screeching Piskies, Morgan heard what sounded like another faint noise in her ears – a different, distant sound. Merlin was examining the shimmering sticky ropes.

"What sort of cobwebs are these?" he inquired of the first spider.

"They're gossamer webs," the first spider said. "We always spin them before dawn. It's part of our duty to the Queen – she expects it of us." Then it looked suspiciously again at Merlin. "If you're a Muryan, you should *know* that."

"Our Muryan land is different," Morgan assured it hastily. The noise in her ears was getting louder. It sounded like a horn or some kind of trumpet. "What's that noise? Can anyone else hear it?"

The other spiders had released Jack and Joan from the webs and were holding them tightly in their grip. They stopped and listened.

"I can hear it," Merlin said.

"You're in luck," the first spider remarked. Its horrible face was twisted in the shape of a grimace; it took Morgan a moment to realise that it was smiling. "The Queen and her Court are coming this way. They're out for the Rade of the full Moon."

"A raid?" Merlin said. He sounded curious, not alarmed. "Like the tribesmen of Éireann? Are they going to attack someone?"

"Not that kind of raid," the first spider said. "Come and see for yourselves."

It crawled off into the grass. Morgan and Merlin looked at each other, hesitant for a moment.

Should we follow it? Morgan asked.

It'll take us to the Muryan Queen, Merlin replied. *Isn't that what you want?*

I suppose so. Besides – she looked back at Jack and Joan, held captive by the other spiders – *we can't leave them.*

She made her way in the wake of the first spider, following

the trail it left but careful to keep her distance. The sound of the trumpet was getting louder, its call silvery and captivating. As they got closer, they heard bells jingling. A strange, eerie whistling accompanied voices singing a beautiful song. When the spider stopped and indicated for them to go forward, Morgan and Merlin parted the high stems of two tall, closed-petal poppies in front of them and beheld a splendid sight.

A procession of amazingly beautiful people were riding by on horseback, all of them dressed in spectacular colourful cloaks and gowns tinged with gold. They looked far richer than anyone Morgan had ever seen at Tintagel. Many of them wore jewels and gemstones that glistened like stars. The light that followed them was much brighter than the moonlight. Their hair was mostly golden – long and flowing for the women, short and curled for the men – with a few raven-black and fire-red headed people among the company. They were singing in unison, a wistful song that reminded Morgan of songs she had heard in Elfodd's chapel.

Amidst the rainbow array of coloured garments, all of them wore one item of a particular shade of green – the green of the banner the rider at the front of the procession was holding up high. They rode upon white horses that were far more noble and elegant than any in Gorlois' stables, though not as stunning or unearthly as the ones of Diana's Wild Hunt. These were like mortal horses, the only difference being that their tails were longer, their necks more highly arched and their manes decorated with small wooden pipes that whistled as the breeze caught them. Their bridles and trappings were richly embellished, many hung with silver bells that jangled out a curious melody. Slender hound dogs trotted proudly alongside them.

So dazzled was Morgan by the beauty of these Small People that at first she didn't notice the creatures accompanying them. It was Merlin who lightly touched her arm and with a nod of his head silently pointed them out to her. The creatures that walked instead of rode were not beautiful like the riders. They weren't like the skinny Piskies, either – many of them were heavier and hairier, with wide, ugly faces.

In the middle of the procession rode a young girl who was taller than all the rest. Her hair was golden and her gown was cloth-of-gold; both she and her gleaming white horse held their heads proudly.

Although the girl – who looked about sixteen or seventeen – was very pretty, she had a haughty expression that Morgan didn't like. She was surrounded by attendants, all on horseback and all dressed in green. Four of them held a luxuriant canopy over her head as they rode along.

That must be the Queen, Morgan thought to Merlin. He didn't reply but she could sense him agreeing with her. Sure enough, the first spider crawled forwards, urging the children to follow it by snapping its pincers at them. The other spiders followed, clutching the hapless Piskies who protested, squealing, "No! She's evil!"

The golden-haired girl caught sight of the odd party of spiders, Piskies and children making their way towards her. She pulled on her horse's bridle and held up her hand. Instantly one of her attendants blew on a horn and the singing and processing ceased. The bells died down as the riders stopped and drew their horses round to face the Queen. She in turn faced the first spider.

"What is the meaning of this, Kevnys?"

"Forgive me, Your Highness," Kevnys the spider said. "We found these intruders trapped in our gossamer webs. These two claim to be Muryans. They say they captured these Piskies and were bringing them to you."

Hostile chatter broke out amongst the other Muryans in the procession. Jack and Joan stared back at them all with hatred, still squirming in the grip of their captors. The golden-haired girl held up her hand again and there was silence. She looked coolly and suspiciously at Morgan and Merlin.

"You say you are Muryans? You look very young. I haven't seen any such young-looking Muryans for a very long time."

Morgan stepped forward and bowed. "Greetings, Your Highness," she said formally, in the manner of the ambassadors to Tintagel. "We are from a Muryan land far away from here. Things are different there. We've come to ask you to be friends with us."

The golden-haired girl laughed. It was not a nice laugh. "Why would I want to be friends with you?"

"Because you're fighting the Piskies," Merlin said. "If you're going to win, you need friends."

The Queen looked at him. Interest flickered in her eyes.

"I am Queen Caelia," she said to him. "What's your name?"

Don't tell her our real names, Morgan thought.

I shan't, she heard him reply, and then he said aloud, "I'm Prince Stone-Heart. This is Princess Light-Eyes."

"You're a Prince and Princess?" Queen Caelia demanded. She sounded outraged. "Are you after my throne? Is that why you're here? Come to trick me?"

"No!" Morgan protested. "We don't want your throne! I told you – we're here to be friends."

"Prove it," Caelia said. There was a murmur of excitement among the Muryans. "If you're what you say you are, prove it."

"How?" Morgan asked.

"Do you have wings?" Caelia asked. Her cloak behind her suddenly lifted and with a sudden crack and a buzz she unfurled a pair of delicate, diaphanous wings on her back like those of a dragonfly. She rose up from her horse, her wings whirring, and flew down from overhead to alight on the ground. Simultaneously, many other Muryans unfolded their wings and did the same, some flying the length of the procession and back again. However, Morgan noticed that others did not. Some of the Muryans simply dismounted from their horses like mortals.

"But all Muryans don't have wings, do they?" she said to Caelia and pointed to the Muryans who dismounted. "We're like them. We don't."

Caelia's eyes narrowed.

"Indeed," she said scornfully. "So you claim to be old, not young. Very well, then. All Muryans can do magic. Show me your magic."

"Alright," Morgan said as calmly as she could, although her mind was racing. What could they do? An unsought image flashed into her head: Joan the Piskie as a tiny blue light. Terrified screams coming from the blue light as the girl Piskie was being burned inside. She knew where the image had come from and who had shown it to her.

No, she thought.

If we do that to one of them, they'll know we have magic, Merlin argued. *I'll show you how. Then they'll be afraid of us.*

And then they'll kill us! Morgan replied angrily. *We have to show them we're friends, remember?*

She thought of when she had used magic. Helping Merlin out of the mire. Chasing away the clouds blocking the Moon. Calling Arcile. The night of the storm. The daffodils.

Then she knew.

"Alright," she said again to Caelia. "Watch this." *And follow me,* she thought to Merlin. *Do what I do.*

She turned behind them to the towering closed-petal poppies from which they had emerged to greet the Queen. She closed her eyes and focused her whole being upon them, remembering how Sebile had told her some flowers closed their petals in the dark after the Sun went down. *Make the petals open,* she thought. *Make them think it's daytime. Make the petals open.*

She felt her thoughts' energy swell with the force of Merlin's mind joined to hers. They both saw an image of poppies with their petals slowly opening. Morgan concentrated with all her might.

But when she opened her eyes, the poppies' petals remained closed. She tried again. *Make the petals open,* she thought more forcefully. *Make them think it's daytime!*

Still nothing.

She heard muttering behind her and a whirring of wings. Several Muryan knights were moving towards her and Merlin with grim faces, their swords drawn. Queen Caelia hovered in the air behind them, her face dark.

Frantically, Morgan tried a third time. Something different. An image of the bright golden Sun in a clear blue sky. Hundreds of scarlet poppies in a field beneath it, dancing in the sunlight. She reached out to Merlin's mind and shared the picture with him.

The Sun is out, she thought fiercely. *The Sun is shining. It's bright and light and hot. It's lighting up everything. The Sun is shining!*

A warmth glowed on her face and the darkness behind her eyelids lightened. When she opened her eyes, a yellow light hovered over the tall, scattered poppies in the long grasses. One by one they opened their petals to welcome the light, brightening the wood with a colourful burst of red.

Morgan felt triumphant. She looked over at Merlin in delighted complicity. The boy half-smiled back at her. She then turned proudly back to Caelia, expecting exclamations of praise and welcome. But the golden-haired Queen did not smile or give praise. She looked very unfriendly.

"So you have magic," she said. "And you say you are ambassadors from a Muryan land and want to be friends with us. Very well. You will accompany us back to our city, where we will talk further." She gestured with her hand and spoke in a louder voice. "Kill the Piskies. Tear them limb from limb and leave them at the border of our realm as a warning to the others."

"No!" Morgan cried above Jack and Joan's shrieks of anguish. Caelia stared coolly at her and Morgan thought fast. "We brought them for you as prisoners, Queen Caelia," she went on hurriedly. "You should keep them as servants. That's a better way to show the Piskie King you're stronger than him."

The Queen's eyes narrowed.

"So that's how *you* would do it, is it?" Caelia addressed her guards. "Bring the Piskies along. Clap them in irons and throw them into the dungeon."

The Queen looked back at Morgan and smiled cruelly. "I'll have them executed after the feast."

XII

HIDDEN CHILDREN

The Muryan Queen nodded at her attendant, who blew his horn once again. Caelia spread her wings and flew back to her horse. All the other Muryans went back to their horses, either flying back like the Queen or remounting their steeds in mortal fashion.

The spiders carried the Piskies forward and placed them into the hands of several of the heavier, uglier creatures in attendance. Jack snarled at his captors and stared with fearful eyes at Morgan. She shook her head slightly at him, willing him not to say anything while at the same time trying to reassure him with her eyes. The Piskies were chained to the backs of two of the Muryan horses to be pulled along on foot. Morgan saw the glisten of a tear on Joan's grey cheek and, to her surprise, felt sorry for her.

Another of the creatures brought forward two beautiful white horses, indicating that they were for Morgan and Merlin. Merlin made his way towards one and was helped onto it by the creature. Before going to her horse, Morgan turned to face Kevnys the spider, who was beside her. She forced herself not to flinch with disgust or feel sick at the sight of him.

"Thank you," she said to him.

The spider looked astonished, as if he had never heard those words before. "Why should you thank me?" he asked at last. "We would have eaten you, you know."

"Yes, but you didn't," Morgan said. "You gave us a chance and brought us to the Queen. So thank you for that."

Kevnys' eight black eyes gazed at her. His face grimaced again in a smile. "You be careful at the court of Queen Caelia, Princess Light-Eyes. If that's who you really are."

The spider turned away and crawled back into the grass, followed by the others. Morgan went to her horse and mounted it with the strange creature's help. The creature looked oddly familiar and she wondered what it was. Merlin was waiting for her on his horse, watching her.

What did the spider say to you?

He said to be careful.

Without needing to be guided, the children's horses moved off to follow the procession. Morgan looked back to see if the spiders were still there, but they were nowhere to be seen. She noticed that the horses left no hoof marks behind them. Even though they had been processing through the grass, not one blade was bent or broken or even touched. The poppy petals were closed once more to the night. There were no signs of anything at all; the wood looked peaceful and undisturbed. It was as if the Muryans were never there.

As the Rade made its way along, the woodland gradually began to slope upwards. Queen Caelia's green canopy swayed from side to side ahead of them, and the Queen's golden gown and hair gleamed in the bright faerie light.

Riding alongside Merlin in the midst of the procession, Morgan observed the Muryans all around her. They really were quite lovely. With the exception of Diana and some of the maidens and young men among her entourage, the Muryans were the most beautiful people she had ever seen. But she couldn't help noticing that their beauty made the ugliness of the creatures who walked alongside them even more apparent. As she had observed before, they were very ugly indeed – heavy-footed and hairy with brutish features. She now noted that many of them walked with a stoop or a limp. Watching the creature who had helped her onto her horse, she wondered why it looked familiar to her. She had never seen anything like it before. And yet …

The enormous trees stretching high into the sky above them began to thin out. Soon there was nothing but the occasional wind-ravaged blackthorn tree and yellow-flowered gorse bush. The sky twinkled with stars and for the first time since arriving in the Muryans' realm Morgan could see the full Moon shining once again. They were riding up what appeared to be a mountain, but because of their small size, Morgan realised that it must only be a round hill, probably not that big to human eyes. She saw what looked like hundreds of sparkling, multi-coloured lights dotted about the crest of the hill. She had seen so many strange things that night that the lights hardly seemed surprising at that point.

But then, to her amazement, the top of the hill itself began to rise up on glass pillars like a large domed building. Beneath the dome more faerie lights blazed. Shadowy figures danced and ate and drank, and played sweet music so enchanting it seemed to swirl visibly around them on the breeze.

Within the dome were glittering crystal fountains of water, cascading into silver lakes full of sparkling coloured fish. Smooth pathways wove through an underground realm built on circular levels descending further and further into the earth.

The highest level was dominated by a splendid pointy-towered structure, similar to the Piskie King's castle of stalagmite rock, but the Muryan palace was made of grey and white crystal. There were beautiful gardens and orchards with all kinds of delicious-looking fruit – red apples and purple plums and green pears hanging from ornamented trees. Morgan's mouth watered, until she remembered Diana and Arcile's warnings. Merlin was riding next to her, gazing at the fruit with a hungry expression.

Don't eat any of it! she warned him.

Merlin turned to her, his dark eyes suddenly cold. *Why not?*

Because they'll make you their prisoner. If you eat anything of theirs, you'll never be able to leave here ever again.

As Queen Caelia passed through on her horse with her head held high, the Muryans inside the faerie hill bowed and curtsied before her. They were all just as beautiful as the ones in the Rade, dressed in silks and satins of all colours and a hint of green, with luminous hair and jewels. Two of them carried forward what looked like a pair of very young children; human babies, a boy and a girl of the same age, both with wispy fair hair, rosy cheeks, blue eyes, and chubby arms and legs. The boy was clad in the petals of a bluebell and the girl in the yellow furls of a primrose.

Morgan's own young heart melted at the sight of the tiny twin babies. But seeing them both for the first time made her wonder. Twadell was adamant he wanted them both returned to him. So why had Diana told her only to bring her the boy's soul? Why hadn't she told her to bring her the girl's soul, too?

That must be them, Merlin broke into her thoughts.

Morgan nodded silently. *Mabon and Maglore.*

The Queen dismounted and greeted the babies with joy, surprising Morgan by smiling with the first sign of real happiness she had seen in her. The other Muryans also got down from their horses and Morgan and Merlin followed suit. Morgan looked around them for the ugly creatures who had accompanied the Rade, but now that they were inside the hill she couldn't see any of them.

More alarmingly, Jack and Joan, shackled to Muryan horses during the procession, had now also disappeared. Morgan knew they couldn't leave without the Piskies. King Twadell might hurt or kill Arcile if they left Jack and Joan behind. Caelia had ordered them to be thrown into the dungeon, Morgan remembered with a sinking heart. They'd somehow have to find that dungeon in this many-levelled Muryan city, rescue the Piskies, then escape with them and Mabon and Maglore in tow.

"Come, Stone-Heart and Light-Eyes." Caelia beckoned Merlin and Morgan forward and, after a glance of trepidation between them, they complied.

"These are my children," the Queen said proudly, stroking the hair of baby Mabon and gently touching baby Maglore's cheek. "Did you ever see such beauties?"

Morgan thought quickly. "They are beautiful, Your Highness," she said. "They look like you, don't they, with their fair hair."

At once she sensed a coldness in the air. None of the Muryans were smiling and there was an ominous hush. Caelia's eyes had narrowed.

"What I mean is," Morgan hastily continued, realising that she had made some kind of mistake, "that they're beautiful enough for you. You're a Queen so you have to have beautiful children."

Caelia still looked suspiciously at her. But after a minute her face cleared and she turned to address one of her attendants.

"Have one of the servants escort the Prince and Princess to my palace so they can prepare for our banquet." She eyed the two children, Merlin in particular. "I will have Prince Stone-Heart seated beside me as we toast the rise of the full Moon."

The Queen swept past with the two Muryans carrying the babies behind her. The attendant she had spoken to clapped his hands and a tall, pale, sad-looking girl appeared. She didn't seem to be like the other Muryans. For one thing, she was very plain. Her hair was lank and mousy, her clothes ill-fitting and roughly hewn, her movements slow and ungainly. Most tellingly of all, there was no light in her eyes.

"Take Prince Stone-Heart and Princess Light-Eyes to the mirror room," the attendant ordered. The mousy-haired girl inclined her head without a word. With one look at Morgan and Merlin, she indicated that they should follow her. Merlin raised his eyebrows in query at Morgan, as if he expected her to refuse. But Morgan thought they should go to the palace and have at least a few minutes alone, away from the Queen and the other Muryans. They needed to think of a plan. So she turned to follow the girl and soon felt Merlin close on her heels.

Why are we going in there? he thought to her. *We know where the baby is. Let's just follow the Queen, grab the boy when she's not looking and run for it.*

They'd catch us, Morgan argued. *We have to think of a plan so they won't notice. Besides, we have to find where Jack and Joan are, and get them out, too.*

Why?

Morgan was taken aback. *What do you mean?*

Why should we get Jack and Joan out? Merlin asked. *Diana wants that boy, Mabon, doesn't she? He's the one we've come to get. Why should we care about the Piskies? They were going to kill us. Let's just get Mabon and get out of here.*

No! Morgan was insistent. *We can't leave them here.*

She couldn't explain it, but she knew there was something not quite right about Caelia. And there was something else.

The beauty of the Muryan realm was so giddying that it was starting to make her feel slightly sick. It reminded her of the time the year before when she, Anna and Blasine had snuck into the castle larder, found a stack of bright sticky sweetmeats, and gorged themselves until they felt stuffed and sick. It had been too much, had made their stomachs ache and had given Morgan a bad feeling.

The Muryan realm was making her feel exactly the same way now. Something here was very wrong. It was all too much – too beautiful, too sweet, too rich. The spider had told her to be careful and for some strange reason his words resonated with her, even though she had always hated spiders, always been afraid of them. But there was something real and true about him, something *right*; something that Morgan did not feel anywhere within the Muryans' faerie hill.

She knew at once that Merlin had heard her thoughts, sensed her bad feeling and shared the memory of gobbling the sweetmeats without her having to express any of it. *Alright* was all he thought, but she knew he understood.

* * *

The mousy-haired girl led them into the crystalline palace and up a shiny staircase to a room filled with silver and gold-plated mirrors draped with silky gossamer threads. Feeling the sickness of too many sweetmeats again, Morgan determined to find out whatever she could about the place, starting with this girl.

"Are you a Muryan?" she asked her. "You're not like the others."

The girl looked startled, then scared for a moment – the first sign of emotion she had displayed. "Forgive me, Princess," she said in a low voice. "I'm not allowed to talk to you."

"Why not?" Morgan demanded.

"Because you're right," the girl replied. "I'm not a Muryan."

"What are you, then?" Merlin asked.

"I was once human," the girl said. "A long, long time ago."

"How did you get here?" Morgan asked her.

The girl looked at her with her dead eyes. Her ripple of feeling was gone. When she did not reply, Morgan said as reassuringly as she could, "Don't worry, you can talk to us. I allow you to."

"It was a long time ago," the girl repeated dully. She looked as if she was struggling to remember. "I went walking on the moor one day and I heard … music. Such lovely music." She sighed. "I saw a beautiful garden full of fruit trees. I picked some of the fruit and ate it. The next thing I knew I was surrounded by faeries and they told me I could never leave. I realised I was no longer human and that they had enchanted me to make me as small as them. The Muryans. I've been their servant ever since."

This made Morgan angry. "They made you their prisoner!" she exclaimed indignantly.

Again, the girl showed no emotion. "Yes. But it was my fault. I ate the fruit. I shouldn't have. I was greedy. I deserved it."

"No, you didn't!" Morgan glanced at Merlin, who was listening intently but in his typical way showing as little feeling as the girl. "Look ... what's your name?"

"Name?" the girl asked, sounding bewildered. She raised her head as if hearing the call of a distant memory. "My name ... uh ... I was called Agnes. When I was human. No one's called me that for ages."

"Look, Agnes," Morgan began, but then Merlin intruded on her thoughts. *You're not going to tell her about us?* he demanded.

Yes, I am, she can help us, Morgan retorted and continued aloud, "... we're like you. We're not Muryans, we're humans. We're children. We can get you out of here if you help us."

Agnes didn't react. "I can't leave. I'm a prisoner. The Muryans made me as small as them. I can't leave. If I do, the spiders and birds and animals will eat me."

"No, they won't!" Morgan insisted. "I told you we're human! We made ourselves small and we can make ourselves big again. We'll make you big again, too. Then you can go home again."

"We have magic," Merlin added by way of explanation.

Agnes looked from one to the other. Morgan thought she saw a pinprick of light ignite in the girl's eyes – or was it only a reflection from the mirrors? "I'm not the only one who's a prisoner here," Agnes said at last. "There are many of us. That's what the Muryans do. They trick people and take them away and keep us here to be their servants. Most of us were taken as children."

"Where are the children?" Morgan asked.

"You've seen them," Agnes said. "On the Rade."

Morgan and Merlin looked at each other. Merlin spoke what

they were both thinking: "We didn't see any children on the Rade."

"They walk. They don't ride."

Then Morgan understood. Horror dawned upon her. "Those ugly things, those creatures – they're human? They're *children*?"

"They were once." Agnes' eyes were dead again. "That's what we become. That's what I'll become."

Morgan recovered her breath. "No," she said firmly. "We're going to get you out."

"Wait," Merlin argued. *We came here to get Mabon. Now you want to get Jack and Joan and this girl and all these other children out, too?*

Not just them, Morgan answered. She said to Agnes, "If we promise to get you out of here, will you help us?"

Agnes hesitated. "You don't know Queen Caelia." The ripple of fear had returned. "She's cruel and wicked. She has powerful magic. If she finds us trying to escape, she'll have us all killed. She's killed others before for trying to leave."

"But why?" Morgan asked, genuinely bewildered. "Why is she so horrible? And why does she want you all to stay so much?"

"The Muryans don't have any children," Agnes replied in a low tone. "Not the Queen, not any of them. They've haven't had children for many, many years."

"Why?" Morgan asked again.

"I don't know." Agnes hesitated, as if afraid to continue. "I've heard it whispered that it was because of a crime the Muryans committed long ago – so long ago that none of them even remember what the crime was. That's why they take human children. It's fine when we're young, but when we grow old we can't stay the same. It isn't natural for us here. We become those things you saw on the Rade. The Muryans hate us for it."

"What about those children we saw?" Morgan asked. "The babies – Caelia's children. They were taken when they were dead, weren't they?"

"Yes, but the Queen had them stolen from the Piskies," Agnes said. Talking to others was obviously not something she did or was allowed to do very often, but Morgan's questions and interest seemed to animate her. "Only the Piskies can take the souls of stillborn babies. Many of them were once stillborn souls themselves. Queen Caelia thinks she can take Mabon and Maglore and turn them into her children. She's tried before with others. But it doesn't work. They'll become the same as the others eventually." Agnes' voice shook. "None of us can grow here, alive or dead. We become monsters."

"We've come here to get Mabon and Maglore," Morgan told her. "We've come to get them out and take them to someone who can help them. To where they're supposed to go."

Them? Merlin questioned in her head.

"Them," Morgan affirmed aloud. "Both of them. We're taking Maglore, too."

"Diana told you only Mabon," Merlin argued.

"I think she'll be happy if we bring her Maglore as well. Why shouldn't Maglore get another chance to live like Mabon?"

"But you can't!" Agnes exclaimed. "The Queen will show you no mercy if she finds out. Her magic is the most powerful of all the Muryans' and her punishments are terrible." A tear fell down the girl's cheek.

"She has powerful magic because she's the Muryan Queen?" Merlin asked.

Agnes looked around her, as if fearful of being heard. She was trembling now. She moved nearer to Morgan and Merlin, and the children leaned in close to listen.

"Caelia isn't really the Queen," Agnes whispered. "She stole her magic from the real Muryan Queens."

"Who are they?" Morgan asked, also in a whisper.

"They were called the Elven. The others whisper about them sometimes. I never knew them. They were the three Queens of the Muryans long ago, before any of us children ever came here. Some of the Muryans still talk about them. Not all of the Muryans love Caelia, but they don't dare say so. They just accept her. They say the Elven were powerful and beautiful faeries, like Caelia, but that they were good and true. They ruled the Muryans for many years and lived in peace with the Piskies, but then something happened. I don't know what."

"So what happened to the Elven?" Merlin asked.

"A lot of the Muryans were angry with the Elven. A wicked group led by Caelia decided to overthrow them. Caelia was the lady-in-waiting to one of the Elven and they were very kind to her. But she tricked them and stole their magic and their charms and spells, and then turned them into terrible monsters – too terrible to look at. Then she fought the war with the Piskies. They've been fighting each other for as long as anyone here can remember."

While Morgan was digesting this, Merlin questioned Agnes again. "Is that really true? How do you know the Elven were turned into these terrible monsters? Have you ever seen them?"

"The Muryans say they sometimes see them in the bottommost depths of the realm," Agnes replied. "Did you see the pathways of the city when you arrived? They go all the way down deep into the dark. The Queen and the high-born Muryans live at the top near the opening of the hill. The rest live further and further down. We children who aren't children anymore live below, where it's darkest and the light can't reach. We only come up to serve the Muryans but we live in the shadows. Right down at the bottom is where the monsters live – the things that crawl in the earth that will kill you and eat you if you get too close."

Morgan didn't like the sound of this at all. But one thing in particular she couldn't ignore. "If the Elven are still down there, then maybe they can help us," she said to Merlin. "They could help us against Caelia and get the children out."

She expected Merlin to argue again, but to her surprise he agreed. "If Caelia stole their magic and became Queen instead of them, they'd want to fight her," he said. "We could help the Elven get their magic back and in return they could help us."

"You can't!" Agnes protested again. "I told you. The Elven are monsters now! Terrible, frightening things. They're not Muryans anymore."

"From what you've told me, I don't like Muryans," Morgan retorted. "And I don't think the Elven would anymore, either."

Agnes opened her mouth to protest again and then stopped. The three children paused to listen to footsteps coming up the staircase outside towards the mirror room.

"They're coming to get you," Agnes said. Her whole demeanour shrank into dullness again. "You're to go to Caelia's banquet."

"Let's get out of here!" Merlin said urgently. He turned to Agnes. "Is there another way out?"

"Wait!" Morgan grabbed his arm and he flinched involuntarily. She let go immediately, remembering how he hated to be touched. "Listen, Merlin. You have to go to the banquet. Caelia specially said she wanted you to sit next to her. You have to go there and talk to her and make sure she doesn't think anything's wrong. I'll go and find the Elven."

"What?" Merlin sounded incredulous, then angry. "You can't go on your own! And I'm not going to sit with that horrible Queen by myself! Besides, she'll see you're not there. She'll know something's wrong."

"No." Morgan had a plan. "I'm not going to go. You're going to say that I'm tired from the journey and I need to rest. It's something my mother's been doing. She hasn't been to any feasts for visitors because she feels tired or sick and just stays in her rooms. My father says sorry to everyone and tells them she isn't feeling well and needs to rest. You can do that for me now. Say sorry and pretend I'm tired and I need to rest. Then when everyone's at the banquet I'll go and find the Elven."

"I don't want to," Merlin said through gritted teeth. "I hate Caelia. I don't want to sit next to her. What am I supposed to say to her?"

"I think she likes you, Merlin," Morgan told him. "So sit next to her. Say nice things to her. Tell her how pretty she is. Say how lovely this place is. And" – another quick thought came to her – "find out where the dungeon is. Find out where she's keeping Jack and Joan, but try and do it so she doesn't know why you want to know …"

She broke off as a couple of Muryan courtiers entered the room. One was a very beautiful lady with pale red hair and the other a young fair-haired gentleman. They each had delicate, diaphanous wings like their Queen. They both bowed to Morgan and Merlin. "Princess Light-Eyes, Prince Stone-Heart," the young gentleman said. "Queen Caelia requests your presence at her table."

Morgan looked meaningfully at Merlin. His face was darkened

with a mutinous scowl, but at her gaze it cleared and he spoke as lightly as he could.

"Princess Light-Eyes is tired and needs to rest. She'll stay here in this room tonight. I'll go to the banquet and sit next to the Queen."

The Muryans inclined their heads again. "As you wish," the young gentleman said. The lady addressed Morgan: "The Queen will be disappointed not to see you, Princess, but she is wonderfully wise and she will understand. Is there anything I can do for you?"

"No, thank you," Morgan said and indicated Agnes. "I'm sure this servant can help me with everything."

The lady and gentleman did not even acknowledge Agnes. They stepped aside to let Merlin pass through the door before them. With a last reproachful glance at Morgan, Merlin turned to leave. *Be careful*, she heard him think. *Tell me what's happening to you. Keep thinking to me like this. Tell me what's going on.*

I will, Morgan replied. *And you tell me what's happening with the Queen, too.*

If you get in trouble, tell me. I'll come and help you. And with that he left, the Muryans with him.

Morgan was left alone with Agnes. The once human girl had shrunk back into herself – lustreless, faded and broken in the wake of the colourful, beauteous and proud Muryans. Morgan ached with pity for her.

"Please, Agnes," she said gently. "Can you take me to where the Elven are?"

Agnes stared at her. A hint of fear glinted behind her dead eyes. Then she nodded.

* * *

The downward pathways seemed to go on forever. Morgan hurried after Agnes along poorly lit passages that ran in between bright little villages with coloured stone houses and crystal windows, encircled by prettily arranged flowers as big to the Muryans as trees. The lovely-looking Muryans themselves milled about their little houses, many of them seeming to have arranged mini-banquets of their own, bringing food and drink to communal tables of stone set in the centre of each village.

The tiers of the Muryan realm were connected by tube-like tunnels plunging steeply down into the earth as if almost vertical. Occasionally the tunnels opened onto flat caverns into which more pretty houses were tucked, before narrowing into another descending passageway.

Where are you? Morgan heard Merlin's voice. *What's happening?*

We're going deeper into the Muryan realm, Morgan replied. She sensed Merlin's mind seeing the tunnels and caverns through her eyes as she rushed past. *Where are* you?

At the banquet. She knew he was grimacing as he said it. *Caelia's here.*

The images in front of Merlin opened into Morgan's mind's eye. Against her own surroundings of gloomy passageways and occasional cluster of modestly adorned houses, a sight rose before her that took her breath away. She saw through Merlin's eyes a riotous blaze of colour under the roof of the faerie hill dome. The scene sparkled with star-like lights and was dominated by large leaves of green, the Muryans' favoured hue, with outbursts of red, purple, blue and white. Huge flower heads of roses and foxgloves and bluebells and cow parsley decorated round tables of stones and mushrooms, rivalling the Muryans' splendidly bright garments in rich silks and satins.

Upon the tables, the food and drink looked equally wonderful: fruits and cakes and puddings, and a flowing reddish drink that looked like wine served in gold cups. Morgan's stomach turned over.

Don't eat or drink anything! she reminded Merlin.

I won't, he responded, sounding a little exasperated with her. *I remember. I'll pretend.*

The Queen was seated in the centre, underneath the highest point of the dome. Now dressed in gold velvet, she sat on a throne made from a full-bloom yellow rose at a round red table covered with white dots. Morgan and Merlin realised at the same time that it was a toadstool – a poisonous one; one Morgan had always been warned by Sebile never, ever to touch. Those who were clearly Caelia's favourite courtiers sat with her at the poisonous table; among them, with a red-haired lady-in-waiting, sat the human twin babies Mabon and Maglore.

Caelia looked up as Merlin approached her. "Welcome, Prince Stone-Heart," the Queen said. It was very disorientating for Morgan to hear herself addressed like that, looking out from behind Merlin's eyes.

"Hello," she heard Merlin reply.

"But where is Princess Light-Eyes?" Caelia asked.

"I'm sorry but she's feeling tired and sick," Merlin replied. "She has to stay in her room tonight."

"I see," the Queen said quietly. "Tired and sick is she?"

She had her suspicious and unfriendly look on her face again. *Tell her we had a long journey from our country and that's why I'm tired*, Morgan urged Merlin.

The boy dutifully did so, but Caelia's expression did not change. However, she did not comment further. "Come and sit next to me," she invited Merlin. Morgan felt a sudden wave of revulsion from Merlin at the thought of sitting so close. Nevertheless, he did so. In front of him, Morgan could see the delectable food and drink spread out on the toadstool table and her mouth watered.

"Are there more like you in your Muryan country?" Caelia inquired of Merlin.

"What do you mean, more like me?" Merlin asked, somewhat curtly.

"More children." Caelia smiled, but it was not a nice smile. "I know that you and Princess Light-Eyes are children. It's clear that you are both very young. It's very interesting to me. I have never seen Muryan children before – in our realm, you see, we have not had children for a long time. At least, not real children; not children of our own."

Merlin's eyes looked across the table at Mabon and Maglore. The babies were being fed what looked like honey, sucking it from the fingers of the red-haired lady-in-waiting. Morgan was horrified. The twins were eating faerie food! Would she be able to get them out? "So, they're not your children, then?" she heard Merlin ask, in what sounded like one of his typical challenges. *Stop it!* she warned him. *Say nice things to her, remember?*

So focused was Morgan on the scene she was witnessing through Merlin's eyes that she had lost all sense of her own situation. When she stumbled and fell to the ground, she blinked away the images of Caelia's banquet and took stock of where she was.

She and Agnes were in a tunnel that seemed longer than the others they had been through. In fact, the tunnels seemed to be getting longer and longer the further down they went into the ground. Agnes had not stopped or looked back, so Morgan picked herself up, brushed herself down and hurried after her.

This tunnel was definitely the longest of them all so far. When they eventually reached a wide cavern opening, the dwellings there were markedly less bright and pretty. There were no coloured stones, no flowers and no banquets. They were sparsely lit, and looked more like holes and openings carved into the earth. The people she saw there were not beautiful, but plain and drab like Agnes, and some even had the gait and shape of the ugly, brutish creatures on the Rade.

"Are those the other children?" Morgan asked, trying to control her instinct to flinch at the sight of them.

"This is where we live," Agnes said.

Out of the corner of her eye, Morgan saw something scurrying into the shadows, but as soon as she turned it disappeared. It didn't look human in appearance. In fact, it had looked alarmingly similar to the spiders she had encountered earlier.

"What was *that*?"

"The things that live down here with us," Agnes said. There was a hint of emotion in her voice again. "I told you, you can't get too close. I can't take you any further."

"Why not? Are the Elven here?"

"Some of the others say they've seen them here sometimes, but they don't live here. If you want to find them you'll have to go further down." Agnes indicated another tunnel off the cavern that sloped steeply downwards.

What's going on? What am I seeing? Morgan heard Merlin's voice in her head, much fainter this time, and felt his eyes looking out behind her own. *Where are you?*

I'm where Agnes and the other children live, Morgan thought. *She won't go any further. I have to go on by myself. What's happening there?*

I can hardly hear you, Morgan. I can see you're in a dark place. What are all those things around you? Why can't I hear you properly?

Maybe because we're too far away. Morgan chose to answer only one question and thought back to him with all her might. *I think I'm very deep in the ground. Merlin? What's happening?*

I know ... where to find ... the Piskies. Morgan could barely make out his thoughts. *Caelia ... wants us to stay ... with her ...*

Merlin's voice in her head was only coming to her in fragments. She looked at Agnes, who stood mutely watching her, and then at the final tunnel through which the girl refused to go. She caught another tantalising glimpse of Caelia's beautiful faerie banquet through Merlin's mind and for an instant she felt resentful towards him. It wasn't fair that she was down here in the darkness while Merlin was up there in the light.

She suddenly felt very tired and hungry and alone. The enormity of the situation overwhelmed her. She wondered if her parents and Sebile and everyone at Tintagel had missed her yet. Were they looking for her at this very moment? She longed for her strong father, her kind mother, her wise tutor. But now she was on her own. Arcile was a prisoner. Merlin couldn't help her. Even Agnes wouldn't go with her. And she knew she had to brave that dark tunnel to find the Elven. They were the only hope she had of ever getting the children away from Caelia and dealing with the Piskies afterwards. If she didn't do this, all of them would be prisoners here forever, and Jack and Joan and Arcile would all be killed. And she would have failed Diana.

I'm going further down to find the Elven, Morgan told Merlin as forcefully as she could. *I might not be able to hear you anymore. When I find them, I'll bring them back and tell you. Don't let Caelia find out.*

Morgan ...!!! It was the last thing her mind heard as she ran towards the tunnel and made her way inside.

There was next to no light at all and she could barely see in front of her, or make out the walls on either side as she hurried along down the passage. The tunnel was made of compact earth, smooth and cool and rounded. Morgan wondered who had built it. The Muryans? But it couldn't have been more different from their beautiful realm of lights and flowers, crystals and colour.

Morgan felt the familiar bad feeling wash over her as she contemplated the stark contrast between Caelia's palace and city and gardens directly underneath the faerie hill, and the tunnels and dark holes and crannies here deep in the earth. Something about it was all wrong, but again she couldn't think what.

She heard a scuttling noise ahead of her and stopped, her heart pounding. At first she thought it was footsteps coming towards her, but it was much too fast and sharp for that. As it came closer, Morgan realised there was nowhere to go. There were no places to hide in the tunnel and she couldn't go back. So she shrank up against the wall and waited, steeling herself for whatever was coming.

A shape loomed up ahead. In front of her appeared a monstrous head with huge circles for eyes. It had what appeared to be two soft horns on top and a pair of fangs protruding from its mouth. As it came closer, she saw the head was attached to a grotesque thin body with six spindly legs and a bulbous posterior. It wasn't a spider. Morgan had thought the spiders were ugly, but she decided this was even worse.

The disgusting creature, as large to her as the spiders had been, came clattering towards her, but it stopped a little way away and moved its head as if it smelled something. Was it blind? Morgan moved ever so slightly and the creature shot forward, pinning her to the wall with its two forelegs.

Up close it was shiny and slimy. Morgan's heart and body seized in terror as she remembered Agnes' words about the creatures that lived in the darkness. But at the same time, a small corner of her mind recalled that she had a power she could use. Taking an idea from what she had seen Merlin do, she stared into the creature's hideous face with ferocious concentration fuelled by her own fear, wishing terrible pain upon the horrible thing. After a few moments there was a humming noise. The creature's soft horns shook and it quickly withdrew its forelegs, freeing Morgan from the wall. It made no sound, but Morgan knew she had hurt it. In the narrow confines of the tunnel, she could sense its pain and shock.

"What are you?" Morgan asked, attempting to control the trembling in her voice. She fully expected the creature to talk to her just as the spiders had.

But the creature was silent. Morgan tried again.

"Tell me – what are you? Do you live down here?"

Again, the creature said nothing. Could it not talk? Morgan stepped closer to it and looked into its face. "Do you understand what I'm saying?" she asked.

The creature raised its head and nodded.

"But you can't talk to me," Morgan said, realising that this thing was not like the spiders.

The creature silently affirmed again. Morgan was thankful it could at least communicate. She had an idea.

"I need you to help me," Morgan said. "I need to find the Elven. Do you know where they are? Can you take me to them?"

The creature reacted violently to her words. Its whole body shook as its head moved quickly from side to side. It was clearly terrified at the very thought. But Morgan didn't care. The Elven were her only hope. "You must take me to them!" she exclaimed.

When the creature shook its head fiercely a second time, Morgan desperately focused her mind on hurting it again. The humming noise returned and the creature shook with pain once more. Morgan felt a stab of remorse but, she reasoned to herself, she had to do it. There wasn't much time. She had to make this thing help her whether it wanted to or not.

Reluctantly, the creature turned its entire body and headed slowly back down the tunnel. Morgan hastened after it. This tunnel was another long one and it seemed ages before the little girl saw a speck of sombre greyish light up ahead. The creature led Morgan from the tunnel into the lowest depth of the hill, made up of a wide space which was almost as high as the dome at the top.

The cavernous hole she found herself in was dismal and the air hung heavy with an unspoken dread. Nothing but brown earth and grey stone could be seen, save for a single brooding black pond in the centre, which lay as still as a mirror. Getting used to the dingy light, Morgan saw other dark passage entrances all around the walls, branching off from the main chamber, and some sticky, slimy things on the ground she couldn't identify. A steady *drip-drip-drip* was the only sound coming from a corner of the cavern.

"Is this where the Elven are?" Morgan asked the creature in a horrified whisper.

Her creature guide shuffled nervously, the soft horns on its head twitching. Had it heard something? Sensed something? Morgan couldn't see much and she could hear nothing except the dripping sound. But the silence frightened her. It was watchful. Predatory. Something was in the cavern with them.

Then she heard it. A faint whirring sound turned quickly into a sharp buzzing. A large, shiny blue streak came skimming across the black pond like lightning, bearing straight at them.

Much bigger than the creature that had brought her here, this monster had a long gleaming rod-like body patterned with segments of blue and black, and two pairs of lucent wings beating so fast they were merely a blur. Morgan glimpsed a repulsive round head and bulging eyes on either side before the monster flew into them, scattering her and her creature guide. Morgan fell to the ground instinctively, scrambling to get away.

But her creature guide was not so lucky. Before it had a chance to react, the blue-black monster grabbed it with its sharp forelegs and stabbed it straight through the torso with its jaws. For a few seconds Morgan felt the excruciating agony of the hapless creature guide. Its body convulsed and her ears rang with its silent screaming. Still on the ground, she backed away in terror as the blue-black monster began tearing the flesh of its prey. A transparent liquid burst out from the creature guide as it quivered helplessly in its last dying moments.

Unable to bear the sight, Morgan turned away and crawled as fast as she could towards one of the passage entrances in the wall. Before she could get there her stomach heaved and she was sick on the floor. Wiping her mouth and her streaming tears, she resumed her frantic crawl towards the dark passage, propelled solely by her need to hide. But then she heard the sharp buzzing behind her. Sick with fear, she turned back to see the blue-black monster hovering in the air directly behind her, its bulging eyes fixed on her, its legs twitching, its fangs snapping.

"No!" was all Morgan could muster. Desperately, she tried to focus her energy on the monster to hurt it, to protect herself, in the same way she had hurt the poor dead creature she had made bring her here. But she couldn't. Her terror made her weak and her eyes were blurry. "Please! Don't!"

The buzzing noise stopped. The blue-black monster planted its crooked legs on the ground and folded its gauzy wings alongside its slender body. It stared curiously at her and made no sound. Morgan did not dare move.

"What are you?" the monster said eventually. It had a hostile, sonorous voice that didn't sound like a man or a woman.

Morgan had been so sure the monster wouldn't be able to talk that she was stunned into silence for a moment. Then she swallowed and tried to stand up, but her legs were too shaky and she fell back down again.

"I'm here looking for the Elven," she said.

"What do you want with them?" The monster sounded suspicious.

"I need their help." On her second attempt Morgan managed to stand up unsteadily. She was briefly aware of how dirty her clothes and face had become. "I'm here to rescue the souls of two children that Queen Caelia stole. I need the Elven to help me."

If the blue-black monster had had an expression, Morgan would have said it was astonished.

"You're here to steal children from Caelia?" It regarded her with something akin to interest, though it hadn't let down its guard. "Answer my question: what are you?"

"I'm human," Morgan said earnestly. "I'm a girl."

Nasty laughter echoed from around the chamber. It didn't come from the blue-black monster in front of her.

"You're no more human than we are," said another strange voice.

"Let's make her tell the truth," said a third.

From either side of the blue-black monster emerged two other monsters, equally strange but quite different in appearance.

The one that had spoken first was pure white all over, with a long slim body and legs, soft thin horns on its head, and two pairs of wide, fan-like feathery wings. If it hadn't looked so scarily strange, Morgan would almost have said it was beautiful. The other one was more frightening. It had thin bright-red wings covering a shiny black body and stick legs, with black jagged horns on its head.

As the white monster, the blue-black monster and the red monster stood side by side towering menacingly over her, the realisation suddenly came to Morgan in a blaze of clarity.

"You're the Elven," she said.

XIII

Lost and Found

"I'll ask you one more time and you had better answer me," the blue-black monster said ominously. "*What* are you?"

"She's not a Muryan, that's certain," the white monster said.

"And she can't be human," the red-winged monster remarked. "No human could be that small."

"But I *am* human!" Morgan protested. "I'm different, that's all. I can do magic! That's how I got this small! Really, I am human!"

"She's not, you know," the red-winged monster said to no one in particular.

But the blue-black monster continued to observe Morgan with keen interest. "You do have magic, don't you?" it said. "So that's what I can smell about you. You *are* different. So, tell us. Why do you want to rescue these children's souls?"

"A lady called Diana sent me," Morgan told them breathlessly. "She's a powerful Queen. She leads the Wild Hunt riding through the sky. She was supposed to save the souls of the children when they died, but they were stolen by the Piskies before she could. I went to the Piskies, but then I found out that Caelia and the Muryans took them. The Piskies sent me and my friend here to get them back. But I really need to get them away from the Piskies and the Muryans and take them to Diana."

The atmosphere had changed. The three monsters were all staring at her now with astonishment and another feeling Morgan didn't recognise. When they didn't respond, she went on hurriedly: "I know Caelia stole your magic from you and turned you into … this. My friend and I both have magic. If you help us get the children out, we'll help you get your magic back."

"You'll help us how?" the white monster asked. "You're very young, whatever you are. You don't have the power to restore our magic."

"No, but Diana does," the blue-black monster mused. It cocked its head to one side, assessing Morgan, who was astounded.

"You know Diana?"

"We know *of* Diana," the blue-black monster said. It sounded bitter. "We were all the same once. But we grew apart. We lived in very different worlds. What do you know of the Muryans and the Piskies?"

Morgan remembered what Agnes had told her. "They're at war with each other. The Piskies take the souls of dead babies. Some of them *are* the souls of dead babies. The Muryans can't have children, so they take human children, too. They say it's because of a crime they committed long ago."

"You *have* learned a lot," the red-winged monster commented.

"And what do you know of *us*?" the blue-black monster challenged.

"That you were the three Queens of the Muryans," Morgan said boldly. "That you were beautiful and good and true. That you lived in peace with the Piskies."

The three monsters were silent, glancing at each other.

"And then something happened," Morgan went on. "The Muryans were angry with you, and Caelia led a group and overthrew you and stole your magic and turned you into monsters." She looked at the creatures, who were twitching – whether with anger or something else, she couldn't tell. "*What* happened?"

"To understand that, you have to understand what the Muryans and the Piskies really are," the blue-black monster said at last.

"What are they? Or you, I mean?"

The blue-black monster paused again, as if trying to find the words. "We were once among many who were condemned to live on earth for a crime that was committed long, long ago," it said. "Before the mists of time began. We were all condemned together. When humans arrived in this world, long after we did, we worked together to take the souls of their unbaptised children for ourselves."

"Why?" Morgan asked.

"Not to harm them, if you can believe that," the blue-black monster replied. "We didn't want to harm anything then. We wanted to keep them on earth with us in the hope that we would be able to use them, to go back to the place we came from with them. But this did not come to pass. You see, after they died, humans were able to go back to the place we originally came from, but we could not. We weren't able to get back to where we had once been, even with the children's souls to bargain with. A faction of the Piskies, led by one called Twadell, grew twisted and bitter and turned on us, the Elven, even though we were their allies."

"Twadell began a war with us," the white monster continued bitterly. "He began fighting us over children's souls to augment the Piskies' dwindling numbers. The Muryans in turn grew angry and jealous. They were led by Caelia, who we had taught and nurtured, and they rose up against us."

"That's when Caelia stole our magic and cast a spell on us," the red-winged monster said. "She transformed us into these creatures we are now. Since then she has made the Muryans as bitter and twisted as the Piskies. She even started kidnapping living children to serve her. The Muryans and the Piskies are now enemies, each dependent on changeling babies, kidnapped children and the souls of the unbaptised to survive."

Morgan hadn't fully understood all of this. "What do you mean about their numbers?"

"As time goes on, there are fewer of them," the white monster asserted. "Eventually they disappear. Both Muryans and Piskies."

"That's why they steal children," the red-winged monster said. "They need them to keep themselves in existence. But it doesn't work."

"They are growing fewer and fewer in number, smaller and smaller in size, weaker and weaker in strength, and less and less powerful," the blue-black monster reiterated. "The dwindling of the Piskies and the Muryans is a sign of their diminishing power. That's why they're both so eager to get hold of human changelings and human children's souls. They need them to reinforce their stock. They prey on humans and take neglected young souls that fall outside the protection human children are granted."

Morgan had a sudden memory of the black crows in the courtyard at Tintagel, pecking at the seeds that spilled from the sacks on the carts. Only the crows saw the seeds that fell onto the ground. No one else did, nor did they pay any attention to them. The crows laid claim to them and snatched them up as their own – just as the Piskies and Muryans did with the lost children. But Morgan had found these children now.

"I want to rescue the children," she said. "All the ones that are here."

"Even the ones Diana didn't send you to save?" the white monster said sceptically.

Morgan nodded. The three monsters glanced at each other again. A frisson of energy hummed between them. Then the blue-black monster came up close to her, its fangs enormous, its hideous face almost touching hers.

"Do you even know what you're dealing with here?" it asked. "Do you have any idea of the forces you're meddling with? Do you know *anything* about this world you have entered?"

Morgan recalled how only a while ago this disgusting monster had savagely killed and ripped apart her creature guide. It was impossible to believe it had ever been beautiful or good. She felt the sick rising in her throat again and tried to control her trembling. "I want to help the children," she said feebly.

The blue-black monster observed her for a long moment. Then it stepped back, smoothly unfolding its wings.

"We will help you," it said. "We will help you rescue the children. But in exchange for our help you will get us back our magic and turn us back into the Elven. Either you will restore us yourself or you will persuade Diana to do it. If you do not, the consequences will be dire for you. I promise you that."

Morgan nodded again, unable to speak. The blue-black monster continued to watch her closely.

"And remember, little one, the truth about this world of ours here. Nothing is as it seems. Don't be surprised if things do not happen the way you expect. The Muryans are not what you think they are. Nothing in this queendom is what it appears to be. Now, we must go."

"Where are we going?" Morgan asked.

"Above ground," the blue-black monster said. "We have a way

to get from here through the tunnels out into the open air. If you want to rescue the children you're going to have to return to the top of the hill. Climb onto my back."

"Wh – a – t?" Morgan gasped.

"We're going to move quickly. You won't be able to keep up with us. If you want to do this, climb onto my back. Now."

The white monster and the red-winged monster both emitted strange noises. It sounded to Morgan as if they were giggling. Swallowing her revulsion, she approached the rod-like body of the blue-black monster and determinedly took a hold of it, hoisting herself up. The blue-black monster's unfolded wings began whirring on either side, creating a draught all around her.

"Do you have a name?"

The red-winged monster was looking sideways at her. It didn't have an expression, but Morgan felt it was interested. "I'm P – " she began, about to say "Princess Light-Eyes." But then she looked into the inscrutable black face of the red-winged monster and the thought of this realm where nothing was true made her change her mind. "*Never trust a fae*," Diana had said. Yet she found that this time she could not lie.

"I'm Morgan."

She could have sworn that the red-winged monster smiled to itself. "Hello, Morgan," it said. "I'm Una." With one of its forelegs it indicated the white monster. "That's Cleena." Then, finally, the blue-black monster. "She's Aynia."

"Come away, now," Aynia said. "Let's do this."

Morgan felt herself rising on Aynia's back as the blue-black monster hovered above the ground. She clasped her arms around the creature's body and held on tight. Then, with a sudden extraordinary rush, they shot forward through the air at head-spinning speed into one of the outer passages, leaving the dark, murky chamber far behind them.

* * *

Whizzing up through the tunnel on Aynia's back, Morgan held on tight. The blue-black Elven zoomed and swerved at such speed that everything became a blur. Morgan was only aware of the gossamer wings around her beating so fast they just appeared to be mist in the air. Before she knew it, a cold breeze hit her lungs and they shot out of the tunnel into the open air.

It was still night-time. They had emerged out of the side of the faerie hill yards below the crest. Above them, some way away, the faerie hill dome was still raised; the gleaming lights and pillars could be seen and raucous feasting and dancing heard from a distance. Morgan thought of the banquet and everybody there – Merlin, Caelia, Mabon, Maglore. *Merlin?* she thought, wondering if he could hear her, but there was no response.

Aynia hovered with her in the air, flanked by Cleena and Una. All three Elven were staring intently at the dome. In stark contrast to the celebrations going on inside, everything where they were was very still and quiet. The full Moon was still shining out high over the hill and the sky remained scattered with stars. Morgan was surprised that it was *still* night-time after all she had been through and everything that had happened. Time seemed to be passing very slowly.

The Elven flew towards a blackthorn tree on the hill slope. Its dark spiny branches were densely tangled and twisted into a massive black web. Aynia flew through the interlacing boughs and alighted on one of the inner branches, with Cleena and Una following her. They could still see the faerie dome through the thicket but were hidden from it.

Morgan slipped off Aynia's back and cautiously stood still on the branch, wobbling a bit before she steadied her balance. For a moment she marvelled that she was actually able to stand on the branch of a stunted tree that would normally be no bigger to her than a hedge.

"What do we do now?" she asked.

"*We* don't do anything," Cleena said. "*We* can't. *You* have to do it."

"If you want to save the children, you must do as we say," Aynia asserted. "You have the magic, but we have the knowledge. To release the children and reveal the truth, you must first create a fire. You have to burn that which burns fastest and brightest."

Morgan didn't know much about making a fire. She'd never been allowed near the great fireplaces at Tintagel and had certainly never been permitted to help build or light one. Still, she'd observed enough to know the basics. "We need logs," she declared. "And sticks. And leaves."

The Elven all made the strange noises again. She realised they were laughing at her and felt a jab of anger.

"No, you little fool," Una told her when she'd stopped chuckling. "The things that will burn fastest here are thorns. Look around you."

Peering through the darkness, Morgan saw that the wrinkled branch she was standing on was virtually covered with tall, wickedly sharp thorny shoots, some of them almost as big as she was. The Elven had landed on a smoother part of the branch, but even underneath them budded smaller, hidden thorns. If she had stumbled or lost her balance, she would have been cut. She grimaced in dismay.

"This isn't going to work," Cleena said to Aynia. "I've had a feeling for a while that this is an Undine. She's not going to be able to set these aflame."

"I will!" Morgan said at once. She rubbed her hand, remembering how the brambles on the moor had sprung from the ground and torn at her skin. "I just hate thorns, that's all."

"There isn't a single being on earth that likes thorns," Una said. "That's the point. If you'll pardon the pun."

"There's a reason for that," declared Aynia. "Thorns weren't part of original creation. You know what I mean, child? The beginning, when the world was created?" Morgan nodded and the blue-black Elven continued. "It was only when sin and evil came into the world – only then were thorns thrown on the ground and made to grow, in amongst all the world's beauty of trees and flowers and birds and animals ... and people."

"But why?" Morgan demanded. "Why did God put thorns in to spoil the world when they're so nasty?"

"To remind us of the nasty," Aynia replied. There was something like anger in her voice. "They were put here to remind us of the pain of doing bad things."

"The pain of sin," Una added, so quietly Morgan barely heard her.

"But what you need to know now is that thorns burn quickly and they burn bright. The burning of thorns on top of this faerie hill will release any children held captive here. If you light the thorns on this tree, the wind will carry the smoke across the top of the hill. We'll take some of them to the top ourselves once they're set alight and drop them there."

Morgan looked anxiously and helplessly at the black spiked thorns along the branch beside her.

"Don't worry," Una said, anticipating Morgan's next objection. "All you have to do is create a spark. The rest will take care of itself."

Next to her, Cleena suddenly twitched. The white Elven ruffled her feathery wings and her horns prickled.

"What is it?" Aynia inquired impatiently.

"I hear something," Cleena said. "Coming up the hill." She scuttled a little way along the branch and peered through the thicket.

"Probably stragglers from the Rade," Una said.

"We must focus." Aynia turned to Morgan. "You have to light a fire. You must conjure up a spark that will ignite this tree and its thorns into flame. To do this you have to understand that fire is one of the sources of all life. It is at the heart of everything created in this world; it is an ancient, primal magic. It is the source of all light. After the creation of the heavens and earth came that light, and with it darkness."

"*Then God said 'Let there be light'; and there was light,*" Morgan remembered.

Aynia's ugly jaws moved in what looked like a smile. "So that's how they tell it now. Very well. So God made two great lights in the sky – one to rule the Day and one to rule the Night."

"The Sun and the Moon," Morgan said at once. She could just see the round white Moon through the maze of black boughs, twigs, thorns and shoots twisting and branching out in all directions.

"What you don't know is that the Moon itself is dark," Aynia said. Morgan looked at her in amazement and the blue-black Elven continued: "The Moon doesn't have its own light. It has other, darker powers – powers that can't be seen but can be felt. The light you see coming from the Moon is the Sun's light reflected. And the Sun is made of fire. To set this blackthorn alight with your magic, you must draw on the power of that reflected light and conjure the Sun's fire."

This amazed Morgan too; she had never thought about what the Sun might be made of. "But how do I do that?" she asked.

"How do you usually use your magic?" Aynia inquired.

"I just … think about something," Morgan told her. "I think very hard and I – I try to make it happen."

"Well, do that now, then!" Cleena said angrily. The white Elven moved threateningly towards her, wings outspread. Morgan tried to back away hastily and nearly stumbled over a thorn, losing her balance. She felt Una grab her with her two thin forelegs before she fell off the branch.

"We'll help you," the red-winged Elven said, more kindly. She turned her head to Aynia. "We can give her an incantation, can't we?"

Aynia walked up to Morgan, who was still wrapped in Una's spindly black legs. Una let her go and Morgan took a deep breath, determined to stand her ground as the blue-black Elven came close to her. "Concentrate," Aynia commanded, indicating a tall, particularly vicious black thorn in front of them.

Morgan gazed at the thorn and then up at the light of the Moon, reflecting, as Aynia said, the Sun's fire. "The Moon you see is full," Aynia said in her ear. "The world is in between the Moon and the Sun. Draw that fire from the Sun through the Moon's light."

Morgan focused her whole mind and body on the moonlight's reflected fire, the memory of the Sun's bright light in the daytime sky, and the tall black thorn. "Repeat after us," she heard Aynia say, and then all the Elven chanted in unison:

"Sun King and Moon Queen, oh hear me this night
Send me your sunfire through wild moonbeams bright
Hear me, oh wise ones, both golden and white
Send me the spark to set blackthorn alight."

Morgan repeated the incantation several times over, concentrating hard, closing her eyes to see.

She saw the Moon no longer bright but dark, hidden in shadow, moving slowly and watchfully around the earth. She saw the Sun's golden rays lighting the Moon up silver and white, exposing it to the world with all of its dark marks and patterns. She saw sunfire streaming down through moonbeams onto the whole of the earth, the moor, the hill, the tree, right down to the single, stark, sharp black thorn.

An extraordinary feeling welled up inside her, a sensation that made her feel very, very old, but strong and powerful beyond imagining. An ever-growing, overwhelming force was building up and coursing throughout her entire body.

There was a *whoosh* sound and a sudden blast of heat. Morgan opened her eyes to see the thorn had burst into flame, shooting up into the tree and making higher branches catch fire. Cleena squealed. She had been forced to fly up into the air to avoid getting singed.

"Did you *see* that?" cried the white Elven in disbelief, fluttering her wings furiously. "She was only supposed to make a spark!"

"Water *and* fire," Una said. The red-winged Elven was staring at Morgan in wonder. "That can only mean one thing."

"It can't be!" Cleena scoffed. "That's impossible!"

Aynia said nothing, but looked at Morgan inscrutably with her bulging monster eyes.

Morgan was shaken by the intensity of it all, but she felt strangely happy and proud, as if she'd jumped off a very high place and landed safe and sound. "What do we do now?" she said eagerly.

"We let the tree burn," Aynia declared. "We'll carry some of the thorns to the top of the hill. You, take one of the tall thorns that isn't burning yet and light it as you would a torch. We'll take you inside the Muryan realm to free the children."

Her heart hammering with excitement, Morgan made her way along the branch, careless of the upgrowing thorns still trying to catch her feet. She placed her hands upon one of the taller thorns and pushed with all her might. The thorn snapped and she tugged at it until it was ripped from the branch. Using one hand to hold it like a torch, with the other she tore strips off an as yet not-sharp small shoot sprouting from the bough. As she wrapped the strips around the top of the thorn, the tree around her crackled. The fire was spreading.

"Hurry!" Aynia was hovering in the air beside her, wings humming. She was holding a thorn by the tips of her spindle legs. Her thorn had just caught fire.

Morgan leaned over and lit her torch from the flame of Aynia's thorn. Then she quickly hoisted herself onto the Elven's back once more.

They sped forward towards the dome, Cleena and Una on either side. The three Elven carried their burning thorns beneath them; Morgan held hers high. She glanced back at the blackthorn tree. Its ebony branches were turning orange in the dark. Curls of smoke wafted into the night air. The wind was blowing mildly; the smoke drifting slowly. Closing her eyes again, Morgan saw the smoke and silently urged the wind to get stronger. *Blow the smoke over the faerie hill.*

The Elven flew to the top of the dome. At Aynia's signal, they dropped the three burning thorns upon the highest point. The thorns looked like beacons in the night as they blazed away.

Then the Elven dived, turned, and flew straight into the faerie dome. Just before the turn, Morgan caught another glimpse of the blackthorn tree burning against the night sky. The grass was moving oddly on the hill – what *was* that? – but before she had time to think further they were inside. So thrilled at the speed and power she was feeling, she felt as if she were flying on her own. She held on firmly to her torch as Aynia winged and swerved their way through the pillars and orchards and fountains of the Muryan queendom.

The thorn-torch burned high and fast now, trailing thick black smoke. As the smoke billowed around them, an invisible veil covering everything inside the faerie hill lifted. Morgan's giddy excitement gave way to sudden shock.

The glass pillars of the raised dome stood exposed as nothing but common rock. The sparkling crystal fountains and their shining waters were revealed as piles of dull stones in dirty puddles. The luminous coloured fish shrivelled down into squiggly slimy tadpoles. The luscious orchard trees bearing ripe apples and plums and pears shrank into dry sticks of bilious haws and blackberries and sloes, all putrid and oozing mould.

Morgan's jaw dropped. Her head began to ache. She couldn't believe what she was seeing. They had warned her that nothing was as it appeared to be. But *this*? She looked down at Aynia, then sideways at the other two. None of the three Elven returned her look.

Into the pointy-towered palace they flew, grimly and purposefully. Their trail of smoke began exposing the place as nothing but tall burrows made out of dry mud. Whizzing through the corridors, they revealed passage after passage of mud-burrows until they reached the main hall. The faerie banquet itself.

As they flew faster and faster round above the feasting tables, the trail of smoke from the torch blotted out the suspended faerie lights. Cobwebs of illusion were swept away to reveal the truth.

The formerly colourful flowers and leaves adorning the banquet hall were dead. The mushrooms being used as tables were rotten. The gold plates were nothing but scraps of wood; the silver glasses shards of tin. Worst of all was the food. The fruits and cakes and puddings vanished and there lay exposed the body parts of flies and earwigs, worms and snails. The half-eaten carcass of a moth. The crooked legs of a frog. The tail of a mouse. Grasshopper wings. Fleshy worms. Wriggling maggots. The flowing red wine turned into a frothy goo that looked like spittle.

Morgan's head was spinning. Sick rose in her throat again and her sight blurred. Blinking furiously and gripping the torch with all her might, she clutched at Aynia with her free hand, willing herself not to fall from the Elven's back.

The Muryans didn't know what was happening at first. They continued eating and drinking and laughing, tearing into the dead creatures on the table with relish. When they felt the rush of air from the Elven flying past, they looked up to see a mist of smoke descending. The smoke swirled around them, peeling off the lavish layers of beauty to reveal what was really underneath.

No longer were they the lovely, richly dressed faerie courtiers of the Rade. Many of them, to Morgan's horror, looked similar to her creature guide that Aynia had killed in the underground chamber – six-legged, lean-bodied, lumpy, long-horned monsters. Even worse, most of them were in various stages of transforming into the creatures. Grotesque bodies grew out of beautiful human-like faerie heads and limbs, horribly disjointed and hideous to behold.

Speechless, unable even to cry out, Morgan couldn't do anything but stare at them in revulsion. Amongst the chatter, a screech suddenly rang out. Then another. And another. The Muryans' glamour dissipated. Panic broke out as the creatures began overturning the banquet tables and scuttling frantically in all directions, terrified, desperate to escape. Morgan suddenly realised what they really were. She had seen this kind of thing before. Tiny creatures rushing backwards and forwards in the stone courtyard at Tintagel and out on the cliff path.

Ants. They were ants.

High-pitched cackles rose above the chaos erupting in the hall. It was the Elven. They were laughing with glee. Caelia on her yellow-rose throne had not yet seen them, but her beautiful face was distorted by an ugly scowl. Morgan looked for Merlin at the table, but he was nowhere to be seen. The Queen looked angry about something, but her anger was nothing compared to the fury of the Elven themselves. Aynia's whole body was quivering with rage. Caelia looked up and saw the three Elven bearing down on her, Morgan on Aynia's back brandishing the torch. The Queen's scowl turned to a look of astonishment and then absolute terror.

When the smoke hit her, the Queen's beautiful golden dress melted. Before their eyes was revealed an ugly, shiny black creature body, wings on her back and a round posterior larger than the others. Her golden head remained the same, but sprouted black creature horns on top. The Muryan Queen scrabbled at the dead remnants of her banquet in a frenzy and scurried away from the Elven, running for her life. Cleena and Una shot after her in pursuit. But Morgan grabbed Aynia's neck as she would to stop a horse.

"No! There!"

Below them the fair-haired baby twins sat in the wreckage of the faerie feast. The only beings in the hall unaffected by the thorn's smoke, they stared up at Morgan with frightened little faces.

"We have to get them!" Morgan urged Aynia. "You promised!"

Aynia said nothing, but dived down towards them. The red-haired lady-in-waiting with them looked the same … except the bottom half of her body was an ant. She shrieked and ran from Aynia, leaving the twins on the floor. The blue-black Elven skimmed along the ground and Morgan dropped the burning torch onto the centre of the toadstool table. She grabbed the babies, one in each arm, and placed them in front of her on Aynia's back, holding them close. Again she looked around wildly for Merlin. Where was he?

Merlin! I'm here in the hall. Where are you?

Silence. Then the door swung open.

Morgan? You're back?

Yes! I'm here. Where are you? Why aren't you at the banquet?

I had to get away.

Why?

Caelia wanted me to stay with her. Morgan could feel the boy's disgust. *She was saying things to me. She was getting too close. I found out where the dungeon is and I ran off. She sent her Muryan knights to chase me. I'm going there now.*

Morgan was annoyed with him. *I told you to stay! What are you doing?*

I'm going to rescue Jack and Joan. In her head, Merlin sounded puzzled. *Isn't that what you wanted?*

Yes, but … Morgan didn't know how to explain. *The Muryans aren't what you think they are. I'm here with the Elven. We used magic to light a torch and a thorn tree to show what they really are. And to rescue all the children. I've got Mabon and Maglore.*

She sensed Merlin looking at the scene in the hall through her eyes and his sudden jolt of shock.

What…? But … what …?

Morgan looked through his eyes to see he was running down through the pathways where she had been before. *We'll come and get you.*

Aynia had risen into the air again with the three children on her back. "We have to go and get my friend," Morgan said in a loud voice above the mayhem. "He's gone to the dungeon to rescue the Piskies."

"Hold on." Aynia flew across the hall, out of the mud-burrows of fleeing ants, and towards the tunnels. The smoke from the blackthorn tree was enveloping the hill and all inside it. Clutching the twins, Morgan could just see the passageways through the murk as Aynia sped through.

Shadowy figures came running towards them. As they got closer, Morgan recognised Agnes. She was leading a group of children. Her demeanour had completely changed. Colour bloomed in her cheeks and she was smiling. When she saw Morgan, her face lit up.

"We're free!" she cried. "Look! We've all changed back!"

Though dimmed by the smoke, the crowd of captured children with her looked normal. There were no more ugly, hairy, limping creatures. They were children again.

"You used your magic!" Agnes exclaimed. She shrank at the sight of Aynia. But Morgan nodded at her to reassure her and the girl looked up with eager desperation. "Can you get us out of here?"

"Yes," Morgan replied at once, as Aynia hovered impatiently. "But we have to go and get my friend first. Wait for us under the hill."

Aynia and Morgan zoomed off, Agnes looking wistfully after them. They flew downwards at breakneck speed, darting through the different levels of the Muryan nest. Aynia swerved into a stony hollow deep underground where dozens of miniature holes were carved into the wall of rock.

In front of the rocky wall, revealed by a surge of smoke, four menacing Muryan-ants stood guard. Merlin was standing before them, staring fixedly at one of them as they bore down on him. The fiery glint in his eye told Morgan he was trying to do what she had done – hurt them with magic. But four would be too much for him.

Merlin's ant made the humming noise Morgan had heard before. It flinched and curled up in pain. Without stopping to think, Morgan focused her mind on one of the others, willing it pain.

After a moment it too trembled uncontrollably and scampered away into the outside passage. Aynia charged at the third and pierced it between her sharp jaws until it went limp. The fourth, seeing what was happening, tried to run away.

Morgan's and Merlin's eyes locked. Then, as one, they directed their minds' energies towards hurting the creature. Humming turned into high-pitched screaming. The creature shook violently. Then it went rigid and keeled over, finally lying still.

Merlin was gazing up at Morgan. His dark eyes were alight. Then he stared at the Elven. He didn't seem afraid. He looked fascinated.

"Where are Jack and Joan?" Morgan said to him without preamble.

"We're here!" Jack's twangy voice came from one of the holes in the rock. Merlin scrambled up and went inside. Morgan hugged the twins tight as she and Aynia waited for Merlin to emerge with the Piskies. When they did, Jack and Joan were astounded to see Morgan seated with the twins on the back of the airborne Elven.

"You came back for us!" Jack exclaimed.

"Why?" Joan asked quietly.

"We weren't going to leave you," Morgan said earnestly.

The Piskies looked at each other, then back at Morgan.

"Our chains vanished," Joan told her. "We were chained to the wall and then they just ... disappeared."

"Like smoke," Jack added. "We couldn't get out because the Muryan guards ..."

"The Muryan magic has been broken," Aynia interrupted. The Piskies fell silent, awestruck at the sight of her. But the Elven had no time for them. "We must go. Now. Bring the boy."

She turned and flew back out into the tunnels. Glancing back, Morgan saw the Piskies on either side of Merlin. They took him by the arms and leapt into the air, flying after the Elven as she winged her way upwards through the labyrinth.

Under the faerie dome chaos had spread. Morgan could barely see through the blackthorn smoke, but something was happening. Wings whirring, Cleena and Una joined them in mid-air.

"Did you catch Caelia?" Aynia demanded.

"Almost," Una replied. "But then we didn't need to. The usurper will pay for what she did."

"We left her to her fate," added Cleena. There was a smirk in her voice.

Through the haze emerged a terrifying sight. The Muryans were not alone. And they weren't panicking anymore. They were fighting. The spindly stick-like figures of their opponents were instantly recognisable.

Piskies had entered the dome. Surging in by their dozens from the hill outside and spilling into the cavern, they were attacking any Muryans in their path. Among them was Twadell, the Piskie King himself, his wrinkled face scrunched up in angry triumph as he beat down on the faerie-insect Muryans with relentless hatred. The green Piskie with grass-like hair was alongside him, fighting and screaming and wrestling with a half-faerie, half-ant Muryan knight.

A ferocious battle was being waged. The Muryans lunged at the Piskies with their swords or tore at them with their fangs. The Piskies clubbed the Muryans with sticks and stones, attacking them with sharp teeth and claw-like nails. Caelia was in the middle of the mayhem, defended by a circle of Muryans. Occasionally she blasted the oncoming Piskies with magical sparks from her horns, stopping the attackers in their tracks.

"How did the Piskies get here?" Morgan shouted above the noise. She turned to Jack and Joan, who looked as stunned as she was. Merlin, suspended between them, seemed riveted by what was going on. It was almost as if he were enjoying it.

"We've never been able to get this far by ourselves before!" Jack yelled. "The Muryans' magic always stopped us!"

"But now the Muryan magic is broken," Morgan said to herself, echoing Aynia's words. Suddenly remembering, she looked around urgently for Agnes and the other children. She had told them to wait for her there. Had they been hurt?

In the midst of the battle below, a flash of white caught her eye. A white arm. Red-brown curls. A familiar face. Freckles.

"Arcile! ARCILE!"

Arcile was on the ground among the Piskies, signalling

feverishly. Morgan leaned down to Aynia and pointed. "That's our friend! We have to go to her!"

"What *is* that?" the blue-black Elven inquired with distaste.

"She's a Wisp," Morgan said. "She helped us get here." Then she added archly, "She's one of Diana's girls. She'll take us back to Diana."

The Elven didn't reply, but Morgan could tell she didn't need to say anything else. Aynia, Cleena and Una dived down towards Arcile. "Give the boy to Una and follow us!" Aynia commanded Jack and Joan. The Piskies obeyed, depositing Merlin on the back of the red-winged Elven and following in their wake.

Cleena swooped to the ground and grasped the astonished Arcile, lightly throwing the Wisp onto her white back before ascending into the air with the others once more. The Piskies were so busy fighting the Muryans they didn't notice.

Morgan was immensely happy and relieved to see her. "Arcile!" she exclaimed. She wanted to reach out her hand but dared not let go of the twins. Arcile caught her balance on Cleena's back as the three Elven faced each other, wings humming. The Wisp smiled at Morgan.

"You found him," she said proudly, looking at Mabon. "But who's the girl?"

"She's his twin, Maglore," Morgan said. Then, before Arcile could react, she changed the subject. "But how did *you* get here? And how come the Piskies are here? Did they hurt you?"

"They brought me with them," Arcile said. "They didn't hurt me. You remember the yellow-haired Piskie? The one who wanted us killed? I recognised him. He was the boy from my village I told you about – the strange one everyone was afraid of. The one whose parents beat him and threw him into the fire and left him in the snow to die. The Piskies found him and took his soul. He's one of them now. He remembered me. He remembered I was kind to him. He spoke for me. They were going to let me go. But I made them come here. I told them that if you could break the magic, they'd be able to get inside the realm and attack the Muryans. That way we'd be able to get Mabon out while they were all fighting each other. I came up the hill with them and we saw the faerie hill was open. But, Morgan – why did you bring the girl?"

"I can't leave her," Morgan said. "She should get another chance to live, too."

"Morgan ..." Arcile began, but Aynia interrupted them.

"Enough of this," the blue-black Elven ordered, addressing Arcile. "We agreed to help this ... whatever she is ... get the children out in exchange for her getting us our magic back and returning us to our natural forms. If she cannot do it, then she swore to us Diana would. If you are one of Diana's spirits, we demand that you take us to her."

"I will, my lady," Arcile said, momentarily startled. "But first, Morgan" – she turned back to her former little mistress – "Diana's task was only to bring the boy's soul to her. We can't take the girl's as well."

Morgan suddenly felt furious. After everything she had seen and been through, she had had enough. "No! Maglore is coming with us! And not only her. All the other children here are coming too!"

"Morgan, you can't!" Arcile said in alarm.

"She doesn't understand," Aynia remarked as Cleena made a sound like a snigger. Una was silent but Morgan sensed sympathy from her. Merlin, seated upon Una's back, also said nothing, but his watchful eyes stayed on Morgan.

"Wait." Jack the Piskie, bobbing in the air behind them, spoke up. "You're taking Mabon and Maglore with *you*?"

"That's right," Merlin told him curtly before Morgan could respond.

"So you never *meant* to bring them back to us." Jack's voice took on a nasty tone, like when they had first heard him on the moor."

Morgan didn't care. "No!" she snapped, still angry. "I came here to get them for Diana. She's going to make them live again. They don't belong to you!"

The boy Piskie's eyes narrowed. He made as if to lunge at her. But Joan put her hand on his arm.

"No," the girl Piskie said quietly. "Let them go."

Jack was dumbfounded. "*What*? Why?"

"Because they came back for us," Joan said. She nodded at Morgan, who gave her a small grateful smile. Jack looked sullen, but made no further protest.

The battle beneath them was still fraught with violence. Muryans and Piskies continued fighting fiercely. Many of them lay on the ground, torn into pieces as a cat would tear a mouse. Morgan couldn't bear to look.

They had to get out. She caught sight of Agnes and the other children huddled together under some stones that had once been glittering fountains.

"There!" she said to Aynia. "Let's get them out!"

"Morgan!" Arcile sounded desperate now. "Wait! You don't know what you're doing!"

But Morgan ignored her. The Elven glanced at each other and flew towards the hidden children without a word, leaving Jack and Joan behind them.

A shriek rose from below. Into the air leapt the little yellow-haired Piskie and he hovered before them, his old-man face contorted with fury. It was hard to believe he had once been a human boy.

"You're not going anywhere!" the Piskie hissed.

"Oh, yes we are," Morgan said defiantly. "We're leaving."

"Mabon and Maglore are ours!"

"No, they aren't!"

The Piskie looked away from Morgan to stare at Arcile in rage and disbelief. "I helped you! I stopped the King from hurting you. I got him to *listen* to you! Is that why you wanted us to come here? So you could help this girl rob us and betray us?"

"I'm sorry, Yallery," Arcile said. She sounded tearful.

"Get out of the way!" Cleena bellowed at him.

The Piskie looked wary for a moment, but then he stared at Morgan. A look of such intense hatred crossed his face that she was alarmed. "You're all the same," he snarled. "All humans. You're cruel, treacherous, evil. There's nothing good in you. You don't deserve what you've been given. You torture your children. Torment your loved ones. Betray your friends. Those children are better off with us! Give them to me!"

"Enough!" Aynia signalled the other two Elven and the three of them charged at Yallery. He darted out of the way, but tried to knock Merlin off Una's back as they sped past. At the same time, Morgan and Merlin directed their minds' energies at him and the Piskie was blasted back down to the ground. Without looking back, Morgan focused on Agnes and the other children. As soon as she saw her, Agnes emerged from her hiding place and came running towards her. The other children followed.

"Princess Light-Eyes!" Agnes cried.

Morgan had forgotten her silly Piskie name up till then. There was no time to explain. "We're going," she told them. "Follow us."

Holding Mabon and Maglore close, Morgan rode out on Aynia, flanked by Arcile riding on Cleena and Merlin on Una. With Agnes and the children running after them, they flew out from under the faerie dome onto the windswept hill.

The smoke-filled air of the moonlit night hit them with full force. The Elven flew towards the bonfire of burning blackthorn, now a shell of a tree with the wind crackling shards of glowing orange flames from its branches into the sky.

The Elven landed softly on the ground, and Morgan, Merlin and Arcile slipped off their backs. Morgan lifted up baby Mabon and gave him to Merlin. Arcile looked at her, but Morgan didn't look back. She held on to tiny Maglore, determined not to let her go. Arcile seemed about to say something but thought better of it.

They waited in silence in the glowing light and heat of the tree's fire. The Elven spread and fluttered their wings impatiently. After a while, the grass began to move and the formerly captive children emerged one by one from the tall blades, Agnes among them. They crowded round Morgan expectantly, eagerly.

"Look!" Merlin held Mabon clumsily in the crook of one arm. With the other he was pointing up the hill.

The rocky cavern that had been the faerie dome was silhouetted with figures. Muryans and Piskies. Together.

Clearly they had been alerted that the children had gone. The battle had been abandoned. Instead, they were coming down the hill after them. The grass blades were twitching. Dozens were moving towards them. Shouts and screeches and other horrible sounds were carried on the wind. Morgan suddenly remembered Yallery's look of hatred. She blanched.

"Quick!" she said. "We must get big again. All of us. Arcile!"

The Wisp didn't reply. Morgan rounded on her angrily. "*Arcile!* We have to get big! Now! Help us!"

"Reverse the spell you said before," Arcile said reluctantly. "Like this:

By the glow of the Moon's full light
Give us the will to change this night
Wise true ancients, near and far
Shift our shapes to what we are."

Morgan and Merlin chanted the spell together. Agnes and the children moved closer to them, wide-eyed and scared. Morgan looked up at the full Moon, her constant companion throughout this seemingly endless night. (Could it really still be the same night?) She hugged baby Maglore and closed her eyes.

Her legs and arms and neck began to stretch and elongate. Her head expanded outwards. Her body was being pulled out as far as it would go. The pain was intense, but she would not make a sound. She heard the other children whimpering around her.

When the pain stopped, she opened her eyes. The first thing she saw was Maglore, a normal-sized baby girl in her arms. Then she saw Merlin awkwardly holding Mabon, both of them normal size. The burning blackthorn was an ordinary-sized tree. A white flicker of light told her that Arcile was back to being a Wisp to her. She couldn't see the Elven; they would still be in the grass. The Muryan domain was nothing but a small hillock harbouring an ants' nest.

A crowd of children stood before her. Some were her size, some taller. At first they were mesmerised, staring at each other and then down at their own selves, unable to believe what they were seeing. Then they started laughing in wonder. Agnes was among them. A pretty, rosy, brown-haired girl with shining eyes and a merry smile. "You did it!" she said. "We're back! We're human again!" She laughed in delight.

As Agnes laughed, Morgan started to smile too. Then her smile faded. Something wasn't right.

Unlike her and Merlin and the two baby souls, the captive children didn't stop growing. They shot up into older children. Then they became young adults. Then grown-ups. Agnes changed from a young girl into a young woman in a matter of seconds.

"What's happening?" Morgan cried, afraid.

No one answered. Agnes grew into a mature woman, then an older grown-up. Her hair grew longer, lanker, less brown, streaked with grey, finally white. Her rosy complexion turned ruddy, then pale, then grey. Lines spread across her smooth skin until she was wrinkled and shrivelled.

Agnes' laughter sputtered and died. She and the other children grew old and gnarled and ancient before Morgan's eyes. Their bodies shrank. Their flesh rotted. In the end they were nothing but skeletons. Their bones crumbled to dust. The wind blew the ashes of the hidden children away into the vastness and emptiness of the night.

XIV

A Dying World

"*NO!!!!!*"

Morgan's scream flew away into the wind in the wake of the remnants of the children. Her breath felt as if it had been punched out of her.

"What happened to them?" Merlin demanded. He sounded as shocked as she was. His own face was ashen.

"I'm so sorry, Morgan." Arcile's bell-like voice was sad and sombre. "The children were already dead. They were captured many years ago when they were still alive – maybe even hundreds of years before now."

"The only reason they were still on this earth was the Muryans' magic." Aynia's strange voice was much fainter.

Through her tears Morgan saw the three now tiny Elven humming in the air before her. She realised dimly through her shock and horror that they were very pretty, delicate insects – Aynia a slender blue damselfly, Cleena a white-plumed moth, Una a red-winged beetle.

"Even the Muryans' magic couldn't sustain the children completely," Aynia said.

"That's why over time they became those ugly brutes you saw," Cleena added.

"Their mortal lives were prolonged unnaturally," Una said, buzzing close to Morgan's face. "It turned them inhuman. They weren't able to grow up properly as children should."

"I only wanted to save them," Morgan said. Her tears were choking her.

"Why didn't you tell us before?" Merlin said to Arcile and the Elven. His voice shook.

"The Wisp tried," Aynia replied before Arcile could answer. "Morgan wouldn't listen. But it's too late now. We fulfilled our end of the bargain. You have the souls of the two you were sent for. Now you must fulfil your side. Either you restore our magic and our original forms, or you get Diana to do it."

Morgan, Merlin thought.

He didn't communicate anything else, but looked towards the hill and the moving grasses. Morgan felt so devastated at what had happened to Agnes and the other children she could barely move. But she could still hear the shrieks of the Piskies and the Muryans bearing down on them. She knew they had to hurry.

"We have to get to Diana," she said, wiping her eyes. "Arcile, we have to go to her and tell her we've got Mabon."

The Wisp floated up to her. "You don't have to go to her," Arcile said earnestly. "You can use the blackthorn tree before it burns out to summon the Wild Hunt to you. Circle the tree three times. Then stare into the dying fire and ask to see the Hunt."

Still stupefied from shock, holding Maglore and catching her breath in sobs, Morgan did as she was bidden. She stumbled around the tree three times, as fast as her quaking legs would carry her. She then stopped and stared into the remains of the fire. The blackthorn was long since dead. The flames engulfing its charred husk were sinking lower and lower, flickering in the wind. Soon they would be no more.

Suddenly Merlin let out a yell. "Hurry!"

He was clutching Mabon and fighting off screeching Piskies. They had caught up and were leaping into the air to attack him. Merlin was trying to balance holding Mabon in one arm while beating the flying Piskies off with the other. Threatening Muryan-ants were encroaching upon him and crawling up his legs. He was losing his balance and was about to drop the baby boy.

The Elven dived at the Muryans and Piskies, trying to protect both Merlin and Mabon.

"Do it, Morgan!" cried Arcile, still at her side.

Morgan whirled round and stared back into the flames with a ferocity that matched that of fire itself. *Bring me the Wild Hunt! Come to me again! Come to me now! Bring the Wild Hunt to me!*

A far-off rumbling sounded across the moor. Softly galloping horses' hooves grew louder as the riders of the Hunt materialised one by one in the moonlit sky. Calls rang out and the eerie yet familiar blast of a trumpet resounded in the air.

As the Hunt approached, they filled the sky with glistening horses and banners blazing. The small Piskies and Muryans fled terrified in all directions, their power and menace abated in the face of the oncoming Hunt's warriors and maidens, children and hounds, half-animals and half-humans.

Leading the pack was Diana. Her silver chariot flashed and sliced through the night sky like a steel spear. The Queen drove her black and white winged steeds round and round overhead above the smouldering blackthorn. As the last flames from the tree went out, the Huntress landed her Moon-chariot on the hill.

At the sight of Diana, Morgan's sick guilt and shocked misery were swept up in a wave of such enormous relief that she felt giddy. Here at last was a grown-up. Someone who could help. Someone who could advise. Reassure. Comfort. She might be a faerie or Goddess or whatever people wanted to call her, but she was a grown-up, and a wise and powerful one. She would know what to do and what to say. Morgan could let her decide everything. Diana could take control. She could make everything better and make the horrors of the night go away.

The Moon Huntress looked as breathtakingly beautiful as ever. Her black eyes shone with warmth and affection as she descended gracefully from her chariot and glided over to Morgan. "My beloved child," she said happily, and caught Morgan and baby Maglore together in a tight embrace.

Morgan felt the tears flow again as she cradled Maglore and nestled in Diana's arms. Murmurs of approval and glad laughter spread through the company arrayed in the air above them.

Diana released Morgan and looked upon her and the baby girl. Her smile froze.

"What is this?"

Morgan swallowed. "This is Maglore," she said eagerly, blinking away her tears. "She's ..."

"This is not the child I asked you to bring." The Huntress' voice had turned to ice.

"No," Morgan faltered nervously. "He's there." She pointed to

Mabon, in Merlin's arms. "Maglore was with him. She's his twin. She was stolen too. I couldn't leave her."

"And who is that?" Diana's eyes were now cold and forbidding as she looked upon Merlin. "Did I not tell you that you were to do this alone?"

"Yes, but …"

"How *dare* you disobey me!"

Diana's reprimand was like the lash of a whip. Gone was the reassuring beauty and loving presence. The wrathful Huntress was suddenly terrifying, towering ominously over her like a shadow.

Morgan cringed. "I *did* do it alone!" she protested. "I found the Elven by myself! *I* rescued the children!"

"My lady." Arcile's white light expanded and she stood before Diana as a young girl again. "My lady, Morgan didn't ask this boy to come with her. He followed her. She tried to leave him, but he wouldn't stay behind."

"And why did you do that?" Diana's cold voice addressed Merlin directly.

Throughout the appearance of the Wild Hunt and the exchange with Diana, Merlin had stayed completely silent. The expression on his usually unreadable countenance was one of absolute awe. There was something else there, too. He seemed resentful. Of what, Morgan couldn't imagine. When Diana addressed him, a brief flash of fear crossed his face. But he controlled it and answered her in a steady voice.

"Because I'm Morgan's friend."

Diana looked at him for a long moment. Merlin dropped his gaze hastily and could not meet her eyes.

"That's not the only reason, though, is it?" the Huntress observed. She looked at him as if she saw right inside him. Merlin said nothing, but clutched Mabon tighter and squirmed under her penetrating stare.

Morgan was trembling. She held Maglore close, determined not to let the baby go. Diana turned back to her. Looking at the frightened little girl, the Huntress' eyes and voice softened.

"I understand why you did what you did, Morgan. I know you want to help people. But it isn't always possible. It is Mabon's soul that is destined to live again. He has a new life I can give him. He has a fate to fulfil. But there is nowhere for Maglore to go. It was her time. I cannot help her."

Morgan couldn't believe what she was hearing.

"But you *must* help her! There *must* be something you can do! Please! It's not fair!"

"Perhaps we can help."

The three Elven were hovering in the air beside them. Aynia, in the middle, had spoken up.

Diana looked surprised. "Aynia?" she said in disbelief. "Is that you?"

"We didn't think you'd remember us," the damselfly replied. "It's been a long, long time, hasn't it?"

"What happened to you?" the Huntress demanded of the fluttering insects in front of her.

"A long story. Our powers were stolen by one of our own and we were turned into these. The child here promised to restore us if we helped her with the task you set her." Aynia paused. "But she's still too young and too new to her magic. It is down to you to honour the bargain."

Diana frowned. Then, without saying a word, light energy surged out of her, radiating from her body. The energy was so pure, so tangible, it was almost fluidic. Liquid. An irresistible magnetism emanated from the Huntress – so strong that Morgan and the others felt pulled towards her by an overwhelming force, powerless to stop it. The liquid light washed over the insect Elven in a flash of blinding white.

The next moment, three stunningly beautiful girls stood in their place. Cleena, the most exquisite, golden-haired and blue-eyed. Aynia, the most striking, her hair blue-black in colour, her eyes a deep brown. And Una, the most approachably lovely, with flame-red hair and moss-green eyes. All of them had shining, transparent wings.

Aynia gazed at her outstretched hand and laughed softly. Cleena broke into a satisfied smile and Una grinned with delight.

"Thank you," Aynia said to Diana.

Diana did not smile. "What happened to those whom you led?"

"They fell into corruption and greed," Aynia replied. "They were destroyed by their own illusions and their refusal to accept the truth."

"There's nothing we can do for them now," Cleena asserted.

"No trace remains of what they once were," Una said.

Morgan was listening to this anxiously. Shyly, she stepped forward to the three grown-up sized Elven. "Won't you go back to the Muryans?" she asked.

"The Muryans are finished," Aynia said. Her tone was harsh and unforgiving. "There's nothing we or anyone else can do to stop that."

"If we'd been able to break Caelia's spell a long time ago, we might have been able to help them," Una told her.

"It's too late now," Cleena declared, somewhat nastily.

"But what will happen to them?"

The Elven looked at each other.

"They will diminish until they are nothing but ants," Aynia said at last. "Mute and blind and crawling in the depths of the earth forever. It won't be long now." She turned to address Diana again. "You must be aware of what's happening. We can't stay here."

"Where do you intend to go?" the Huntress asked.

Morgan wondered why Diana didn't ask them to stay with her. Couldn't they join the Wild Hunt? A little smile played upon Aynia's lips.

"We'll leave here for the emerald island across the sea. There our kind still stand strong, at least for now."

The black-haired Elven turned to Morgan. "We'll take the soul of the girl-twin with us." Her eyes looked deep into Morgan's. "Who knows? Maybe we or the child here will find a place for her one day."

"What makes you think either of you can?" Diana asked coldly. She sounded angry. Affronted.

Aynia looked directly at Diana. For the first time, Morgan realised that Aynia and the Huntress didn't like each other. Even though Diana had restored the Elven and their magic, their unfriendliness to each other was obvious.

"If this child is truly her mother's daughter, there's no reason why she couldn't," Aynia said evenly. "Besides, we were always the ones who took care of the unwanted souls."

Before Diana could respond, the black-haired Elven held out her arms for Maglore. "Let us take her, Morgan. We'll look after her."

Morgan looked nervously at Diana, but the Huntress was staring at Aynia. Reluctantly, Morgan handed the baby girl over to the Elven. Aynia cradled Maglore and the baby cooed happily.

"Let's go." Cleena unfolded her shimmering wings and rose into the air. Aynia, with a last parting look at Morgan, followed. "I know who you really are, Morgan," she said as she rose higher and further away. "Remember us."

"Wait!" Morgan grasped Una's arm, just as she was about to ascend with the others. "What does she mean? Who am I? Why do you have to go? Why can't you stay in Belerion?"

Una sighed.

"You saw what became of our realm, Morgan. We failed. Our world is dying. And there is no one to save it."

Una gave her a sad smile and rose into the air to join the others. Without looking back, the three Elven flew up into the sky amidst the gathered riders of the Hunt, then across the moor and out of sight.

"Take the baby boy."

Diana's curt command startled Morgan. The stag-headed Smertullos descended from above on a dark grey steed and landed in front of Merlin. So shocked was the boy at the sight that he almost dropped Mabon.

Merlin and Smertullos stared at each other for a few seconds without moving. Then Merlin slowly handed the baby over. The boy shuddered.

So captivated was Morgan by Smertullos and Mabon's return on horseback to the watchful retinue in the sky that she hadn't noticed Diana was observing her again. The Huntress' beautiful face had softened once more. There was a warmth and intensity of feeling in her expression that made Morgan's insides tingle.

"I'm sorry I was angry with you," Diana said gently. "You did well." When Morgan didn't answer, the Huntress added, "But you're still unhappy, aren't you?"

"The other children," was all Morgan could say. "The hidden children. The ones the Muryans took. They died. They" – she choked up, remembering the awful way they had crumbled to dust – "were blown away in the wind. I couldn't save them."

Diana was sympathetic. "I know, Morgan. I told you at our first meeting that there are many things in this world that are cruel and unjust. Not everyone can be saved. Do you think I didn't want to save the baby girl, too? It isn't a question of not wanting to do the right thing."

The Huntress knelt down in front of the little girl and took both her hands. To Morgan's surprise, Diana sounded tired. "But I will tell you this. I am happy that you tried. I used to be like you. I wanted to save everyone. I wanted to change the world. But I couldn't change everything I wanted to change. Even I don't have the power."

"But you should still try," Morgan argued. "You said so. You said never stop fighting to make unjust things right." She struggled to put into words what she wanted to say. "Diana, the Muryans had a horrible world. They had magic and they could have changed it. They could have got the Elven back. The Elven could have helped them. But the Muryans just pretended everything was good. They pretended their Queen was beautiful and good and it was all pretty and nice. Why didn't they try to make the real world better, instead of making a pretend one? Why do it ... why have it ... if it's not real?"

Diana broke into a smile. "That's a very good question." She paused. "You'll find this is something common to all beings, in the mortal world and in ours. When people don't want to face the truth, they often pretend. They create a world for themselves that they pretend is real. Instead of, as you say, trying to make the real world better, they create an illusion they can pretend is real."

"Why?"

"Many reasons." The Huntress looked up at her company of riders in the sky. "It's difficult for you to understand now. You're very young. But, sometimes, people who have been fighting to change things for a long, long time can become tired and disillusioned. Pretending the world is better than it is – creating an illusion that it is better – makes it easier to bear. Even if it's just a dream, it can lift us up out of a dark place. That dream, that illusion, can sometimes give us the strength to continue to fight. It can give us something to fight *for*, a better world.

"But other times illusion is used to serve the lazy and the selfish. Like the Muryans. They prefer easy, unchallenging gratification to facing up to the truth. That way they don't *have* to fight. That way they don't have to do anything themselves to make the world a better place. The illusion does it for them. They wilfully delude themselves and do nothing, and point to their illusion to convince themselves and others that everything is right with the world, that nothing is really wrong. That way they fool themselves into thinking that they don't have to do anything to change things. That they don't have to accept hard truths. That they don't have to make every effort to *make* everything right with the world."

Morgan found this hard to understand. She was so very tired and her head felt so thick and dull and heavy that she thought she would faint. The words all sounded very far away. Her clothes and skin were thick with dirt and grime, her hair felt matted and tangled, and she was suddenly aware that she was very, very hungry. She hadn't eaten for hours and hours and hours. What time was it? What *day* was it? She looked up at the sky. It was still night-time. But it couldn't be the same night, could it? So much time had passed. So much had *happened*.

She could barely keep her eyes open. The riders of the Hunt above her were blurred, as though she were seeing them through ripples of water at the bottom of a pool. She looked over at Merlin and he was blurry too. How long had they been here? How long had they been away? Were they looking for them at Tintagel?

"It's time for you to return." Diana's voice cut through Morgan's stupor. "Dyonas! Summon the horses." The Huntress put her arms around the little girl and looked into her eyes. Morgan tried to summon her strength to face her one last time.

"Your horses are here," Diana said. There on the hill stood Dyonas, holding the steeds they had lost and left behind. Swiftback and Windbane. "Follow them back along the paths that lead out of the moor. From there they will carry you home."

Slowly, Morgan went over to Swiftback and reached up to stroke his neck, hardly daring to believe the horse was real. But Swiftback was warm, solid, his horsehair smooth, his mane scratchy. Merlin hurried over to join her, standing beside Windbane. Arcile folded back into her white light and flickered around Morgan's head, bidding her a silent farewell.

The winged black and white horses drew Diana's silver chariot forward and she stepped into it, grasping the shining reins. She looked back at Morgan.

"Until next time."

The Huntress and her chariot rose into the sky. Her retinue of riders parted smoothly to allow her through and closed ranks behind her. Dyonas gave an impish grin as he placed his silver trumpet to his lips. Setting off to the trumpet's blare, the Wild Hunt galloped across the sky, led by their Huntress Queen, briefly passing as shadow silhouettes upon the white surface of the full Moon until they disappeared into the night.

A stillness fell. The burned tree stood blackened and lifeless. The hill was deserted. The sky was empty. Away into the distance stretched the moor, vast and unyielding. There was no movement, no presence, no sound save that of the wind, blowing softer now.

Merlin was staring at her. He didn't say anything. Morgan was too weary to meet his eyes. Swirls of inky black clouds spread over the Moon until its light was smothered. The land descended into darkness, as if a torch had been snuffed out.

XV

The Oncoming Storm

"Don't you believe me?"

Looking around at her friends, Morgan was frustrated that she couldn't hear what they thought. After she had breathlessly related all her adventures on the moor that night, she had expected exclamations of astonishment and excitement and wonder. But they stayed silent.

They were in the stables. Safir was cleaning Gorlois' armour on a wooden trestle table. Taliesin was standing beside her, polishing a bejewelled gold neckpiece Morgan had never seen before. It must be something belonging to his new master Cadwellon, since he was no longer doing page boy chores. Fleur was sitting on a small bale of hay, unaware that bits of straw were sticking to her pretty red dress as she stared at Morgan, her chin cupped in her hand.

It was Fleur who spoke first. "I don't know, Morgan. I don't like it. All of this sounds horrible, whatever it is. It doesn't sound good."

"What do you mean, good?"

"Well." Fleur hesitated. "It sounds like what Father Elfodd was telling us about. It sounds like all these things were demons trying to trick you. To trap you."

"But they weren't demons," Morgan protested. "They were Piskies and Muryans. They were faeries, like the ones Cadwellon told us about. And Diana's not a demon. She's beautiful and good."

She appealed to Taliesin. "*You* must know. Cadwellon's your master now. He must be teaching you these things."

"I don't know." Taliesin's strange gold-flecked eyes looked directly at her. He seemed uncomfortable. "Grand Master Cadwellon hasn't told me much yet. I'm still learning how to be an apprentice. But … I don't know. I've heard about magic. But I've never seen it."

Morgan couldn't contain herself. "Yes, you have!" she said indignantly. "That day we came back from your village, you and me and Merlin saw the Wisp on the path. The little white light? That was Arcile. We all saw it. I know you did!"

Taliesin pursed his lips. "I don't know what I saw that day," he said stubbornly.

"Is this a game, Morgan?" Fleur asked suddenly. She was frowning.

"Is what a game?" Morgan asked, genuinely puzzled.

"Pretending you have magic, I mean. Saying you made yourself small so you could meet faeries. All the stuff about Diana and Arcile and the faerie queen, and the – the Muryans in their underground realm and them really being ants. And the Elven who were really insects who turned into beautiful faeries. And the Piskies."

"It's *not* a game," Morgan protested.

"You told Father Elfodd that you think your maid is still here, even after she died," Fleur said. "Maybe you want her to be here. But it isn't true."

"Father Elfodd said it could be true," Morgan retorted. "He said people's souls could come back to see them after they died. And it *is* true. Arcile *is* still here."

"And it can't be true that you have magic," Fleur went on. To Morgan's annoyance, the princess seemed determined to argue with her. "Magic is evil. Anyone who has magic is evil. That's what the Church says. Anyone who has magic is a witch."

"I'm not a witch!" Morgan was upset. "And I do have magic. I do!"

"Why don't you show us, then?" Taliesin asked. "If you have magic, show us."

Morgan hesitated. She had to admit that now she was in daylight, surrounded by everyday smells and sounds, she didn't feel at all magical.

"Well ... I can't do it right now," she said feebly. "When I was on the moor, Arcile helped me. I used the Moon's power to get small and then big again. And the Elven helped me set the blackthorn tree on fire."

Fleur and Taliesin didn't say anything. They just exchanged

furtive glances.

Morgan continued hurriedly, in a futile attempt to explain. "Also, there's magic in the faerie world. It's like … I *feel* magic. I felt it when I was there. It isn't here now, so I can't do it."

When they still didn't reply, she felt angry again. "So you think I'm lying?"

Safir spoke up for the first time. "I don't believe you are lying." She looked over at Morgan. "I understand of what you speak. I know of creatures like the ones you saw."

Morgan was thrilled and grateful at the same time. "You know about Piskies and Muryans?"

"Not exactly." The squire stopped working for a moment and turned to the others. "In my country we have many stories about Small People. They're tiny people or spirits that are not from our world but live in it. We call them Peris. Sometimes they can be good, sometimes they are bad. They have magic like you say. They can control things in nature – the movement of the Sun, the clouds, the rivers, the crops."

"So you have magic and faeries in Babylon, too!"

Safir smiled. "And other things also. When I was in Armorica, I heard tales like the stories my mother told me. You have what you call angels and demons and other spirits, yes? So do we. We have Yazatas and Djinns and Devs. Yazatas are beings of goodness and light. They are spirits of the earth and sky, gods and goddesses, who protect our world and serve Ahura Mazda, the Great One. Djinns are creatures of the wind. They rebelled against Ahura Mazda, and now they have to live in the desert and other dead places. They can change into any shape they want or be invisible to our eyes."

"Djinns are like demons, then," Fleur said. "They rebelled against God."

Morgan was fascinated. This was the first time she'd ever heard of this. Demons had rebelled against God? *Why?* she wondered. What had God done to make them rebel against him?

"But Djinns are not always bad," Safir told them. "They can give great gifts and magical power to the people they like. Sometimes they fall in love with humans and have children with them."

"They can be bad, though?" Morgan asked.

Safir nodded. "Very bad. But not as bad as the Devs. They are very, very bad. They serve Ahura Mazda's enemy, Ahriman, the Destroyer. They are always fighting with the Peris. The Devs hate everything that is good and beautiful." She paused for a moment. "I saw a Peri once."

"Where? How?" Morgan asked eagerly.

"Many years ago. In my country. When I was very young."

"Really? What was it like? Was it like a Piskie or a Muryan?"

"She was like one of your Muryans – at least before you saw what they really were. She was very beautiful, very tiny. Shining with light." Safir's eyes grew distant at the memory. "So, yes, Morgan. I believe you."

"But ... how do you know they're real?" Taliesin asked cautiously, clearly not wanting to annoy Morgan further. "You say they can be invisible and we can't see them all the time. How do you know you didn't dream it?"

But Morgan was still annoyed with him. "I know I didn't!" she snapped. "You heard what Safir said. *She* saw a faerie in her country, too. And anyway, Merlin was with me the whole way. He saw everything. How could we ...?"

She stopped suddenly as the thought struck her. After all, there *had* been a time when they had dreamed the same dream.

"Yes, but just because Merlin says it doesn't mean it's true," Fleur countered with a knowing smile.

"Why not?"

Fleur's smile widened. "Merlin likes you, Morgan. He'll say anything you tell him to if you ask him."

Morgan's face felt strangely hot. "That isn't true!" she said fiercely.

Safir grinned along with Fleur and soon the two were giggling. Morgan's blush deepened. More than anything, she hated to be laughed at. She felt cross with Fleur for saying such a stupid thing. And for not believing her story. Why was she being so mean? Taliesin didn't join in with the laughter. Instead, he frowned.

At that moment, Merlin walked down into the stable from the steps leading to his family's rooms above. He was leading Ganieda, holding her arm through his. As Safir and Fleur smothered their giggles, Morgan felt herself unable to say anything.

She hadn't seen him since their long journey back to Tintagel across the moor. They hadn't said a word to each other all the way back. The horses Swiftback and Windbane hadn't needed any guidance, knowing exactly how to get home. The Moon had gradually sunk lower until it disappeared altogether, while one by one the stars gradually faded to nothingness in the brightening sky.

When they had arrived back in the castle courtyard, the Sun was just rising over the horizon, the guards were still asleep and the first faint stirrings could be heard from the servants' quarters. Morgan and Merlin had taken the horses back to the stable, then Merlin had left her and returned to his rooms without a word or a backward glance.

Morgan had puzzled over his silence and attitude as she made her way back through the castle hall and corridors. What was the matter with him? Was he angry? Upset? Grumpy? Tired?

Fleur had been still asleep when she crept back into their room. Morgan had scrubbed herself clean in a tub of water brought by a servant before her friend had woken up. Since Arcile had gone, Morgan no longer had a personal maid. She didn't even know the name of the servant who had brought the water. The woman had said nothing to her, had not even commented on her dirty and dishevelled appearance. In fact, she had barely even looked at Morgan, but stared into space as if not seeing anything around her.

The servant's blank expression had reminded Morgan of Agnes and her dead eyes, and the shock and horror at what had happened to the captured children had come flooding back. She could hardly think about the awful thing that had happened to Agnes. The mousy-haired girl's terrible death, growing old in the blink of an eye and crumbling to ash in the wind – just when she was so happy and finally free. It wasn't fair. It wasn't right. Just the ghastly thought of it had made Morgan's eyes sting with tears and she had felt sick to her stomach. It had been like something out of a nightmare.

But the appearance of Merlin and Ganieda in the stables gave Morgan a feeling to hold on to, something that told her everything she knew and had seen was real. Recounting her adventures to her friends in the stables wasn't helping her make sense of the extraordinary things she had seen and done. Alarmingly, the more she tried to remember it all, the more it all became hazy and confusing.

However, the sight of Merlin in the stable now focused her mind. The way he had left abruptly when they got back and had not spoken to her upset her. The way he was now back to his typical habit of staring unsmilingly at her while avoiding her eyes irritated her. The friendship and connection she had felt for him during the adventure was leaving her, and the old annoyance was returning.

Are you alright, Morgan?

It was Ganieda's voice inside her head. The little girl's white eyes seemed to be looking directly at her. Probably seeing through her brother's mind, Morgan thought crossly. She was also still angry at Ganieda for sulking because she couldn't go with her. And for telling Merlin about Diana and her task when she knew it was supposed to be a secret.

Why did you tell your brother about Diana and about me going away from the castle? Morgan demanded, determined that Ganieda should know how angry she was.

But Ganieda looked stricken.

Morgan, I didn't mean to …

Another thought cut across Ganieda's voice, abruptly and violently. Morgan felt a sudden searing pain in her head.

My sister and I tell each other everything.

It was Merlin. His dark eyes glinted as Morgan stared at him. She hadn't been communicating with him – how had he got into her mind like that?

Ganieda was silent. Standing beside him, her arm held tightly through her brother's, the little girl's lips trembled.

Safir, Fleur and Taliesin were looking curiously at Morgan, Merlin and Ganieda. Safir eventually broke through the uncomfortable silence to address Merlin.

"Morgan's been telling us what happened to you both out on the moor, Merlin. About how you rode far away, how you crossed the moor together, and made yourselves small by magic. How you faced the Piskies and the spiders and the Muryans. How you rescued the children's stolen souls. How you met Diana and the Wild Hunt and the Elven. It must have been amazing."

"If it's true," Taliesin said under his breath. Morgan shot him an angry glare.

Merlin looked at Taliesin with dislike. "It *is* true," he retorted. "But Morgan couldn't have done it without me. She would have been lost if I hadn't gone with her."

Morgan's anger redirected itself back to Merlin. "That's a lie! You were the one who got tricked by the Piskies into the marsh! I had to save you!"

Merlin's eyes narrowed. "I would have got out without your help."

"You didn't do anything!" Morgan scoffed. "You didn't even stay and talk to Caelia like I asked. You were too scared!"

"I was not! I went and found out where the dungeon was!"

"I would have found them without you! *I* was the one who found the Elven!"

"But you both came back safe," Safir interjected hastily. "That's what's important. And something else very important is happening today."

Morgan scowled furiously at Merlin, who coldly averted his eyes from her again.

"What's happening today?" Morgan asked, acknowledging Safir's change of subject.

"Your father ordered me to prepare," the squire said, indicating the armour on the table. "The High King Vortigern and his Queen are coming to Tintagel."

"They're coming *here*?" Morgan said in surprise.

"Many nobles of Belerion are coming too," Taliesin told her. "To pay tribute to the High King. Some are already here."

"But why is King Vortigern coming here? You said before he was trying to get all the rulers of the tribes together."

"Some of the men say the High King is coming here because your father doesn't want to join him in the fight against the Pendragon brothers," Safir said. She sounded uncomfortable. "He's coming to make sure the Duke and his men fight with him."

A faint shadow crossed Morgan's vision again. "The Pendragon brothers," she remembered. "Ambrosius and Uther."

"That's right." Safir looked at her, concerned.

Morgan sat down next to Fleur, her annoyance with her friend forgotten, and Fleur reached out and held her hand. Merlin had seated Ganieda down on a stool nearby and was watching Safir, listening intently.

"Ambrosius and Uther are in Britain," the squire went on. "They've returned from Armorica with an army and landed in the far west. Just like the High King was afraid they would."

"Grand Master Cadwellon is summoning the Druid Council of Twelve to Tintagel," Taliesin added. The new apprentice had a touch of pride in his voice. "They're going to advise King Vortigern what to do against the Pendragon brothers before he meets with the Saxons."

Morgan felt another stab of pain inside her head. She looked across at Merlin. An intense surge of feeling hit her. She knew it was from him. He was now staring in his fixed way at Taliesin. Was he still cross about the page boy being the Grand Master's apprentice, even though he'd told her he was going to be apprentice to Myrddin?

Morgan recalled how she had agreed to keep Merlin being a Druid apprentice a secret. For a second, still angry at his boast, she was tempted to tell the others anyway just to spite him.

But she decided against it. After all, Myrddin wasn't an important Druid. He was only Cadwellon's assistant, Morgan thought with satisfaction. Taliesin had a much more important position than Merlin.

Merlin suddenly turned his head and looked at her. She sensed a flash of something indefinable from him. Then it disappeared abruptly. He had closed her off somehow. She couldn't feel him anymore. But there was another presence inside her mind. A different one. Ganieda. The little girl's expression was worried. Though she heard nothing, Morgan felt concern and a different kind of feeling. Her own head was aching.

* * *

All the way up to the chapel that afternoon, Morgan thought about everything she and the others had talked about. It was a blustery day; the Sun was still shining bravely but a chill wind was blowing towards Tintagel from the west. White clouds tinged with grey raced overhead, spreading slowly across the sky. The green headlands were gradually fading to brown, the bracken was crisp and crimson, and the long-stemmed grasses bent in the wind, topped with gold made brighter by the Sun. The sea had darkened to a rich blue-green, frothing and foaming white against the cliffs and rocky bays below. Amongst the circling grey and white sea-birds were several newcomers that stood out glaringly with their sleek black feathers, red legs and curved red beaks.

How different it all was compared to the Piskie and Muryan worlds beneath the earth! How strange it was to compare the lovely autumn day at Tintagel with the faerie realms! How odd it was to think of Tintagel compared with the cavernous passageway and underground stalactite chamber of the Piskies; Tintagel compared with the beautiful, dome-dominated hill of the Muryans that hid tube-like vertical tunnels containing so much ugliness underneath. Morgan gazed at the ground as she walked, gently nudging it with her foot and marvelling at what she knew she had seen, what she could still smell in her nostrils, what she could still feel on her flesh. And yet, out on the cliff path, with the autumn Sun on her hair, the westerly wind on her face and the familiar scent of sea salt on the air, both the bizarre and frightening faerie realms seemed distant now as a bad dream.

Fleur was chatting away but Morgan didn't feel much like talking. She wanted to think. Before she knew it, they had reached the chapel. Standing alone on the cliff, its stone walls seemed to reflect the increasingly grey clouds scurrying overhead. Morgan hadn't noticed before how lonely the little chapel looked. The stark stone cross outside and long windswept grasses around it only seemed to make its loneliness worse. Against the overcast sky, the wild headland and the crashing sea beyond the cliff, the chapel looked like a forlorn and forgotten sentinel, standing alone against a world that was hard and mean and cruel.

As Father Elfodd taught them about how Jesus talked about forgiving people even when they had done bad things, Morgan found she couldn't concentrate as she usually did. She gazed round at the hand-painted carved statues around the walls, letting Elfodd's voice wash over her. The statues' odd-looking oval faces stared sternly back at her, their eyes big and strange, their small mouths pursed and disapproving. She wondered who they all were. The more she gazed at them, the more their bizarre faces looked weirdly inhuman. The faces of the beautiful faerie Muryans came back to her. They had looked more human than these statues – and yet they hadn't been real; they had been hiding their hideous ant bodies and horns and legs with magic. Unlike the disguised Muryans, the statues in the chapel didn't look like humans. They reminded her more of the Piskies with their inhuman faces. Fleur had said that faeries were like demons. And now that Morgan thought about it, the Piskies *had* reminded her of demons when she first saw them. Demons, who had rebelled against God.

But why? Why had they rebelled against God?

"And Jesus said, '*If you forgive others their sins, your heavenly Father will forgive you yours; but if you do not forgive others, your Father will not forgive your sins either.*' And as Jesus taught us, God is all-forgiving ... Do you understand that, Lady Morgan?"

Morgan jumped guiltily. Elfodd was looking at her, but he didn't seem to be angry or upset. He was asking her a real question.

She chose to answer with a question of her own. "Is that really true, Father? Is God is all-forgiving?"

"That's the message of Jesus, yes," Elfodd said gently.

Morgan gave a sideways glance at Fleur, who was eagerly following Elfodd's every word.

"But what about demons?" she asked. "Demons who rebelled against God? Was God all-forgiving with them?"

"Ah, you mean the fallen angels," Elfodd said, interested.

"The fallen angels?"

"That's what demons are," the priest told her. "All demons were angels once. But you're right, Lady Morgan – they rebelled against God. Saint Peter himself tells us in his second epistle, '*For God* spared not the angels that sinned but cast them down to Tartarus and delivered them into chains of darkness, to be reserved unto judgement.'"

"What's Tartarus?" Fleur wanted to know.

"It's an old name for Hell," Elfodd said. "It's from the old Hellenic language. The Hellenic people are from a land far to the south east of ours. Their language was the first to be used to write down the life of Jesus; that's how we first came to know about him."

But Morgan had remembered the word "Tartarus." Almost without thinking, the lines from Sebile's book came back to her and she recited them, instinctively, from memory.

"Chaos was first of all, but next appeared
Broad-bosomed Earth, sure standing-place for all
The gods who live on snowy Olympus's peak
And misty Tartarus, in a recess
Of broad-pathed earth, and Love, most beautiful
Of all the deathless gods ..."

Elfodd closed his Bible and placed it down on the wooden bench beside him.

"Where did you learn that?" he asked in a voice that was hard to read.

"In a book Sebile gave me," Morgan told him. "It's called *Theogony*."

"Not that horrible book!" Fleur exclaimed in disgust.

But Elfodd was looking at Morgan with an extraordinary expression on his face. His eyes were shining.

"Your tutor gave you *Theogony* to read?"

"Yes." Morgan nodded. "I was reading it. It's a lot like the way God created the world in the Bible. Except that they had all different names of gods – even bad ones like Kronos. It says he was the most terrible of sons. He was his vigorous father's enemy." The words she had read were flooding back, tumbling out of her. "I thought he sounded like the Devil – the way the Devil is God's enemy."

"I know the story of Kronos," Elfodd said. "I've read it, too. It also comes from the Hellenic people; *Theogony* is the tale of their old gods. Many of the old gods have similar stories to those of the angels. In fact, our word 'angels' comes from the Hellenic language as well – '*angelos*' is the Hellenic word for messengers. Angels are the messengers of God."

"The angel Gabriel was the messenger of God to the Virgin Mary," Fleur said proudly. "He told her she was going to have Jesus."

"That's right," Elfodd affirmed. "And the angels even spoke to Jesus himself. God created angels long before he created people. They serve him and carry out his will. Peter tells us that the angels have greater authority than anything here on earth and they are immortal, which means that they never die. But there are still limits to what they can do. Angels don't understand everything the way God understands everything. They don't know the future the way God knows the future. They can't know human thoughts the way God knows human thoughts. There are many mysteries that angels don't understand, just as there are many mysteries we humans don't understand."

Again, Morgan felt pleased by the way Elfodd talked to her as if she were a grown-up.

"But why did angels become demons?" she asked him. "Why did they rebel against God?"

"It's said that it was envy of mortals that made them rebel," Elfodd said. "They were jealous of humans. Angels were created first, but when God created his second children, mortal men and women like you and me, he gave the angels his own knowledge of the future. The angels were allowed to see what mortals would be like. They saw that we wouldn't be as powerful as the angels themselves. But the angels were also allowed to see that God loved mortals so much that he would send his only son, Jesus, to become one of them."

"But why weren't they happy about that?" Morgan asked, puzzled. "They could see Jesus! They could see the future!"

"It made some of them happy, but not all of them. The greatest and brightest and most favoured of God's angels was Lucifer, but he wasn't happy when he was given this knowledge. He grew angry, because it meant he would have to worship a man, a simple mortal, and he thought mortals would be inferior to him. He was proud and arrogant, and so were many other angels like him. So they rebelled against God and tried to take the throne of Heaven. That's when God threw them down into Hell. Lucifer was once so bright, so beautiful, so good, he was known as the Morning Star. But when he sinned against God he became the Dark One – Satan, the Devil, everything that was evil. The Book of Isaiah tells us how he was cast down. Jesus himself says he saw Satan fall like lightning from Heaven."

Fleur gasped. Morgan could see it in her mind's eye. Angels falling down from Heaven. Hundreds of them, streaking across a dark, thunderous sky like streams of fire.

She *had* seen it. Not in her mind. In her dream. In her nightmare. In the nightmare she had had on the night of the storm, the night the *Sea Queen* was lost.

She remembered it vividly. It was as if she were seeing it in front of her eyes right then and there. Angels whose brilliant beauty had turned to unbearable ugliness, their faces contorted in terror, howling and screaming as they fell to earth, down into the sea. Their wings caught fire in the circle of light around the world and streamed across the sky in a blaze of red, white and gold, before crumbling into a nothingness of black ash scattered in the storm wind.

Elfodd's eyes were scrutinising her. Morgan tried to say what she was feeling but it was difficult to find the words. The terrible images of the falling fiery angels brought back something Merlin had once told her. About how God had rained fire from the sky on two cities because the people there had been bad, so he had killed every single one. She repeated this to Elfodd, recalling Merlin's words.

"Is it true, Father? Did God kill all those people because they were sinners? Because if he did ..." She hesitated to say it. "If God did that ... then he's not all-forgiving, is he? In that story, God was really angry and horrible. Like a monster."

"Morgan!" Fleur was horrified. "You mustn't speak about God

that way! Must she, Father?"

But Elfodd was looking at Morgan curiously. He didn't seem angry at all. He actually seemed pleased with her. Fascinated, even.

"It's true that the Old Testament God did a lot of cruel things," the priest said. "But he did them to bad people and he always tempered his punishments with mercy. Right after Saint Peter tells us how the angels were cast down into Hell, he tells how mortals too were punished here on earth for their terrible sins. '*And he spared not the old world but saved Noah the eighth person, a preacher of righteousness, bringing in the flood upon the world of the ungodly.*'"

"What does that mean?" Fleur asked.

"It's here, in the Book of Genesis." Elfodd picked up the Bible, leafed through it and held it out to show the two little girls. There was an illuminated picture of a man in a strange-looking brown boat floating on blue-green water. Above him flew a white bird carrying a green branch in its beak.

"When the human race became so bad, so sinful, God sent the Great Flood to wash the world clean and to build a new world," the priest told them. "But he was merciful and he spared the one good man who was left. That man was called Noah. God told Noah to build an ark for himself and his family, and fill it with two of every kind of animal on earth so that when the water went down, they could all survive and begin anew."

"But what happened to all the other people in the world?" Morgan queried. She knew the story of Noah's Ark and knew with a sick feeling what Elfodd was going to say, but she wanted to hear it anyway.

"They drowned, Lady Morgan," Elfodd said quietly. "That was God's punishment. Remember – God always does things for a reason."

But all Morgan could think about was people drowning. Again she could see them, vividly, just as she had before in her dream. Ragged people of all kinds; old, young, grown-ups, children. Struggling, terrified, exhausted, hopeless. Crying out for help. Fighting against the waves trying to pull them into the dark ocean depths.

"I don't understand!" she said fiercely, trying to banish the horrible images from her head. "Why didn't God forgive the people and the angels if he's supposed to be all-forgiving? Jesus said you should forgive, so why didn't God?"

"You need to listen and to read carefully what Jesus said," Elfodd told her. "He said you can only be forgiven if you forgive others yourself. The wicked people of the flood didn't forgive others – they were evil and cruel and unjust. The bad angels didn't forgive others – to this day, they still hate God and all humankind, and seek to corrupt and destroy God's children. They didn't forgive and they didn't repent. You cannot have forgiveness without repentance. You cannot be forgiven unless you're truly sorry for what you have done. Only if you're really sorry for what you have done can you be granted forgiveness. And bad angels and demons and wicked people aren't usually sorry for what they do."

"But what about intercession?" Morgan argued. "You said that people's souls go to Purgatory when they die and they wait there to pray for their sins. You said that we can inter – intercede for them and pray for their sins to be forgiven and help them get into Heaven. Why doesn't anyone pray to God for demons and bad people so that he can save them, too?"

The image of Agnes crumbling into dust came into her mind. It was an image she couldn't banish, no matter how hard she tried. Had Agnes been a bad person? Agnes had thought she was bad because she had eaten the faeries' fruit; because she had been greedy. Agnes thought she had deserved what had happened to her. But Morgan refused to believe that.

To her astonishment, Elfodd was smiling at her. He seemed delighted that she was arguing with him. Fleur was looking at them both somewhat fearfully, not liking the way the conversation was going.

"That's a very good point, Lady Morgan," Elfodd conceded. "But tell me this: do you think demons and bad people *want* to be saved?"

Morgan was taken aback. "What do you mean?"

"Just what I said. Do you think demons and bad people *want* to be saved by you and me? Do they want us to intercede for them?

Do they want us to pray for them?"

Morgan thought for a few moments. "I don't know," she admitted at last.

Elfodd gave her a sympathetic look.

"You see, Lady Morgan, it isn't as simple as that. Demons and bad people aren't wicked just like that. It isn't something that they can't help. On the contrary – they have *chosen* to be bad. They have *chosen* to turn against God and all that is good. Just because you and I want them to be saved doesn't mean that *they* want to be. That's why being sorry for your sins is so important; that's why repentance is such an essential part of being forgiven. Any sin, however bad, can be forgiven in the eyes of God – but only if your repentance of that sin is true. You have to want to be forgiven. You have to want redemption in order to find it."

Morgan said nothing. Fleur looked askance at her, her eyes bright.

Elfodd closed the Bible gently again. He was looking at Morgan kindly, but there was something else in his expression. Interest? Understanding? Watchfulness?

"You cannot save those who do not want to be saved," the priest said finally. "Demons and bad people have to want to be saved, Lady Morgan, before they can *be* saved. Whether they be angel, demon or mortal, they have to *want* salvation if it is ever to be granted to them."

* * *

On the way back to Tintagel, the Sun's light was fading as heavy clouds billowed overhead, coming together in the cold wind and oozing into a sea of gloomy dark grey that spread across the sky. Morgan and Fleur hurried along the path side by side, wanting to get back to the castle as quickly as possible. Both little girls were quiet. Fleur didn't seem to want to say anything this time. And Morgan was too busy turning things over and over in her head, trying to make sense of all of them.

Father Elfodd had said that you couldn't save those who didn't want to be saved. On the Moon Moor, Morgan remembered,

Diana had said something similar. She had said that you couldn't save everyone. Diana had once wanted to, she had once tried, but she couldn't. Even Diana, the powerful Moon Huntress herself, couldn't save everyone, so she had stopped trying. It sounded to Morgan as if Elfodd was saying that Diana was right, that you shouldn't try to save bad people – or demons – because they didn't want to be saved.

But were Diana and Elfodd really right?

"You should still try," Morgan had said to Diana. She still believed that. And she felt deep down that Diana and Elfodd were both wrong. Even if you couldn't save everyone, you should still try. And even if people didn't *want* to be saved, you should still try.

She recalled again her nightmare on the night of the shipwreck. With a clarity brighter and more vivid than the wind and sea and dark swelling clouds around her, she remembered the dream-feeling of hovering above the drowning angels and people in the stormy ocean. She recalled the iron manacles binding her wrists. She recalled how she had fought against the invisible force holding her up in the air; how she had squirmed and kicked against the wind in her dream, fighting to be with the desperate creatures in the water below her; fighting to be with them, to help them, to be among them.

The sound of crashing waves beneath the cliff path brought her back from her nightmare into the present. The sea around Tintagel was turning slate-coloured, dotted with specks of shining silver as far as the eye could see. Swirling storm clouds above merged as if into a mirror of the ocean itself; the sky's visual echo of the sounding silver-grey waves, frothy white foam and misty spray. Tintagel Castle stood upon the cliffs like a lone rock, proud and unyielding against the wind and sea now battering its coast. Like a protector, Morgan thought, just as she had thought before. But this time another thought came to her: a protector against whom? Against what?

Something odd attracted her eye. Something that wasn't meant to be there.

A figure was standing on the small island that separated from the mainland just beyond the castle. The island that nobody ever went to.

Morgan had never really thought about the island before. It was just there. It had always been there, part of the landscape and coastline that surrounded her home. She had heard its name once or twice from servants. They called it the Black Head. But she had never given it a second thought. Until now.

A tall figure was standing at the very tip of the Black Head, right on the edge of the cliff.

Morgan had seen that figure before. It was a man, but not a man. It was a man who had the antlers of a stag growing out of his head. Horns.

A Horned Man, with a pointed beard and deerskin cloak. The Horned Man she had seen on the night of the last storm. The Horned Man, whose shape and silhouette looked like the Devil. The Horned Man who looked like Lucifer, once the brightest of the angels, the Morning Star, who had rebelled against God and become Satan. Satan who had fallen like lightning from Heaven and had brought the other bad angels down with him, screaming from the sky.

"Fleur!" Morgan yelled into the wind. She grabbed her friend's arm. "Look! Look! Do you see him?"

"Who? Where?" Fleur demanded, staring round.

"There! On the island! The man, there! With horns!"

"A man with horns!" Fleur exclaimed. "Where? I don't see anything!"

"But he's there! On the cliff! Right there!"

The Horned Man turned slowly to look at Morgan.

She felt as if she couldn't breathe. His black fathomless eyes were gazing into her very heart. Even though he was far away, standing at the furthermost point of the Black Head, she could see right into his eyes. And into his face. It too was dark, as if burned by the Sun.

The Horned Man smiled, showing teeth whiter than the sea foam.

"Morgan!" Fleur was shaking her. "What's the matter? You're scaring me!"

Morgan turned to face her and gestured wildly. "*Look* at him!

268

Over on the island!"

Fleur stared out over to the island for a minute. Then she looked back at Morgan with troubled eyes.

"There's no one there!"

Morgan gazed back at the island.

Fleur was right. There was no one there. Nothing on the island but a thin mantle of golden-brown grass spread over cliffs and rocks of dark granite. The Horned Man was gone.

"Come on," Fleur said, tugging at her arm.

Morgan allowed herself to be pulled back to the castle. She kept staring at the Black Head until they entered the courtyard, but she saw no sign of anything else.

Once inside the courtyard, the earthly rush of human noise and activity hit her as if she had just come up from under water. In the grimly greying gloom of the day, a number of servants were hurrying about, carrying food and utensils and bedding. Others were sweeping the cobblestones, chasing stray chickens back into wooden huts, dragging the hunting dogs back to their kennels, lugging straw into the stable. They were trying to clean the courtyard, but their efforts were stirring up disgusting smells of droppings and dregs and debris that were being carried on the wind. Squires were running back and forth carrying freshly polished saddles and swords. More soldiers than usual, all wearing chainmail and wielding spears, were standing guard both at the foregate and high above on the castle battlements.

"It's because of High King Vortigern!" Fleur declared in wonder. "He's coming to Tintagel, just like Safir said! They're getting ready for him!"

High King Vortigern. Morgan had never seen him. He'd never been to Tintagel before. But he was coming now because Ambrosius and Uther, the Pendragon brothers, were in Britain with an army from Armorica. Ambrosius and Uther, the sons of Constantine, whoever he was. They were coming to fight Vortigern. Vortigern wanted Gorlois to fight on his side and many nobles of Belerion were coming too.

If Ambrosius and Uther wanted to fight Vortigern, that must mean there would be a war. A human war. Like the faerie war of the Piskies and the Muryans, only with people. The people of Tintagel. People she knew.

Horrific images suddenly filled her mind again. This time they were vivid memories of the Piskies and the Muryans fighting each other in the underground realm, tearing each other into pieces with their claws and fangs, like beasts savagely ripping other animals apart.

Morgan shivered. What would it be like if that kind of war was fought with humans?

Amidst all the hustle and bustle of the courtyard, rising above the smells, the dirt, the greyness, the people rushing about and the cold wind blowing in from the west, something starkly different caught Morgan's eye. Something bright. Something white. Something familiar.

A flickering round white light bobbed up and down in the encroaching gloom. No bigger than a pinprick, the small white light fluttered like butterfly wings across the courtyard, and then flew up, up, up the castle walls towards the high battlements. It seemed to struggle against the wind, falling downwards now and then, but bravely bobbing back up again in its determination to soar to the top of the castle.

"We should go in," Morgan heard Fleur's voice saying. "Aunt Igraine will be waiting for us in her chambers."

"I have to talk to Sebile about something," Morgan said, not taking her eyes off the small white light. "Tell Mother I'll be there in a minute."

She left Fleur looking at her strangely, as if she thought Morgan was going to do something bad. Morgan didn't care.

She ran into the castle, through the corridor, past the main hall, up the stairs and along the passageway. Dimly aware of an endless flow of grown-ups moving backwards and forwards in a seeming frenzy of busyness, Morgan dodged round them and between them as best she could. Being such a little girl, it was easy to stay out of their way. Most of them barely noticed her. When she got to the stairs leading to the battlements, she climbed them carefully, hoping she wouldn't meet anyone in the winding stairwell. The stairs were very steep and weren't easy to climb. But Morgan remembered the time she had done it before. The night she had met Diana for the first time. The night after the dark Moon.

Out on the battlements, the bracing gusts of salty wind were much stronger than down in the courtyard, bringing with them all the fresh, tangy, sea-weedy smells Morgan knew so well. Now that she was high up, the sky was much closer and it was vast. Huge fuming storm clouds churned overhead. Grey and white sea-birds had spread their wings and were riding on the wind, suspended in mid-flight, crying plaintively. Among them glided a few of the strange red-legged, red-beaked black birds, silently and ominously circling the castle. Way down below, at the foot of the cliffs, the dark grey sea seemed to be getting angrier, lashing ferociously at the rocks and the shore. Furious white waves were frothing higher and higher out to sea, until they looked like a range of snow-capped watery hills rising up from the ocean to surround Tintagel.

The soldiers she had seen standing guard were on the battlements looking out over the parapets. They all towered over her and their chainmail armour clinked as they moved. Not only were they carrying sharp spears that to Morgan seemed as tall as trees, but on their belts hung sinister iron swords that were almost as big as Morgan herself. When the soldiers saw Morgan, they didn't speak to her, merely acknowledged her with slight nods of their heads or recognition in their eyes. None of them smiled.

Away from the hectic bustle of castle and courtyard, Morgan could sense that the air around Tintagel had changed, and not just because of the wind. The atmosphere felt tight, heavy. Uneasy. The soldiers on guard were silent and solemn. They weren't interested in her. All their focus was in the other direction as they kept keen-eyed vigil on the world outside.

Morgan hurried along the battlements, peeping through the crenels to see if she could see the small white light anywhere. She knew instinctively that it had flown up there. She knew she had to find it.

The battlements seemed to go on forever, corridors of grey stone in the open air, running straight ahead for the longest time before they curved slightly until you couldn't see round the corners. Passing the occasional soldier on guard who paid her no attention,

Morgan clambered up and down narrow steps, running all the way round the top of the castle while desperately looking out for the small round light. When she reached the side where the castle looked out onto the ocean, she stood on tiptoe to peer through the crenels once more. And gasped.

She'd always known Tintagel stood right on the edge of the cliff, but she'd never seen the dramatic drop so clearly before. Only a narrow ledge sloping ever so slightly downwards stood between the castle's outer wall and the edge of the precipice. The waves crashing against the cliffs seemed to be climbing higher each time, like white sea-spray arms stretching upwards one after the other, trying to reach all the way up to Tintagel.

"Hello, Morgan."

Morgan turned round sharply. Arcile was standing behind her on the battlements. Her former maid's reddish-brown hair and pretty green dress were billowing in the wind and she was grinning her toothy grin.

Morgan didn't stop to think this time but ran to hug her. She felt Arcile hugging her back, alive, warm and solid just like anyone else.

Morgan stepped back and looked up into Arcile's freckled face, anxiously searching to see if she looked any different.

"Arcile ... are you really a spirit? Are you really a soul?"

Arcile laughed. Her laugh sounded like the tinkle of bells, just as it always did. But Morgan realised for the first time that Arcile had never sounded like that when she had been a mortal girl. Her bell-like voice was something different.

"Why do you ask me that, Morgan? You know what I am."

Morgan's mind was whirling like the storm clouds above. The cold wind was blowing her hair about and she tried to push it back, tuck it behind her ears. She remembered Elfodd talking about souls in Purgatory, but then the Druid Grand Master Cadwellon's words came to mind as well. He had said the Druids believed the soul didn't leave the earth but was reborn into another body. Just like Diana had saved the soul of the little boy Mabon so he could be reborn.

"If you're a soul, why aren't you in Purgatory waiting to go to

Heaven?" Morgan asked her. "And if you're a soul, why aren't you going to be reborn like Mabon is?"

"I'm not going to be reborn because I don't *want* to be reborn," Arcile said. There was something strange about her voice.

"Why not?"

"Because I want to stay with Diana."

Arcile's grin had vanished and there was an odd look in her eye. "Don't you understand, Morgan? I'm a faerie now! I'm a Will o' the Wisp! I have magic! I can change my shape, fly through the air, go anywhere I want to! I can fly to the stars with Diana! I can sleep in the hollow of the tiniest leaf! I can ride on the wind and dance on the clouds! I can skim the seas and flit from one land to another faster than it takes you to blink!"

The Wisp's voice had suddenly turned harsh. Gone was the tinkling prettiness of her former bell-like tones; instead she sounded jangly, discordant. The look on her freckled face was contorted; it wasn't the warm, friendly, kind Arcile Morgan had always known. It was a look that Morgan knew she had seen before, though she couldn't think where.

Before she could answer, Arcile was speaking again. "Wouldn't you choose this, if you had the choice? Wouldn't you choose to be a faerie? Instead of coming back to all" – the Wisp gestured round the castle with her arm and almost spat – "*this?*"

"But what about Heaven?" Morgan said.

Arcile didn't reply. Her eyes only narrowed.

"Heaven!" Morgan said again. "You said you weren't baptised so you couldn't go to Heaven and you were sad about it – "

"I'm not sad about it anymore."

Not only was Arcile's voice jangly, it was now cold; colder than the wind, rougher than the sounding sea. "I don't want to go to Heaven. Not anymore. Why would I want to go there? If there's a God who did this to me and to the others, leaving us here on earth, punishing us when we haven't done anything wrong, then he's cruel and vicious and unjust, and I don't want anything to do with him. And I don't want anything to do with his horrible world either – the world mortals live in. Mortals are just as cruel and hateful and evil as God is."

The wind suddenly gusted so fiercely that Morgan was nearly blown off her feet. Afraid, she held on to the battlement wall and crouched down next to it so the wind wouldn't get her.

She knew now where she had seen the look on Arcile's face before. The yellow-haired Piskie who hated humans had had the same look. He had had exactly the same expression when he had looked at her and Merlin. The yellow-haired Piskie who had once been a human boy, a strange-looking boy, whose parents had beaten him and thrown him in the fire and left him to die.

Yallery. That was his name. Arcile had known him. She had recognised him. She had got him to help Morgan and Merlin against the Muryans. Together they had brought the Piskies to fight the Muryans.

And now Arcile was becoming like him.

"Listen," Morgan began desperately, "it isn't true that you can't be saved! I don't believe that! You can – "

"But I *have* been saved, Morgan." A smile touched Arcile's lips. "Look at me."

Standing before her, Arcile suddenly went all blurry. At first Morgan thought there was something wrong with her eyes. But then blurry Arcile began to shrink, slowly folding in on herself in a hazy white glow. The white glow grew smaller, sharper, rounder, brighter. In the space of a moment Arcile in the green dress had vanished, replaced by the small fluttering white light of the Will o' the Wisp.

"I'm magical!" Arcile's voice exclaimed triumphantly from the white light. "I told you I'd been saved! Diana saved me. Diana is the true Goddess, the Great Goddess of Light. She is good and kind. She looks after us, she protects us. She's saved all of us."

"Not Agnes," Morgan said.

The small white light floated down to where Morgan was huddled by the wall.

"What do you mean?"

Strong feelings were welling up in Morgan's chest. She couldn't tell if it was rage or distress; all she knew was the feelings were so strong they were about to choke her.

"Diana didn't save Agnes!" she blurted out. "And what about

Maglore? Diana didn't want me to save that little girl – she only wanted the little boy, Mabon! She told me she couldn't save Maglore even if she wanted to! How can she be the Great Goddess like you say if she can't even do that?"

The small white light fluttered close to her face.

"But *you* saved Maglore, Morgan."

Morgan was close to tears. Whether with anger or sadness, she didn't know or care. "So? What's that got to do with it?"

"Diana couldn't save Maglore. But you could. You did. Diana sent you into a place where she couldn't go and *you* saved Maglore. Maybe she knew you would. Maybe you were meant to. That's what gods do sometimes. They send messengers to do things they can't do themselves."

"Messengers?" Morgan wiped her hand across her eyes. "You mean like angels?"

Arcile's laughter rang out from the small white light.

"Not just angels, Morgan. People too. Diana sent you into the world of the Small People to perform a task for her. That's what gods do, too. They test people. To see if they're worthy. If they're good. If they're strong. If they keep their promises. You performed the task she set you and more. You didn't just save the little boy, you saved the little girl too."

"But what about Agnes?" Morgan insisted. "I didn't save *her*. No one did. Where is she? Why was she kept prisoner in that horrible Muryan hill for hundreds of years with no one to help her? Why didn't anyone get her out? Why didn't Diana send someone to get *her* out?"

"Diana told you she couldn't save everyone," Arcile's voice said. The Wisp was starting to sound annoyed.

"So where did Agnes and the other children go? Where did their souls go? Who saved them?"

"I don't know!" Arcile snapped. "Probably no one!"

Morgan's throat tightened. This was horrible. Arcile was being horrible. She hardly recognised this Arcile anymore.

The small white light hovered in front of her, light as a feather, invisible wings buzzing like a hummingbird's.

"I didn't come here to argue with you, Morgan," the Wisp said, her voice a little softer now. "I came here to warn you."

Morgan was startled. "Warn me? Warn me about what?"

"About the Piskies and the Muryans, of course."

The heavy storm clouds in the sky over the battlements had turned almost black. Only tiny cracks of daylight penetrated the dark smoky swirls threatening to smother the castle and its coast. The sea was lashing at the rocks and cliffs with such fury that it seemed it was trying to beat them down. The westerly wind was blowing winter-cold, beginning to bring with it the odd droplet of icy rain. Tintagel Castle suddenly seemed very small and exposed; no longer a protector standing proud, but something small, weak, all alone, standing precariously close to the edge of a cliff.

"What about the Piskies and the Muryans?" Morgan managed to say.

"Did you think this was the end?" Arcile's voice said, her small white light hovering fixedly in front of Morgan, refusing to be blown away by the gusts of wind. "The Piskies and the Muryans were enemies once, but they're united now in their hatred for a common enemy. You, Morgan. You tricked them. You got the better of them. And you stole the children from them. There's nothing more valuable to them than children. You're in danger now. They've sworn revenge on you. And their revenge can be terrible. They'll be coming after you. They know who you really are."

The icy rain was spitting down now. In the shelter of the battlement wall, Morgan could still feel the drops on her head and her cheeks, wincing as they hit her skin.

"They know who I really am?" she asked fearfully. "What does that mean? Who am I?"

The small white light glowed suddenly. Morgan couldn't see her face but she knew Arcile was smiling. All the Wisp's warmth, her friendliness, her kindness, was back.

"All I can tell you now is that you are special to Diana, Morgan. Very, very special. Remember I told you how wonderful it is to be magical. You are more magical than any of us."

"MORGAN!"

Morgan almost jumped out of her skin. She leapt to her feet.

Sebile was standing a little way away from her.

The old tutor was holding onto her white headdress with one hand, protecting it as the wind blew around them. She was looking at Morgan with the oddest expression on her face.

Morgan stared round in panic for the Wisp's small white light. Could Sebile see it?

But it was nowhere to be seen. The small white light had disappeared into the oncoming storm.

Arcile had gone.

* * *

"Who are you talking to, Morgan?"

Icy rain droplets were lashing into Morgan's face, falling faster now. Angry storm clouds rolled and spiralled overhead, blotting out the daylight, bearing a charcoal shroud of heavy rain with them. The sea had turned almost as black as the sky, its raging rise and swell propelling the roaring force of white foamy waves higher and higher. The wind was blowing so strongly that Sebile had had to raise her voice to be heard over its whistling and howling.

For a mad moment, Morgan wanted to tell Sebile everything. All about Arcile, Diana, the Wild Hunt; the Piskies, the Muryans, the Elven. Of all the grown-ups she knew, Sebile would understand, wouldn't she? Sebile would listen, wouldn't she?

But would Sebile believe her?

Morgan couldn't do it.

"No one!" she shouted back.

But the old tutor looked at her with shrewd eyes. Morgan knew that look. It was the look Sebile always gave her when she knew Morgan was lying.

"Come along." Sebile held out a hand, still holding onto her white headdress with the other. "Your mother's been looking for you. You must come back to her chambers now. The whole castle's getting ready."

"Getting ready? For High King Vortigern, you mean?"

Sebile gestured over the battlements. "Look down there, child."

Morgan struggled over in the wind and stood on tiptoe to look down through the crenels. Below, beneath the driving downpour of icy rain, men on horseback were fast arriving at the castle foregate. Some were wearing chainmail armour like the guards on the battlements; others were richly dressed in vibrant colours that stood out even in the eerie dim light. But the strong, gusting gale was making them all look bedraggled and dishevelled.

Covered wooden wagons were also arriving. Descending hastily from them, hurrying into the castle out of the storm, were elegant ladies: some young with their long hair blown loose and untidy in the wind; others older, holding onto headdresses similar to Sebile's. On one wagon, uncovered and exposed to the rain, sat a number of older men, their beige and brown robes billowing in the wind. These older men were all straggly-haired and bearded; some grey, some black, some white, some a mixture of all three. A stark figure all in white came out of the foregate to greet them. Though she couldn't see his face, Morgan recognised him from his robes and staff: Grand Master Cadwellon, the old Druid Master.

"The Council of Twelve," Sebile said, watching Cadwellon greet each older man as he descended from the uncovered wagon and urge him on quickly through the castle foregate. "Like everyone else, they're here to see High King Vortigern and his Queen Rowena. The High King should be here any minute now."

But Morgan was thinking how strange and small all the people down below on the ground seemed. They were all scuttling about, trying to get inside, hurrying to escape the power of the storm. Looking down on them from such a great height, she felt as if she were suspended in the air, floating high above them, watching them from a great distance. They reminded her of something; something she had seen not long ago.

"They all look like ants," she said loudly, half to herself, half to Sebile.

"Perhaps that's all they are, really," Sebile said. The tutor was smiling.

In the corner of Morgan's eye there was a flash, a glimmer; the glare of a shade darker even than the black water of the storm-tossed sea. She ran back to the side of the battlements that looked out onto the ocean.

Behind the misty veil of rain, amidst the rolling waves, small shadows bobbed up and down. It took a few seconds for Morgan to make out the shapes of boats tilting and keeling in the wind. The boats were full of men, shadowy figures silhouetted against the white foam of the dark waters, rowing towards the shore. Beyond the bay, further out to sea, Morgan could see the shapes of ships anchored off shore, their dark sails flapping as the howling gale blasted around them.

"What about those boats?" she called out to Sebile. "Are those men coming to see High King Vortigern, too?"

When Sebile didn't answer, Morgan turned round to find the tutor looking at her with squinted eyes.

"What boats?" Sebile said loudly in a hoarse voice.

"Why, those ...!" Morgan pointed back out to sea, then stared.

The boats had vanished. So had the ships.

There was nothing out there. Nothing but huge black waves crashing into torrents of frothy white spume, pounding the cliffs and shoreline without mercy. Nothing but an endless tumult of dark, gale-driven rainy mist and thrashing white-crested waves surging forward, smashing into the coast with relentless rage. Roaring wind and pounding sea were drowning out every other sound. The wind-whipped ocean and black cloud-swirling sky seemed to become one; the waves and clouds collided with each other, melded into one another, until she couldn't tell which was which. The storm was spreading out to every corner of the world beyond the horizon. Stinging salty spray flew into her face, blinding her eyes and cracking her lips.

She had never felt so happy. The spiralling dark clouds lifted her up and carried her away, making her as one with the raw power of the storm. Her blood rushed with the surge of the ocean; her heart pounded with the power of the waves; her mind reeled with the force of the wind. Her flesh was alive with the sting of salt-spray; her whole body was soaring, spiralling, melting into the dark rainy clouds. She wanted to lose herself forever in the twisting black swirls of darkness wrapping themselves around her like a blanket.

Sebile grabbed her shoulder.

The shock of it brought Morgan back to Tintagel with a thud; to the freezing cold, wind-beaten, rain-swept battlements. To the sogginess of wet clothes. To the buffeting of the gale. To the painful jabs on her skin of icy rain and salty spray.

The thrashing waters of the sea below parted for a moment. They pulled back to reveal a giant face. A man's face.

It was the man's face she had seen once before, the night of that other great storm. A man's face wrinkled with ripples, framed with a beard and hair of white foam. Dark eyes of whirling water looked up at her.

Two enormous waves smashed against each other, sending the white spume in opposite directions.

The man's face smiled.

She knew it was all real now.

The world of the Small People. The Piskies. The Muryans. The Elven. The Horned Man. Arcile. The Wild Hunt. Diana.

All of it. All of what Father Elfodd called the spiritual world, where God and the saints lived, full of angels and demons. All of what Grand Master Cadwellon called the faerie world, the world of all the different gods and the power of nature. She was beginning to see these new worlds open up all around her. They were always there, with her all the time. Right alongside the world of Tintagel and her everyday life, the life she lived as a simple little girl.

One part of her loved the idea and was so excited by it that she wanted to dance and spin. Another part of her felt sick and terrified at the thought. And yet another part of her was so confused and in such turmoil, it didn't know how she felt about it.

"Morgan! What is it? What's the matter? What can you see?"

Sebile had crouched down, had taken her by the shoulders and was gazing into her face. Morgan struggled to put into words what she was thinking, what she was feeling.

"Everything's changing, Sebile."

Sebile squeezed her shoulders in sympathy. There was a light in the old tutor's eyes.

"Of course it is, child. Everything always changes, sooner or later."

"Why? Why do things have to change?"

"Because the world we live in, the universe, the cosmos, and all things in it are always changing, always transforming, always evolving."

Sebile gave a wry smile. "Life is all about change, Morgan. Some people don't like it. They want everything to stay the same because they think they're safer that way; because they're afraid that change will make things worse. But change is inevitable. It can't be stopped. Change will happen whether you want it to or not."

With difficulty, the tutor straightened herself up, grabbing her headdress with one hand to stop it from blowing away in the gale. She took Morgan's hand and began pulling her to the stairwell leading back inside.

But Morgan wasn't finished. "So you can't do anything about it?"

"I didn't say that." Sebile looked down at her. "Old worlds die and new ones are born, Morgan. That has always been the way of things and it always will be. The old always has to make way for the new. You have to accept the natural flow of things, but it doesn't mean you can't do anything about it. You have to decide if you want to go through life pretending that nothing will ever change; but if you do you'll get swept away by a tide over which you have no control. Or you can decide to be happy that change is coming and act to influence the course of things to come. Once you accept that change is going to happen, you can help effect that change yourself – help make things better. What you choose to do can play a great part in *how* the world changes, if you're clever enough."

"You can make the real world better if you face the truth," Morgan said, finally understanding what Diana had said on the Moon Moor.

Sebile smiled again. "Exactly."

The currents of Morgan's mind were coursing once more. So was that what it all meant? She had to face the truth?

But what *was* the truth?

Arcile had said the Piskies and Muryans knew who Morgan really was. She had said that Morgan was more magical than any of them. "Them" had to mean the faeries.

If she, Morgan, was magical, then she could use her magic. If the Piskies and the Muryans came to find her looking for a terrible revenge, she could use her magic against them. She could use her magic to find out what they knew. She could find out who she really was.

She could use her magic to help people, to save people. Little children like Mabon and Maglore, who hadn't been saved. People like Agnes, who hadn't been saved and had wanted to be saved. Even spirits, souls, like Arcile, who hadn't been saved and *didn't* want to be saved. It didn't matter. Morgan would save them anyway.

As Morgan and Sebile ducked inside the doorway, the black storm clouds lit up bright white, crackling with sharp lightning. A crash of thunder roared across the sky, seeming to rip the clouds apart and with them the storm itself. The wind tore through the air, screaming as the storm broke. The spattering of icy rain turned into a cascading, gushing, torrential ocean unleashed from above.

But Morgan wasn't afraid of the storm. Not anymore. She would never be afraid of any storm ever again.

She would do it all.

She would find out who she really was. She would learn about her magic and use it to make things better. She would accept the natural flow of things, all the worlds that lived side by side, and she would be happy that change was coming. She would face the truth.

She was going to change everything.

Now Available

MORGAN LE FAY: CHILDREN OF THIS WORLD

Book Two in the Fata Morgana Series

Extract from Chapter I

It didn't seem as if it would ever stop raining. The water bucketed down, plummeting to earth in torrents from the dark sky. It flooded the courtyard and gathered in great pools of water, soaking into the green and brown headlands beyond. It even started dripping in through the roof. Wooden pails were placed directly underneath to stop the water spreading, but the river rushes and straw strewn across the floor still got all damp and soggy. The rain seemed to be doing all it could to get inside, drumming relentlessly and remorselessly on the roof, pounding at the battlements, lashing at the walls.

Tintagel Castle stood on the edge of the cliff in lonely defiance against the ferocity of the storm. A western wind swept around the castle, howling and gusting with fury. From time to time, jagged forks of bright white lightning shot across the sky, lighting up the black clouds, followed by deafening crashes of thunder so loud they threatened to shatter the walls. It felt as if the storm were trying to beat and blow and smash Tintagel into pieces, attempting to sweep the castle off the edge of the cliff into the raging ocean below. Beyond the castle window the steel-hued sea was in turmoil. Huge roaring waves lurched themselves at the cliff faces, crashing against the granite rocks in misty mountains of spray so high that they almost reached the castle itself. The waves were joining in with the rain and the wind, the thunder and lightning; attacking Tintagel, trying to drag it all down into the depths of the dark waters.

Morgan sat in her mother Igraine's chambers, gazing up at the window from the cushions she was sitting on. A fire was blazing in the hearth but Morgan didn't want to be near it. Strangely, she didn't mind the cold, or the wind, or the occasional spurts of rain that splashed in through the window. She preferred to be where she could see as much as possible – the brilliant flashes of lightning, the churning steely ocean, the sheets of rain billowing against the grey stone walls.

Everyone else in the room seemed to be uninterested in the storm, or at least was studiously ignoring it. Igraine's lady-in-waiting, Halwynna, was seated on a chair by the fire darning a woollen dress with great concentration. Morgan's two younger sisters, the twins Anna and Blasine, were sitting on a bear rug by the fire at Halwynna's feet. Blasine was playing with a couple of her straw dolls, while Anna was waving a small wooden stick around mouthing words silently to herself. Morgan had no idea what game Anna was playing, but she didn't much care either. Morgan's best friend Fleur was on the cushions beside her, reading her beautiful gold-illustrated Bible. She didn't look up from her book or out at the storm at all.

Igraine herself wasn't there. The Duchess had gone to help her husband with the visitors arriving at the castle. As the Duke and Duchess of Belerion, it was the duty of Gorlois and Igraine to greet all the people who came to visit them; especially now, as many nobleman and ladies were coming to see High King Vortigern and his Queen Rowena, who were soon to arrive at Tintagel. Morgan recalled the richly dressed men on horseback and elegant ladies either on horses or in covered wooden wagons that she had seen from the storm-swept battlements. She remembered that many of the men had also been wearing armour, and she thought of the guards armed with spears and swords whom she had seen standing sentinel on the battlements.

Vortigern and Rowena and all those other people weren't just coming to Tintagel to visit. They were all coming to the castle because Vortigern's enemies, the Pendragon brothers, had landed in Britain with an army from Armorica across the sea and they wanted to fight Vortigern.

Morgan still didn't know quite why Ambrosius Pendragon and his brother Uther wanted to fight Vortigern, though. She wondered if her father Gorlois would fight on Vortigern's side. Safir had told her some of the men said Gorlois didn't want to join Vortigern in the fight against Ambrosius – and as Gorlois' squire, Safir would know.

She and Fleur had talked about it together in low voices. "Do you really think my father doesn't want to fight on Vortigern's side?" Morgan asked her.

Fleur frowned. "I don't know. Why shouldn't he?"

"Maybe he doesn't want a war," Morgan said. She remembered what she had seen of the terrible Muryan and Piskie faerie war, and winced. "Lots of people could be killed."

"Maybe it's because of the Saxons," Fleur suggested. "My father always says you can't trust the Saxons. He says Vortigern should never have joined with them."

The Saxons. Morgan had heard about them all her life, but she only knew vaguely who and what they were. She knew they were people, but they weren't like the people of Belerion. The Saxons came from lands far to the east and that was where they lived – a long way away from Belerion in the west. She had never seen or met a Saxon. They weren't part of her world.

Morgan hated sitting in the chamber hour after hour. She wanted to move about, go where she wanted to, *do* something. She wished she could have gone with Igraine to greet the visitors. But she was only five years old and she knew little children didn't really matter to grown-ups at times like this. She didn't have Sebile's *Theogony* with her, which she would have liked to read more of. She peered over Fleur's shoulder at the Bible and saw her friend was reading about Noah's Ark. Father Elfodd had just been telling them about that in their lesson at the chapel earlier that afternoon. People had become so bad and sinful that God had sent the Great Flood to wash the earth clean and build a new world.

Morgan had seen how God did that. In her nightmare, on the night before the last terrible storm, she had seen people drowning in a sea that turned to blood. In that same dream she had seen angels falling from the skies, their wings on fire, into that same ocean. Then, when she had woken up, she had seen the ship, the *Sea Queen*, wrecked on the coast of Tintagel and people dying and drowning.

Out of that terrible storm and shipwreck had come new arrivals, new friends from outside her previously closed-off world. Fleur, the princess of Ynys Môn and cousin of her own age, who had come to live with them; the adopted daughter of King Pellinore and Queen Sardoine, Igraine's sister. Taliesin, the fisherman Elffin's adopted son, a former page boy who was now a Druid apprentice to Grand Master Cadwellon himself. Safir, the eight-year-old Saracen girl who'd run away from her home in Babylon, had stowed away on the wrecked ship, and who now lived disguised as a boy because she worked as Gorlois' squire. And Merlin and Ganieda, the twins, also of Morgan's own age; the children of Lady Aldan, who'd been sent into exile by her father King Einion of Gwynedd because of Merlin and Ganieda's strange ways.

But the storm and shipwreck had brought other things, too. Things Morgan never could have imagined. Things she found hard to talk about. The death of Arcile, her young maid, who had drowned in the storm flood. Morgan had seen Arcile's dead body, lying all cold and stiff among many other dead bodies who had drowned that night. But then she had seen Arcile again – first in the shape of a small round white light, a Will o' the Wisp; then as a young girl again, in the faerie court of Diana.

Diana. The Moon Goddess. Morgan recalled the night after the dark Moon when Diana had come to her on the battlements of Tintagel, just as the herald Dyonas had said she would. Diana had taken her across the night sky on her chariot to a mountainside far away, where she and her strange, scary, yet wonderful Wild Hunt danced and revelled all night. Diana had told Morgan that she was special. Unique. That there was no one else like her and there would never be anyone else like her. That she had been granted many gifts. Morgan hadn't understood that until later. Arcile had told Morgan she was precious to Diana and that Morgan was more magical than any of them. That was what Diana had meant.

And that was why Diana had chosen Morgan to perform a dangerous task for her. Morgan had had to go into the realms of the Small People, a whole other new world, where Diana could not go. Morgan had had to go to rescue the soul of a stillborn baby boy, Mabon, who was destined to be reborn.

Morgan had gone with Merlin and Arcile down into the underground cave-like realm of the beastly Piskies, horribly ugly and revolting little creatures ruled by their king Twadell. Twadell had threatened to kill her and Merlin, and had taken Arcile captive. But the baby boy Mabon and his twin sister Maglore, who like him had died at birth, had been taken from the Piskies by their enemies, the Muryans. The Muryans were beautiful-looking faeries who lived in what looked like a lovely faerie hill. However, underneath all their beauty, the Muryans were just as horrible as the Piskies, if not even more so. The Muryans used magic to hide the fact that they were turning into hideous ants. Their queen, Caelia, had betrayed their three former queens, the Elven, had stolen the Elven's magic and had turned them into insects.

Morgan had sought out the three Elven, Aynia, Cleena and Una. With their help, she had used magic and had saved Mabon and Maglore. For that, Arcile had told Morgan, the Piskies and the Muryans were angry with her. The faeries knew about her now. They would be coming for her. To seek a terrible revenge, Arcile had said.

But the Muryans had taken other children too. Human children, including a girl called Agnes, keeping them prisoner and using them as servants. Morgan had tried to save Agnes and the others, taking them with her when she escaped from the Muryans' realm. But Agnes and the other children had been in the Muryans' realm for a long time, maybe hundreds of years. Without the Muryans' magic, Agnes and the other children had grown old in the space of seconds and crumbled to dust.

It was so painful to think of Agnes that it made Morgan feel sick. She may have saved Mabon and Maglore, but she hadn't saved Agnes. Agnes had had a horrible life and, because of Morgan, a horrible death too, with no chance of getting another life, either in this world or in the faeries' world. Diana had taken Mabon to be reborn into *his* new life. The Elven Aynia, once again a faerie queen, had taken Maglore to look after. But Agnes had gone. Disappeared into nothingness. No one had come for Agnes. No one had saved Agnes. Agnes had been left. Abandoned. Forgotten.

And there was no one to remember her.

"What's wrong with you?"

Morgan's little sister Anna was standing in front of her, waving the stick she'd been playing with in her face.

"You look like you're going to be sick!" Anna exclaimed in glee. There was laughter and jeering in her voice. It sounded as if she was pleased.

"Morgan? Are you alright?"

Her other little sister, Blasine, chimed in from across the room, seeming scared and worried. Halwynna looked over at them and Fleur raised her head from her book.

"Nothing's wrong with me!" Morgan said crossly. As usual, Anna annoyed her intensely. She wished the horrid little girl would leave her alone.

But Anna scowled back at Morgan and pointed the stick directly at her. Normally her little sister would have looked quite pretty with her fair hair like Igraine's and dark eyes like Gorlois'. But now, with her face all scrunched up, she looked ugly.

"Do you know what this is?" Anna said, waving the stick at her threateningly. "It's a magic stick like the Druids have. It's got great magic. I'm going to use that magic on you! I'm going to kill you!"

Anna looked so stupid that Morgan burst out laughing.

"Magic!" she scoffed. "You! You don't know anything about magic! And you never will either! You're just a baby waving a silly little stick!"

Anna's frown deepened even further with fury. The little girl looked as if she were about to hit Morgan with the stick. But Morgan was older by a whole year. She was fully prepared to pull the stick off Anna and hit her right back. She was about to do just that when Halwynna intervened.

"That's enough! Lady Morgan! Lady Anna! What would your mother say if she saw you behaving like this? You know she has raised you to be young ladies – you must behave as such. Young ladies don't fight."

Anna's mouth twisted. Morgan glared at her little sister right in the eyes until Anna looked away and stomped back over to the rug by the fireplace.

There were times when Morgan really hated Anna. Most of the time she ignored her. But whenever they spoke, Anna was always annoying her, always saying nasty things, always arguing with her. It was as if Anna *wanted* Morgan to hate her. Morgan knew she should love Anna because she was her little sister. She loved Blasine – but it was easy to love Blasine because she was sweet and gentle and never said horrid things or annoyed anyone. But Morgan found it very difficult to love Anna. She decided the only way she could ever love Anna was by ignoring her and not speaking to her. Ever.

By late afternoon the wind, thunder and lightning began to die down. All that was left was the rain, still pounding hard on the castle roof and walls. Just when Morgan felt she was so fed up with being in the chamber that she wanted to scream, Sebile entered the room.

The old tutor was wearing her usual white headdress and carrying a large brown leather satchel, the one she always used when making her rounds. Tintagel Castle had no official physician, but Sebile was such a skilled healer and had such wide knowledge of herbs and medicines that everyone had come to depend on her. Sebile had so many talents – not only was she Morgan and Fleur's tutor and the castle healer, she also kept a library of scrolls and books in her chambers. Morgan would always rather be in Sebile's rooms than in any other place in the castle.

"Greetings," Sebile acknowledged Halwynna, who had stood up as the tutor entered. "I just came to see Morgan and Fleur. I'm on my way to visit Lady Aldan, children – would you like to accompany me?"

Fleur wrinkled up her nose in distaste.

"But it's still raining, isn't it, Sebile?"

"I'm afraid it is," Sebile agreed.

"Then, no, thank you," Fleur said politely. Fleur was always so good and neat and beautiful. Morgan couldn't imagine her ever getting dirty or wanting to go out in a rainstorm. No matter what she did, Fleur always looked perfect and acted perfectly; so exquisite, graceful and sweet. The little princess didn't look like anyone else, either. She stood out from everyone at Tintagel with her very delicate, unusual features, her long, silky, straight jet-black hair and her eyes as black as ebony.

But Morgan couldn't wait to go outside in the rain. She jumped up from the cushions immediately. Sebile looked at her with a hint of a smile hovering on the edges of her lips. But all the tutor said was, "Go to your room and put on a cloak if you're coming, child. I'll wait for you at the stairwell."

Morgan rushed back to her chamber and pulled on the first cloak she saw, a dark blue one with a hood. The upstairs corridor was glowing orange-gold from the lit torches in their iron holders on the walls, giving the damp interior a warmth to counter the dark grey rainclouds surrounding the castle outside. There were a number of soldiers in mail shirts standing guard, and several servants were rushing to and fro carrying pots and buckets of water, cloths and brooms.

Downstairs, the castle was even busier, with more people outside the main hall than Morgan had ever seen before. They were all milling about, greeting one another, calling out to each other and talking animatedly. Most of them she didn't recognise; they must be the visitors she had seen from the battlements. They looked even more impressive close up. The men were wearing dark trousers, some loose, some fitted, and a variety of colourful tunics both long and short, pinned at the shoulder with distinctive metal brooches, some of which had coloured jewels of red, blue, green, orange and black. Morgan noticed that it was older men who wore their tunics long, while younger men wore their tunics shorter with belts and long trousers tucked into boots. The tunics were all very elaborate and embroidered, made of rich materials often trimmed with silk.

The women looked even more stunning; beautiful flowing tunics and wide-sleeved dresses in reds, blues, greens, yellows, purples, pinks – all colours mixed together, shimmering with silk embroidery and glittering gemstones. Younger women wore their long hair in plaits that fell to their waists – women with hair of fair gold, raven black, copper red and chestnut brown – and metallic diadems like crowns on their heads. Older women wore their hair pulled back off their faces and light headdresses held in place by diadems similar to those of the younger women. A few even older women wore white headdresses that covered their hair entirely, as Sebile did. Even the soldiers among them were dressed more finely than Morgan had ever seen Tintagel soldiers dress, wearing black and brown leather tunics and rich cloaks together with their metallic mail shirts.

Morgan was so mesmerised by all the new grown-ups that at first she didn't hear someone shouting her name. When she finally heard it, she turned to see Taliesin waving at her and moving through the crowd, dodging around the grown-ups in his way. It was easy to follow him, a very pale-skinned little boy with curly hair so fair it was almost white.

She wasn't sure if she was happy to see him. When she had told her friends about her adventures with the Piskies and the Muryans, neither Fleur nor Taliesin had believed her. She had been upset about Fleur, and upset *and* surprised about Taliesin. After all, at only seven years old, Taliesin had gone from being a page boy to becoming apprentice to the leader of the Druids, Grand Master Cadwellon himself. If anyone should have believed her about the faeries, it was Taliesin. Morgan decided she was going to be unfriendly to Taliesin since he wouldn't believe her. However, Taliesin seemed so pleased to see her that she couldn't help but warm to him again almost immediately.

"Morgan!"

Taliesin came right up to her and grinned. In the past he had been cautious around her, afraid that someone might see them talking and he would get into trouble. But now he seemed much more confident.

"What are you doing here?" Morgan asked him.

"I'm here with Grand Master Cadwellon," Taliesin told her. There was pride in his voice. "He's called a meeting of the Council of Twelve before High King Vortigern gets here. He's letting me go with him."

"Your master is going to meet the Druid elders now?" Sebile said. The tutor was looking down at the two children, listening.

"That's right, Lady Sebile," a man's voice answered behind her. Standing there was Grand Master Cadwellon himself. He was wearing an all-white robe that matched his hair and long beard exactly, and the bejewelled gold necklace Morgan had seen Taliesin cleaning in the stables that morning. The Druid master carried his long staff in his left hand and acknowledged both Sebile and Morgan with an incline of his head.

"Good to see you again, *athrawes*. And you of course, Lady Morgan."

"You'll be discussing what you're going to say to the High King, I imagine," Sebile said.

Cadwellon sighed. "We're in a very difficult situation, as I'm sure you're aware, my lady. If Ambrosius and Uther have crossed the sea and landed in Britain, it means they intend to go to war with Vortigern and all who support him. It's rumoured that, after all these years in Armorica, the Pendragon brothers now favour Christianity, which means that they are no friends to the Druidical Order." He then gave Sebile an odd look Morgan didn't understand. "Or indeed any of us who follow the older faiths."

"From what I remember of the Pendragon brothers, they won't care who or what helps them or hinders them," Sebile said dryly. "They'll do whatever it takes, use whatever means they deem necessary, to ensure they're victorious."

Morgan wasn't sure she had understood this right. Sebile remembered the Pendragon brothers? Ambrosius and Uther, the enemies of Vortigern? Sebile *knew* them?

She and Taliesin exchanged looks. Taliesin's hazel eyes were wide; he was as stunned as she was.

"Then we must ensure that High King Vortigern does the same," Cadwellon was saying. "But he cannot achieve victory without help. Not only does he need the Duke and the men of Belerion, he needs the help of his Saxon allies."

The Saxons again. Morgan listened intently, not wanting to miss a word.

"Do you really trust the Saxons to help?" Sebile asked in a tone which made Morgan realise that Sebile herself didn't trust them.

Cadwellon gave the tutor another odd look.

"Well, the Saxons at least respect our faith," the Grand Master said. "They have a similar faith – or, at least, they aren't Christians, either. They have no time for that man from the eastern lands who called himself a prophet. In fact, they have paid homage to our gods. When Vortigern and Hengist first forged their alliance, Hengist and his men offered up gifts and sacrifices to our Oakfather and to Belenos as a token of good faith to seal the bargain."

Sebile said nothing for a moment.

"What's the matter, *athrawes*?" Cadwellon asked her, again addressing the tutor with the word Morgan didn't know.

"Be wary of those from outside who offer gifts to your gods, Grand Master," Sebile said in a strange, strangled voice that didn't sound like her. "They can use those gifts as a trick, as a means to gain your trust and then strike from within when you least expect it – like a viper taken to the breast. I have seen it happen, time and time again. What you might think is a holy gift, an offering to the gods, or even a gift from the gods themselves, may be a catalyst for your betrayal. What you might think is a kindness, and a token of faith and friendship, may be the seed of your own destruction."

Morgan felt a tingling going all the way down her back. She had never heard Sebile talk like that before. Taliesin was staring up at the tutor, open-mouthed.

Cadwellon was looking at Sebile with great respect and, Morgan thought, some sadness too.

"I hear what you're saying," the Grand Master said gently. "But what choice do we have? With the kings of Cambria taking a neutral stance, and the Pictish warriors and Éireann raiders poised to attack us from the north and west, Vortigern doesn't have the forces to fight them all. We on the Council of Twelve must advise him on all matters military as well as matters of faith."

Cadwellon put his hand on Sebile's arm. "I assure you, *athrawes*, we take every precaution with Hengist and his Saxons. Why else do you think we only gave them rough lands in the bogs and marshes around Londinium – far away from the richest and most fertile lands of our island? Why else do you think we use Hengist and his hordes to keep the Picts at bay? It satisfies their lust for fighting and keeps them so busy that they cannot turn west to attack us. Do not fear. We know how to deal with them."

"Grand Master."

A lean, dark-haired man was standing behind Cadwellon, dressed in strange Druidical robes that looked almost black. It was Myrddin, the dark Druid, Cadwellon's right hand man.

Morgan suppressed a shudder. There was something about the man that made her feel very bad. Once, when she had caught Myrddin staring at her in the courtyard, she had realised that the dark Druid really didn't like her and she had no idea why. She did know, however, that she really didn't like him, either.

But Myrddin didn't look at her now. He didn't look at Sebile, either – the tutor may as well not have been there. The dark Druid gave Taliesin a cursory glance, then focused his full attention on Cadwellon.

"I have shown the Council into the Duke's chamber," Myrddin said. "They are waiting for you, Grand Master."

"Very well." Cadwellon made as if to leave, but Myrddin stepped quietly in front of him, blocking his path.

"What is it?" the Druid Grand Master said, sounding surprised and rather irritated.

"Forgive me, Grand Master, but I wish to ask you, in all humility, if I may attend the meeting of the Council of Twelve with you. I understand" – here Myrddin glanced again at Taliesin – "that your apprentice is to accompany you. I have some suggestions that I feel the Council needs to hear."

"*You* have suggestions?" Cadwellon was astonished now. "May I remind you, Myrddin, that you are not on the Council of Twelve. Our deliberations must be secret until we come to a decision."

Myrddin's face twitched.

"But your apprentice – " he began.

"My apprentice is coming to the meeting because he serves me," Cadwellon interrupted him. "He's just a child and he is sworn to me. But you, Myrddin, are a Vate and you know only Mages can sit on the Council. Let us have no more of this."

The dark Druid bowed before Cadwellon. The Druid Grand Master bade Sebile and Morgan farewell, but Morgan was watching Myrddin. His face had a curious shadow upon it, a shadow that seemed to flicker across his features. His lips were tightly pursed. As Cadwellon passed, he gave Myrddin an appraising look – a look that reminded Morgan of the way grown-ups would look at her when they thought she might do something naughty. Taliesin, trotting after Cadwellon, was looking strangely at Myrddin as well.

When Cadwellon had gone, Myrddin straightened up, turned on his heel and walked swiftly away without a backward glance. He had not looked at, spoken to or acknowledged Sebile or Morgan even once. He acted as if they were invisible to him. Yet Morgan knew he had been very aware of them the whole time.

"He's trouble, that one," Sebile mused. "Come along, Morgan. Lady Aldan is waiting for us."

Morgan wondered if she should tell Sebile the secret she knew about Myrddin. She had never liked keeping secrets. Ever since she had found out that Merlin was studying with Myrddin to be his Druid apprentice, she had been tempted to tell someone. Merlin had asked her to keep it a secret. But if Myrddin was trouble, like Sebile said, then maybe she *should* tell someone. If Myrddin was trouble, he could get Merlin into trouble too.

But she decided against it. So what if Myrddin got Merlin into trouble? She was still annoyed at Merlin and his weird ways. She had never known anyone who could sway so quickly from being friendly to being unfriendly, from being loyal to being hostile, from being kind to being mean. Merlin was so puzzling, so infuriating, so hurtful. If he got into trouble because of Myrddin, it would serve him right.

DRAMATIS PERSONÆ

(in alphabetical order)

AGNES *Servant girl*

ALDAN *Princess of Gwynedd, daughter of King* **EINION,** *mother of* **MERLIN** *and* **GANIEDA**

ANNA *Twin sister of* **BLASINE,** *younger sister of* **MORGAN,** *daughter of* **GORLOIS** *and* **IGRAINE**

ARCILE *Maid to* **MORGAN**

AYNIA *An Elven, sister of* **CLEENA** *and* **UNA**

BLAES *Christian monk of Gwynedd, tutor of* **MERLIN**

BLANCHEFLEUR *known as* **FLEUR,** *Princess of Ynys Môn, adopted daughter of King* **PELLINORE** *and Queen* **SARDOINE,** *niece of* **IGRAINE**

BLASINE *Twin sister of* **ANNA,** *younger sister of* **MORGAN,** *daughter of* **GORLOIS** *and* **IGRAINE**

BORMOVO *A spirit*

BRASTIAS *Knight of Belerion, seneschal to* **GORLOIS**

CADWELLON *Grand Master of the Druid Order*

CAELIA *Queen of the Muryans*

CLEENA *An Elven, sister of* **AYNIA** *and* **UNA**

DANDO *A Cynocephalus*

DIANA *The Moon Huntress, leader of the Wild Hunt*

DYONAS *A spirit, herald of* **DIANA**

ELFFIN   *A fisherman, adopted father of* **TALIESIN**
ELFODD   *Christian priest, tutor of* **MORGAN** *and*
BLANCHEFLEUR
GANIEDA   *Twin sister of* **MERLIN**, *daughter of*
ALDAN
GORLOIS   *Duke of Belerion, husband of* **IGRAINE**,
father of **MORGAN**, **ANNA** *and*
BLASINE
HALWYNNA   *Lady-in-waiting to* **IGRAINE**
IGRAINE   *Duchess of Belerion, wife of* **GORLOIS**,
mother of **MORGAN**, **ANNA** *and*
BLASINE, *sister of* **SARDOINE**
JACK   *A Piskie*
JOAN   *A Piskie*
KEVNYS   *A spider*
MABON   *A child soul*
MAGLORE   *A child soul*
MERLIN   *Twin brother of* **GANIEDA**, *son of*
ALDAN
MORGAN   *Eldest daughter of* **GORLOIS** *and*
IGRAINE, *sister of* **ANNA** *and* **BLASINE**
MYRDDIN   *Druid Master, attendant to*
CADWELLON
SAFIR   *A runaway, squire to* **GORLOIS**
SEBILE   *Physician and herbalist, tutor of*
MORGAN *and* **BLANCHEFLEUR**
SMERTULLOS   *A Pooka*
TALIESIN   *Adopted son of* **ELFFIN**, *page boy to*
GORLOIS, *apprentice to* **CADWELLON**
TWADELL   *King of the Piskies*
UNA   *An Elven, sister of* **AYNIA** *and* **CLEENA**
YALLERY   *A Piskie, formerly a human boy*

UNSEEN CHARACTERS

(in alphabetical order)

AMBROSIUS   *Enemy of* **VORTIGERN**, *rival claimant to the title of High King of Britain, brother of* **UTHER**

CONSTANTINE   *Former High King of Britain, father of* **AMBROSIUS** *and* **UTHER**

EINION   *King of Gwynedd, father of* **ALDAN**, *grandfather of* **MERLIN** *and* **GANIEDA**

GERMANUS   *Christian bishop*

PELLINORE   *King of Ynys Môn, husband of* **SARDOINE,** *adopted father of* **BLANCHEFLEUR**

ROWENA   *High Queen of Britain, wife of* **VORTIGERN**

SARDOINE   *Queen of Ynys Môn, wife of* **PELLINORE,** *adopted mother of* **BLANCHEFLEUR**

UTHER   *A warrior, brother of* **AMBROSIUS**

VORTIGERN   *High King of Britain, enemy of* **AMBROSIUS** *and* **UTHER**

Printed in Great Britain
by Amazon

17721060R00178